D1553902

RENEWED FAITH

CSA Case Files, Book Three

Kennedy Layne

RENEWED FAITH

Dedication

Elsie—you will forever be remembered.

Jeffrey, my loving husband…you give me faith every day. I love you.

Prologue

Crest walked across the living room floor of his penthouse apartment, the dim lamp in the living room casting just enough light to guide him. Satisfaction flowed through him as the warmth of the hardwood soaked into his bare feet. The under floor heating system that he'd had installed last winter was well worth every penny that he'd paid. December had certainly brought with it the colder weather and once again, he questioned his decision to base his investigative agency in Minneapolis. Minnesota was the state he'd been born in, but Florida was sounding better and better.

Walking around the obsidian quartz topped island which separated the kitchen from the living space, Crest opened the refrigerator and steeled himself against the chilly mist-filled draft that wafted over his bare chest. He let the brushed nickel door swing open as he tightened the belt on his favorite luxury men's robe that had been a present from a woman he'd had a previous casual intimate relationship with. She'd surprised him with an all expenses paid weekend at a Catskills exclusive spa, which included the robe. He still stopped in to see her whenever he was in Washington for business.

Crest pulled a bottle of Lauquen mineral water off of the bottom shelf and then closed the door. He heard the whirl of the coffee grinder echo through the stillness as the five o'clock morning hour struck. The aroma of the rich select Jamaican Blue Mountain ground beans filled the air as they were released into the custom coffee maker. He contemplated waiting for the coffee to brew, but then he heard the distinctive ringtone of his cell coming from the bedroom. He unscrewed the cap of the bottle and took a swill of the chilled water as he walked back from where he'd come from. The uniquely refreshing liquid was exactly what he needed after the last few hours. It was bottled from an aquifer fifteen hundred feet below the Andes Mountains and no purer water existed on the planet.

Crossing the threshold of his bedroom, Crest ignored the rumpled brown Egyptian cotton sheets and matching down-filled comforter along with the various articles of clothing that were strewn across the floor. He made his way to the nightstand and picked up his phone. Seeing Jessie's name on the display had him tightening his jaw. Her calling him this early was never a good thing. He entered his ten-digit pin along with his index fingerprint for the embedded scanner and answered.

"Has Taryn found something on the search?"

"No," Jessie replied, the noise of car horns honking in the background almost obscuring the sound of her voice. She was obviously in the vicinity of the office. "Kevin just called me though. He's been at a murder scene for the past two hours and is requesting that we get in touch with that profiler you worked with on both the Karnes and Sweeney case. I just wanted to run it by you before I placed the call."

Crest set the bottle of water down on the nightstand and then rubbed the back of his neck, relishing the coolness of his fingers as he tried to knead away the tension that was beginning to mount. The search he'd been referring to was in regards to a freelance contractor that cost a great deal of money in exchange for his services as a hired assassin. An extremely cunning and manipulative man who went by the name of Ryland who was a danger to Crest and his team. Ryland had somehow managed to escape a federal supermax prison six months ago. No one had any indication as to how he'd orchestrated such a feat with regards to his exodus. The safety of Crest's personnel was essential and this extended pursuit had taken up most of his daily life. Unfortunately, their lives did have to go on in the interim.

His team of six associate members, not including Jessie and numerous support staff on call, had become family over the years. Connor, Jax, Kevin, and Ethan were former Marines that he'd selected specifically to come and work for him. The same could be said of Taryn, with the exception that she was former Navy Intel. Lach was the latest addition to the group, although he'd been a Bureau Hostage Rescue Team Leader before needing a change in pace. Although Crest intentionally kept Lach's past a mystery to the other team members, they each in turn knew that Crest wouldn't have selected him to join the agency unless he met his own special list of criteria. It was unfortunate that the past caseloads hadn't provided much of a change.

"Go ahead," Crest instructed, his eyes zeroing in on the bathroom door as it slowly opened to reveal a petite brunette wearing nothing but one of his plush terry cloth towels. For a brief moment, he swore it was Jessie standing there with the steam billowing around her feminine form. A flash of embarrassed irritation shot through him. He'd already established boundaries when it came to Jessie. The age difference alone would have been enough to cross her off of his list of potential mates. This reaction hammered home the fact that he was definitely burning the candle at both ends. Something had to give and soon. "I missed that. What did you say?"

"Do you want Fallon Canna flown in or just have the case files sent to her?"

As the lovely brunette sauntered towards him, sliding her fingers underneath the soft fabric, Crest turned away. He clenched his jaw to prevent himself from snapping into the phone when Jessie had done nothing more than ask him a reasonable question. Hell, she'd kept her distance from him since the wedding of one of his team members when he'd basically spelled things out for her. It would be easier on everyone if he just fired her, but Crest couldn't bring himself to do that. This was his burden to bear and he would damn well man up and be the professional that he was.

"For now, just send Fallon the case files along with Kevin's AME2000 number. Fallon can contact him directly after she's written up a profile. Remind me to have Kevin change out his secure phone once the case wraps and have Taryn network update his new number into the other members' devices." Crest could hear the sound of the sheets rustling, indicating that his guest was waiting for him. "I'll be into the office within the hour."

Crest disconnected the call without waiting to hear if Jessie had anything else to add. He'd originally planned to make his guest breakfast, enjoy the coffee that was now brewing, and return to bed to continue what had been a very pleasurable night. That wouldn't happen now, for his mind was running at a thousand beats per minute. He also refused to allow something that had little significance to ruin a perfectly good start to the morning. It was still salvageable. He walked back around the bed and placed his phone on the nightstand.

"I think you might have missed a few spots," Crest murmured, holding out a hand. Her smooth fingers slid into his and her beautiful smile brightened. Pulling her to stand directly in front of him, he allowed her hands to slip under the lapel of his robe. He tried his damnedest to forget everything outside of this room, but staring into the emerald green eyes before him made that difficult. "And I think I have just enough time to make sure every inch of your body is thoroughly washed."

Chapter One

Kevin Dreier was kneeling in the corner of an abandoned warehouse, observing the crime scene while a forensics team finished processing the evidence. The body of a young woman lay sprawled out on the frigid faded concrete, as if she'd been garbage to be discarded. Her clothes were ripped, her skin had cuts and bruises in every exposed area, her dull brown hair was matted, and it was obvious that she fought like hell. She hadn't known it was a losing battle and the single bright ligature mark around her pale neck left a blaring message for all to see. The scumbag who did this thought he was entitled. It took time to manually strangle another human being. Their killer had time to consider what he was doing and he had tossed her away, intent on this purpose.

"They're about to remove the body," Taggart said as he came to stand next to him. Kevin glanced down at the scuffed black dress shoes, mentally shaking his head in disbelief. There was easily seven inches of snow on the ground and more to come, if the weatherman was to be believed. Taggart's motion toward the victim brought Kevin's gaze back to point. The sight was brutal and had him gritting his teeth. "She looks nothing like the previous victim. No physical resemblance at all. That will only make it harder to pinpoint this son of a bitch."

Taggart Macon was the typical old-fashioned police officer, maintaining a polished image that the public liked to see. One thing in his favor was that he was one of the best damn detectives that the Minneapolis Police Department had on staff. Short on common sense if his shoes were anything to go by, but Kevin knew Taggart had the intelligence to close this case. Unfortunately, the killer kept upping the ante and changing his MO.

"No, but everything else corresponds with the last victim. The way she's laid out, the ligature marks, and his personal touch."

Kevin inwardly groaned when he stood up, feeling pain radiate through his bad knee. The pins and plates made it more difficult in that that they didn't react well to the cold weather. At least he wore his brown military issued boots that kept his feet insulated. Having grown up in the backcountry of Wisconsin on a dairy farm, sound judgment was vital. Regrettably, they needed more than that to solve this case.

The parents of a rape victim had hired Crest Security Agency to find their daughter's rapist. Kevin was the ideal member of the team to take the case, as he was the one who maintained street credo and was known for keeping his word among that particular element. This case hit a little too close to home, as the second victim was someone he'd known. Unfortunately, the perp escalated in his anger and within three months committed murder. That was back in June and here it was in late December. They still hadn't caught a break.

"Let's go grab a cup of coffee and go over what we know," Kevin suggested, resisting the urge to lean down and rub his knee. "It's better to pool our resources, and at some point this morning I'm going to have to give an update to my clients. I'd really like to avoid us both looking like some stand up routine."

"If that's your way of thanking me for working with you, I'll take it. I'll even let you buy me coffee. Let me finish up here and I'll meet you over at the Caribou in the skyway."

"Caribou? Seriously?" Kevin shook his head in disgust. He liked his coffee black and preferably with a substantial breakfast. Not some frilly-assed drink laced with sugar and fortified with only a scone. He had to remind himself that Taggart was a city boy through and through. "I'll be at the Uptown Diner. Ethan and Lach will meet us there. Maybe they can give us an insight to the evidence that we're missing, because I'm coming up with jack shit."

"You and the lab both," Taggart muttered, already walking across the cracked cement. Before reaching one of the crime scene investigative personnel, he turned back around. "Just so you know, you're messing with my chance to ask a cute barista out to lunch."

"I'm saving you from yourself," Kevin called out, his voice echoing off of the steel beams embedded into the ceiling. "Skimmed latte? Really?"

Taggart just laughed as he then entered the fray, already being asked numerous questions from the CSI unit. Civilians would never understand what law enforcement employees went through when dealing with vicious, cruel and brutal scenes like the one in front of them. Humor got most of them through it, while others remained emotionally unattached and treated the victims as if they were pieces on a game board. There was no right or wrong way to do one's job.

Kevin took one last look at the woman whose lot in life had been carved out from the very beginning of her teenage years. The existence she chose as a prostitute had unfortunately put her into the crosshairs of one sick son of a bitch and now here she was, dead at what he assumed was roughly twenty years of age. If Taggart was able to get a full identification of the victim, Kevin had to wonder how her parents would react. Would they be saddened by their daughter's death? Or would they not give a shit and carry on with their daily lives as if she'd never existed?

He didn't relish what Taggart would have to do, as Kevin had to pass this information on to his own clients. There was no doubt this was the same perpetrator. The personal touch that the killer liked to leave was smeared across the victim's lips. The striking red color against her pale skin looked like one of those Picasso pieces. Knowing it was a generic brand of lipstick didn't help their cause and they were no closer to catching this scumbag now than they were before.

Kevin finally turned from the horrific sight and continued to cross the floor until he was able to walk through the outer door. The frigid cold that hit him immediately sucked his breath away. The stationed officer, whose cheeks were as ruddy as his lips, nodded his head and prompted Kevin to do the same. Pulling the keys from his jacket, Kevin walked the distance to his black four-wheel drive truck making sure that he didn't limp. Weakness wasn't shown. Ever. He kicked his running board, knocking off the remaining snow on his boots before folding his large frame into the driver's seat.

Once the engine was started, Kevin used the time for the large vehicle to warm up in order to survey the area. He dismissed the patrol cars, the unmarked police cars, and the two forensic vans and concentrated on the city elements. The media had started to descend in various vehicles and other than the two girls huddled together behind the yellow tape; the scene was still quiet due to the hour.

Concentrating on the women, Kevin knew they worked the streets and were Bee's girls. He'd follow up with them later tonight, as well as their pimp, when they were back on the job and easier to access. He watched one of the detectives working with Taggart walk up to them and start the interview process. The victim wasn't someone that looked familiar, so he was relatively certain she hadn't worked for Bee. That didn't mean these women didn't know her. What should have been an open and shut case had turned into an elevated crime that was escalating quicker than a combat element descending on a battlefield.

The ringing of Kevin's cell drew his attention. Reaching into the pocket of his black insulated jacket, he withdrew his phone and saw Ethan's name on the display. He glanced at the time exhibited on his dashboard and he knew that his friend was waiting for him.

"Hey, grunt, I'm on my way."

"I wouldn't bother," Ethan said, his voice a little rough around the edges. Although his tone was naturally deep, it was apparent he was sick. "Lach was just sent to the airport to take that hostage rescue case Crest informed us about yesterday. You know, the hospital volunteer that was taken prisoner by the rebels in Africa?"

"I thought Crest told the victim's family to call up Red Starr HRT?"

Kevin was referring to the hostage rescue team that worked outside the confines of the federal government run by a biracial woman of Native American and Caucasian descent. She had no need to advertise her business, as word of mouth kept her calendar full. Her reputation preceded her. He never had the pleasure of meeting Catori Starr, but Crest thought highly of her and that was as critical an endorsement as there was.

Before Ethan could respond, movement to Kevin's right caught his attention. Hash slowly made his way up the street, his back to the wind and snow. He was a low-level drug dealer who usually stayed away from the street girls. He didn't like the doubled odds of potentially landing his ass in the slammer. Kevin found it interesting that Hash was out at this hour, when he would normally be calling it a night and returning to his rundown apartment in the seedy part of town.

"Apparently, no one can get a hold of Catori Starr." Ethan coughed hard enough to cause Kevin to wince. "I'm going back to bed for a couple of hours. I'll see you at the office later."

"Better yet, don't," Kevin said, all the while keeping his attention on Hash as the scrawny male seemed to be comforting the two women. They were all huddled together, unsuccessful in trying to keep the wind at bay. What did they expect to find out? It was sheer stupidity to stand out in this weather unless they had a damn good reason. More coughing from the phone brought his attention back around. "You sound like shit. Crest will kick your ass if you infect the rest of us."

"I'll text Jessie." Ethan went into another coughing fit. Kevin pulled the phone away from his ear until it was over. "If I'm not in the office tomorrow, make sure I'm still alive."

"Yeah, yeah." Kevin smirked as his friend's voice became almost non-existent. Ethan wouldn't be seen for days at this rate. "Just get some sleep, buddy."

Kevin disconnected the call and watched as the detective who had been questioning the two women turned his attention on Hash. Whatever was said was quick and to the point, for the three walked away shortly thereafter. Kevin shook his head, knowing that the officer had no idea how to speak with someone like Hash. Kevin had no doubt that Taggart would share the interviews and whatever else he had in connection with the case, but it was more the other way around that they would get the answers they sought. Kevin would touch base with Hash tonight. Right now, the snow was starting to fall a little heavier and since Ethan and Lach weren't meeting him for breakfast, Kevin knew what he had to do. A mixture of unease and anticipation rushed through him. It was an odd combination, but there just the same. Elle Reyes had that affect on him.

Have to take care of something first. Meet me at the Uptown Diner in an hour.

Kevin sent the text to Taggart and then tucked the phone back into his jacket. He'd faced the fact that he would have to contact Elle when he'd first received the call about another murder. It had to be him that let her know that he thought their suspect had struck again. He wouldn't have it any other way. She wouldn't take the news well.

It was just over a year ago that Elle had been one of those women on the street. A prostitute. She cared deeply and continued to go to the shelters, seeking ways to help them turn their lives around. Kevin had even caught her talking to one of Bee's girls on the street a couple of weeks ago. It didn't go over well when Kevin told her how dangerous it was to return to her old haunts. His attempts at keeping her safe were as discarded as his efforts to get her to smile.

Kevin couldn't for the life of him figure out why Elle felt responsible for the working girls. She couldn't save everyone. He should know. It was obvious in her actions that she had unresolved issues from her past life. On one hand, that kept him at a distance. He knew she needed time to heal and he wanted to give her that. On the other, he hoped like hell that she would open up to him soon, needing to help her in any way that he could. It was torture to maintain this void that she'd put into place. Elle had gotten to him in a way that no other woman had.

Kevin wrapped his fingers around the cold leather steering wheel, his determination just as unyielding. That didn't mean he would get what he wanted, which was Elle in his life. It was a matter of how much patience he had and he prayed that he wouldn't fuck it all up.

Chapter Two

Elle groaned in frustration upon hearing the pounding on her door. She squinted one eye at her clock, seeing that it read a little after six in the morning. Everyone that knew her was well aware what her hours were at the club and that her internal schedule was turned around. It didn't help that she suffered from insomnia as well. When she could fall into a light sleep, she grabbed a hold of it with both hands. When the pounding continued, she mentally threw the counting sheep over the fence and she knew any attempt now would be futile.

"Shit."

Elle tossed the covers off and grabbed the flannel pajama bottoms that she'd tossed on the floor. Hopping on one foot, she slid her left leg through the soft material and then did the same with her left. She shoved her feet into her pink fuzzy slippers that were a gift to herself for Christmas. The cold hardwood floor was too much to take in the winter. While she liked to sleep in nothing more than panties and a tank top, the temperature she could afford to keep her apartment at was a little too brisk to walk around in them.

Finally on the path to the door, Elle quickly glanced around the open space. She had a couple Chinese wall partitions to separate where her bed was situated. A bathroom was to the far left and was the only *room* to have a door. A few pieces of clothing were scattered about on the couch and floor. The small kitchen area, consisting of a sink, stove, and small countertop with a microwave, had dishes that still needed to be washed. She winced and hoped like hell it wasn't Jax or Connor.

Jax Christensen and Connor Ortega were owners of a kink club called Masters, which just happened to be right below Elle's small apartment. They'd made some type of agreement with the landlord and they had somehow finagled a way to include this space as hers while she managed their club. Elle didn't look a gift horse in the mouth, no matter how charitable it sounded. She made sure she did the best damn job in management and paid her rent on time, regardless of their protests. Even she knew that she wasn't paying close to what the landlord could probably get. They compensated her well, too well, but that didn't mean that this gig couldn't be taken away in the blink of an eye. It was better to save as much as she could, just in case of the worst scenario.

Pounding sounded once more and Elle reached for her ponytail, which sat high on her head to keep her long hair contained while she slept, tightening the band. Finally reaching her destination, she turned the knob and threw open the door. The last person she expected to see was Kevin Dreier.

"You didn't check to see who it was."

Kevin stood in front of Elle with his hands on his hips looking irritated. Well, he could just join the club. Ever since he'd helped her get the management position at Masters, his attitude had changed toward her and she didn't like it one bit. When they'd first met, she'd been working the streets. It wasn't something she was proud of, and to his credit he never made her feel as if she were lower than dirt. He had some sort of relationship with Bee, the man she'd worked for, and Kevin had seemed to take an interest in her. Not physical, by any means, but more of a casual friend. The one thing she'd liked and respected about Kevin was his brutal honesty. Unfortunately, his mannerisms had changed the minute she cleaned up her act and it made her damn uncomfortable. She didn't like how his voice transformed from no-nonsense to tenderness when he dealt with her. And this overprotective shit was getting on her nerves.

"There are two security doors a person would have to get through, Kevin. And even then a card key is required." Elle didn't bother to hide her frown. She turned away and retreated back into her apartment, knowing that he would follow. Since sleep was now out of the question, she made her way to the small counter where a four-cup coffeemaker sat beside the microwave. She did her best to ignore the fact that his presence behind her made her apartment feel like a tin box. "It was either Jax, Connor, or the landlord. Speaking of which, how did you gain access to the club?"

"I swung by Jax's place and picked up a key."

Kevin leaned against the wall, making no pretense that he was watching her as she made coffee. Elle had no doubt that had she lived another life and had been the girl next-door type they might have hooked up. As it was, life was a bitch and so was she. This six foot three inch man deserved a hell of a lot better than a washed up hooker. It wasn't that she was ashamed of who or what she was, but some things were just a basic fact. In addition, him treating her lately like a little sister was downright degrading and only cemented their stations. He certainly didn't handle her like the submissives the kink club catered to. Not that she wanted him to. She wasn't sure why that even crossed her mind.

"And you got the key to come see me why?" Elle asked crossly as she hit the brew button with a little too much force.

"I needed to talk to you."

Kevin's statement grabbed her attention and she paused long enough to look his way. Her heart stuttered just a bit and the empty pit that was her stomach lurched as the reason for his visit finally dawned. His grey eyes met hers, and from the rawness within she knew what he was about to say. To give herself more time before hearing the horrifying news, she concentrated on his appearance. His brown hair was almost fashioned in a crew cut, but a little longer on top and glistening with what must be melted snowflakes. It gave him a boyish look, which was ludicrous, because his aura was anything but. His shift in stance signaled his need to tell her his news. She tried to brace herself.

"Was it someone I knew?"

Elle held her breath as she waited for his answer. They'd had multiple discussions about her apparent need to help the women that were still working on the street. He didn't understand and it wasn't her job to make him. It was her life and she would do what she needed to do. From the time she was seventeen, the only way she knew how to survive was off of her body. It was rare that one got out of the profession and even rarer that they were offered the chance. At the age of twenty-five, Elle now knew better. She didn't kid herself that she could help them all, but she damn well knew she could save some. Now there was some sick son of a bitch raping and murdering prostitutes. It could have well been her that had been raped or murdered.

"I don't think so," Kevin answered, his voice soft. The hint of tenderness was right underneath, as if she needed to be coddled. Elle ignored it, but she still felt relief run through her body while at the same time sorrow for the girl who lost her life. She forced herself to listen to the rest of what Kevin had to say. "She didn't work for Bee. I did find it odd that Clarisse and Rachel were on the scene though. The victim could have been new to town or visiting one of the other girls."

"If you didn't recognize her, why are you assuming she's a working girl?" Elle asked, leaning a hip against the countertop. She knew that came across a little spiteful and that wasn't how she meant it. "We know the two rapes and the murder back in June were all call girls. What makes you think this one was?"

Kevin didn't break their eye contact and his confidence was a little intimidating. She didn't let that get to her though and she refused to be the one to look away first. If there was something that the women should know that would somehow keep them from being a target, they had a right to know. They were already terrified but having more information would only aid in their safety.

"There are details that only the police are privy to that won't be shared with the public unless they deem necessary. I can assure you, this was a victim of the man we are looking for."

Elle tilted her head and she gave him a quizzical look, her mind already running a thousand miles per minute. She worked closely with the shelter in town, as well as keeping in contact with most of the women. No one mentioned a new girl, but maybe Kevin had a point about a visiting friend. She didn't doubt that the girl's occupation was what he assumed, but she refused to feel guilt over calling him on it.

She glanced at the time on the microwave and knew that Cam would be on shift at Reformation this morning. Cam and his brother Eric ran the women's shelter and they split their time evenly so that someone was always present. She'd purposefully stayed away from the center during her years on the street. It wasn't until this last year that she'd seen how much Eric had changed and though she still didn't feel comfortable around him, she respected his work ethic in helping the girls turn their lives around.

"I'll check with Cam," Elle said, spinning away from the scowl that crossed Kevin's face upon her declaration. He'd just have to deal it. She was as invested in this case as he was. After all, she was the one who referred Becky Rattore's parents to CSA. The eighteen-year-old girl had run away from home, thinking she could hack it on the streets. It didn't take long for reality to set in. Elle opened one of the three cabinets above the counter and pulled down a mug, hoping to avoid an argument. "Maybe Cam heard something about her or knew of her."

"I didn't come here to enlist your help, Elle." Kevin's voice had deepened into censorship and Elle did her best to reign in her temper. To give herself something to do, she poured the steaming black liquid into a plain white mug that she'd pur-chased from the grocery store. If she'd had a second, she might have offered him one. Then again, maybe not. She slid the pot back onto the miniscule burner. "You'll only put yourself in danger. I came because I wanted you to hear from me that there's been another murder. It's best that you stay away from the streets and the shelter for awhile. The police haven't pinpointed how this guy is choosing his victims and until he's apprehended, I think you should stay clear."

"Just say it, Kevin." Elle slammed her mug on the laminate counter and faced him, crossing her arms. "You think because I was a hooker that I could be a target."

From the twitch of Kevin's jawline, it was obvious he was suppressing his response and something inside her jumped for glee. She would love to see him lose a little of that control that just irritated the shit out of her. She knew that she baited him a little too much for his comfort, but she couldn't seem to help herself. Dealing with abrupt, concise, and blunt people she could handle. It was what she was used to. This veiled kindness and affection that he seemed to have adopted this last year confused her and she wanted nothing to do with it or him.

"You have a habit of putting words in my mouth," Kevin replied, pushing off of the wall and standing to his full height. An advantage for her was that she wasn't as small as the average woman he was used to and she squared her shoulders as well, using her five foot eight inch stature to challenge him. For some reason, he still made her feel feminine, but she pushed it aside to listen to the remainder of what he had to say. "We have no idea who this guy is, how he's picking his victims, or when he will change course. Until we figure that out no one is safe."

"I appreciate your concern."

There. Simple and to the point. Elle watched as Kevin tried to formulate more words and she raised her chin another fraction of an inch. It wasn't like she was hiding anything from him. He knew damn well that she would do what she wanted. He didn't seem to understand that she could actually help him. He was intelligent enough to know that his snitches didn't tell him everything. But someone like her, who they claimed as one of their own, was a different matter. This killer had to have made a mistake somewhere and been seen by someone. It was just a matter of finding out whom.

"Is it so hard to have someone care about you?"

Kevin's words, as soft as they sounded, were like ice cold water being thrown in her face. It took a moment to gather her composure, and even then she wasn't sure how to respond. Elle slowly dragged oxygen into her lungs after having realized that she wasn't breathing. She wasn't sure exactly what he meant and she didn't want to. No matter how she answered, it wouldn't come out right. The best course of action was to pretend it was never said. Feeling as if she were on autopilot, Elle grabbed her mug and somehow managed to walk around him without touching.

"I appreciate that you came to tell me," Elle said, trying to keep her voice even. She walked to the door and opened it, although she didn't take a sip of her coffee for fear that her hand would tremble. "If you find out anything more, you can just call. The club is closed tonight, so I'll be doing inventory for the bar."

Kevin slowly turned to face her, and for a moment she worried that he wouldn't let it go. As he walked toward her in a predatory way, she found herself holding her breath once more. Since when had she turned into such a weak specimen of the female race? Elle tightened her grip on the cup and waited for his reaction when what she wanted to do was shout that she didn't need an older brother watching out for her. She refused to think he meant it any other way.

"Be careful if you go to the shelter," Kevin said, his voice registering an octave lower. He was also inches from her with his head tilted down, giving her a view of his full lips. She didn't look up to meet his gaze for fear of what she would see. More apt, what she wouldn't see. "I'll be in touch."

With those four words, Kevin was out the door, leaving only a slight hint of woodsy aftershave in his wake. She quickly shut the door to seal it outside versus in. Elle didn't need any reminders of his visit. The news he'd left was enough and that prompted her to quickly cross the floor and walk behind the wooden wall partition. She set her mug down on the nightstand, although not before she fortified herself with a long swallow. The day proved to be a long one if she was going to spend it at the shelter. She'd catch a few hours of sleep later this evening before she did that inventory she mentioned.

Is it so hard to have someone care about you? Kevin's words rang in Elle's ears as she got dressed, causing more frustration than she thought possible. If she'd answered him honestly then he'd learn that she didn't know if it was hard. It was something that she never had. She didn't pity herself by any means. It was just the way it was. But Kevin would pity her and that was something she couldn't allow.

Elle turned her focus on the shelter and the women who sought help. Some were young runaways, some were prostitutes trying to turn their life around, and then there were the women who were either single moms or victims of domestic abuse. They each had the courage to reach out and try to change the course of their lives. It had taken her a long time to find that resolution within herself, and if she could give them even an ounce of hope, then she'd done what she set out to do. This killer wasn't about to take that away from any of them.

Chapter Three

"Heads up!"

Kevin turned around just in time to catch the yellow stress ball that Jax had thrown his way. He caught the sucker inches from his face and immediately threw it back. Jax kept walking to his cubicle as if nothing had happened, leaving Kevin shaking his head in amusement. Ever since his wife, Emily, had hit her third trimester and the morning sickness had evaporated, Jax was one happy man. Seeing as Kevin had enough nieces and nephews running around in Wisconsin, he knew Jax's good nature was about to take a nosedive when Jax Jr. was born.

"When do you think reality will hit?" Taryn asked, pulling his attention toward her as she placed a mug of water inside the microwave. Her addiction to tea was becoming a problem because whatever the hell those leaves were made of had the entire office reeking of wet dog. "You know Ethan will have a tub of popcorn with his feet up the first day Jax comes in here after a sleepless night."

"I'm more worried that while he's struggling with father-hood, Ryland will make his appearance and blow shit sky high,"

Kevin replied wryly as he poured fresh coffee into his battered Vikings mug. He spared a glance Taryn's way to find her adjusting her black-rimmed glasses as if she wasn't comfortable with his turn of the conversation. Considering she barely came up to his chest, it was a cute gesture. "Have you or Crest located him yet?"

Ryland had caused trouble for every single member of CSA and their families when he'd been hired to kill Emily Weiss, Jax's wife. Whereas Kevin and the rest of the team were on high alert at all times, especially Jax and Emily, Taryn seemed confident that Ryland was lying low in Switzerland. Her sole purpose for the last six months had been monitoring every entrance into the country and locating their target. Kevin was well aware that it was more personal to her, but he was also aware of the reason and he wasn't one to pry into another's business. If Taryn wanted to talk about it, she would. In the meantime, he had his own shit to worry about.

"He's not on U.S. soil, if that's what you mean," Taryn replied, picking up a pencil that had been left next to the packets of sugar and sticking it behind her ear and in her spikey blonde hair that fit her feisty personality so well. He could tell by the sparkle in her brown eyes that she was about to change the subject. "How's Elle by the way?"

Fuck. Everyone on the team knew that Kevin had a thing for the raven-haired beauty whose lot in life seemed to be keeping him at arms length. This morning was a perfect example. What made him try and push her out of her comfort zone was beyond his rational thought process. Elle had made it perfectly clear that she thought of him nothing more than a friend. Hell, more of an acquaintance at this point.

"You suck, like all squids." Kevin picked up his mug and ignored the chuckle that came from their resident former Navy intel specialist. Her nickname was just a way to rub it in, but considering her out and out laugh, she didn't give a rat's ass. "Think you could get back to work and maybe match up something to the file I left on your desk? Taggart gave me everything he had at breakfast this morning. We're at another dead end."

"I'll run the info through its course," Taryn said over the ding of the microwave. She pulled out her cup and then started back to her office. "I've connected with the database of the forensics lab that Taggart's been using. I'll let you know when any results are posted."

Kevin watched her walk back to her workspace, which was located directly across from Crest's office. All of Taryn's equipment started taking up too much space in the cubicles, so it made sense that she had her own area. As for the *connected* shit she just referenced, Kevin was well aware that she'd hacked into the lab's database and hoped like hell she was covering her tracks. Crest would have her ass strung up on a flagpole if she had federal charges brought against the agency.

"Did Ethan make the coffee?"

Kevin didn't bother to stifle a groan of annoyance when Connor walked up behind him. He'd never get to his desk at this rate. All he wanted was a little solitude while he looked over his case notes one more time and entered the details of this morning onto his whiteboard. The sucker was overloaded with everything but who the actual killer was. That fucking spot still sat empty.

"No, he's got the crud." Everyone knew that when Ethan made the coffee that Jessie would end up making a Caribou run. Kevin walked to his cubicle, which he shared with Ethan. He spotted the Lysol can right away. Jessie was always on the ball.

"I told him to stay home and not bring his ass in. The last thing we all need is to get sick."

"I heard that you're sending your case files to that profiler Crest has in his back pocket," Connor said, his voice drifting over the partition. Kevin sat his mug on his desk while reaching for the can of disinfectant. Spraying mostly Ethan's side of the cubicle, Kevin placed his arm over his mouth so he didn't inhale the shit while Connor kept talking. "She seems good. Has a great reputation with the bureau."

"We'll see," Kevin replied, finally satisfied that he'd covered every square inch of where Ethan might have touched. He slid out his chair and finally sank into the black beat up old leather. He ignored the creaks and rasps that came from the wheels below from his large frame. "It can't hurt to have an extra set of eyes. The victim today wasn't a working girl from our neck of the woods. Taggart's following up on some leads now. Not sure where she came from, but she definitely got the same treatment as the others."

Connor appeared in the opening with his worn Marines ball cap on backwards and a cup of steaming hot coffee in his right hand. His Cuban heritage shown through, giving him a healthy glow instead of the rest of them with their winter pale and pasty skins. Well, with the exception of Jessie. She was always tan. Connor raised his mug toward Kevin's whiteboard.

"That information included on there?"

"No," Kevin answered, tapping the folder on his desk. Maybe having Connor to blow ideas around with wasn't such a bad idea. It might shake off his negative attitude about what happened with Elle this morning. Did she go back to bed or did she go against his wishes and visit the shelter anyway? He shook his head slightly, trying to get her off of his mind. "I was about to plug it in. This victim was staged in the same manner as the previous one. Her clothes were ripped to shreds, her hair matted as if she hadn't been taken care of for days, and the bruising and cuts were similar although there appeared to be more this time around. Either this victim fought harder or the scumbag is continuing his escalation with each victim."

"Well, it seems likely." Connor leaned against the partition, studying the board. "Look at the timeline. First rape was in the beginning of March. Second rape three weeks later, yet more physical damage to the girl. By June, your perp murders the third target. Now you've got your fourth victim with substantial injuries to her body. God only knows what he's going to do next."

"The only thing any of them have in common was that they worked as hookers." Kevin leaned back in his chair and studied the whiteboard as well. "Each had diverse features, such as hair and eye color. Their backgrounds are all different. There is nothing linking them together."

"Bee?"

"Nah," Kevin replied and then took a sip of his coffee. It reminded him of this morning with Elle. She hadn't even bothered to offer him a cup. For some reason that irked him. He tried to focus on the written words in front of him. "Only one of the victims worked for Bee and she was the first rape victim. She remembers nothing. Zilch, which isn't unheard of considering the emotional, mental, and physical trauma she went through. The second girl operated in St. Paul under Larry the Limey, but she was unconscious by the time the rape occurred. The first casualty, Daisy Scott, had just arrived in town. The bus ticket that had been on her person stated she'd gotten here the day before. Taggart spoke with her family and they informed him that she was a runaway, but had previously been in Chicago where she'd gotten into prostitution."

"Are you thinking this morning's victim was trying to set up shop here?"

"Yeah. Either that or she was visiting a friend." Kevin thought back to early this morning when he'd spotted Hash standing with Clarisse and Rachel behind the yellow tape. Something about that just didn't sit right with him. "Hash and two of Bee's girls were at the scene this morning. I'll take a stroll this evening and see if I can dig up any information."

"And Elle? Does she know about the murder?"

Kevin didn't answer right away, as hearing Elle's name threw him off kilter. He stared down into his coffee as their first meeting well over a year ago seemed to materialize in the deep brown liquid.

"Miss? You dropped this," Kevin said, picking up the black scarf that had fallen to the cold ground.

The tall woman with a glorious figure turned at the sound of his voice, her head tilting just so in question. Her black hair fell around her shoulders and seemed to cover most of her with the exception of her cleavage. The strands were as black as the leather corset she was wearing. The rest of her was just as beautiful and the black tights did nothing to hide her long legs beneath a short matching skirt. She had some type of jacket over her shoulders, but the waist seemed to stop right below her breasts. He had to wonder how she was walking around in this cold with hardly anything on.

"Are you talking to me?"

Her voice had a slight tremor to it and he had his answer on whether or not the weather affected her. She was downright freezing, but tried not to show it. It was obvious she worked the streets and that she was looking for her next john. The protective edge that was embedded within him roared to the forefront, taking him by surprise. Kevin had the urge to keep her warm, keep her safe, and he would damn well make sure that she never had to live this type of life again. It was that moment that started his downfall.

"Isn't this yours?" Kevin asked with a small smile, holding up the scarf.

Her eyes left his face to look at the item in his hand. Nodding in answer and taking the soft fabric from his hands, she then wrapped it around her neck. Again, the color of the material and her hair blended together until he couldn't tell which was which. It was her rich brown eyes that captivated him the most. Long lashes that seemed to never end framed them just right, yet something inside of them seemed locked up tighter than a pirate's chest. What secrets or treasures were lying within?

"Yes, sorry." The raven-haired beauty returned his smile. "I'm just not used to being called 'Miss'."

Kevin's gut tightened upon hearing her matter-of-fact tone as if there was nothing wrong with her statement. He'd been raised by a mother who would have smacked the back of his head if he so much as forgot to open a door for her let alone address her properly. He knew that times were different, but his upbringing was so engrained in him that he always reverted back to his manners. He wanted her to know what it was to be treated like a woman.

What astounded Kevin the most was the fact that she didn't have that weathered look women in her profession usually acquired over time. Her skin was flawless, her pearl white teeth were captivating, and her eyes still contained a little life that seemed to dim in the prostitutes he'd come to know.

"Elle, get back to work."

The words were like explosions. Kevin shot Bee a sideways look to let him know he didn't care for the man's tone. It didn't help that the low level pimp shooed her away as if she were some unwanted pest that had gotten too close. Kevin had to remind himself that this wasn't the time or place. He had no right to interfere with Bee's business or with Elle's life.

Elle...the name suited her. Simple and unique. He sought out Elle's gaze to see how she would react to Bee's ignorant manner. Elle gave Kevin another puzzling look that made him realize she knew no different and he *resisted the urge to wipe Bee's existence off of the street in question. Unfortunately, this was their world and he had no part in it. That didn't stop him from continuing their conversation.*

"Elle? I'm Kevin Dreier." He couldn't resist keeping her there a moment longer. He held out his hand and patiently waited for her to take it. It took longer than a few seconds as her gaze went from his outstretched hand to his face, as if trying to find a reason for his politeness. Finally, her cold fingers slid into his. Her touch changed everything. "It's nice to meet you."

"I'll take that as a yes," Connor said, his voice laced with wit as it cut through the memory.

"She's got it in her head that she can ask questions with results that I can't get," Kevin said, irritated that he got caught reminiscing. He rubbed his right knee to ease the ache. He wished it were that easy to do with other parts of his body. Elle had no idea the wreckage she left with every conversation they had. "By the way, I borrowed Jax's security key to gain entrance to her apartment. Just grab it out of my jacket."

"Yeah, I heard you knocking on his door at some ungodly hour of the morning." Connor made no attempt to reach inside Kevin's coat, which was draped over Ethan's chair. Probably not the smartest place to put it. "Let me just say that Lauren was not happy."

"Emily's always up at that hour," Kevin answered with a shrug. "I swear Jax gives us a play by play of her piss schedule."

Connor threw his head back and laughed. Kevin heard Jax mumble something from his cubicle, but couldn't make it out. Whatever he said had Connor laughing even harder. Kevin wished he could join in but the thought of Elle on the street, asking questions that would only put her in danger pissed him the fuck off.

"No worries about Lauren," Connor said, his blue eyes hinting on what he was about to say. "She was happy when I left."

"I'm glad to hear that all is well with your sex life, Connor," Crest said with a deadpan voice as he walked up behind him. Jax's laughter rang out over the partition loud and clear. "It'll make it easier to send you to Switzerland and check out the lead that Taryn has on Ryland."

"Wait. If Lauren gets pregnant, do I get a free pass like Jax does?"

"Fuck you, boyo." Jax's muffled voice carried over the cubicle. "You have to marry her first."

"That's not the order you did it in," Connor called out.

"When Lauren is in that state, we'll talk about it." Crest slid one hand into his trouser pocket while the other had his suit jacket slung over his shoulder. It was obvious that he was heading out of the office. "For now, Jessie's making your travel arrangements."

"I've already made them." Jessie seemed to materialize between Crest and Connor with her usual cheerful smile in place. She was technically Crest's personal assistant, but she aided them all when needed. For such a young sprite, she was the most efficient person that Kevin ever had the privilege of working with and she had certainly saved his bacon a time or two. If she weren't the type to worry about breaking a nail, she would have been great to have on the farm. "And it's not called a state. A state is Minnesota. Pregnancy is much more than that and you should be careful. We seem to be gaining in numbers around here."

Crest gave her a sideways look, but didn't speak. That was probably the route to go, considering it was a no-win situation. Jessie was obviously referring the word *we* to *women*. Jax mentioned months ago that the men seemed to be dropping like flies when it came to relationships. Jessie said it was the way the stars were aligned and no one was inclined to argue. She was always right and would hammer the topic into the ground just to prove a point. Kevin really wanted to state the obvious in the fact that his stars must have not gotten the memo, but it wasn't worth the hassle of dealing with her answer.

"Did you send Kevin's case files to Fallon?" Crest asked as he stepped to the side to shrug into his suit jacket. It fell over his holster with ease and his weapon disappeared from view as he secured one of the buttons. "She's in between cases right now, so time is of the essence."

"Nice way to sidestep that conversation," Connor muttered as he brought the mug up to his mouth. The look that Crest shot Connor was just as efficient as if he'd given him the bird. "I'm going, I'm going."

Connor backtracked out of the cubicle, leaving only Crest and Jessie in the opening. Kevin felt a little uncomfortable as those two stared at each other longer than what was necessary. This sexual tension that covered the office wasn't good for morale. Everyone knew that Jessie had a thing for Crest while it was obvious he did anything he could to keep her at a distance. Connor mentioned that it was the age difference, but Kevin wasn't so sure. Whatever the reason, he felt a kinship to Jessie. They both wanted what they couldn't have. Kevin was relieved when Connor's voice could be heard.

"Jax, tell Emily she's not allowed to have Junior while Uncle Connor is out of the country."

That seemed to cut into whatever the hell was going on in Kevin's cubicle and he couldn't be happier. He still wanted time to go over the case, head home for a few hours of sleep, and then hit the streets later tonight. It did cross his mind that since

Connor didn't take the key to the club that paying another visit to Elle might be a good idea, just to make sure she was minding her own business.

"I did get the files emailed over to her," Jessie said, bringing the conversation back around. "Kevin, Fallon replied that she would like the photos of today's crime scene as well."

"I'll scan them to you before I leave the office."

"Great." Jessie's focus turned to Crest. "Gavin, I need to speak with you before you leave for your appointment."

The only being on the face of the planet that Crest allowed to call him by his first name was Jessie. At least as far as Kevin knew. None of them had the honor of meeting Crest's parents. Hearing his first name always brought a smile to Kevin's lips, although it was obvious it had a totally different effect on Crest.

"I've got three minutes."

"I'll only need two," Jessie replied, her tone indicating that she would take his challenge.

Kevin turned his chair back around, leaving those two to walk back to Crest's office and have whatever duel they were going to have. The day was going by faster than anticipated and Kevin needed to get his ass in gear. He opened the file, but instead of grabbing the pictures he needed to scan, a sentence in Taggart's report caught his attention.

Three weeks. Three months. Six months.

Kevin started looking around on his desk for a calendar, but couldn't locate one quick enough for his liking. He resorted to using his computer and pulled up a yearly calendar. Using the mouse to backtrack to the first date in question, he began calculating and came up with their first solid lead.

Oorah.

Kevin felt satisfaction roll through his veins as the whiteboard confirmed his suspicions. What was that saying? Measure twice, cut once. Sure enough, the second rape happened exactly three months to the day. The first murder happened three months to the day, according to time of death. The victim this morning was killed sometime last night, placing her homicide exactly six months to the day. Either they were missing a victim three months ago or their killer had a timetable he was observing.

"Now all we have to do is figure out which one," Kevin muttered as he reached for his office phone. He dialed Taggart. As he waited for the detective to answer, Kevin couldn't help but wonder where Elle was right now. Had she heeded his advice and stayed home or was she at the shelter, putting her nose in where it didn't belong? "Taggart, I've got something. Are you at the station?"

Chapter Four

"What are *you* doing here at this time of the morning?"

Elle looked up from taking her coat off to see Cam Bennett stepping into the kitchen of the shelter at Reformation. Coffee and what smelled like cinnamon rolls saturated the air. A few pans and dishes sat in the sink. The kitchen table was a little cluttered with hand towels that had yet to be folded and sections of the newspaper were scattered about, looking to have been well read. It was unlike Cam to leave the kitchen in such disarray, as he was meticulous in making sure that everyone pulled their own weight.

Cam was no taller than she and had short, red, perfectly styled hair with a close-cropped full beard. He wasn't what anyone would call handsome, yet his immaculate appearance and perfect smile carried the day for him. He had a heart of pure twenty-four karat gold, which made every woman who crossed the doors of this shelter feel quite comfortable. It was as if he was their long lost older brother who only wanted to protect them. It might have to do with the fact that he was a way over the top overt homosexual, but in the end these women didn't feel judged by Cam. In return, they didn't feel the need to judge him or question his motives. They felt safe here.

"Morning, Cam," Elle replied, removing her scarf and laying it on one of the kitchen chairs. She then proceeded to drape her jacket over the back. "I just wanted to check on the girls. Did you hear about the murder this morning?"

"Rachel showed up here a few hours ago with the news. It's horrible. I gave her the back room for as long as she needs it." Anguish and concern crossed Cam's features as he turned to the counter and made himself busy by pouring her a cup of coffee. One of Cam's many talents was remembering exactly how every single woman whom had ever passed through his door had taken their coffee. Only his regulars knew these little secrets. "Maybe this will scare her enough to return home."

"Did Rachel know the girl that was killed?" Elle asked, taking the proffered drink. Lord knew she needed it to keep herself going.

"Apparently. The girl's name was Francie and she was strangled in the same way that Daisy was." Cam pulled out a chair but didn't sit, motioning for her to find a perch as he indulged his OCD cleaning fetish, picking up this and that. "Rachel went to the scene with Clarisse when word got out there was another murder."

"Who was she?"

Elle sank in the chair diagonally from Cam's unused seat and pushed away the feeling of satisfaction that she was finding out information that Kevin hadn't known. It wasn't the time nor did the situation call for it and sometimes Elle had to wonder if she hadn't lost all compassion.

"A new girl that wanted in on the action, I guess." Cam reached for one of the hand towels and started to fold it. It was such a mundane task, but it seemed to balance the horror of the conversation. Sometimes normalcy was all they had. "After some detective gave them a description, Rachel knew who it was. She and Clarisse admitted that they'd only seen her once. Apparently, Bee tried to get Francie to work for him, but she wouldn't go for it. He went on to explain who owned what part of town and that was the last they saw of her."

"What about Larry? Did she end up working for him?" Elle was well aware that Bee ran the south side of Minneapolis and Larry the Limey kept to the north, as well as having territory in St. Paul. The girls' paths would sometimes cross, but the lines were clearly marked to make sure there wasn't any confusion. "This Francie could have also worked in St. Paul."

"I'm sure the police will figure it out." Cam had stacked three towels on top of each other and was working on the fourth. "In the meantime, Eric said something this morning that had me in agreement…and you know that rarely happens."

Elle smiled over her cup, knowing full well that Cam and his brother Eric didn't see eye to eye on many things. If one of them wanted the kitchen blue, the other wanted it yellow. It was a constant battle that entertained the women who sought help within these walls. For all she knew, the brothers kept up the ruse on purpose to keep the atmosphere lighthearted.

Eric was the total opposite of Cam, all the way down to their sexual preferences. Eric stood a good six inches taller than Cam, as well as having blonde hair, although only on his head. The minute Cam had facial hair was the same day Eric kept himself clean-shaven at all times. Cam drove a car, so Eric drove an SUV.

"And what did the oh-so-insightful Eric have to say?" Elle asked, trying to keep her sarcasm on the down low. She and Eric had their issues, but as long he stayed out of her way, she stayed out of his.

"Just that in the midst of all this horror there is a silver lining. The girls might realize how dangerous the streets are and turn their lives around."

"Cam, I know that you and Eric don't want to hear this," Elle said, pausing long enough to formulate the words, "but some of these women prefer this life. It's what they know and all they'll ever know. They don't want to change."

Cam looked at her with sorrow and Elle's heart ached for him. She didn't know anything about his or Eric's past, but whatever led them to open this shelter and lobby for funding at every fork in the road had to have been fundamental. She reached over and squeezed Cam's hand, which now rested on one of the hand towels that he'd given up folding.

"What are you always telling me?" Elle asked, encouraging him to see the brighter side.

"One saved soul at a time."

"That sounds like a bad country song." Eric barged through the kitchen and went straight to the coffee. He hummed a tune that reminded her of Willie Nelson. "Damn, it's cold out there. Miss Elle, always a pleasure."

"Eric," Elle replied in a civil acknowledgement, all the while hating how he used the title. The only time that she ever felt it was used correctly was when she had first met Kevin. She gritted her teeth, not knowing if it was Eric's presence that had set her on edge or thoughts of Kevin. Either way, it didn't matter. All Elle wanted to do was talk to Rachel and see how she was holding up. "How goes the battle?"

"I think I have a donor lined up, so I'd say I'm winning at the moment. If we can bring in money before the end of the year, it will certainly help at tax time. I take it you heard about the murder?"

Before Elle could answer, a couple of young women walked in wearing business suits that were provided by Reformation. It was Liv and Molly, both of whom had forged a friendship. Liv used to work the streets in St. Paul and Molly was just down on her luck, trying her best to get away from a domestic abuse relationship. They both wore suits that had come from the interview wardrobe, which Cam and Eric provided to them in outfits for all sizes. From the smile on Liv's face, she'd had a good morning.

"Elle, I'm so glad that you're here!" Liv leaned down and gave Elle a hug, not giving her a chance set down her coffee. A little spilled over the rim. "Oops. Sorry, but I'm so excited. The construction company hired me to be their part time reception-ist."

Cam tossed Elle a towel. While she wiped her hand off and then the droplets on the table, Liv went on to say that she would be starting next week and all that her job description entailed. Elle noticed that Molly seemed a little distracted but she managed to look enthused anytime Liv glanced her way. Another round of hugs commenced, this time including Eric and Cam.

"Liv, I am so proud of you," Elle said, truly delighted for Liv. What Elle had told Cam wasn't a lie. Some women actually preferred life on the streets, as it was within their comfort zone. It was the majority that just needed a chance to get out from under the uncertainty and hand-to-mouth existence. Sometimes all it took was someone believing in them to give the confidence they needed to actually reach out for hope. "Molly, how did your interview go today?"

"I interviewed for a secretarial position at a trucking opera-tion," Molly replied with a shrug. "They said they'd be in touch."

"Do you feel the interview went well?" Cam finally sat down in his chair and leaned forward, with his elbows on the table. "Did they ask anything that I didn't cover?"

Elle hid a smile behind the mug of her now lukewarm coffee. Cam prided himself of instructing the girls in certain things, such as interviews, finance, and cooking. His eager expression for details was amusing as Liv and Molly delved into the particulars. Knowing this was the perfect time to excuse herself, Elle did so and walked back to the counter. Eric reached behind him and refilled her cup without even offering cream or sugar. Not that she took it sweet.

"I'm going to go check on Rachel," Elle murmured, keeping her voice low so as to not interrupt the conversation at the table. She nodded her head toward the door, which led to the stairway. "Cam said that Rachel has the back room?"

"Yeah. We're packed, especially with the amount of snow we're supposed to get over the next few days." Eric turned slightly to replace the carafe back on its burner. When he finally faced her, she could tell that he wasn't as cheerful as he let on. Those were definitely stress lines around his eyes, not laugh lines. Elle wasn't sure what to say, as they usually didn't talk about personal stuff. Each of them avoided that like the plague. She was glad when he kept speaking, thus preventing her from saying anything. "A couple of new girls came in last night. We couldn't refuse them, but I know they just wanted a place to crash because they hadn't paid up on their rent. Within the next week they'll be gone."

Elle was relieved when he'd stayed on the topic of Reformation. The housing was a specific type of shelter that aided women in getting back on their feet. They weren't a homeless shelter and they weren't there to be taken advantage of. Unfortunately it happened, and when it did, space was scarce.

There were only eight rooms, yet Cam and Eric did their best to weed through the ones that weren't serious in turning their lives around. Liv, Molly, Teresa, Sue, and Angela all had different back stories, but each of them was committed in reforming their existence. With the additional two women from last night, that left one more room. Elle needed to see how steadfast Rachel was in achieving something more than daily survival.

"You can only go by what they tell you, Eric. Look at it this way—the next time they come seeking help, you can refer them to the homeless shelter down the street. Reformation has a strike out policy, which I'm sure Cam lectured them on."

"He did," Eric conceded, nodding his head. "It didn't deter them at all, but maybe I'm mistaken and they'll see how good Liv is doing."

"Faith, Eric. They just need a little bit of faith." Elle didn't need to say anything else as they both knew that with just a little renewed faith, a person's outlook could change on a dime. An uncomfortable silence descended when he didn't reply. Yep, it was time to go. "Would you please pour me another cup? I'll take one up to Rachel."

Elle silently left the kitchen when she was armed with both mugs. She ignored the feeling of being watched as she walked through the doorway and up the stairs. The first time that Elle had offered to volunteer to help in any way she could, she'd met Cam. Had she met Eric first, she wasn't so sure she would have continued volunteering here. She hadn't made the connection that they were brothers. She'd met Eric previously years before when he'd been a totally different man. He'd never said or done anything wrong in the past year, but Elle's instinct never steered her wrong before. Cam was the reason she still came to Reformation.

Teresa's voice could be heard through her bedroom door and Elle was happy to hear that it sounded as if she were talking to a representative of a local community college in White Bear Lake. They'd spoken about it at length and it seemed as if Teresa was going for it. Good for her.

Finally reaching her destination, Elle kicked the door softly so as not to spill the coffees. Within seconds, the door opened and revealed one tired young girl. Rachel was no more than nineteen or twenty years old, her brown mousy hair hanging down her back. The blemishes underneath her dull brown eyes blaringly sent the message of missed sleep and stress. A disturbing feeling settled in Elle's stomach. Did Rachel know something more than she was letting on?

"Hey," Elle said softly, holding up a mug in gesture. "I heard about what happened and thought this might help."

"Come on in." Rachel's smile didn't quite meet her eyes as she took the proffered drink. She turned and took a few steps to where a small desk sat in the corner and placed the mug down on the worn surface. "I thought you might be Clarisse. She said she would stop by today."

"Just me." Elle crossed the threshold and took in the layout of the room. As much as she came to Reformation, it was rare that she ever set foot in the privacy of the girls' rooms. Usually she kept her visits to the community area or the kitchen. "I thought you might want to talk."

"There's not much to say," Rachel replied with a defeated shrug. She crossed her arms as if to ward off a chill but Elle was relatively sure it was meant to do more than that. "It's just not safe on the streets anymore."

"Honey, it was never safe to begin with." Elle gave her a wry smile and joined Rachel when she sat on the single bed. "There isn't a day or night that goes by that we're not watching over our shoulders. We might pick up a john that gets his kicks out of knocking us around or we might not do enough business for Bee. Let's face it—he has his anger issues when he's not seeing the cash."

"You make it sound like you're still a part of us, but we all know the sweet deal you got from that cop or whatever he is." Rachel's voice was laced with bitterness. Elle reached out a hand in comfort but it was scorned. Indecision seemed to linger in Rachel's eyes. "Is there a job opening at that club you work at?"

"Rachel, it's not that simple," Elle said, not knowing how to explain her situation without it sounding like her ass had landed in a pot of gold at the end of the rainbow. "Kevin and I had been…friends…for a while before he mentioned that the club was looking for a manager. Please don't think that it was given to me any other way than through proving myself."

Damn it. Elle's explanation was coming out wrong and sounding entirely different than what she actually meant. Her hesitation over what exactly she and Kevin were only seemed to make Rachel pull away even further. Elle realized that she'd taken hold of her necklace and started to worry the small locket that dangled from the chain. Her old habit was blatant and she released the silver accessory to let it fall back against her gray sweater.

"All Kevin did was set up an interview for me, Rachel. I never thought to come here or any other shelter where I could borrow nice clothes and look reasonably well put together." Elle thought back to last year when she'd first met Connor and Jax. She'd never been so nervous in her life. "I showed up in my nicest pair of jeans and a top that didn't reveal too much, if you know what I mean. The one thing I had going for me was that I had graduated high school. Believe it or not, I had a good GPA. But I'll be honest with you and tell you how I got the job."

"How?"

Elle could tell that she had one hundred percent of Rachel's attention now. Good. Maybe a little of what Elle said would actually stick with her.

"Desperation. In the eight years I was working the streets and living in run down apartments, I'd never been presented a chance to get out. I never even thought about it really. Sitting in front of two men who didn't look at me like their next fuck or expect anything from me other than to answer their questions honestly was something I'd never experienced. And you know something else? A part of me will always be that girl who sold her body on the streets. I will always be looking over my shoulder. That fear of the unknown never goes away."

Rachel's resentment seemed to fade just a bit, but it was enough to let Elle know that she'd made the right call in being totally honest. There were times when revealing too much of oneself was only opening up vulnerability that would be used against you later. Elle had been working hard to get herself out of that habit.

"I want out, Elle. I can't take the anxiety and fear of thinking the next guy that wants to pay for sex will be the one who kills me." Elle's heart broke as a tear slid down Rachel's tired face. "I don't want to die like this. I want so much more."

Elle was relieved when Rachel leaned into her and allowed herself to be comforted. The next couple of hours were spent listening to Rachel's hopes and dreams. Some were attainable and some wouldn't be possible right away. They spoke of the murders and the fear that this killer had instilled within the community. It was when Rachel spoke of Bee and what she'd seen a few nights ago that had Elle's heart racing. Her admission about Hash was just icing on the cake. Was this the break that Kevin needed to solve the case?

Chapter Five

"Shit," Kevin said, leaning back in the booth of an all night diner. Grease lingered in the air while it stuck to their plates. The naugahyde vinyl booths were nauseating paisley patterns and spoke of an earlier time. There was no better breakfast than at one o'clock in the morning. "No one's going to be out in this weather."

"I don't know how you guys work it, but when we have snitches, we usually just call them up." Taggart held up his hand to the waitress, signaling for the check. "Max, you're buying."

"Fuck that." Max shook his head while he wiped his mouth with a napkin and then threw it on his empty plate. "You left me with the last two meals when you suddenly *got a call*. It's your turn."

Kevin finished his orange juice while the two men sitting across from him argued about the check. He'd probably be the one picking it up, but he didn't tell them that. Max Higgens was a DEA agent that frequented Masters. He was a good man and even better agent. It was by happenstance that Kevin and Taggart had run into him.

"Hash isn't one to carry a cell phone. For how paranoid he is over the fact that devices can be tracked nowadays, you'd think he was an eighty year old man who'd built himself a bunker in the middle of bum fuck Egypt."

"He's got a point," Taggart replied with nod of approval. "You know where he lives?"

"You know the rules as well as I do." Kevin leaned back against his seat wishing he could stretch his legs. This table was too damn small for the three of them. "I go to his inner sanctum, all trust is violated. I'm not a cop. I can't just bring him in for questioning."

"I don't know what you think he'd know." Taggart finished off his coffee. "If you're right about the rapes and killings taking place exactly three months apart, a low level drug dealer doesn't strike me as the type to be that organized. By the way, we're looking at all possible Jane Does that were reported three months ago. If the body's been found, we'll link it through the autopsy reports."

"So you think Hash knows something about your case?" Max had gotten much of the low down throughout the meal, and since his specialty was drugs and alcohol, it made sense that Hash's connection would garner his attention. "I know he's a low level drug dealer, but you should be aware that his ass is getting caught up in some serious shit. He's been seen with Gibson."

"Hash told me that Gibson was trying to run a couple of lines through the city, but I thought Carlos had his area sealed off." Kevin noticed that since the conversation had technically steered off the case, Taggart was busy texting someone on his phone. "Hash mentioned a few weeks ago that Gibson was looking at some dealers in St. Paul."

"Carlos' supplier isn't meeting the demand of his clients. Word has it that he's thinking of teaming up with Gibson." The waitress finally showed and placed the check on the edge of the table. Max silently slid the small piece of paper over so that it was situated in front of Taggart. "We have some people in place should that happen. If we can get Gibson's supplier, we can take down multiple routes through the Midwest."

"Interesting," Kevin said, looking out the window of the diner. The snow was falling at a steady rate, and by morning another five inches would make rush hour traffic fucked up. He didn't mind snow, but it was the aftereffect that he didn't want to deal with. "I was hoping to catch both Hash and Bee tonight. As Taggart said, Hash was with two hookers earlier this morning. Told the detective who'd tried to question him that he was just there to walk the women home. The Hash I know isn't known for his manners."

"At least we know the victim's name," Taggart cut in, sliding his phone in his suit jacket. "Francie McQueen. I highly doubt that's her real name, but we're running her through the system now. According to Rachel and Clarisse, Francie wanted to work the area but Bee explained how his territory worked. I've been trying to track down Larry the Limey to see if he or his girls had any encounters. In the meantime, a cute barista is waiting for me. Move your ass, Max."

"Not until you pay for the meal, Casanova."

"Fine," Taggart mumbled good-naturedly, reaching into his back pocket. He pulled out his wallet and threw a fifty down on the table, which would cover not only their meals but the tip as well. Kevin let him have this one, knowing Max wouldn't let it go. "There. Happy?"

"Extremely."

Max laughed and then stood up, allowing for Taggart to maneuver out of the booth. One would think that a man would look rumpled after such a long day, but there wasn't a wrinkle in the man's suit. Max and Taggart shook hands and patted each other on the back. Kevin just shook his head at their antics and then turned his gaze back to the windowpane.

Before leaving the office around two o'clock this afternoon, Kevin had made sure to pass the information he'd discovered over to Taryn. She said she would input the specific dates and see if they matched up with any other murders in the country and then if needed would broaden the scope. He'd even scanned in the photographs so that Jessie could send them off to Fallon. Maybe the profile that she was going to provide them would shed clues as to what type of scumbag they were looking for.

"I'll touch base with you tomorrow morning." Taggart's words pulled Kevin's gaze away from the street. "It should prove to be a busy day, so I'm going to go and enjoy the company of a nice young woman."

"Made time to stop by Caribou, did you?" Kevin smiled, knowing that Taggart wasn't one to let an opportunity pass him by. "Go get her, Casanova."

Taggart laughed as he made his way to the door. Max sat back down, but something caught Kevin's gaze and made him look outside once more. What the hell? Elle was walking down the opposite side of the street, bundled up in a white ski jacket with the same black scarf that she wore when he'd first met her. Her black hair was still pulled back and sitting in a high ponytail, making her look younger than her twenty-five years. And even that was young compared to his thirty-two.

"She's still giving you a run for the money, huh?"

Kevin unfolded his frame from the booth and slapped his friend on the shoulder. Max attended Masters on a weekly basis and was well aware of Kevin's fascination with Elle. Everyone busted his balls over the fact that he didn't play at the club. It felt too uncomfortable to him to do that in front of Elle. Had either of them been in any other situation, where she didn't manage the club his friends owned, it might be different. They certainly didn't have a relationship and she made it abundantly clear that she didn't want one. Kevin was free to sleep with whoever the hell he wanted…unfortunately, he wanted her.

"I'll see you this weekend, buddy."

With those words, Kevin snatched his jacket from the booth and was out the door. The cold hit him but didn't really register in his brain as he looked both ways to cross the snow-covered street. He shrugged into his coat and had just about caught up with her when she quickly turned on him, light glinting off the blade of the knife she was holding.

"Jesus!"

"What the hell are you doing?" Elle yelled, practically stomping her foot. "I could have stabbed you."

"Stabbed me? You could have killed me, woman." Kevin's chest finally loosened to where he could breathe. The first instinct that came over him when being confronted with a knife was to disarm his opponent and immediately get the upper hand. She was damn lucky that his brain kept registering that it was her and not some stranger. The likelihood of her actually having gotten the knife that close to him was nil. "You're damn lucky that I didn't hurt you."

"You just said two different things with opposite meanings," Elle replied in irritation, seemingly having caught her composure though. She folded the knife and slid it back inside her pocket. She wore no gloves, so her hands remained inside what must be warm material. "And yes, I could have killed you. You should know better than to sneak up on a woman."

"I wasn't sneaking up on you." Kevin put his hands inside his pockets as well, the cold finally registering. "What are you doing out on the street at this hour? Didn't I warn you that it's dangerous right now?"

"As opposed to every other day?" Elle was being a little too snarky for Kevin's liking, but he clenched his teeth to prevent himself from saying something that he would regret. Dealing with the submissives at the club was a hell of a lot easier than talking to Elle. He felt like he was back in Afghanistan walking through a minefield. "I was actually looking for you. I figured you'd be talking with Hash after what you said this morning."

"You should know that no one's out in weather like this." The minute the words were out of his mouth, Kevin knew he'd made a mistake. Had he not been looking, he would have missed the flash of pain that tore through her brown eyes. The minefield had been a hell of a lot easier to navigate. "You took that the wrong way, but nothing I say right now will make you see that. Instead, I'll walk you back to your apartment while you tell me why it is that you were looking for me."

Kevin didn't give her a chance to say no as he gently took a hold of her arm and led her back from the way she'd come. Once Elle was by his side, he kept a hand on her lower back regardless that the wind chill bit into his fingers. It was well worth the pain, or numbness as the case may be, to touch her in some way.

"Isn't that Max Higgens?"

Elle's question had him looking over her head and across the street. Max was just exiting the diner, holding a hand in the air in salute. Elle returned the gesture, while Kevin just gave a nod of his head. Max continued to walk the opposite way, the snow eventually hiding his form.

"Yeah, that's where I was when I spotted you. We had a bite to eat. Taggart and I were going to have a chat with Hash and Bee tonight, but it'll have to wait until the weather clears."

"Who's Taggart?"

Elle looked up at him, snowflakes falling on her lashes and making her look like one of the beautiful women in those jewelry commercials that were getting engaged. Wouldn't she be a sight to see in that situation? Kevin mentally kicked himself in the ass.

"He's just a detective that I'm working with on the case." Kevin let his fingers sink into her jacket as they came to an intersection. Holding on tightly while he slowed his steps, he waited for the orange light to indicate it was okay to cross. "He works homicide, but since all the cases are related, my best shot at helping solve who raped Becky Rattore is through him. Again, this brings us back to the reason you were looking for me. Unless it was personal?"

"What?" Elle's gaze once again swung up to meet his. Why there was surprise written across her features, he didn't know. Kevin had made it blatantly obvious that he was interested in her from the get go, dropping clues as many times as the opportunity allowed. "Of course it's not personal."

"Of course," Kevin replied wryly. Not giving her a chance to follow up on that, he continued. "Then we're back to square one."

"I went to the shelter today and Rachel was there." They rounded the corner of a building and Kevin nonchalantly scanned the area while listening to what Elle had to say. He refrained from commenting on the fact that she purposefully went against his advice, but he knew it would get him nowhere. "I got information that I think will help you out."

Kevin couldn't repress the smirk that lifted one side of his mouth. He made sure she couldn't see by looking ahead of them, but damn if she wasn't just an enigmatic nymph all proud that she obtained information she thought he didn't have. He knew all about Rachel and Clarisse, having double-checked the detective's interview statements that Taggart had sent over to the office. He'd let her enjoy her little moment for a while longer.

"And what would that be?"

"Well, for starts, Rachel and Clarisse knew the victim. Her name is Francie and she was looking for an area to pick up johns. Bee confronted Francie and told her how the territories were split. Rachel never saw the girl after that."

The wind and snow were picking up and Kevin didn't like that the weather put them at a disadvantage if someone were to come up upon them. Regardless that there was a killer still roaming the area, Ryland was never far from his mind. It wouldn't surprise Kevin if the man decided to take them out one by one in order to make a statement to Crest. Kevin was going to have to cut off her bragging a little sooner than he wanted. Her apartment was only one block away as it was.

"City girl, I hate to break it to you, but I knew that almost the minute I left your apartment," Kevin stated, looking both ways as they crossed the final street to their destination. "As I said, I don't want you putting yourself in danger by asking questions. You have a job, which is managing Masters. My job is to find out who is raping and murdering these girls."

They were now standing directly in front of Masters and he allowed her to come to a standstill in front of him. They were facing each other and when his gaze landed on Elle's upturned face, Kevin knew he was in trouble. Any satisfaction should have been wiped away by his statement. Instead, she looked like she was ready to deliver a final blow in their battle of wills.

"Then I'd say you're not doing your job properly," Elle replied, her brown eyes lightening in her delight. "If you were, you'd know that Bee was seen leaving the same warehouse where Francie's body was found the night before."

Chapter Six

Elle couldn't help but feel a little victorious when the look of disbelief had crossed Kevin's face. She let him stew just a little more on that tiny bit of information as she used her keycard for access to Masters. She never used the backdoor, which was located in the parking garage to the left of the building. It wasn't like she drove or had a vehicle, so that entryway was pointless. Wanting to get out from the cold and knowing she still had a lot to cover with Kevin, she led the way through the small foyer of the club.

The small hall was usually dimly lit with gas lamp sconces to give off an air of sensuality, while Latin music ordinarily drifted from the speakers. At the moment, one canister light did shine down on the wooden oak hostess stand. It was well lit enough that she easily swept her card key and gained access to the inner sanctum of the club.

Whereas usually the sounds of low murmurs and carnal moans enveloped a person as they entered the main area, silence descended as the empty play spaces hid themselves in the shadows of the after hours lighting. The orange scented wood soap hung in the air and teased Elle's nostrils. She bypassed the bar to the left of her, sneaking a glance in the mirror that hung toward the back. Kevin's eyes were on her.

"There's a lot more information where that came from," Elle added, trying to ignore the BDSM equipment and implements as they walked past them. Each play station was cordoned off by black velvet rope, which was slung between antiquated brass poles. She maneuvered around the sitting quarters which consisted of booths and couches, privacy gained from the palms and ferns situated just so. Her apartment was located at the top of the backstairs. She usually never gave the club a second glance, but for some reason having Kevin behind her made it stand out more. She ignored the niggling feeling and pushed it to the back of her mind. "Rachel said she would touch base with the detective who interviewed her."

"Trust me, after I tell this to Taggart he'll question her himself."

"He won't get answers if he comes on too strong," Elle warned, using the keycard to gain access to her apartment. She liked the security system that Jax and Connor had set up. She walked through the doorway and grimaced, knowing she would have to turn the heat up just a tad. She hated wasting money on a few degrees. "It's better if she speaks with the detective who questioned her in the first place. Rachel felt comfortable with him."

Elle turned just in time to see the frown on Kevin's face. He didn't like someone other than him or this Taggart to be lead in this investigation. Was it vanity or just a sense of control? She didn't picture Kevin as narcissistic in any way, but then again, she really didn't *know* him. She quickly took off her jacket and scarf then made her way to the small kitchenette. She refused to admit the reason of why she'd purchased a few more mugs on the way home from the center this afternoon.

"I'm making coffee. Would you like some?"

"Whatever other information you have must be a doozy," Kevin replied. She didn't have to turn around to know that he was taking off his jacket. Before she could ask what he meant, he continued. "You're offering me coffee? Usually you show me the door."

At that she did turn around. Elle could see how serious he was and she tried to think back to the other times when he was in her apartment. It was rare, but there had been times that he would drop by with Jax or Connor. She wasn't the type to be rude so much as matter of fact. They technically didn't run in the same circles. Had he taken her attitude a different way?

"Kevin, I never meant for you to feel that you're not welcome here." Elle struggled for the right words as she leaned against the counter. How could she explain that it wasn't her who had changed once she'd cleaned up her life? "You know that I appreciate how you helped me, but it's not as if you and I have the type of relationship where we just drop by each other's places. I don't even know where you live. Regardless, I didn't mean for you to feel that I was ungrateful."

Kevin's gray eyes never wavered from hers, as if he was trying to gauge if she was telling the truth. Elle figured she should have been insulted, but then thought better of it. Hearing him say out loud that he felt unwelcome was just a testament that he recognized her change in behavior toward him. He stood in the middle of her sitting area with his legs spread just so and his arms crossed over his chest.

"You used to talk to me."

Elle started to feel confined, similar to how he made her feel this morning when he asked about allowing people to care for her. He was making this personal when it was just the opposite. Kevin had done a good deed by setting her up an interview. Nothing more, nothing less. The words he just spoke made it sound as if he thought she took advantage of him.

"I still talk to you," Elle argued, feeling unsettled. She needed to do something with her hands. The four-cup coffee maker was the perfect excuse, so she turned around and went to work. "You were helpful to me when I needed it. I will always be grateful. When I started working for Jax and Connor, I poured my heart into being the best manager they could have. You had your life and I was building mine. Let's face it, we still run in different circles."

Silence descended over the small apartment. Elle finally hit the brew button and then went about washing the new mugs that she'd purchased earlier. It had nothing to do with the fact that she didn't want to turn around and face him yet. Would he see that she hadn't told him the full truth? Elle was pretty damn good at lying if the situation called for it.

"I live in Eden Prairie."

The change of topic threw her off course. Elle looked over her shoulder to see that he'd taken a seat on her couch. It looked more like a loveseat with his large frame on it. Add on top of that him stretching out his legs and he looked mighty comfortable. The altered conversation drew her attention away from being concerned she'd revealed too much. The slight grin on Kevin's face made her wonder if he'd done that on purpose.

"Eden Prairie? You drive every day into the city?" Elle quickly rinsed off the mugs and then grabbed a dishtowel. She faced him once more, feeling more comfortable and wanting to find out a little more about him. "Why don't you rent an apartment like Ethan or live on the edge of the city like Connor and Jax? It would certainly make your commute easier."

"I was raised in the country," Kevin replied, resting a hand on his right knee. "My parents still own a farm in Wisconsin, although my brothers mostly do the daily chores. The city is fine to work in, but not to live. I own a couple of acres of land and the house sits toward the back end of the section. It's peaceful."

Elle studied him, a hundred questions racing through her mind. A farm boy? She never in a million years would have guessed that Kevin Dreier—the man who maintained street contacts for his job—grew up in the backwoods of Wisconsin. Asking about his upbringing would only prompt him to do the same to her. It was second nature to most people, but she'd learned not to put herself in that position. For the first time in her life, she found herself tempted to break that rule.

"So what else did Rachel have to say?"

Kevin's inquiry took away her decision to ask more questions. She should be grateful, but she found that she wasn't. Just when she thought the day couldn't get stranger, here she was with Kevin sitting in her living room about to serve him coffee. In the beginning, he resonated a blunt attitude. Then he became tender and caring—something she couldn't handle—which made her keep her distance. Now he was acting as if they were long lost friends. This change of personality was worse than a woman PMSing. Elle didn't like it, but she still poured both of them coffees and walked over to where he sat.

"Rachel was having trouble with a trick not paying her the full amount, so she went looking for Bee a few nights ago." Elle handed him one of the mugs. She couldn't bring herself to sit next to him on the couch, so she took the chair. "Clarisse mentioned that he had business in or around that area, so Rachel headed that way. And before you ask, I know that Bee carried a cell phone around, but Rachel doesn't. She can't afford one."

"And she found Bee coming out of the warehouse?"

"Yes." Elle paused long enough to take a sip, letting the warm liquid spread through her. She'd forgotten to turn up the heat but didn't feel like getting up again. "The thing is this. When Rachel mentioned it to Bee this morning, he said she was mistaken. That he'd never been there."

"This morning?" Kevin leaned forward and placed his drink on the small coffee table that she'd bought at the thrift shop on the corner. "Bee wasn't at the crime scene, so I'm assuming that means Rachel spoke to him afterward. Why didn't she…never mind, stupid question. She wouldn't have told the detective because she feared what Bee's response would have been."

"Right." Elle noticed that he was rubbing his right knee and couldn't help but think that he'd hurt it somehow. Kevin's hand pulled away and when she looked up, she realized that it was something he hadn't wanted her to see. She was well aware of the saying that curiosity killed the cat and tried to heed that advice by continuing their course of focus. "I tried to explain to Rachel that if she's going to turn her life around, she needs to start by making things right. Francie didn't deserve to die like that and if Bee is the one who killed her, than he should be brought to justice."

"Whoa, hold on a second," Kevin warned, holding a hand up. "You can't just jump to the conclusion that Bee is the one raping and murdering these girls."

"Why not?" Elle didn't understand his reluctance to see the truth. "The man sells out women for money. He's got anger issues that make the Tasmanian devil seem like a tame house cat. He was seen leaving the crime scene. What more do you want?"

Kevin's rich laughter filled the air and instead of being offended, she found herself captivated by the laugh lines around his eyes and the ripples through his upper body. Elle had seen him do the same during club hours, when one of his friends or even a submissive said something in humor. She wasn't sure she'd ever found something that amusing.

"Okay, farm boy, you tell me who's killing those girls." Elle kicked off her boots and then pulled her feet up underneath her. "I just gave you a prime suspect."

"I don't see a television in here," Kevin said, pretending to look around. He knew damn well that she didn't own a TV. "Seriously, solving murder cases is nothing like you see on the screen. You have circumstantial evidence. That doesn't mean that Taggart won't bring him for questioning. This is totally different than me wanting to have a conversation with Hash over why he was there this morning. Taggart will run this by the book and have Bee in an interrogation room the minute Rachel comes in to revise her statement."

"Good." Elle took another sip of her coffee. "Then you'll have to check his alibis."

Kevin sat back against the couch once more, studying her. His gray eyes didn't seem to miss a thing and she squirmed a little under his gaze. Elle didn't like to think that he could see more than she wanted him to, so she glanced down at the contents of her cup. She was about to tell him her other news to keep the conversation going when he spoke.

"Do you remember the day I told that if you didn't get out from that life, that it would eventually swallow you whole and spit your corpse out as if it was nothing more than a piece of leftover garbage?"

Kevin's question startled her and she wasn't sure how to answer. She remembered his words as if it were yesterday. Elle had been walking down the street when she happened upon him and Bee in a deep conversation. Her intention had been to keep walking, as the black eye that had been given to her by an overzealous john had still been very much discolored. It wasn't how she'd wanted Kevin to see her.

The anger that had spread across Kevin's face didn't scare her, for he also radiated restraint. Elle had never once seen him lose control, although Bee did like to push his buttons every once in a while. Why Kevin continued to use the pimp as one of his snitches to get information on the happenings of the city were beyond her. She would think other people would have access to more info than Bee.

"Yes," Elle replied, uncertain as to where he was leading this discussion.

"What made you listen to me?"

Here she'd been worried that if she asked too many questions, he would do the same. It hadn't mattered and now here they were, with Kevin asking personal questions. It wasn't that she wouldn't answer him because his topic was more artificial than actually delving into her personal life. Unfortunately, one inquiry usually led to the next.

"Well, that statement wasn't the only thing you said that night. The lecture you gave was at the right time and place." Elle struggled to find the right words without giving too much away. "You weren't telling me anything I hadn't heard, but it was the way you said it. You wanted nothing in return. You detailed cold hard facts and after having been in a situation where I didn't know how far that guy would end up hurting me, fear was a big motivation as well. I guess it was a combination of things. You aren't like you are now or else I—"

Shit. Elle hadn't meant to spill that much detail and from the way Kevin was looking at her, he'd caught her slip. This was the problem when answering questions. She suddenly felt bad for Rachel should Taggart get a hold of her.

"And how am I now?"

"You know," Elle said, waving a hand to try to dismiss her mistake, "just that you seem to be careful of what you say to me. Like I'm going to break or something. It's no big deal, really. I needed somebody to lay it on the line and you did that."

"So it wasn't Bee?" Kevin seemed to get the hint that he was treading water and relief surged through her that he was willing to let it go. Her respite didn't last long as his question sunk in, followed by more. "He didn't hurt you in any way? You're not keeping something from me that I don't know?"

Reality dawned and Elle felt a spark of anger flick off of her skin and ignite the emotion so that it trailed through her tense body. Kevin had a way of causing her to react without first thinking it through. Her fingers tightened on the mug as she tried to keep her feelings contained. She gave up trying as the words flew out of her mouth.

"You think I want to throw him under the bus for the rapes and murders to get back at him for being my pimp?" Elle sat forward and slammed her mug on the coffee table. "You have some nerve to accuse me of being some spiteful bitch who doesn't take responsibility for her own actions. I sold my body for sex because it was the only thing I was good at. As long as I brought in the money, Bee was fine. The man does have anger issues, although they were never directed at me. Rachel told me what happened and it doesn't take a fucking genius to see that it makes Bee a likely suspect. You can—"

"Elle, it was just a question…not an accusation." Kevin sat forward, resting his elbows on his knees after he picked up his coffee. Through it all, he never wavered in his scrutiny. "Again, you're putting words into my mouth. I never accused you of anything, so don't go and change my mind about you being spiteful. Understand?"

The way he said that last word had her stomach tightening in response and deflating whatever anger she might have felt. Elle sensed something that she refused to name as his tone dropped an octave. Kevin sounded like the Doms did when speaking with their subs. Secretly Elle wanted nothing more than to be one of those women whose Dominant took over his submissive's pleasure. She'd always been the one performing, making sure she made her money's worth. Sure, the johns told her what they wanted, but it was still her that was executing the acts. Pushing that loose thought aside and knowing that those kinds of considerations were nothing but trouble, Elle didn't answer. She did what she was best at and changed the subject.

"Hash has a vested interest in Rachel." Elle finally unfolded her legs out from underneath her and stood up, not bothering to look at him. She went into the kitchen and placed her cup into the sink with the other dishes she needed to wash. "They've been seeing each other for a couple of months. That's why he was there at the crime scene."

Elle wasn't sure what he would say or if he would allow her to get away with avoiding, well, all of the things she'd side-stepped tonight. It wasn't like she didn't have his cell phone number, so why she felt the need to go looking for him tonight made absolute no sense to her. Maybe she needed to take some of the money that she'd saved by being frugal and go on a mini vacation. The moment she discarded that idea something else immediately took its place. Kevin never mentioned why it was so cool in her apartment. Was he just being polite?

"There will eventually come a time that you and I will be truthful to one another," Kevin murmured, his low voice humming in her ear. Elle's fingers tightened on the countertop to prevent herself from turning around into his body which now melded with hers. It was the first time that she'd been so close to a man since she'd left the life. "Right now, I'm going to give both of us some breathing room before I do something that I'll regret."

The heat of Kevin's body vaporized the second he stepped back from her. Elle turned her head slightly to see that he was walking over to her small kitchenette table for two. It came from the same thrift shop as the coffee table. As was becoming her typical reaction, she wasn't sure what to feel or say, so she remained silent while he shrugged into his jacket.

"You're going to drive in this?" Elle closed her eyes at the foolish question. It wasn't her right to be concerned for his safety and she hoped that he didn't take that as an invitation to stay with her. She quickly thought of an escape. "Wouldn't it be better for you to drive to Connor or Jax's house? The roads have to be covered by now."

Kevin's left side of his mouth lifted up in a smile, but she didn't return the gesture. Elle was well aware that he found humor in her attempt at correcting the mistake. Leaving him to the investigation was probably a sound idea and one she should have listened to. She wouldn't make that mistake again.

"My truck has four wheel drive. The snow is no problem, plus I like my bed." Kevin walked to the door and opened it, stopping to look at her once more. "You may not want to hear this, city girl, but this thing between us is not going away. We've ignored it for over a year. That might come easy to you, but for a man like me, it's bringing me to the end of my rope. I don't like it there, Elle, so something has to change now."

Chapter Seven

Elle managed to get through an entire week without seeing Kevin. It wasn't like she had to go out of her way. The only time she'd left her apartment was when she'd volunteered her time at Reformation, talking to the girls who were still there and making sure that Rachel was still on the right path. She got her information on the investigation through Rachel, who'd contacted the police just as she said she would. Elle knew that Bee had been brought in for questioning, but not the outcome. It wasn't as if she were going to call up Kevin to find out either, specifically after his parting words the last time they'd been together.

"Elle, why is the front door open?"

Jax appeared in the doorway of the storage closet with Emily, whose belly was the size of a basketball. His usual smile had now been replaced with a scowl while his wife was practically glowing with happiness. Elle felt a twinge of envy, but quickly pushed it aside. Her life had dramatically changed in the last year and she couldn't be more content with her good fortune. She stood from where she was rearranging some of the boxes of liquor, non-alcoholic beverages, and additional inventory that had arrived not thirty minutes before their arrival.

"The delivery man just left," Elle explained, wiping her palms down the front of her denim to get rid of the dirt. "I was just about to lock things up."

"I don't mean to be harsh here, but you can't be too cautious." Jax took a step back, leading Emily to one of the stools that were situated at the end of the bar. "We're still in the crosshairs of an assassin and until he's caught I don't want to take any chances."

"Jax, she knows that," Emily said, taking his hand and holding it to her thigh. Elle didn't press the issue on this threat that was mentioned every so often, but now that he reminded her, she wondered if Kevin's life was at risk as well. "How are you doing, Elle?"

"Good." Elle walked back behind the bar and reached for a glass. She poured Emily a glass of orange juice and set the tumbler in front of her. "Jax, I've been careful, I promise. I'm not getting careless. The deliveryman had just literally walked out the door."

"I saw him." Jax reached up and removed the skullcap he'd been wearing, leaving his blonde hair mussed up. Elle could see a few little stress lines around his eyes and she wondered if it was due to the fact someone was still out there with the intent to kill Emily or was it because his firstborn child was scheduled into this world within the next few weeks. "I know you're not going to like this, but I think having either Connor or myself here for the deliveries might be a good idea. All it does is provide this predator with easy access into this part of our lives. We can't be too careful."

Elle didn't have the heart to argue with him even though that was her gut instinct. She'd been taking care of herself for a long time and she didn't need someone else to do that for her. The rational part of her brain knew that Jax needed to have his bases covered. Emily had become this core for him and Elle didn't blame him in the least for doing his damnedest to keep her safe.

"Whatever you feel is best. I'll make sure you have the delivery schedule." Elle turned her attention to Emily, whose blue eyes sparkled with happiness. They'd been sweet and invited her to their wedding, although Elle had remained to herself as much as she could. She worked for Jax and Connor, but that didn't mean she socialized with their women and friends outside of that circle. "Emily, how are you feeling? The date is getting close."

"Other than having to pee every half hour, I'm doing good." Emily took a sip of her juice and then set the glass back down onto the countertop. "Listen, we didn't just stop by to visit. There's something we want to run by you."

Elle didn't want to hurt her feelings by saying that she hadn't thought their visit was anything but social, so she just nodded her head for either one of them to continue. Emily seemed to be the one who was uncomfortable as she shot her husband a look, whereas Jax's signature smile started to appear. Her heart began to stutter at the trouble that implied.

"It's no secret that you and Kevin have been dancing around whatever the hell is between you two." Jax took a couple of steps behind Emily until he pulled out another barstool and made himself comfortable. He folded his arms on the countertop, holding his cap in between in large hands. His look became somber for a brief moment. "Kevin's grandfather passed away this morning. He's cleaning up his shit at the office before driving to Wisconsin in order to be with his family."

Elle wasn't sure how to react to the news, so she crossed her arms over her chest and waited to see what this had to do with her. She felt sympathy for what Kevin must be going through, but it wasn't like she could do anything for him. The best thing for him was to be with his family and friends. She glanced at Emily to see that the woman was nibbling her lower lip and watching her closely. An uneasy feeling started to ascend her spine.

"Connor isn't here." Jax's voice caught Elle's attention and she turned her focus back on him. "He's checking out a lead on this threat that's been hanging over CSA and won't be back into the country for another few days. In the meantime, I can't leave Emily, as we're too close to her due date. Lach is somewhere in the jungles of Africa, which leaves the rest of the team covering the cases that we do have."

"I'm not sure I'm understanding what this has to do with me." Elle mentally cringed, knowing how heartless she sounded. It wasn't that she wouldn't lend a hand when needed, but she had a feeling that Jax and Emily were going to ask more of her than she could give. "I have the club under control. It's not like you need to be here. There have been numerous times that you and Connor were gone at the same time and I handled management just fine."

"Elle, we're not questioning your management skills," Emily said softly, leaning forward and placing her elbows on the hard surface. "We're worried about Kevin and we don't think he should make the drive by himself. He was very, very close to his grandfather and this is hitting him hard. He's made it no secret that he has feelings for you and we thought that maybe as a friend—just a friend—that you would go with him for support."

Elle didn't reply right away, mostly because she was speechless. She switched her gaze back and forth between them, trying to figure out if this was some sort of prank. Her breathing became rather stinted when it appeared that it wasn't. They really thought it would be in Kevin's best interest if she were to accompany Kevin to his family's farm in Wisconsin and attend a family funeral. Jax and Emily were delusional.

"Whatever you think Kevin feels for me is nothing more than pity." Elle busied herself by putting the cap back on the orange juice and storing it back into the mini fridge underneath the bar. "I owe him a lot for what he's done for me, but that doesn't give me a ticket to pry into his personal life. I wouldn't even say that we're friends so much as acquaintances. You know that. You're his friends and he isn't going to want me with him for something so private."

"Is that how you see it? Pity?" Jax asked, his deep voice expressing disappointment. Elle refused to be kowtowed just because he saw things differently. She straightened and met his gaze straight on. Emily placed a hand on Jax's arm, but he saw her stare for stare. "Kevin isn't one for pity, Elle. The man almost lost his leg when an IUD went off beside him during his tour in Afghanistan. He came back to recover but instead of lying in his own bed of misfortune, he dug his way through four years of college to obtain his bachelor's degree. He used it to help others in a program similar to the Wounded Warriors Project. He's seen people learn to live without their limbs and he watched those men and women deal with PTSD. Never once did he look upon them as some kind of charity case or them needing his pity, so don't think you're any different."

"Jax." Emily's voice cut through his lecture, but she shouldn't have felt like Elle needed saved. She didn't. This type of honesty was something that Elle could deal with and respond to in kind. "I don't think—"

"Emily, it's fine." Elle felt like she finally had some footing in what was being asked of her. CSA wasn't just a team of members doing their job. They were family, similar to how she felt about the girls at Reformation or those still on the street. Sort of. She wouldn't call them family, but that didn't mean she didn't understand the concept. "I appreciate your honesty, Jax. I'm not too proud to admit that sometimes I view kindness as charity. And I'm not one to turn that down, as long as I'm working for it. Hearing some of Kevin's history gives me assurance that he doesn't feel sorry for me, but that doesn't give me the right to have access into his personal grief."

"If you're too chickenshit to be there for someone who's been there for you, so be it. But let's call a spade a spade." Jax stood up and surveyed the room. Guilt attacked her from every vantage point, just as he'd intended. He took his time putting his skullcap back on and then sighed as if in acceptance. "You do an exceptional job here, Elle. Connor and I couldn't ask for a better manager. But this isn't a life. You have qualities in you that all of us see, but no matter how much we extend our hand, you only see charity when what we'd really offered you was our friendship. Not everyone in your life is angling for an advantage."

"Jax, would you give Elle and me a minute?" Emily asked, all the while Elle gritting her teeth against the brutal honesty of Jax's words. Talking with Emily might not be such a bad idea, seeing as how she might understand where Elle was coming from. "Alone?"

"I've got to call the office anyway." Jax brushed a kiss on Emily's forehead, but instead of walking out into the entryway, he paused and looked at Elle once more. "You've always been upfront with me. I'm just returning the favor."

Elle and Emily watched as Jax meandered through the club and out into the entryway. He kept the door open while placing his call, not letting Emily out of his sight. Elle didn't blame him and although she knew there was more to Emily than met the eye, it was her business.

"Is he right? Do you hold yourself at arms length from the rest of us because you feel we view you differently?"

Elle sighed in resignation, knowing that Emily wasn't going to let this go. The woman was like a dog with a bone and had somehow tamed the wildcard pacing back and forth in the entryway. What had started off as a reasonably okay day with four hours of sleep had slowly disintegrated into muddled crap.

"We're different." Elle tried to formulate her words right without hurting Emily's feelings. "It's not that I don't like you, Lauren, Taryn or Jessie. You're all very kind and have always treated me with respect. I—"

"We're not so different, Elle." The way Emily spoke the words gave Elle pause, for she heard the underlying pain in the woman's voice. "I may not have sold my body for money, but the choices I made affected my soul just the same. We all have some kind of guilt to assuage from our actions but no one says we have to do it alone."

Emily slid off of the stool, albeit not gracefully as were her usual movements. She placed one hand on her lower back and slowly pushed the empty glass toward Elle with her other. For a woman who appeared to have everything and lived life to the fullest, Emily seemed to be full of secrets.

"Kevin needs a friend." Emily glanced to where Jax was waiting for her before finishing what she wanted to say. Elle remained silent, not knowing what to add to the conversation.

Between Jax and Emily, they were making her arguments seem selfish. "Would it really be so bad if that friend was you?"

"It's complicated, Emily." Elle struggled to find a way to explain it, but in the end, all of her excuses sounded petty. Her heart started to race and her breathing became a little shallow as her mind accepted the only decent decision that could be made. "I – shit. Shit, shit, shit."

Elle looked at Emily to see a small smile playing on her lips. The woman knew a victory when she saw one. Even though Elle knew it was inevitable, she still grasped at the last straw that was left.

"What about the club?"

"What about it?" Emily asked with a shrug. "It's closed for the next two nights. Jax and I can handle it for a couple more if need be."

"So…that's it?" Elle wasn't sure exactly what to do now. What was the protocol for something like this? "I'm just supposed to show up at his place, which I don't even have the exact address, and declare that I'm going with him?"

"You'll figure it out," Emily replied, her smile as large as the one Jax usually displayed. "And maybe, when you return, we can grab a bite to eat and share some stories. I'm not opposed to having a new friend either."

Elle's chest tightened as she felt her barriers being tugged on all sides. She straightened her shoulders to try and relieve the pressure. She wasn't at all too proud to admit relief when Jax finished his call and started to walk across the club. Emily nodded her head slightly and when Jax arrived at her side, he snatched a napkin and jotted down something in ink. Elle realized it was Kevin's address.

"If either of you need anything, just call."

Elle nodded her head, as there was no need for words. She watched them walk out and heard the outer door close behind them. Slowly crossing the floor to the entry door, she shut it and wished it were as easy to close out the emotions they'd left her with. Elle turned back and faced the club, the white napkin practically glowing underneath the lights of the bar. How the hell was she going to deal with this?

Chapter Eight

Kevin finished packing his duffle bag and zippered up his best suit in his Valpak. He used his helmet bag for those items he might need access to before he got a chance to unpack. He did this all the while doing his damndest not to think about his grandfather. It wasn't as if Kevin hadn't been expecting the call, but all the same it was difficult to hear the news. His mother had sounded devastated. He could hear the rest of the family in the background, asking to speak with him. There was no need and when he'd hung up, he'd taken a moment in Crest's empty office to gather his composure. There would be time to deal with the grief later. Right now, his family needed him and the five hour drive would clear his head. Just as he'd grabbed the canvas handles of his bags, the doorbell rang.

Cursing under his breath, Kevin decided to lug his belongings through the bedroom and down the stairs anyway. He had everything he needed for his trip and time was of the essence. He dropped the heavy load at the door and then swung the thick oaken frame open. It took a moment to register that it was Elle standing out in the cold.

"What happened?" Kevin barked, looking behind her to see if anyone else was around. To his disbelief, a taxi was driving away. Looking her over, there didn't seem to be a hair out of place. She was bundled in her white jacket with the infamous scarf wrapped around her neck. White gloves encased her hands and while denim covered her long legs, her black boots covered the material up to her knees. There was an edge to her that had him immediately on alert. He took her by the arm and pulled her beside him, shutting both of them inside. "Are you okay?"

"I'm fine and nothing happened." Elle's brown eyes drifted away from his, as she seemed to be fascinated by his home. Her eyes fluttered from one object to the next. He was more concerned about what the hell brought her here to begin with. "I have to tell you this is not how I pictured your place. It's stunning."

"Elle," Kevin said, drawing out her name so his impatience would register, "you wouldn't be here if it weren't important. If you're fine, then is it Rachel? Do I need to touch base with Taggart?"

"Oh, you think I'm here about the case?" Elle was leaving him exasperated, which was unusual. She was a bright woman, but at the moment all intelligence seemed to have fled. She had pretty much already turned to face the living room, seemingly enamored with the two long panes of glass on either side of the fireplace that went from ceiling to floor. Any other time he would have taken pride in the fact that his home impressed her, but this wasn't the moment and he needed to be on his way. His touch on her shoulder finally stole her attention and when her eyes liquefied into a deep melting pot of chocolate, his gut churned. "Jax and Emily came by the club this morning and told me what happened. I'm really sorry to hear about your grandfather, Kevin. I, um, thought I could accompany you. You know, to Wisconsin."

"Accompany me?" Kevin felt like he'd been sucked down the rabbit hole. Anger was starting to form that she would choose now to play some sort of game. The resentment started to fade as her words finally penetrated. Elle's phrase was way too proper, almost like she needed to keep an emotional distance. Having her offer herself up to spend more time with him was counterproductive to what seemed like her intent. He finally connected the dots. "Son of a bitch. Did Jax ask you to come here? He just doesn't learn his lesson, does he?"

Kevin could see her confusion but he didn't take time to explain. He walked through the hallway and into the kitchen, determined on getting to his phone. His parents always kept a large wooden bowl to place their keys next to where they commonly entered their home. He'd kept up the tradition and added his wallet and phone to the mix. Snatching his cell up into his hands, he immediately hit Jax's speed dial.

"Kevin, what do you mean? What lesson? Jax was just trying to be helpful." Elle had followed Kevin into the kitchen, and when he turned around he saw that her attention had been grabbed by the updates he'd just completed on the cabinets. "My God, this is beautiful."

"Elle, I'll give you a tour some other day, I promise. Now just isn't a good time." Ringing could be heard on the other end, but the son of a bitch didn't answer. Jax's voicemail picked up. "Listen to me, you jackass. I thought you learned your lesson about meddling into other people's lives. Do me a favor and stay the fuck out of mine."

One thing about having a landline is that you could slam down the phone and make it mean something. A cell phone just didn't give Kevin the same satisfaction when he pressed the disconnect button. He was left simmering and wasn't quite sure what to say without hurting Elle's feelings. She didn't seem like the type to have her arm twisted by Jax…under any circumstances.

"Jax and Emily are just looking out for you." Elle pulled off her white gloves, shoving them inside her pockets. Her attention was now solely on him, and for the first time since he'd met her, Kevin felt a little unsettled by her scrutiny. It was as if she was studying him. "You mentioned that you were close with your family. I know that Ethan would be your choice to have as a road buddy, but you got me."

"I have you?" Kevin worded the question the way he meant it, even though he was chancing that it was the wrong time and place. Elle's lips parted and it was obvious he'd surprised her. Tough shit. He'd known who he'd wanted the first time he laid eyes on her. His grandfather's death definitely hit home that life was too short. "Exactly what does that mean, Elle?"

"Just that I'll go with you." Elle shifted her weight to her other foot, unmistakably agitated by his question. He didn't care. The tables had turned and he felt more confident, more stable than before. He wanted answers and she was evading the entire situation, as usual. "Do we have to break everything down? Can't we just go?"

"No, we can't." Kevin wasn't in the mood to give an inch, let alone allow this chance to pass them by. It was as if he could hear his grandfather cheering him on. "I'll make this easier on you though. A simple question really. Why are you going?"

"That's easier?" Elle was getting annoyed, which wasn't a bad thing. He found the more worked up she got, the more she revealed. He wasn't one to quibble about how he got the information he needed. "I'm going because you shouldn't be alone. How's that for simple?"

"We're both big boys and girls, Elle. I can handle loss, although I know it won't be easy." Kevin closed the distance between them and came just short of where she stood by the large island. She tilted her head just so, revealing her uneasiness. "But we're not going anywhere until you answer some questions. Are you going as a friend? Something more? I already told you that I'm done skirting around this thing between us. You coming with me has multiple meanings, but none of them alter the fact that you'll be around my family. You'll meet my parents, my siblings, my nieces and nephew. You'll be seeing into my life. Are you prepared for that?"

"I don't know, Kevin!" Elle's voice had risen enough to let Kevin know he'd pushed her as far as she was going to go today. As anticipated, her armor cracked just enough for him to get a glimpse of the uncertainty that lay just beneath the surface. Her voice lowered to almost a whisper, although not once did she let on that she couldn't handle the reality that he'd pounded home. "I don't know what this means. Maybe it's my way of repaying you. Maybe I'm being selfish and I want to be able to say that the slate is wiped clean after this. Will it lead to friendship? I think we'll both see that I don't fit into your life, but that doesn't mean we won't be given an understanding of how each other works. Just let me do this for you, without question or judgment. One day at a time."

Kevin felt the turmoil rise up inside of him. The rational side of his brain told him to drop Elle back at the club on his way out of town and they could deal with this at a more appropriate time. Handling his grandfather's death was going to be tough enough. He shouldn't be heaping on this type of emotional shit, but he knew he'd already made his decision. He'd let her come with him. It wasn't him who would end up regretting it and he hoped like hell they could salvage whatever was left after this.

"I'm not promising anything, city girl." Kevin reached up and brushed a loose strand of hair that caressed her cheek. A small gasp escaped her lips and he couldn't wait until the time came when he would claim them. She was entering his neck of the woods and he would do everything in his power to prove just how wrong she was. Fit into his life? She would do more than that. She would belong. "Let's get on the road."

Chapter Nine

Elle tried to settle back comfortably against the black leather seat, but nothing she did felt right. The cab of the truck felt stifling and she'd shed her coat within twenty minutes of the drive. Not sure of what to say, she'd remained silent and let Kevin concentrate on the highway. Her thoughts kept drifting to when he'd tucked her hair behind her ear. His fingers brushing her face felt as if they had seared her skin. Since then she'd made sure that no loose strands from the clip were visible. That kind of tenderness and lure mixed together wasn't something she could handle.

"You can turn down the heat if you're hot."

Elle jumped slightly at Kevin's voice as it rebounded throughout the truck. His deep tone seemed to up the heat and she was tempted to turn the dial on the dashboard, but knew it was just her. He was the one driving and she didn't want to make him uncomfortable. She shook her head slightly.

"I'm fine."

"Fine, huh?" Kevin ran the wipers, smearing away the snowflakes that left watermarks on the windshield. He looked her way, but instead of following up their previous uncomfortable conversation, he surprised her by asking her opinion of his house. "You seemed shocked, although I'm not sure why. I told you I lived out in the country."

"Country," Elle repeated, feeling a little more at ease with such an artificial topic. "Which means farmhouse. I wasn't expecting a million dollar home."

Kevin's rich laughter vibrated the windows and Elle tensed, ready to take offense. Was he laughing at her? Just because she grew up on the streets didn't mean she wasn't aware of how much things cost. She hadn't been exaggerating. His house was at least that much, if not more so.

"The house didn't even cost that much, I'm afraid." Kevin shifted and rested his left arm on the door, keeping both hands on the steering wheel. "It was a run down piece of shit until I got a hold of it. Everything you saw I remodeled with my own two hands. Back home you either do it yourself or barter with neighbors for specialty work such as plumbing or electrical. I've got a handle on most of it. I still have the back of the house, but I'll get to it eventually. Then I'll start the remodel on the barn."

If Kevin was talking about the ramshackle of wood that sat off to the right side of his property, then he had a lot of work ahead of him. Had that been the shape of the house too? Elle breathed deeply for the first time in…well, she couldn't remember. She settled back and let the relaxed atmosphere envelop her. This she could handle.

"Will you sell it when you're done?"

Kevin's eyebrows rose as if that wasn't the question he thought she would ask. If he believed she was going to delve any deeper, he was sadly mistaken. Elle was about to meet his family. Odds were she'd get to know Kevin through them without having to ask him herself and find that he wanted something in return. She reached for the water bottle that he'd supplied her with before they'd gotten on the road.

"No. I take pride that I renovated my home with my own hands. It means something now. Something I can pass on to my children. Who would I be if I didn't make better the place I call home?"

Elle choked as the water got trapped in her windpipe. The casual way he said the word *children* had surprised her. After a couple of moments where she wasn't sure she'd ever get oxygen again, she was grateful when he didn't comment on her reaction.

"Drank too fast," Elle murmured, placing the bottle back into the console that sat between them. "So how's the investigation coming along?"

Elle glanced at the clock on the dashboard and she calculated the illuminated green numbers. Four hours and twenty minutes left, if they'd been around five hours out like he'd said. Keeping to non-personal topics wasn't going to be as manageable as she'd thought.

"Before we delve into that, I think it's best I forewarn you about my family." Had Jax not mentioned Kevin's injury that he'd sustained in Afghanistan, Elle wouldn't have thought twice when he casually rubbed his right knee. She'd seen him do that from time to time, but never really thought anything about it. If Jax was right about the extent of the damage, she would have thought he'd be in more pain. "My mother and father will dote on you. Just accept it and everything will be fine. As for my three brothers and little sister, they'll try and see exactly how important you are to me. I have no doubt that you can stand your ground, but you might want to have something at the ready so they aren't constantly hounding you. My two nieces will finagle a way to get their hands on you for a makeover. As for my nephew, well, he's only six months old. As long as somebody's holding him, he's content. It's a good thing you have a predilection for sweaters. He's still on his momma's breast and he might get overfriendly if you show him yours."

Elle's mind tried to keep up and suddenly, the cab of the truck once more felt a little warm. This talk of family meant they'd be in their company quite a bit. She never really thought to ask where they were staying and now it looked as if she might be holing up in a hotel by herself. She quickly calculated what she had in savings. As long as it was only two nights, it was doable. He was making it hard for her not to ask the questions that she wanted and found herself on the losing end.

"Um, you *are* planning to tell them that I'm just a friend, right? Look upon me as a substitute for Ethan. They wouldn't be asking him those kinds of questions, would they?"

Again, Kevin belted out a laugh. His reaction was starting to irritate her. This wasn't a funny situation as far as she was concerned. Elle twisted in the seat slightly so that she was facing him. She'd had enough of this playing around.

"Seriously. Your brothers and sister wouldn't ask something like that about Ethan. So we'll tell them that I've come in his place for emotional support. I really won't be around them that much, so it shouldn't be a problem. As for children, I'm sure they'll be wary of a stranger. I'll attend the service and anything that might be held afterward in honor of your grandfather. I'm not going to intrude on your family time, so when it's time to head back home, just swing by my hotel room and pick me up. See? There's no reason to forewarn me."

Elle didn't like the way he was smiling, but she felt like if she continued she'd be prodding a hibernating bear and that just wasn't on her agenda. He didn't argue with her, which should have made her feel better, but instead ended up doing the opposite. Regardless if things went smoothly, at least she could say she'd paid it forward. That should give her comfort.

"Can we get back to the investigation? I know Bee was brought in, but not the outcome." Elle remained with her back more against the door than the seat. She liked being able to study him without him doing the same to her. His gray eyes were focused on the road and she would do what she could to keep the conversation from getting too serious. Talking of the investigation would get his mind off of his grandfather's death. It was a win-win for both of them. "Rachel shared with me that he's unhappy his girls are being given an out by Reformation. Throw on the fact that she ratted him out, well, I'm worried about her."

"Taggart checked into it and is keeping tabs on Bee's whereabouts. The interview went as expected and according to Bee, he wasn't anywhere near the warehouse. Until the police can prove otherwise, their hands are tied. As for the other rapes and murders, he can't pinpoint where he actually was during the time they were committed." They were behind a semi and it didn't surprise Elle when Kevin turned his signal on. He was confident in his driving, regardless that the snow was coming down at a faster pace. "I watched the recording of his interview and you're right. Bee's not too happy with Eric and Cam Bennett. That's still not a motive. Why would Bee kill his hard won source of income? There are too many unanswered questions, but as long as he stays away from you, then we won't have a problem. As it stands, Taggart's scheduled a patrol car to swing past Reformation every now and then to make sure things don't escalate. It's just not in the budget to give Rachel round the clock protection, not that I truly think she needs it. She's more likely to be talked back into working for Bee, in which case putting herself at risk because of her occupation."

Elle played with a string that must have come from a snag in her sweater. She spun the white thread, questions circling through her mind. Kevin had hit on a point that she never really followed up on in this last year because she didn't really want to know the answer. Curiosity was getting the best of her today.

"I was able to get out relatively easy," Elle admitted, going back to studying his square jaw. He used to have longer hair, but now he kept it short in addition to his sideburns. There was no question that he was a handsome man, along with a very wide protective streak. She'd wondered if that extended to her and was about to find out. "That life…I guess what I'm saying is that Bee isn't the type to just let his girls walk without doing everything in his power to make them stay. He likes them to be dependent upon him, whether for drugs, money, food, or a place to stay. When I told him I was out, he didn't say a word. Did you have something to do with that?"

"It depends," Kevin replied, shooting her a sideways look as if to gauge her reaction. "If it's going to put further distance between us and make the rest of this trip harder for me than it already is, then I'll plead the fifth."

Elle couldn't stop the small smile from forming on her lips. She could understand why he would think that would be her reaction, but it was far from the truth. What she told Jax earlier that morning hadn't been a lie. She didn't mind being given a helping hand as long as she worked damn hard for it. Jax and Connor had given her a chance and she'd repaid them twofold. Kevin had done the same and as far as she was concerned, she was settling a debt with this trip. Upon their return, she was hoping she wouldn't feel so loaded down with gratitude.

"Pretty."

Elle found that she was once again studying the little thread she held between her fingers. Her eyes flew to his upon hearing that one word. A heartbeat later, he broke their connection by concentrating on the road. What was pretty? She looked out the windshield, but only saw the snowflakes coming at them like angry hornets.

"Did I miss something?"

"You smiled."

Elle lost her breath for a moment and she didn't have the oxygen to reply. She wouldn't react, for that would defeat the purpose in what this trip was intended for. When he started talking about mundane things, such as why he was a Vikings supporter instead of a Packers fan, she settled back into her seat to enjoy the stories of his youth. Apparently she'd been wrong and Kevin talking about his grandfather was his way of letting go. A niggling of worry that she was learning too much was pushed away as she marveled at what a different life he'd led compared to her. She felt like a sponge that had been on the sand for too long and the water was now just nipping at her edge. Elle soaked it up.

Chapter Ten

Kevin didn't bother to hide his smile as they drove farther into the country. If Elle thought she was staying at some hotel versus with his parents, she had another think coming. That wasn't the type of people his family were and it was just something she'd have to accept. If one of their children brought someone home, regardless of the relationship, his parents would see to it that they were comfortable and welcome in all regards. He noticed Elle's brows furrowed a little deeper as she studied the area and he knew it wouldn't be long before she put two and two together.

"Kevin, how far away are we from your parents' house?"

"Oh, probably another eight miles." It had stopped snowing a couple hours back, but the landscape around them showed plenty of white powder as they slowly cruised down what was once a two-lane road. The plows only removed what was needed in this area. Kevin had no doubt that more snow would come before they headed back to Minneapolis. "We'll have missed dinner, but I'm sure there will be enough leftovers. Besides, at times like these, neighbors keep each other knee deep in casserole dishes. Mom won't have to cook for weeks."

"Neighbors?" Elle looked around, probably to ensure that she wasn't missing something. "There's nothing out here, Kevin. Maybe you should turn around. There was a town around thirty miles back that had hotels."

"We have lots of neighbors out here," Kevin replied, side-stepping what she really wanted to talk about. "Mr. and Mrs. Troyer live around a mile down that drive to your right."

"What drive?" Elle turned her head to the right, obviously missing the turn. "There's nothing there."

"Look back and you'll see the black mailbox. The bottom of it is buried in the snow, but you'll be able to make out the box." Kevin waited a few seconds before pointing out that Mr. Fisher lived two miles down the left hand lane. "His son and I went to boot camp together. Good man. Last I heard he was serving another tour over in Afghanistan."

"I don't know if I'd call them neighbors." Elle finally stopped looking at the area to glance his way. She had one eyebrow raised. "Neighbors are those people that live right next to you, where you walk no more than twenty steps, knock on their door, and ask for milk. I'm pretty sure you need a vehicle to visit these people out here."

"No, city girl. You are referring to the strangers who lived next to you when you resided in that apartment complex. Neighbors help each other when needed, don't ask for favors in return, and will always have your back when things get tough."

Kevin pulled the truck closer to the right side of the road as a pick-up was headed their way. It was Leroy Howe who lived on the north side. When his vehicle slowed down to almost a stop, Kevin did the same and rolled down his window.

"Mr. Howe, it's good to see you. How's Mrs. Howe?"

"We're doing good, son." Mr. Howe's eyes darted past Kevin to obviously get a glimpse of Elle. He tipped his head in acknowledgment before turning his attention back to Kevin. "I'm sorry for your loss. Your grandfather was a good man. The missus and I will be at the service tomorrow."

"Much appreciated." Kevin turned toward Elle to make the anticipated introductions. "Mr. Howe, this is a good friend of mine, Elle Reyes."

"Nice to meet you, miss."

"You too, Mr. Howe."

"You keep warm now," Kevin said, getting ready to roll up the window. The heat seemed to have been swallowed whole by the square outside access. "And we'll see you tomorrow."

"I know you have a lot on your plate, son, but maybe before you leave town you could stop in at the center. Craig misses having you around and I know it would be good for morale." Mr. Howe ran a hand over the rough skin on his leathered face as if he might be asking too much. "Have you kept up your service?"

Kevin knew that Mr. Howe was asking if he was volunteering his time at a foundation for wounded veterans in Minnesota. Mr. Howe was one of the first neighbors to have reached out to Kevin upon his return home from when he'd been injured in Afghanistan. The old vet volunteered his time at the Heroes Benefit Society and he had made sure that Kevin didn't fall into a depression. It was hard enough to deal with the injury that one sustained, but it was another to mentally process that one's future was profoundly altered making it easy to fall into a meaningless self-absorbed void.

"Yes, sir." Kevin shifted uncomfortably, knowing that Elle heard every word of the exchange. His volunteer hours were private and something that he didn't talk about very often. "And I'll do my best to stop in and talk with Craig."

"Alright then," Mr. Howe replied, his satisfaction shining through. "We'll see you tomorrow."

Kevin secured the window and pulled the truck forward, getting them back on the single plowed lane. His parents' ranch was three miles up on the right hand side and he looked forward to being within the comfort of his family home. He waited for the peppering of questions to come his way and when they didn't, he felt the tension of his body ease away. He looked over at Elle to find that she was playing with the locket that she wore around her neck.

"Mr. Howe lives around five miles down this road." Kevin motioned to the area in front of them. "His land borders ours. Mrs. Howe makes the best damn fried chicken this side of the Mississippi. I'm sure she's already loaded my mother up with more than the whole family could eat in a week, but my brothers and I will see to it that it's much appreciated."

"Kevin, I don't want you to have to drive me back to the nearest city tonight. You're not going to want to leave later and it's wrong of me to ask you to. I think it's best to take me now, unless one of your siblings will be headed back that way. I can hitch a ride with them."

If Elle didn't stop grinding that locket onto her chain, she was going to wear it down until the links snapped. Kevin figured now was the time to tell her that she wouldn't be staying anywhere other than his parents' home. At least he had two miles to deal with the fallout.

"Elle, you'll be staying in one of the guest bedrooms." Kevin turned the temperature up a notch, trying to recapture the heat that had escaped. Maybe it would warm her up to the idea as well. "It's pointless to stay in a hotel when I'd waste too much time driving you back and forth."

"No, I won't be staying *with* you. That wasn't the deal. I specifically said I would be sleeping at a hotel." Elle's focus was expressly on him, the beautiful scenery forgotten. So much for the heat notion. "As for wasting your time, that won't be a problem. I told you that I would just be at the viewing and that you could then spend time with your family. There's no need for me to intrude on such a private time."

The turn to his parents' dairy farm came into view. It was bittersweet coming home to family when his grandfather was no longer with them. Pop's hearty laugh over the dinner table would be heard no more. The stories he told would now be relayed by the next generation and his memory would live on. That didn't erase the grief they would go through as they gained acceptance.

"My parents would be offended if you chose to stay in some damn hotel," Kevin said in a low voice, needing to convey the importance of what he was articulating. Every word was the truth and he was about to extend himself out on a limb. "They don't need any more problems just now and to tell you the truth, I need you here. All I would do is worry about you being all alone in a cheap hotel room so far away instead of just down the hall."

Kevin didn't have to look Elle's way to know that her brown eyes widened in shock at his admission. He had flicked his blinker on a few feet back and slowed his truck, taking the right turn carefully onto the plowed drive that led to his childhood home. The sun was setting behind them as he drove down the lane and dusk was descending over the land. Deer could be seen stirring in the distant tree line and the land of his youth amplified his emotions as he audibly sighed. The days ahead would carry enough darkness and he waited for her reaction with unease.

"Okay." Elle's voice shook just enough that he caught the crack at the end. He wished he knew whether it was over having to be around strangers and the given circumstances or if it was that she was afraid to spend too much time with him. The days ahead would be very telling. Elle's shoulders straightened and she reached up to adjust the clip in her hair. "I wouldn't want to cause more distress for your family and I don't want you to concern yourself over me and the case when you should be thinking about your parents. I'll do my best to stay out of the way though."

Kevin shook his head in disbelief at her blatant misconception. She either did it on purpose or she really believed the words that she was emitting from her mouth. What the hell did family and friendship mean to her? The case didn't have anything to do with them an entire state away. Lights shone ahead over the rise, indicating they were getting close to the house. It was for the best he didn't have time to answer for he wasn't sure he wouldn't have chased her immediately back the way they came. As it was, the front door was opening as he pulled the truck behind the other vehicles parked out front of the large wraparound porch. His family waited for them.

Elle took in the Norman Rockwell vision in front of her and stared at it in disbelief. Powdered snow covered the landscape, surrounding a large farmhouse with a white wraparound porch. She had no doubt that during warmer weather there were rocking chairs to accompany the swing that swayed in the bitter wind. The golden rays of light that streamed from the windows cast a "coming home" feeling that she'd only ever read about or seen on Christmas cards. She seriously contemplated waiting until Kevin got out of the driver's side to then hotwire the truck and hightail it out of here.

Elle took a deep breath and reminded herself that looks were deceiving and what was inside rarely matched the façade. These people were no different than those she surrounded herself with. They just hid it better. Kevin had come around the passenger side and was holding her door open before she even had a chance to put her jacket on. Deciding against it since the porch was a short walk away, she grabbed it behind her and started to exit the vehicle.

"Don't even try getting out of this truck without putting your jacket on." Kevin's rich voice had taken on that authoritative tone and she found herself reacting to it. Her fingers tightened in the downy fabric so as not to show any physical response. The more he resorted back to the old Kevin, where his dominance shined through, the more she had trouble controlling her reactions. She reminded herself why she was here as she shrugged into her jacket, making it seem as if it weren't a big deal. Ignoring his outstretched hand, she slid her body down to the ground. "You're on my turf now, city girl. That means my rules."

"Remember that talk of neighbors?" Elle asked, purposely refusing to allow Kevin to one up her. It wasn't going to happen and she was about to let that be known. She looked up into his gray eyes and met him stare for stare, not giving him an inch. She refused to admit to even herself that he affected her physically. This back and forth exchange they had going was just to keep his mind off of the reason they were here. It wasn't like they did this back home. They rarely saw each other. It was only when he nodded that Elle remembered she was making a point. "Well, think of me as a neighbor. I'm helping you out and then I will be on my way. I'm relatively sure that my compassion doesn't give you the right to bark out demands."

"For someone who's supposedly helping me during this hard time, you've yet to touch me in comfort. Do I have that to look forward to?"

Elle didn't know if his way of coping with what he was about to face was to bait her at every turn. What she did understand was that deep down he wasn't serious. If the farmhouse in front of her, along with the stories of his grandfather on the drive here and the interaction he'd had with Mr. Howe was any indication, Kevin deserved to have a woman who had the same naïve upbringing. These people were protected from the horrors of society and turned a blind eye to people like her.

"What you need is the comfort of your family," Elle said softly as she caught movement out of the corner of her eye. "And if I'm not mistaken, one of your brothers is about to provide that."

Sure enough, before Kevin had time to react, a similar looking male wrapped his arms around Kevin's body from behind and pulled him up into a bear hug. His gaze promised that their conversation wasn't over, but Elle wasn't really worried about it. He was about to be sucked back into time with tales and memories of his deceased grandfather. These moments should be with his family.

"It's about damn time you showed up." The man released him and then slapped Kevin on the back before turning him around. "You're looking good, Kevin. It's been way too long. That Crest character been working you too hard?"

"Good to see you too, Kyle." Kevin had grabbed his brother's shoulder and pulled him into what she would consider a chest crushing hug. Elle resisted rolling her eyes at their boyish antics. "It's been less than six months and I've been calling Mom and Dad once a week. I heard you and Molly are building a house on the south side of the property. Congratulations."

"It won't be ready until next fall, but we're looking forward to it. It still takes a four wheel drive to get back to it off the country road." Kyle had been staring at Elle the entire time, not bothering to hide his interest. She shifted uncomfortably, unable to help herself from wondering what he was thinking. She didn't have long to wait to find out. "Mom didn't say you were bringing anyone. There something we should know?"

"Kyle, this is Elle." Kevin stepped back so that he was standing next to her. She expected him to elaborate why she was here, but he didn't. In a way, his silence gave an answer that they had something more significant than what was reality. "Elle, this is my oldest brother, Kyle."

"We're just friends," Elle said, extending her arm and waiting for Kyle to take her hand. "I'm sorry that we have to meet under these circumstances. You have my condolences."

"It's very nice to meet you, Elle." Kyle shook her hand and his familiar gray eyes, although more laced with blue than his brother, seemed to see more than she wanted. It must be a family trait and one she'd have to be more careful around. "I think we should get inside. I don't have a coat on and it's damn cold out here. Kevin, take Elle on in to meet everyone and I'll get your bags."

The brothers exchanged long looks, but Elle was unable to decipher them. She didn't like that she was the subject and as she took a step toward the house, her chest tightened at the thought of crossing the threshold where judgments awaited. It wasn't as if they knew her background, but it didn't wash away the feeling of inadequacy. She squared her shoulders and crossed the distance to the porch.

"They don't bite," Kevin murmured, his hand going to her lower back. She was grateful that the bulky material kept his warmth away. She didn't need to rely on him. "If at any time you need me, all you have to do is look my way and I'll know."

Elle would have replied he needn't worry, that she could take care of herself, when Kevin grabbed the handle and opened the screen door. A woman instantly appeared before them. She was a good five inches shorter than Elle, but the smile of this woman left no doubt she was Kevin's mother. Her blue eyes lit up with delight when they landed on Elle, much to her dismay.

"Kevin, who have you brought with you?"

"Mom, this is Elle." As Mrs. Dreier backed up a few steps to allow them to enter, Kevin led Elle inside and let the door click shut behind them. "This is my mother, Florence."

Before Elle could extend her arm once more, Mrs. Dreier's eyes filled with unshed tears and pulled her into a hug. Feeling uncomfortable, she patted the older woman on the shoulder. Stepping back, Elle was surprised when Kevin's mother slid her hands down and firmly grasped her fingers.

"Thank you, dear, for coming with Kevin. This is a very difficult time for us." Mrs. Dreier squeezed her hands before releasing them and wiping the corners of her eyes. "I was so worried he would have to drive himself."

"It's nice to meet you too, Mrs. Dreier," Elle replied, doing her best to give a small smile. "As a friend, I'm here to offer my support."

Elle felt better having set the groundwork and stepped slightly aside so that Mrs. Dreier could hug her son. It was then that Elle saw the rest of the family in the living room staring at her as if she was holding Kevin at gunpoint. She reminded herself that they didn't know her background and met their gaze head on. She reined in the need to say something sarcastic, knowing that would only make her stay more uncomfortable.

"How are you holding up, Mom?" Kevin pulled his mother in tightly, her small frame being folded into his arms. Elle heard the small catch in Mrs. Dreier's throat as she restrained her tears. "We knew it was coming and he's with Gram now."

"I know, dear." Mrs. Dreier pulled away and then reached up to cradle Kevin's face. "It's still hard, but we'll get through the next couple of days by remembering and honoring the man he was."

"Move your ass."

Elle turned slightly to see Kyle coming through the door with both of their bags. He brushed past them and went right up the staircase to where she presumed would be the bedrooms...separate. These folks seemed to be old fashioned, so there was nothing to worry about.

"Come in, come in," Mrs. Dreier ushered, shooing them into the living room. Family portraits, wreaths, and knickknacks adorned the cream colored walls. Elle would have to look at them another time, for right now she was too busy being on alert for what the rest of the family might think of her. "Everyone, this is Elle. I'll make the introductions."

Sure enough, Mrs. Dreier went around the crowded room. Her husband, Lloyd, came right over and enclosed Elle into another hug. Kevin was the spitting image of his father, height and all. Kane and Keith were the other two brothers who were now standing next to their wives, Paige and Ashley. Kelly was the lone sister, who took after her mother. Her husband was back at their house, which apparently was only a few miles away, getting some diaper supplies. The six-month-old baby boy, Mason, had the same gray eyes as his uncle. The two young girls, no more than four and five, were the progeny of Kane. Their curious gaze made Elle wary.

"Now give me your coats. Your father will put them on the coat rack. Are you two hungry?" Mrs. Dreier had waited for the pleasantries, which turned out to be more personal than Elle would have wanted with more hugs, before the older woman clasped her hands together and played hostess. "We have enough food in the kitchen to feed an army. The doorbell hasn't stopped ringing since this morning."

"That sounds good, Mom."

Elle's mind was spinning as she tried to keep track of who was who and hoped they didn't expect her to remember their names. She was grateful when Kevin once again placed his hand on her lower back. She caught him looking at her neck and she realized that she was playing with her locket. Immediately dropping it, she shrugged out of her coat and handed it over. Instinct had her pulling her sweater lower, ensuring that she looked good enough to pass muster.

"Thank you, Mr. Dreier," Elle murmured, once the older gentleman had taken their jackets.

"Please, call me Lloyd." He winked and looked back fondly at his wife. "We're not much for formality here."

Elle shoved her hands in the back pockets of her jeans, feeling uncomfortable as everyone was still looking their way. Kevin must have sensed it, for he excused them and followed his mother into the kitchen. Elle would eat and then excuse herself for the evening. Kevin needed time with his family without her. Tomorrow would be a hectic day and one she would need to prepare for.

"That was the hard part," Kevin whispered in her ear, his warm breath catching her off guard. "The rest will be easy."

It was obvious that their definitions of certain words were vastly different. Elle didn't reply and made sure she sat on the far side of the table, away from everyone else. Kelly and the two sisters-in-law had followed them in. Kevin didn't exactly allow Elle to get away with sitting so far apart, as he sat himself right next to her and carried on the conversation. Meeting everyone was just a standard thing in her mind. What would be hard for her were the difficult questions that were bound to come her way. She glanced at the clock on the wall. Fifty-nine minutes to go.

Chapter Eleven

Kevin turned the logs in the fire with a poker, all the while keeping his eyes on Elle. The service was over and everyone had retired back to his parents' house. Neighbors had come and gone, but the entire family remained. Elle had been making her way into the kitchen when Kelly had stopped her and the two women were now talking. Elle wasn't looking his way like he'd told her to should she feel uncomfortable, but he knew that she wouldn't. The world could be ending and she would still think she could manage on her own.

"You stare at her anymore and she's likely to catch like that fire in front of you." Kyle sat down in the chair and spread his legs out in front of him. Kevin placed the poker back into its rightful place and then sat on the hearth with his back to the fire. "I've done my best to keep the women at bay, but eventually they'll come at you with canons loaded. Especially Kelly. They want to know how important Elle is to you and why you would bring her here while we're all at our worst."

Kevin stretched his right leg, doing his best not to grimace at the ache that had settled deep inside from standing on his feet most of the day. He did have to hand it to his brother. His sister and the rest of the family had pretty much left him alone, although they did have more important things to deal with than his private life. Kyle had done him a favor. It was time to fess up and he was always upfront with his family about his life. That wasn't going to change now.

"I met Elle over a year ago," Kevin replied, keeping a close eye on her. It was important that she see into his life, but that didn't mean he wanted it to scare her off. He needed her to see that she would belong here, regardless of how different they were. "She's had some hard times but she's managed to overcome them. Unfortunately, I want more than she's willing to give right now."

"I'm not so sure about that." Kyle had a beer in his hand and pointed it in Elle's direction. "She's watched you like a hawk all day, making sure that you were okay. The only time she left your side was when we walked through the front door fifteen minutes ago."

"There's a lot that you don't know and I don't feel comfortable telling you without Elle's knowledge. Suffice it to say, I have my work cut out for me. There's this…courage…deep inside of her that just astounds me. She's got so much pride, strength, and a downright survivor mentality that rivals anyone I've seen on the battlefield." Kevin finally looked at his brother, who had been married for well over five years now. "She's the one, Kyle. Mom always said it would happen this way and as usual, she's right. Elle wouldn't agree and as much as I know that patience is needed, I only have so much."

"What would Pop tell you?" Kyle didn't wait for Kevin to reply. "He'd tell you that if her soul is the other half of yours, you'll find what it takes to do what is needed. He'd also tell you to think outside the box. That old coot was a sucker for unexpected schemes."

"I needed that," Kevin said, nodding his head in appreciation. He reached behind him to where he'd set his beer. Holding it up, he clinked the glass to Kyle's. "To Pop."

It wasn't long after that the rest of the family descended into the living room. The only ones missing were Elle and his mother. It didn't surprise him, as Elle was probably doing her damndest to keep herself away from the chaos. His mother was probably fixing a dessert tray in the kitchen. As for the children, Brianna and Annie had been in the formal dining room, playing with their dolls underneath the table the last time he'd checked. He'd give Elle five minutes and if she didn't show herself, he'd track her down. He'd gotten used to having her by his side all day and since they weren't heading back home until tomorrow afternoon, he figured he'd take advantage of the time they had.

✧ ✧ ✧ ✧

Elle wasn't sure how it happened, but she'd ended up sitting at the kitchen table with two little girls giving her a hair makeover. She'd finally gotten away from Kelly without giving away her life's story, pleading the need for caffeine. Kevin's sister wasn't one to contain her curiosity. Elle thought all was good when she'd poured herself a cup coffee in the unoccupied room, having a little breathing space. If she'd been smart, she'd have hightailed it up to her room. Instead, Kevin's mother had come out of nowhere.

"Would you like cream or sugar?"

"No, thank you," Elle replied, wincing when Brianna got the brush tangled in some strands on her left side. Annie was working on her right. "I'm sure that you want to join the rest of your family. It's been a long day."

"It's kind of nice to have a breather," Mrs. Dreier replied, taking the chair across from Elle's. She set her coffee on the table and smiled fondly at the girls who were now doing something Elle knew would probably make her look ridiculous. She'd never done this as a little girl herself and wasn't sure what the fascination was with long hair. "I do hope they remember their great-grandfather. He was a good man. Kevin is very much like him."

Elle wasn't sure how to reply to that so she reached for her coffee. She'd learned to take it black early on to save money. She held on to the cup to give her something to do and felt herself relax as the girls braided a few strands that felt soothing. How did one go about comforting a stranger? It wasn't that Mrs. Dreier hadn't been welcoming. She had. This one-on-one left Elle feeling a little helpless and she struggled to find the words that the woman obviously wanted to hear.

"From what I heard today, your father sounded like a caring man." Elle swallowed away the envy that had been creeping up on her all day. When she and Kevin had pulled up to the house yesterday, all she could think of was that the exterior was a pretense for what it truly contained. It was something placed on television to give people a fodder of picture-perfect fiction. What she witnessed today proved her wrong and what she really wanted most of all was time to herself to process it. She could return home tomorrow, tell Jax that she'd done her duty, and hope like hell she could return to her normal life. "I'm sure his great-grandchildren will grow up on his stories."

"Do you have a great-grandpa?"

Elle startled a bit when Brianna peeked around the side of the chair with her big blue innocent eyes. Had Elle ever been that naïve? She noticed that her coffee was coming rather close to the sides of the rim of her mug from the slight tremor of her hands, so she set it back on the table. Mrs. Dreier was watching her closely.

"Um, sure." Elle tried her best to give the little girl a smile. This evening was just dragging on and on. "Everyone has a great-grandpa, but sometimes they pass on like yours and we remember them through stories."

"Do you have stories about yours?"

Pieces of Elle's past started to flash through her mind, but she slammed that door shut before those unpleasant emotions filled the very air she was struggling to breathe. The walls of the kitchen seemed to close in on her and she shifted uneasily in her chair. No, she didn't even have stories about her grandfather, let alone her great-grandfather.

"Girls, why don't you two go see if Uncle Kevin will break out the marshmallows? You can roast them over the fire, but only if you bring me back a s'more."

Elle took a deep breath as the girls yelled excitedly, brushes in hand, and ran through the archway. She wanted to follow them and then detour toward the staircase, but she didn't want to appear rude. She'd quickly finish this cup of coffee before stating that she needed to retire for the evening.

"They can be inquisitive," Mrs. Dreier said, leaning back in her chair with a tender smile. "They didn't mean to dredge up unpleasant memories. I can see that it made you restless and that's not what today is supposed to do. We want to celebrate life, not dwell on the past."

There wasn't a question in anything Kevin's mother had to say, so Elle went to work on her coffee. The tightness in her chest still remained and all she wanted was to be left on her own. She'd focused her attention on Kevin all day, doing what she'd come to do. Jax had been wrong and she hadn't really been needed. Kevin's family had given him support. All this managed to do was make Elle realize that Hallmark cards actually came from somewhere. They weren't made up words just to spout gibberish on nonsensical holidays. It made her understand that what she'd always longed for was actuality, but would never be *her* reality. She'd been cheated out of all of it.

"I know that you and Kevin are leaving tomorrow afternoon, but I wanted to thank you for coming with him. I can see in his eyes that he's appreciative of your support." Mrs. Dreier laced her fingers and set her hands on the table. A feeling of foreboding overcame Elle and she knew the woman was about to make the mistake of making more of Elle's presence than warranted. She picked up her locket and started to worry the accessory against the chain to prevent herself from screaming in denial. "Please know that you are always welcome in our home."

"Don't—" Elle shook her head as she broke off the sentence. Mrs. Dreier wasn't to blame for this aimless sentiment that this trip had brought over Elle. She tried to soften her tone all the while feeling like she wanted to throw her coffee cup across the room and watch it smash into tiny pieces. "Kevin and I are friends, Mrs. Dreier. He...helped me at one point and I'm just returning the favor."

"I know my son, Elle." Mrs. Dreier had tried numerous times to get Elle to call her Florence throughout the day, but that wasn't going to happen. It would only personalize this favor that Elle was trying to execute. Unfortunately, Mrs. Dreier proceeded to do just that. "I see the way he looks at you."

"With pity?" The words slipped out before Elle could stop them. She laughed, but knew it came out more of a cruel sound. She stood, causing the chair legs to screech on the tiled floor. "I'm sorry. That wasn't called for. You've had a very emotional day and I think it best if I go on up to my room."

"Pity?" Elle's head whipped toward the living room entrance to see Kevin standing there with disbelief and anger written on his face. "I'm feeling a lot of emotions at this precise moment, but pity isn't one of them. Mom, would you excuse us please?"

Panic flitted across Elle's skin at the thought of being left along with Kevin. She'd only ever seen him look like this once and that was long ago when she'd still been working the streets. His control and his self-confidence was an underlying attraction she hadn't had to deal with after he'd become sensitive to her plight. Seeing this side of him once again was more than she could handle right now. Fear got the better of her and before she could rein in her emotions, did something she knew she would regret.

"Stay, Mrs. Dreier. Maybe if you were aware that I used to be a hooker, you'd have a better understanding of our friendship." Elle crossed her arms and tightened her hold across her abdomen. The words just wouldn't stop. "Your son helped me off the streets. I was living in a seedy apartment with just enough cash for my next meal. I would have offered him sex had I thought he'd pay for it. I'm just here to repay the debt. I—"

"That's enough." Kevin's harsh tone had Elle snapping her teeth together. The damage of what she'd done smacked her in the face as she took in the fury that was within his gray eyes. "Not one more word."

The silence after that was deafening. Elle struggled to swallow against the lump that had formed in her throat. She never cried. Ever. These family members were the ones who should be grieving and it was her who couldn't seem to control her emotions. The clawing of flight seemed to take hold and she would have fled had Mrs. Dreier not spoken at that moment.

"I can see that the two of you have things to work out." Mrs. Dreier stood, but instead of walking out of the kitchen, she took a couple of steps until she was directly in front of Elle. "You are who you are from the decisions that you made and will make in the future. Do you think my father was a perfect man? I hope the stories that you heard today don't convey that. He was very flawed but that, in part, is what made him who he was. He learned from his mistakes, one of those having not lived up to his responsibility of having a child. I was four years old when he came back home to repair the damage he'd done. In that time he learned what was important. It's what we take away from our actions that define us a person. And from what I've seen today, young lady, you are a compassionate, strong, and intelligent woman. You will always be welcome in our home."

With that profound speech, Mrs. Dreier gracefully turned to the table to pick up her coffee and walked toward Kevin. She paused long enough to kiss him on the cheek and then proceeded out of the kitchen. Elle wanted to be anywhere but here. Since Kevin remained where he was, she allowed her lashes to fall in an attempt to conceal the sight of him. If only it were that easy to block out what she knew was coming.

"Look at me." Elle's eyes flew open to find Kevin standing right in front of her. His large frame blocked out everything else and he seemed to be the only thing in existence. He didn't physically touch her, but his intensity had her in his firm grasp. Something had broken loose inside of her and she didn't know how to put it back together. "You're the only one who's holding on to your past. When you're ready to let it go and see what could be your present and future, you let me know."

Chapter Twelve

Elle hugged the pillow closer to her chest as she stared at the bedroom door. Although the room was warm enough, she still felt chilled. She'd retired upstairs last night after Kevin had walked out of the kitchen leaving her standing there to deal with the emotional aftermath. It was as if he'd made a conclusive decision about her and was finally at peace. She wasn't.

She'd sat on her bed, feeling somewhat numb after their encounter, and heard the laughter and tears as their voices travelled through the vents. Her past choices had been easy when all of this had just been an aspiration for people without hope. Keeping Kevin at arms length had been automatic. Not involving herself with Emily, Lauren, and the other women had been self-preservation. She could admit that now. Lying here in bed all night, dissecting her life, she understood why she used the shelter to consume her time. It kept her from living and allowed her to keep a hold of her past. It wasn't that she didn't want to help those girls that were in need, but her reasons hadn't been altogether altruistic.

Giggling came from the hallway outside of Elle's door. The sound still felt like shards of glass to her heart. Had she truly numbed herself to the lighthearted aspects of daily life? Was that the woman that Kevin saw when he looked at her? For the umpteenth time, she used her palm to wipe the tears that escaped as they ran down her cheek.

"Do you think she's awake?" Annie's whisper travelled through the wooden door. "If we wake her up, Nana will be very, very, very mad."

Elle felt a laugh, so unlike her, bubble up as the girls discussed how much trouble they would be in should they go against their nana's wishes. It was obvious they were told not to disturb her, but their light musical voices were a much needed disruption from this despair that had taken hold. She had no idea what happened from here, but knew that whatever snapped within her last night wasn't something that would ever be mended.

"What if we just peek? If she's asleep, we'll close the door," Brianna replied, as if she'd figured it all out. "But if she's awake, we can't get in trouble."

Elle finally shifted, amazed that her body felt as if it'd been used as a punching bag when she'd done nothing but lay here for hours. She'd just put her back against the headboard when she heard the doorknob turn. Sure enough, two little girls with big blue eyes peered around the thick wood. They squealed with delight to see she was awake and came running in.

"Good morning." Elle's voice seemed a little rough around the edges, so she cleared her throat. "What are you two doing up so early?"

"Uncle Kevin and Uncle Kane said they'd build a snowman with us this morning." Brianna hopped on the bed causing Elle to move over just a tad. The girl's energy seemed to know no bounds. Annie, the younger one, stayed standing while holding a carrot. "Will you help us too?"

"We need a hat, but Papa is looking for one now," Annie said, her eyes roaming the room. "Do you have anything shiny for the eyes?"

"Um, I don't think so." Elle wasn't sure which question they thought she answered, but her response was to both. What she wanted more than anything was for her and Kevin to be on their way home. The thought of facing Kevin's mother this morning was just too much. "I'm sure your uncles will find things to decorate the snowman."

"Brianna, Annie. Did Nana say that you could wake Elle?"

Once more, for being such a large man, Kevin had managed to appear out of nowhere without a sound. His large frame was leaning against the jamb, his arms were crossed across his chest, and his gray eyes didn't miss a thing. Elle resisted the urge to make sure her hair was still contained by her hair tie, but didn't want him to think that gesture meant anything. The problem was it would.

"We didn't wake her, Uncle Kevin," Brianna replied in argument. The little girl was very intelligent and knew her way around rationalizing her defense. It must come from being in a large family, because Elle still didn't have that art down. "We checked to see if she was sleeping and found her eyes open. So she was already awake."

"I see." A smile played on Kevin's lips, but his eyes displayed anything but good humor. "Girls, go down and have Nana suit the two of you up in your snow pants."

With an exaggerated sigh, Brianna blew at her bangs and then hopped off the bed. Grabbing Annie's arm, she led the younger girl across the room. Kevin moved out of their way by stepping inside. The girls' chatter could be heard from the hallway.

"I was right," Brianna stated, her voice fading as it got farther away. The diminished words could still be heard. "Elle is Uncle Kevin's girlfriend. He just wants to kiss her."

Elle looked down at her hands, wishing the girls had just stuck to talking about the snowman they were going to build. She needed time to process these last few days and the only way to do that was to resume her normal routine back home. She wasn't looking forward to the five hour trip, but seeing as she'd been awake all night, maybe she'd sleep the entire time.

"I figure we'll head out around noon. I need to make a stop in town before we head out. Shouldn't be more than an hour."

That was it? Kevin wasn't going to mention what happened? Elle sat up a little straighter and looked his way. He'd already turned to go. Why the hell was he being so nice to her after she'd embarrassed him in front of his mother?

"Wait." Elle was glad she'd chosen to wear her flannel pajamas instead of sleeping in her usual tank top and panties. She tossed the covers aside and swung her legs over the side until her feet touched the cold wood floor below. "I'm…I'm sorry about last night. It was wrong of me."

"If I thought you were apologizing for what you truly should be sorry for, then I'd cross this room and join you in that bed," Kevin said as he'd turned around once more to face her. The gray of his eyes that usually resembled soft pillows were now hard as granite. Elle's heart raced a little faster. Finality sunk in that the man who'd walked out of the kitchen last night had been transformed by her mistake. It wasn't that he was closing himself off to her. It just seemed to be a different side of him and one that was a hundred percent determination. "You should shower and get ready for the day. I'll meet you downstairs."

Downstairs. That would mean having to talk with his mother. Kevin didn't give her a chance to reply or ask exactly what he meant by her apologizing for the wrong thing. Elle glanced at the clock on the nightstand. For the foreseeable next four hours it didn't matter, as she needed to deal with the fallout from last night. She let herself drop back against the mattress in defeat. Her calm, familiar, and comforting life had detoured off its tracks and there was no getting back on that train.

Elle had thought she'd be able to apologize to Mrs. Dreier in private, but the kitchen was overloaded with her children. The only ones missing were Kevin, Kane, and the two little girls. Kelly was holding Mason on her hip while eating a piece of bacon at the counter. The others were sitting around the table talking over each other and laughing at the stories being told.

"Elle, perfect timing," Kelly said with delight, walking toward her. "Would you hold Mason for a minute? I'm just going to change clothes quick. I won't be long."

Without waiting for an answer, Kelly thrust the little boy her way. Elle automatically put her hands in the air and ended up with a sturdy baby in her arms. Panic started to shroud every pore on her body as she looked into the innocent face blowing bubbles as if being held by a stranger was an ordinary thing.

"Elle, I poured you some coffee," Mrs. Dreier said, her voice drowning out the ringing that had been resounding in Elle's ears. "Come."

Elle's necessity to apologize and her need to hand off Mason to someone who knew what they were doing raged within her. Seeing as she had no choice, she took faltered steps toward the counter. Shifting Mason farther up on her hip, each stride seemed to become more comfortable. She'd finally taken a deep breath and had reached her destination. Now it was time to execute her plan before anything else went awry.

"Mrs. Dreier, I want to apologize for—"

"Elle, I'm going to stop you right there." Mrs. Dreier waved her spatula in the air. "There will be no apologizing for how you feel. It was a good thing for you to express yourself and it was even better that Kevin was there to hear. Yes, we have a close family, but even we know when to leave matters in the hands of those that are affected. Now wipe that worry off of your face. You and Kevin have a long trip ahead of you and if I'm not mistaken, he said he was stopping at the Heroes Benefit Society before it began. So would you like French toast or pancakes? And before you answer that, it better be with my first name."

"Just coffee for now, Florence," Elle murmured, her voice weakened from having been reprimanded in a distinctive motherly fashion. She couldn't bring herself to contemplate the ramifications of that, so she looked down at Mason, who seemed fascinated by her locket. His tiny fingers were having trouble grabbing hold. Heroes Benefit Society had been brought up many times. "I know that Kevin was wounded, but he had you and his childhood home to recover in. Why go to the center?"

Elle knew her questioning was one of weakness, giving her the chance to find out what she wanted while Kevin didn't get to reciprocate. It didn't stop her though. Concentrating on Mason and making sure her hold on him was tight enough, she silently willed Florence to answer her.

"Kevin really struggled after coming home from Afghanistan. My boy seemed lost." Florence looked out the kitchen window, causing Elle to do the same. She hadn't realized the view included Kevin as he and his brother were showing the girls how to build a large snowman. His smile was breathtaking. "It was Lloyd who suggested Kevin involve himself with the Heroes Benefit Society."

Elle felt a pudgy hand against her cheek and drew her attention away from the outdoor scene. Mason was studying her, much like his uncle did. She gave a smile hoping it didn't seem forced, but then realized he wouldn't know the difference. Would he? The only thing in the toddler's expression was curiosity and determination. Suddenly, it hit Elle why the Heroes Benefit Society had become so important to Kevin.

"It gave him purpose," Elle said, looking up at Florence as understanding fell into place. Kevin's mother had a knowing smile on her face. "He didn't need the center, but rather the center needed him. He took control, didn't he? He saw to it that the men and women who were having trouble acclimating to civilian life got the help they needed. In turn it alleviated the helplessness that had overtaken him."

"She's a smart cookie," Florence whispered, her statement directed at Mason. "Now take this boy over to his father. I'm not allowing you to leave my house hungry."

Elle stepped away, although she found herself reluctant to walk to the table and hand off the bundle of warmth. She'd never been in the vicinity of a child so young and found that it wasn't as bad as she would have thought. Instead of feeling bitterness for recognizing how little it took to mold this innocent being, she found herself feeling grateful that Mason would grow up in a family like this. How different her life would have been had she been a member of this household. How different could her life be now should she accept that?

Chapter Thirteen

Kevin deposited Elle's small suitcase inside the door of her apartment. She must have turned down the heat while they were away for the air was chilled. He opened his mouth to tell her to turn the temperature higher so that she'd be comfortable, but he immediately snapped it shut. It wasn't his place.

"Thank you."

Elle slowly took off her gloves as if she needed time to contemplate what to do. The trip had passed by in relative silence after they'd left the Heroes Benefit Society. She'd followed Kevin around while he paid his respects to the employees and volunteers that he knew. A few of the veterans that he recognized were there and he'd taken time to see how they were doing. Instead of the questions that he thought he'd receive, Elle had remained somewhat silent unless a question was directed her way. She'd seemed lost in her own world.

"It looks as if your debt is paid," Kevin said, his voice containing no sarcasm. He meant it. If this was what she thought would put them on even ground, it wasn't a bad thing. "I did appreciate the company, so thank you. It was a difficult time."

"I didn't make it better though, did I? I have a feeling things would have gone smoother without me." Elle was still looking at the gloves in her hand. Kevin wished she would look at him so that he could read what was in her eyes. "You didn't take my apology earlier, but I do want you to know that I never meant to cause you embarrassment in front of your family."

Kevin felt exasperation fall over him as he didn't know what else to say or do for Elle to grasp that her past didn't embarrass him. If anything, he felt pride and adoration for the difficulties that she had overcome to get to this point in time. He had told himself that the ball was in her court and that he would wait out her decision on where the two of them went from here, but maybe it was time for another tactic.

Kevin unzipped his jacket and then shrugged out of the heavy material before hanging it on the back of the kitchen chair. He noticed that her eyes followed his movements. Her lips parted as if she wanted to ask what he was doing, but she remained silent. Closing the distance between them, he slowly removed the gloves from her hands.

"What are you doing?" Elle asked, her voice no more than a whisper. It was almost as if she were afraid to move. She cleared her throat. "I should go downstairs. The club is in full swing."

"There's no need to go downstairs when Jax said he has everything covered." Kevin proceeded to unzip her white jacket and had just gotten the fastener to the bottom when her fingers encircled his wrists. "I'm just taking care of you, Elle. It was a long drive and I know you must be tired. You're used to being awake at night and sleeping during the day. This trip has to have messed with your internal clock."

"See?" Elle stepped back, dropping his hands. Her brown eyes shot to his, expressing her frustration. Now they were getting somewhere. He could handle whatever emotion she threw his way, but it was when she withdrew that he felt helpless. "This is the problem."

Kevin studied her as she yanked her arms out of the insulated jacket and basically threw it on her kitchen table. She paced to the small kitchenette and then turned to face him with her hands on her hips. Was she finally going to open up enough for him to know the truth of what she was feeling? This guessing shit was getting old. He waited her out by crossing his arms, ensuring that she knew he wasn't going anywhere.

"Damn it, Kevin, I don't need taken care of." Elle's voice rose with each word. The passion she was expressing was everything he'd hoped for and the barriers that she'd set in place were finally coming down. "I've been doing it myself for my whole life. I don't need you to fight my battles for me, I don't need you to take over and make me dependent on you, and I damn well didn't need to see the way that your family lives."

"And how is that?" Kevin asked, taking advantage of her need to breathe. The minute she switched tenses, he knew that now was the time to get to the crux of her issue. "My family depends on each other, Elle. That's how it works."

"I was fine. Do you understand that? I was fine living my life, content with my normal routine, and certainly gratified to be working for a living where I didn't have to sell myself." Elle had pointed a finger his way and emphasized each and every fact. "Now? In a matter of weeks, you've managed to destroy the serenity that I was able to bury myself in."

"Is that how you want to live the rest of your life?" Kevin asked, involuntarily taking a step toward her. They were finally making progress. She was like a fucking magnet and her pull on him was unconscious. "Just being content? Do you not want happiness, enjoyment, or passion? What about sharing moments with someone? What about building something until the outcome is what you've just witnessed with my family? This satisfaction you talk of sounds damn lonely to me."

"It wasn't…" Elle shook her head as if she were at a loss for words. The lost look on her face was just too much. If she were to only really see what was in front of her, he could give her what she truly needed. Her brown eyes rested on him, but she still didn't really *see*. "I was just fine."

"You deserve so much better than just fine, city girl."

Kevin crossed the distance until they were inches apart and she had to tilt her head to look up into his face. Elle's hair had started to come free of the hair band and he brushed the strands away from her cheek. His gaze was drawn to her lips, which had parted upon his touch. He raised his eyes until his could see the darker flecks within her brown eyes and the vulnerability that lay within was his undoing.

"I need to taste you," Kevin murmured, slowly lowering his head without disconnecting their connection. Her breathing become shallow and her pupils dilated in reaction. She didn't pull away. He gently cradled her face within his palms and watched in fascination as her lashes drifted closed. "So beautiful."

With those whispered words, Kevin's lips slowly sealed over hers. He kept it soft, easy, and tranquil so that she had time to soak in their first kiss. He wanted this seared into her memory. Their body heat fused and something rare took hold, confirming what he'd always known. She was the one.

Carefully and refusing to disengage, Kevin lowered his hands and let them drift down her shoulders and arms. The counter was small but uncluttered, and he easily lifted her up so that she was sitting on the laminate surface. He stepped forward until her denim-clad legs separated, surrounding his hips.

Nothing had ever felt so right to him. Needing to feel and taste more of her, he glided his fingers into her hair until the band fell out, letting her black strands fall around her.

Holding her head just so, Kevin used his tongue to trace her lower lip. Gaining access to her mouth, he savored her taste and deepened their kiss. He brought his right hand down until it rested at her lower back and pulled her body close to his. The heat of her core could be felt through both of their jeans and his reaction was immediate. Refusing to give in to his basic desires and knowing this needed to be about her, Kevin reined himself in by using both hands to soothe her arms and legs. Anywhere he could touch without breaking off their kiss, he did.

Kevin felt her tentatively place her hands on his shoulders and willed her to touch him as he was doing to her. She skated her fingers down the sides of his arms and then to the front of his chest. For a brief moment, he thought she was going to push him away, but instead she gathered up the material of his shirt in her fists and pulled him even closer.

Time passed as the two of them familiarized themselves with each other. Their desires escalated, but neither took things further than this invaluable kiss. It wasn't until Kevin felt her move her hips like sinuous waves that he knew it was time to slowly end the beginning of what was to come.

"That was more than fine as well," Kevin murmured, pulling away. Elle's hands still had his shirt fisted in her palms and when her eyes finally opened, heat spread through him at seeing the darkened desire no longer hidden. "It also proves to me that you care. We'll take this one day at a time, as I don't want you to pressure me."

"What?" Elle asked, her fingers finally releasing his shirt as her right eyebrow rose in disbelief. "Pressure *you*? I—"

Elle broke off her sentence when he smirked, having done what he'd set out to do. Kevin refused to leave here with her confused as to where things stood between them. Injecting a bit of humor into the situation would help both of them transition out of the sensual moment they'd created.

"You heard me." Kevin stepped away, although it was damn harder than he thought. The loss of her heat left a chill that only she could evaporate. Forcing himself to walk to the table, it felt as if the pins in his leg had rusted. Even his body was asking what the hell he was doing. He grabbed his jacket and finally faced her. "We'll take this nice and easy, city girl. You say things have changed and you're right. We just need to navigate this new course together and see what it brings."

Kevin strolled to the door, giving her time to respond. There was no going back from this. Only forward. When he reached for the knob and swung open the heavy wood, her sweet voice reached his ears.

"Kevin, I don't think I can give you what you want. You deserve—"

"I'd stop there, if I were you," Kevin replied, consciously formulating his words in a hard voice. "If you ever try to finish that sentence, I'll have you downstairs and over that spanking bench before you do. Just as you pointed out before that you are an independent woman, I'm a man who knows what I want and need. You don't get to do that for me."

Elle didn't say a word, although she never looked away from him. Her lower lip was in between her teeth, as if she wanted to say more but didn't want to take the chance. They *were* making progress.

"Get some sleep and I'll touch base with you tomorrow." Kevin had been about to walk out the door when an idea formed. Elle had yet to move from the counter. "You deserve a first date, but since you work the weekends it looks like I'll have to be creative. I'll pick you up on Saturday around one o'clock in the afternoon. Dress warm."

With that last instruction, Kevin closed the door behind him. He'd had to deal with a lot of emotions over the course of these last few days and he was glad for some alone time. He needed it to compartmentalize everything that had transpired and map out this new course that he and Elle were about to take. The stakes were too high for mistakes. Instead of exiting through the club where he'd have to face Jax and some of his other friends, Kevin chose the back exit, which was connected to the parking garage. The cold air was welcome and by the time he reached his truck, a smile had overtaken his features. This was truly living.

Chapter Fourteen

Friday arrived and as Kevin entered the office, he saw Jessie walking toward the open area in the back where the conference table was situated. Crest stood there with his hands in his trouser pockets, studying some papers in front of him. Yesterday had been spent catching up on the case and having a discussion with Crest about Kevin's emotional status after his grandfather's death. He appreciated the sentiment.

"Something happen?" Kevin asked, unzipping his coat as he joined his other team members who were taking their places around the table.

"Connor's headed back to give a detailed SITREP on the Switzerland run." Crest looked up and pinned his gaze on Jax. "The summary is that Ryland was nowhere to be found."

"He's there." Taryn held a pencil in her hand and pointed it toward the papers. "Those are the locations I've pinpointed after cracking his aliases. All of them were empty because he's working from scratch. He knows that we're onto him."

"What I know is that he's still out there and we're still a target." Jax ran a hand through his disheveled hair. Either he'd been up all night because Emily's due date was any day now or he was obsessing over Ryland. Both were probably the answer. "Ryland will also make this personal, so it's just not Emily he's going to come after. It's the entire team."

Kevin noticed that Crest and Taryn shared a look that was undecipherable. Each member knew there was something more going on and it was just a matter of time before Jax couldn't contain his irritation at being kept in the dark. Trust only went so far when it came to the woman he'd centered his life around. Kevin was just beginning to understand the depth of what his friend must be feeling.

"I pulled Connor out of there to regroup. Sending him on a recon is one thing, but I don't want any of you confronting this man one on one." Crest reached for his cup, causing Kevin to glance to his right and see that a pot of coffee was sitting on the burner. His battered Vikings cup, which his grandfather had given to him, sat empty. "Ethan is the only one free of cases right now, so he's going to help Taryn try and figure out Ryland's new pattern. There's got to be a thread that we've been missing."

"I've already been working on that and I think we need to look into the Yvette Capri angle. She was important to him, which means something in that woman's life might point to where he's hiding," Ethan said, switching his gaze between Crest and Taryn, having also caught the previous exchange. "If that's going to be a problem, then tell me now."

"It won't be a problem." Crest took a sip of his coffee and it was blatant that he was giving himself some extra time before discussing it further. Kevin used the brief respite to remove his jacket and fill his own mug. The warm liquid spread through him, but it was nothing compared to having held Elle in his arms. When Crest started speaking once more, Kevin had to concentrate. He'd be able to enjoy her company tomorrow and with what he had planned, she'd have no alternative but to talk to him and share some of her history. "As all of you know, there is a connection between Yvette Capri and Taryn. It's her story to tell and one I'm sure she'll share with you if the need arises. Until then, let's review the other cases we have on the front burner."

"Then I'll go first," Ethan replied, garnering everyone's attention. "Lach called in to debrief. The Africa kidnapping situation has been contained and the hostage was rescued. However, there were a number of casualties including one of the locals that we hired to assist in the mission. Lach is headed back to the States as well and he will return to work on Monday."

"Good." Crest murmured something to Jessie, who was taking notes. Kevin noticed that Crest didn't look her way when he spoke and wondered when those two would finally hash out this thing between them. "Jax, you're working on that counterfeiting case. Were you able to meet with Agent Cornish?"

Agent Cornish worked with the Treasury Department and while he was overseeing the case, a local business had requested that CSA take a look at the investigation in a more personal aspect. Kevin didn't blame the CEO for hiring an outside agency, as the client's reputation was now front and center with the media as the potential source.

When Jax finally finished giving the details of his progress, he looked at his phone. He'd been doing that every few minutes and it was apparent he thought Emily would call at any moment to sound the alarm. Even Crest seemed amused as he hid a smile behind his mug.

"I received Fallon's profile yesterday and it did have some interesting points that I'll run by Taggart later today." Kevin placed his coffee on the table and finally took a seat, ignoring the ache in his right knee. Crest and Jessie were the only ones left standing. "She feels we're looking for a white male in his thirties or forties. Fallon picked up on the dates as well and feels that specific day is related to an incident in his childhood or is somehow relative to the killer's internal thinking. It could be that his mother was a prostitute or that the occupation is something he'd been around in his youth. He's escalating, which could mean a shift in his life that is beyond his control and this is how the suspect is dealing with it. Fallon is not under the belief that he *wants* to be caught. As for the lipstick that the suspect places on the victim, it's out of character. If we don't nab this guy through DNA, which nothing we've come across at the moment matches anything in the system, Fallon would like permission to visit the next crime scene."

"Let's hope that doesn't happen," Ethan murmured, tapping his thumb on the table. "You have two and a half months left before he strikes again."

"I'm using the date you gave me and narrowing down crimes that seem similar in nature over the past thirty years." Taryn chewed on the eraser side of the pencil she was holding as she looked down at one of her papers, her glasses slipping slightly on her pert nose. "I've even broadened the search to include male victims. You never know."

"Go back further than that," Crest ordered, motioning Taryn's way. "What if he's taking over for a parent? It's apparent that Fallon thinks there's a missing key within this lipstick gesture the perp likes to execute."

"I have a meeting with Taggart this afternoon." Kevin glanced Jax's way to see him looking down at his phone once more. "That is, unless Emily goes into labor."

Jax's head whipped up and when he realized that Kevin was pulling his leg, the yellow stress ball came flying at his head.

Reaching out just in time, Kevin caught the sucker and immediately threw it back.

"You need it more than I do, buddy."

"Fuck you."

"All right, all right." Crest called their attention back to the meeting. After a few more brief highlights, Kevin stood up to head back to his cubicle. Crest's next words had his ass sitting right back down. "I had wanted to do this yesterday, as well as wait for Connor and Lach to be here, but I think now is appropriate. Kevin, we all know that you were close to your grandfather. Condolences and flowers are a nice gesture, but we wanted to do something a little more to honor his place in your life. In tribute to his love of the land and where he grew up, we made a donation in his name to your hometown in order to help with the difficulties that occurred from the drought that occurred there this last year."

Jessie handed Kevin the envelope, which contained a receipt for the amount his team members had donated. The sum left him speechless and he had no doubt that his grandfather would be truly appreciative. Kevin could spout the *you didn't have to* nonsense and even though he would mean it, their gesture should be taken the way it was given…with grace.

"Thank you, not only on my behalf, but that of my family."

Kevin felt Jessie's hand on his shoulder and he accepted her quick hug as she leaned down and wrapped her arms around him. Everyone else either shook hands or slapped him on the back while he gained his composure. Finally standing, he met Crest's stare and nodded once more in gratitude. This team might not be related by blood, but he damn well considered them his brothers and sisters.

The sound of ringing indicated that someone wanted entrance into the office. They all had card keys that allowed them to bypass the security. If a client or visitor came to the door, they had to press a button for entrance. Jessie made her way to the front while some of the others disbanded back to their work areas. He and Crest stayed at the table.

Kevin was surprised to see Taggart being led in by Jessie. From the way the detective was looking at her ass, it was obvious that he was interested in her. Kevin happened to glance over at Crest, seeing that he had observed the same thing. He gathered up the papers in front of him and astoundingly the man walked back to his office. Was he that unaffected?

"Jessie, I have a conference call scheduled," Crest said, stopping short at his door. His next words were more in line with how Kevin would have reacted had he been in the man's shoes. "Would you please clear your calendar to take notes?"

Jessie continued walking past Kevin, unaware of what had truly transpired. Kevin waited until both she and Crest disappeared into his office before turning to Taggart, who was holding out a file. Taking it, Kevin then gave his friend some advice.

"I wouldn't go there if I were you." Kevin motioned for Taggart to follow him to his cubicle. "Don't ask me why, but let's just say Jessie is off limits to you."

"Now you have my curiosity piqued." Taggart pulled out Ethan's chair and took a seat. Ethan had gone into Taryn's office to discuss specifics on their case. "First, you didn't tell me that you worked with such a beautiful young woman. Second, I certainly didn't see a wedding ring on her finger. Third, I thought your interests were wound up with the manager of that club you go to."

"All of your points would be correct." Kevin sank into his leather chair and leaned back, sipping on his coffee. Taggart could get his own. "As I said, don't go there. Just a word to the wise. I'd hate to see you end up getting beaten senseless, at least without being warned off first. Your regular MO could get you killed, if you get my drift."

Taggart's gaze travelled to the outer area of the cubicle, obviously not taking Kevin's advice to heart. Shit, if the poor bastard didn't want to listen to him, that was his unfortunate choice. Kevin set his coffee behind him on the desk and then opened up the folder Taggart had given him. Inside was a statement by an anonymous person who'd called the station. The male gave a detailed account of the night the latest victim was murdered with the exception of one thing.

"Taggart, where is the description?" Kevin glanced up at the detective, who was obviously waiting for his question. "If he saw the perp, why didn't you bring the witness in?"

"The call was disconnected, but the officer was able to trace it." Taggart leaned forward, placing his elbows on his knees. Kevin had a sinking feeling that the shit was about to hit the fan. "It was a pay phone from a gas station near the south end of town."

"And the patrol that was sent there? What did they find?"

"A dead man."

Chapter Fifteen

Elle managed to catch a few hours sleep on Saturday morning, but her nerves were stretched so thin over this date with Kevin that she'd ended up making coffee and studying her measly wardrobe to pass the time. He'd originally said to wear something warm, but when he'd spoken to her on the phone yesterday, he'd changed his mind and told her to just wear something comfortable.

Comfortable? That excluded her five business outfits that she wore when managing the club. All were pantsuits, with tapered suit jackets. Just because the submissives wore erotic outfits didn't mean that was how she should dress. Elle was there to represent the club's management and she did that in the most professional manner. It didn't matter that she felt moments of envy upon seeing the subs wear next to nothing while enjoying the touch of their Doms, letting their responsibilities fade away into the night.

Elle's cell phone rang on the nightstand. Her heart rate instantly sped up and she tightened her grip on the handle of her cup. Was Kevin calling to cancel? That would be for the best, before this went any further. She'd tried to warn him and maybe he'd finally seen reason. Leaning forward, careful not to spill any liquid on her bedspread, she snagged the phone. It was Lauren. Elle couldn't decipher what emotion rushed through her veins. Disappointment or relief?

"Hello?"

"Hey, Elle. I'm coming by in an hour to drop off some new inventory. There was a special order placed by Flint and he asked that it be at the club before he and Shelley arrive." Lauren designed specialized BDSM equipment by adorning gems to the items, giving them a unique look. There was no doubting the woman's talent and many of the Doms and subs placed orders with Lauren. "I have Connor's access card, but if you hear me downstairs, I didn't want you to think someone had broken in. Also, I'll need a secure place to leave it. It's quite expensive, so I was thinking you could put it in the safe for me."

"Oh. No problem." Elle tossed the pillow off of her lap and scooted to the edge of the bed. "With the upgraded security system, I highly doubt even the FBI could gain entrance into the club."

Lauren laughed and in the distance, Elle could hear Connor ask what was so funny. For a split second, she was surprised to hear Connor's voice, as he would normally be at work but then it dawned on her it was the weekend. Her attention was immediately drawn to the open dresser drawers. She would obviously wear jeans today, but she'd worn her nicest sweater in Wisconsin. Kevin had already seen her in it. Shit, why was this even an issue?

"Elle?"

"What? Oh, sorry," Elle replied, cringing when she realized she'd missed half the conversation. "Can you repeat that?"

"I said I was wary to call in case you were asleep, but Connor has special plans for me this afternoon and I only have an hour to drop this stuff off at the club." Elle placed her cup on the nightstand as Lauren continued to talk and then she grabbed a sweatshirt. Holding the phone away from her ear, she slipped it over her head. Tucking the phone back into place and then grabbing her cup, she padded around the partition. "…don't sound tired."

"No worries, I wasn't asleep." Elle opened the microwave door and placed her mug inside. Pressing the reheating button, she leaned against the counter to wait. "I have—"

Elle broke off her words, berating herself for almost having told Lauren about her afternoon plans. The woman was busy herself and didn't have time for another girl's problems. It wasn't as if they were friends. Emily's words came back to haunt Elle, reminding her that Lauren and Emily both had tried numerous times to take her to lunch and get to know her better. It was Elle who kept them at arms length.

"You have…?" Lauren questioned, waiting for Elle to finish her sentence.

"I have a date with Kevin." Elle closed her eyes as the words rushed out and then held her breath. She shook her head, wondering what the hell she was doing. Slowly exhaling, she tried to get things back to normal. She shouldn't have mentioned it. "That's why I'm up. Like I said, no worries about the call. I appreciate the warning. You have a great day."

"Elle, wait," Lauren called out, her curiosity causing Elle to tighten her fingers on her phone. So much for trying to regain some normalcy. "What time is Kevin picking you up?"

"Um, one o'clock," Elle answered distractedly, wondering what that had to do with anything. The microwave beeped and she spun around, grateful to have something to do. She tried again to get things on even ground. "If you just put the inventory behind the bar in the cash box cabinet, I'll make sure that Flint gets his order placed in their personal club storage safe."

"Elle, would you like some company while you get ready for your date?"

The offer hung in the air. Elle wanted to say yes, but the word wouldn't come out. She stared into the microwave and had it been a portal to another world, she would have gladly crawled inside. Instead, she had no choice but to stay here and deal with this life that had been given to her. She always reminded herself that she had choices, whether bad or good, and one was looming in front of her. The speed in which her life was changing was a little much and maybe, just maybe, having a small anchor might not be such a bad idea.

"Yes, I would."

✧   ✧   ✧   ✧

"How's that?"

Elle turned to the standing mirror that was attached to the bathroom door, which was now swung open for full access, and took in her appearance. Her long black hair was left down, something she rarely did. It flowed down her back, while the scarf hung around her neck, giving the front of her some color. The burgundy and brown colors contained rich tones, which brightened what Elle had thought to be a dull brown in the sweater she wore.

"No wonder you're good at what you do," Elle muttered, amazed that something so old could look so new. The scarf had been tucked back into a dresser drawer and the sweater had been in the lower one. She'd have never thought to put the two together. Her eyes met Lauren's in the mirror and Elle tried to convey her appreciation without making this seem awkward. "Thank you for doing this. I know it's silly, but—"

"Nonsense." Lauren turned and walked back to the kitchen table where she had a bottle of water. She brushed her auburn curls over her shoulder, took a seat and smiled. "I have an ulterior motive."

Elle's defenses immediately went on alert and her body tensed. People usually had an ulterior motive, but she would admit to thinking—wishing—that Lauren's offer had been different. She waited.

"I think you and Kevin are perfect for each other," Lauren said, raising her bottle in salute. "Whatever I can do to help, I will."

Elle waited for more, but when Lauren didn't continue realized that was all she meant. Nothing more, nothing less. She relaxed her shoulders and then joined Lauren at the table. If she was telling the truth, then maybe she could answer the question that had been rattling around in Elle's head for days.

"How are we perfect for each other?" Elle crossed her arms in front of her and waited for the answer. If Lauren could tell her, maybe her nerves wouldn't be so chaotic. "I just don't see it, Lauren. We are so different."

"That's what makes you two good for one another." Lauren screwed the cap back on the bottle. "You know the old saying *opposites attract.*"

"Lauren, let's face it," Elle said, trying to get the woman to see reason. Kevin certainly didn't listen and his threat if she finished her thought had Elle thinking twice…about saying it and also believing it. If he didn't see it as an issue, why should she? Because it damn well did matter, that's why. "He's a farm boy at heart and I'm an ex-hooker. That's not just opposite, Lauren. Sometimes that spectrum is too far apart to even contemplate inside my head."

"You put yourself down because of what you've done, yet the way you speak and the words you use defy that you kept yourself limited to that lifestyle." Lauren looked at her quizzically. "You're obviously well educated."

"I have a high school diploma, but I'm not college material," Elle argued, not seeing what that had to do with anything. "I read a lot. I like to learn. And I'm not putting myself down, I'm facing facts. Why would Kevin want to be with someone who sold her body for money? I've made choices that people would find morally, abhorrent, or highly questionable to say the least."

"I'm sure there are judgmental people, but remember the lifestyle we live. The majority of our friends, along with Connor and I, enjoy BDSM and other kinks. We don't judge. Why would Kevin?"

Elle could see the point Lauren was trying to make, but she wasn't privy to Elle's past. She didn't have the upbringing that Kevin had. She was a different person with a separate view on life. How did people accept that? It seemed a hell of a lot easier to just keep to herself. There was still time to back out.

Much to Elle's surprise the last hour had been enjoyable. Lauren was fun to be around, seemingly going to extra lengths to make sure that Elle was comfortable. The first few minutes were awkward, but then Lauren started chatting about random stuff that had happened around the club. When the topic of Kevin came up, along with Elle's predicament regarding her wardrobe, Lauren became a woman on a mission. It was fun to witness and even more fun being used as a model for said experiment. In the end, both were satisfied with the outcome.

"You know what I think?" Lauren asked after Elle didn't answer right away. "I think you're judging yourself way too harshly."

A knock came at the door. Elle would have sworn her heart stopped for that moment. This was it. She wanted to share with Lauren that not only was this her first date with Kevin, but this was her first date period. As in ever, but she couldn't bring herself to speak. She'd never gotten to experience the joys of being a carefree teenager. Instead, she'd been on her back in a seedy motel earning money for food. Another knock sounded. Is this how she was supposed to feel?

"Well, that's my cue to leave." Lauren stood and picked up her jacket.

Elle bit her lip to keep from panicking and telling Lauren to make Kevin go away. That would be cowardly and if there was one thing Elle prided herself on, it was that she was an independent woman capable of handling her own problems. As she'd told Kevin numerous times, she'd done it her whole life.

Lauren leaned down and quickly hugged Elle before heading to the door. She whispered something about having a good time this afternoon and not fretting over the little things. The moment was over within a blink of an eye and Lauren had already opened the door. Kevin stood there with a surprised expression, his gaze going back and forth between the two of them.

"Hi Kevin." Lauren's tone was cheerful, as if she wasn't aware of the turmoil Elle was feeling. She turned and sent a wave Elle's way. "You two have fun."

"Lauren, wait," Elle called out, not ready for what was about to happen. Anything to delay it. Lauren had walked past Kevin and was outside in the entryway before she turned around. "Thank you for stopping by and keeping me company."

"We'll do it again soon." Lauren gave her a thumbs up, partially hidden by her jacket so that Kevin couldn't see. "Have fun."

Elle watched helplessly as Lauren left, leaving her alone with Kevin. He was looking at her expectantly but didn't ask about Lauren's visit, for which she was glad. She took a deep breath, fortifying whatever barriers were left and gave herself a pep talk. One afternoon. How bad could it be?

Chapter Sixteen

A few hours later, after the shock wore off that Kevin had taken her back to his house for their *date*, Elle found herself relaxed on the couch in front of the magnificent fireplace complete with a roaring fire. They enjoyed lunch in the dining room, where another wall of glass adorned the room similar to that of the living room, giving a view of the snow-covered land that merged into a conservation area. The sun only made the vision even more beautiful.

"Here you go," Kevin said, walking into the room with two mugs of hot chocolate. As he handed one to her, she saw that mini-marshmallows floated on the surface. "Careful. It's hot."

Elle murmured her thanks and carefully took hold of the cup. Their fingers brushed, but she purposefully didn't show her reaction. It wasn't the heat from the ceramic that set her flesh aflame. Using the time that Kevin poked at the fire and made sure it continued to burn evenly, Elle thought back over the afternoon. Whereas she thought their time together would be taut with tension, Kevin had kept the conversation light, not even discussing the case. She'd asked numerous times about the progress, but he evaded her questions time and again. She finally gave up and discussed the topics he wanted to cover, which ranged from their favorite foods to their preferred books and then to his friends. Technically, she wondered if she should start calling them her friends, but didn't want to dwell on that at the moment.

"I still can't believe you renovated this yourself," Elle said, feeling the need to contribute to the range of subjects. He'd been carrying it the entire time. "I know how often you were working the streets, talking to snitches back in the day. When did you find the time?"

"There's always time," Kevin responded, finally standing and joining her on the couch. She was grateful when he sat in his own space, not crowding her. He placed his own mug on his thigh as he twisted his body so that he was facing her way. "This is my home. It deserves to be taken care of. I don't know if I mentioned it, but my parents' house is over a hundred years old."

"Really? It didn't show signs of aging. If anything, with all the upgrades, I wouldn't have thought it could be more than ten years old."

"Where did you grow up?"

Kevin's question came out of left field, but it was asked in such a nonchalant and nonthreatening manner that Elle knew she would answer him. It did put her on guard, but all that his gray eyes contained was curiosity. She took a calming breath and hoped that her opening up just a little didn't give him the impression that it was a free for all.

"St. Paul."

If Kevin was surprised in any way, he didn't show it. He sipped his drink as if she'd told him that it was snowing outside. She expected him to follow up with another question, but he patiently waited for her to continue. Reaching up, she felt the locket through the material of her sweater. How much should she share? And if she divulged too much, would this end before it even truly started? Wasn't that what she wanted? He still sat silently, studying her.

"I never knew my mother. My father felt that he'd done his job by providing a roof over my head." Elle felt that same old apprehension start to saturate her pores as the past started to grab hold of her. She pushed on, hoping that once it was out, they'd never discuss it again. "When I graduated high school, he kicked me out. He drank and dabbled in drugs, so I didn't have any close friends that I could stay with. I took the money that he kept in a can in one of the cupboards and hit the streets. You know the rest."

Elle was aware that she'd rushed the words together, but that pretty much summed up her life story. It was very similar to that of the other girls on the street. A loveless home where they weren't wanted. The road was a vicious circle that normally couldn't be broken. She wasn't any different than they were, so there was no need to dwell on it.

"Is your mother's picture in that locket?" Kevin's head tilted toward the ornament she was now tracing. His question didn't surprise Elle, but yet it did. She knew she had a bad habit of fiddling with it, but he'd been taking a wild guess as to what it contained. "It's clearly special to you."

"Yes." Elle took a sip of her drink, thinking of how to switch topics. Hadn't she done her duty and shared a piece of herself? What more did he want? "She died in a drive-by shooting. At least that's what my father told me. We didn't live in the best neighborhood."

"May I?" Kevin gestured toward the locket with a nod.

Elle had never shown anyone and she wasn't sure she want-ed to now. How could she explain to him that the picture within the locket was the only dream of what her life could have been like? She used to stare for hours at the beautiful woman with long black hair so like her own and fantasize about having had a different childhood. It would never be her reality and she knew that, but showing her mother's picture to him meant facing it.

"Sure." Elle's mouth felt dry as she tried to sound normal. For some reason, she didn't want him to know how much this affected her. Without giving herself any more time to think it through, she reached inside her sweater and withdrew the locket. The chain was long enough that all she had to do was pull it over her head, which she did and handed it over as if it didn't mean anything. "Here."

Kevin slowly reached for it, indecision within his gaze. He knew. He knew that it meant more than she was willing to admit and Elle couldn't help but wonder what he would think of the woman within the gold accessory. His fingers once again brushed hers, but they were numb. He placed his cup on the coffee table in front of him and then concentrated on carefully opening the locket. It was as if he were afraid his large hands would break it. She didn't realize how still she'd become until he smiled tenderly at the picture within.

"She's beautiful. You look just like her."

And as simple as that, Kevin handed Elle back her necklace. Instead of putting it on, she held it tightly in her palm and feared that whatever this was between them would never last. It astounded her how her uncertainties had changed on a dime. At first, she hadn't wanted it to progress this far. Now she was worried she'd lose this chance at something more. Lauren had been wrong about opposites attracting one another. It was when couples complemented each other that their relationship lasted. She had nothing to give Kevin that would do that and once he heard how she'd entered the life, he'd wash his hands of her and that would be that. She'd be able to go about her life, albeit changed in knowing that the life she'd always dreamed about did exist…but that was something she'd have to live with. Explaining why she'd traded her body for a warm meal wasn't something he'd want to hear.

Kevin's cell phone rang and Elle breathed a sigh of relief. A part of her wanted to tell him the rest of her story and get this over with, but there was another part of her that wanted to extend this afternoon. Taking away the last fifteen minutes of apprehension, she'd really enjoyed his company and the mundane topics they'd covered. For once, it made her feel as if this was truly a date and that her life had a little normalcy instead of being a woman who hoarded away every penny in terror of having this newfound life ripped from her hands.

"We'll be there in thirty minutes," Kevin exclaimed, standing up quickly while disconnecting the call and shoving it into his front pocket. He was wearing a ribbed navy blue shirt and he pushed the sleeves up to his elbows. "Emily's in labor. We'll swing by the club and post a note on the door that all activities are cancelled tonight."

"What? No, we can't do that," Elle argued, standing up herself. Why would he even suggest such a thing? "There's no reason to cancel. This is why Jax and Connor hired me. To manage the club so they can live their lives. Drop me off and then go be with your friends."

Within seconds, Kevin had taken the mug out of her hands and placed it on the table. Before she could say another word, he was cradling her face within his hands. He hadn't touched her all afternoon and she'd let herself relax, but this heated contact stopped her in her tracks. The indecision she'd been feeling came back full force.

"*You* are included in these friendships, city girl," Kevin murmured, looking into her eyes intently. Had his hands not held her face, she knew her head would have shaken in denial. "Didn't you spend time with Lauren today? You enjoyed it, that much I could see. Don't you think she'd like a friend to sit with her? This is about Jax and Emily sharing a moment with the people they care about. That includes you. We're done with the doubts that float inside that indecisive mind of yours. Now get your ass moving and grab our jackets while I take care of the fire."

Kevin quickly kissed her before taking away his hands and moving toward the fire. He leaned down, his shirt pulling against his wide muscular back. Maybe she had entered some mystic portal when she'd been back at her apartment. The more she was around him the more she wanted to believe that this was the start of something new.

Doubts did float through Elle's mind pretty much every second of the day. They weren't easy to get rid of, but at the accelerated rate her life had taken lately, she felt she was entitled to them. It wasn't until Kevin threw a glance over his shoulder, his gray eyes pinning her with the fact she hadn't moved as he'd requested, that she slowly turned toward the foyer to grab their coats. Regardless that he seemed so confident in what was about to take place, Elle still had time to change his mind on the trip home.

✧   ✧   ✧   ✧

The calls over the loudspeaker, the beeps and noises that came from various rooms, the drone of the television in the background and the low murmur of the people in the waiting room seemed to blend together for a disordered ambiance. Elle had gotten used the antiseptic smell, although it still hung in the air.

What she wasn't accustomed to was the various different conversations that everyone seemed to be following but her.

"Don't let it overwhelm you," Lauren said, leaning back in her chair. "You should know by seeing us in the club that we're one big unrelated dysfunctional happy family."

"It's not that I don't think it's a nice gesture," Elle contended, sweeping her gaze over the room. It had come to her attention early on that there were two or three more waiting rooms, allowing Jax and Emily's family and friends to more or less take over this one. Honestly, it wasn't like these men and women would have given anyone a choice. "But I would have thought that only family should be here."

"Like I said, we are family."

Kevin had basically stayed by her side with the exception of taking a couple of phone calls regarding what she assumed was the case. Elle knew there was something more going on than what she was privy to, especially since he went to great lengths to avoid the subject today. She had seen him speak with Crest a few times as well. She would ask Kevin again for an update when he took her home.

Lauren yawned, covering her mouth with the palm of her hand. Elle glanced at the large black and white clock on the wall above the coffee stand and noticed it was going on midnight. They'd been here for hours. She could only imagine the exhaustion that Emily and Jax were feeling right now.

"Um, may I have your attention?"

The faltering feminine voice came from the doorway and all eyes swung that way. Elle recognized her from Emily and Jax's wedding. The older woman's name was Beatrice and she was Emily's aunt. From the stricken expression on her face and the unshed tears in her eyes, she wasn't here to present the news everyone had been waiting on. The air caught in Elle's throat and she swallowed hard. Lauren shot to her feet and was standing beside Connor within seconds. The team members gathered around.

Kevin was off to the side, pinning his gray stare to her, and holding his hand out with his palm facing upward. He wanted her to join them. Elle slowly nodded, her selfish plight of trying to understand her lot in life suddenly placed on the back burner.

"Emily…Emily had some trouble during the delivery." Beatrice placed a hand over her mouth, as if trying to come to terms with her own words. After a few seconds, her trembling fingers finally lowered and she delivered the boom. "They have her in surgery right now. Jax is with the baby, who is a healthy seven pound, four ounce boy. Once he's made sure that Derrick Connor Christensen is settled, I'll take over so that he can concentrate on Emily."

Murmurs went around, questions went unanswered, and it was obvious that no one was leaving anytime soon. Connor had a stunned expression on his face and it was apparent he hadn't known the name that Jax and Emily had chosen. Crest closed the distance to where Beatrice stood and enfolded her into his arms. He whispered something and then turned her over to Roger Dallen, her boyfriend, who was waiting in the wings.

"Where is Jax?" Connor asked after having cleared his throat. "This floor?"

"The surgery is taking place on the fifth floor. It wouldn't surprise me if Jax isn't already there." Beatrice patted Roger's hand as he rubbed her shoulder. "I'll make sure that Derrick is taken care of, but I think it best for all of you to go on up. Jax will need you."

Connor and Lauren were the first to maneuver themselves out of the crowd, quickly making their way out of the room. Ethan and Jessie held back, gathering up the coats and gloves that had been left behind. Crest and Taryn went deep into a conversation and the only one who wasn't present was Lach, apparently on his way and due at any moment. Kevin's grip was firm and Elle instinctively tightened her fingers around his.

"I can stay here and wait for Lach if you like," Elle said, offering to be the one left behind. "I overheard Ethan say that Lach was on his way."

"Ethan will have texted him by now." Kevin pulled her with him to where their jackets were lying over a chair in the corner. He tucked both coats over his right arm, all the while keeping his left hand secured in hers. "I'm sure he'll meet up with us on the fifth floor."

Elle remained silent as they followed the rest of the group out into the hallway and to where the elevator was located. The stress and worry that laced everyone's features hit home the fear they felt at losing one of their own. She wasn't privy to a lot of Emily's history, but Elle was aware that Jax and Emily had fought long and hard to be together. To be torn apart by what was supposed to have been the most joyous moment of their lives seemed truly unfair.

Within moments they were on the fifth floor, Jessie waving to everyone from down the hall. She and Ethan must have already located the waiting room and more importantly, Jax. Crest veered off to the nurse's station located on the right hand side of the hall and was now speaking with one of the personnel on staff. Events unfolded and by the time all was said and done, the entire group had been allowed to use a private room while waiting for news.

Kevin finally released her hand and threw their coats onto another chair before making his way over to Jax. Elle had never seen her boss look so…terrified. Jax always carried himself in a very self-assured manner that never seemed to waver. Except now. Seeing a shadow in the doorway, Elle noticed that Lach's large frame was crossing the threshold.

Lach's dark eyes took in everyone's whereabouts and it wasn't until he saw Elle that he moved. Coming to stand beside her, he crossed his sizeable arms across his black leather jacket. Even his gloved hands seemed oversized, although she'd personally witnessed him play in the club and it never ceased to amaze her the gentleness that resided within.

"Ethan texted me what happened." Lach didn't speak unless it was direct and to the point. He wasn't one for idle chitchat. "Do we know what went wrong?"

"Not yet," Elle responded, feeling a little out of place. She shifted her stance and grabbed onto her locket to give herself something to do. "We just came up to this floor ourselves. Connor, Ethan, and Kevin are finding out now. I just don't want to crowd him."

Elle could feel Lach's gaze on her, as if he knew the real reason that she was holding herself back, but she wasn't so sure that he'd be right. Everything she'd experienced in the last couple of weeks had altered the way she viewed life. Her life. Right now, any other introspection would have to wait.

"Coffee?"

Elle's lips lifted into a half smile. He really wasn't a man of words, was he? She glanced at Lauren, looking helplessly on as Connor and the men tried to comfort their friend. Ethan and Taryn stood nearby as well while Crest and Jessie were near the door. The man's face seemed to be made of stone until Jessie reached out, placing a hand on his arm. The intimate moment caused a softening of his features as he looked down at the petite woman. Elle hadn't realized there was something between the two of them. As if it hadn't happened at all, Crest pulled away and leaned against the doorjamb, crossing his arms and staring out into the hallway as if protecting them from unseen forces.

"Make that two?" Elle nodded toward Lauren.

"There's hope for you after all," Lach muttered under his breath.

Elle knew it was intentional, although his actual implication could mean several different things. The group knew that she and Kevin were...dating? Is that the term she should use? Again, this wasn't the time nor place to contemplate her life when another hung in the balance. Elle didn't reply to Lach's comment and made her way over to Lauren, hesitantly reaching out her hand. The redhead smiled in appreciation and took hold of Elle's fingers, both settling in to wait for news.

Chapter Seventeen

Kevin sat next to Jax, whose elbows were resting on his knees. His head hung low as he struggled with the fact that his wife was in surgery fighting for her life. It was every man's nightmare.

Connor sat on the opposite side of his best friend, while the rest of the crew gave Jax some breathing space. Kevin had forged a friendship with Jax over the course of their professional life within CSA and wanted to provide him with the support that Kevin knew came from only family. As Jax didn't have any blood relatives around or that he laid claim to, they would have to do.

"Did they tell you anything when they took Emily in for surgery?" Connor asked, keeping his focus solely on his friend. "She's a fighter, Jax. Look at how hard she fought for the two of you."

"Everything was going fine," Jax whispered, his torment hitched to every word that he expelled. "Emily was doing great. Then all of a sudden, her grip on mine just went slack. The machines started to go off, the nurses were trying to push me out of the way, and—fuck—"

Jax pinched the bridge of his nose, his features showing the emotional agony he was going through. When he managed to regain some of his composure, he looked directly at the door as if expecting the surgeon to be standing there. The only one near the doorway was Crest.

"She has the best doctors on staff," Kevin offered, knowing every bit of information helped. Reassurance was half the battle in sustaining hope. "You and Emily did all the research and you know this. Whatever went wrong, they'll fix. You have to believe that."

"I heard someone mention a blood clot." Jax's voice sounded far away, as if he was back in that delivery room. Kevin didn't doubt that's where his mind was. "Crying. I heard crying and there Derrick was, perfectly healthy and wanting to be held. Emily doesn't even know."

Jax's sentences seemed to be random, but Kevin knew they made sense to Jax. That's all that was needed. He looked over to see that Elle had taken up residence near Lauren, who seemed to be in shock. This was a jolt to all of them, but Kevin refused to believe this could end any other way than Emily making a full recovery and leaving this hospital with Derrick in her arms.

"I disagree with you, Jax," Connor argued, shaking his head. "Emily knows that Derrck is here, healthy, and waiting on her. Just like she knows you're sitting here obsessing over what those surgeons are doing and refraining from barging in there to demand answers."

"She fought for us when I didn't." Jax's gaze was now solely focused on the doorway. Kevin saw Crest discreetly step out and knew he was going to check on the progress of the surgery. Jax needed to hear something, anything, to keep his sanity in check. "Two years of her life was spent ensuring that we could be together and this is what she gets? I'm not even close to being the man she deserves and yet she fought every fucking day for a chance at happiness. It doesn't end like this. I refuse to believe it ends like this. Fuck. I need air. I can't breathe."

Jax stood and everyone cleared, giving him a wide berth to walk off the pent-up terror that was coursing through his veins. Unfortunately, nothing was going to be able to flush that feeling out of his body except news from the surgeons that Emily would be all right. Kevin prayed that happened.

"Can I get you anything?" Elle stood in front of Kevin, blocking his sight. Her beautiful face was a welcome change versus the horror that embodied his friend. "Coffee? Water? I don't think Jax could hold on to anything right now or I'd get him something as well."

Kevin had shaken his head at the start of her offer and continued to do so. He wasn't sure he could hold on to anything either, as his hands trembled with fear of the un-known. He refused to think of the worst outcome. He wasn't sure Jax would recover.

"No, thank you," Kevin replied, standing up and pulling Elle into his arms. For the first time, she didn't hesitate and while he noticed it, didn't take time to dwell on it. Getting Jax through this moment was what took precedence. Kevin laid his cheek on top of Elle's head. "Just having you here is enough."

Elle's silence could be taken a lot of ways, but having her body melt into his gave him hope that an instant like this shed important light on what was truly essential. Kevin would have given anything to instill some type of faith into Jax, but unfortunately, this was a demon that he would have to come to terms with. They were all here to wrestle with him, but only Jax could deliver the final blow.

✧　✧　✧　✧

"I can't take this waiting any longer," Jax muttered, the fingers of his right hand rubbing his forehead. He'd sat back down a while ago, his leg bouncing faster than the seconds ticking by on the clock hanging on the wall. The minutes were agonizingly painful, as each second seemed to take an eternity. "I need to see her. To know she's still with me."

"You know she's still with you." Kevin leaned his head back against the wall and stared up at the sterile ceiling. "Emily's doing everything she can to make her way back to you."

"We don't have separate souls anymore." Jax scrubbed his hand down to his unshaven jaw. A faraway look was in his bloodshot eyes. "We're one. Only one. If she were to…let's just say that I would be dead inside. I'd do what I was left here to do and raise our son, but I would never be whole."

Silence reigned and all that could be heard was the ticking of the clock above Kevin's head. It had to be going on three in the morning. Exhaustion had overtaken everyone, but each one of them stood at the ready for whatever they were about to face. It took a moment to register that a man appeared in the doorway and that Crest was standing beside him, his sole focus on Jax.

"Mr. Christensen?"

"Me." Jax's voice caught in his throat. Clearing it away, he quickly stood up and rubbed his hands down the sides of his denim. "Emily…?"

"Is fine," the surgeon said, swiping his surgical hat off of his head. The man was tall and lanky, with a thick load of black hair. His brown eyes were focused on Jax while presenting a tender smile, as if to reassure Jax that his words were true. "We were able to isolate the blood clot and relieve it. I won't bore you with the details now, as I know you want to be by your wife's side. I'll stop in to see you in about an hour to answer your questions. She is in recovery now and they'll be moving her to a room momentarily."

Jax covered his face with both hands while everyone gave him a moment to regain his composure. Kevin knew that the reality wouldn't sink in for Jax until he was by Emily's side, holding her hand and seeing his wife's beautiful smile. Jax took a deep breath, his heavy shoulders having finally lifted after hours of tormented waiting and extended his arm toward the surgeon.

"Thank you."

The words were raw, but certainly expressed the gratitude of what everyone was feeling. A nurse appeared behind the surgeon, waiting to take Jax to Emily. Crest then assured him that they would see to it that Beatrice was made aware of the situation. Lauren offered to stay with Derrick so that Jax felt someone was with his son while Beatrice joined him at Emily's side. Within seconds, Jax had disappeared through the doorway.

Everyone stayed in place a few minutes longer, letting the news settle over them. It had been a close call and one that they all hoped didn't get repeated. Crest was the first to move, walking over to the rack that was situated in the corner. He was the only one to have used it, as everyone else's jackets were scattered around the room. Calmly and efficiently, he shrugged into the long dress coat.

"The fates are fickle. Sometimes the crisis comes from an unpredictable direction. As always, we have to adapt, improvise, and overcome. Take some time and get some rest. We'll regroup Monday morning."

Chapter Eighteen

Elle awoke slowly to the sun streaming into the windows. The dim light gave away that Sunday had passed and the evening hours were approaching. She stretched and then tilted her face toward the receding warmth and was surprised by the idleness that remained in her body after having slept so long. Usually her nerves created an edge that she couldn't shake. Like a slow fog lifting, her eyes finally opened and she took in a room that was not hers. She should have known, considering her bed wasn't near a window. Fuck. She sat straight up and looked around Kevin's bedroom. He wasn't anywhere to be found.

Running a hand through her hair, Elle slowly released her pent up breath. She forced her mind to cooperate in organizing her thoughts. The club was closed Sunday and Monday evenings, so it wasn't as if she was in a hurry to leave. On the other hand, she wasn't so sure she wanted to extend her stay. They'd gotten home in the wee hours of the morning and somewhere in her exhaustion, she agreed to lie down for a few hours in Kevin's bed. It wasn't as if he didn't have a couple spare rooms handy, but both of them had been too tired to really argue.

"I'd offer you coffee, but I'm thinking a hot cup of tea might be in order." Elle's gaze flew to the doorway, where a shirtless Kevin stood looking like no man she'd ever been with. The johns she'd hosted were usually scrawny twenty-year olds looking for anything that would fuck them or fifty-year-old men who couldn't talk dirty to their wives. Last night's epiphanies seemed to fade with the setting sun. Kevin deserved better than her. He deserved what Jax and Emily had. "Herbal or black?"

"Um, I think I'll pass," Elle replied, throwing the warm covers back. She gave a sigh of relief to see that she was still wearing her jeans and sweater, sans the scarf, which must have come off when she'd removed her jacket. She scooted to the end of the bed. "I should get back home. I'm sure you have to get up early tomorrow and I'd just be in the way. I'll just ring a taxi and—"

"No, you won't." Kevin's voice had hardened and disappointment tinged his tone. "You'll take a shower, use my robe while we wash your clothes, and eat the meals that we've missed. The time for doubts has passed, so whatever reservations you're harboring in that mind of yours, wash them out when you shower. I'll be downstairs."

Just like that, Kevin disappeared from sight. Elle stayed there for a while until she started to question why she was still standing in one spot. That wasn't how she'd planned on that going, but it was a nice change of pace not to be given a choice. Not that she wanted that all the time, but there was a slight exhilaration that he didn't allow her to slink away. He was absolutely right when he said that the time for doubts had passed. It was a hard habit to break.

As fast as she could, Elle showered and used his bathrobe that had been hanging on the back of the bathroom door. It was navy in color and though she was tall for a woman, the material still hung loose on her frame. It was as if a child had put on their daddy's robe and been swallowed by it. She rolled up the sleeves as best she could and used her hair tie to bundle her wet strands high up on her head. She'd sung a song to keep from thinking about the rest of the evening. Would he eventually take her home? Or would he want her to spend the night? Slowly padding downstairs, she carried her clothes, uncertain of where his utility room was located.

"Door to your right," Kevin called out from the kitchen, apparently knowing her location from her footsteps. She glanced down at her bare feet. The hardwood floor was cool but nothing she wasn't used to, and she wondered how he'd heard her. "Just leave them in the basket and I'll get to them later this evening."

Elle stared at the new computerized front loading washer and dryer, deciding to take his advice. These machines looked nothing like the ones in the laundromat she used a few blocks away from the club. Seeing a white basket off to the side, she gently laid her clothes on top of the ones in there. It seemed a little too intimate, but again, she shoved that thought away and would worry about it later. She hadn't realized she was so good at procrastination. It was the new Elle.

"Looks better on you than me, that's for sure," Kevin said, catching sight of her in the open doorway of the kitchen. His gaze ran from the top of her head to the tips of her toes. They were warm now. "Hop up. I'll whip us up a couple of omelets and bacon. I decided one cup of coffee wouldn't hurt."

Elle used the rung of the stool to situate herself on the padded leather barstool, the brown color matching the wooden cabinets. Lights hung low from the ceiling, casting shadows across the room and making the ambience serene when she felt anything but. What she originally deferred slowly started to simmer to the surface and she fiddled with her locket.

"Okay. We'll play it your way." With those words, Kevin walked around the island, still shirtless, and didn't stop until he'd spun the rotating stool his way. His chest was nearly devoid of any hair and chiseled to be a perfect match with Michelangelo's *David.* As Kevin stepped into her, she instinctively opened her legs and tilted her head to look up at him, only to have her lips claimed by his. Her thoughts scattered and her mind went blank as her body reacted to his. This kiss wasn't anything like the ones they'd previously shared and the heat practically consumed her. By the time he was done tasting every crevice within her mouth, Elle was pretty damn sure they'd burned the kitchen to the ground. He pulled away and when her lashes fluttered open, she was surprised to see that the kitchen remained standing. "Much better. Now eat before I change my mind and take you upstairs on an empty stomach."

"But—"

"Eat." Kevin took the stool next to her and dug into his food as if he hadn't eaten all day. Technically, she supposed they hadn't and hesitantly she picked up her fork and followed suit. "I just spoke with Connor. He and Lauren headed back to the hospital this afternoon. Emily was just waking up, Jax was about to fall flat on his face, and Derrick was crying for his mommy. I'm sure by tomorrow things will be back on track."

"I'm so glad to hear that things are still going well and that Emily will be all right. They're fortunate to have good friends," Elle said after having taken a bite. The omelet had a smack to it and she found that it also kick-started her hunger. She ate a little more. "I've never seen such solidarity like that."

"Did you ever attend college?"

The question threw Elle and her eyes shot to his. Kevin was serious. Thinking back on it, they never did get to finish their conversation about her teenage years and she wasn't sure she wanted to. What if she did share with him how she got into the business? Would he walk away like she predicted? Her new-found love of procrastination came back in full force. Was it so bad to want to have a taste of the closeness she'd witnessed last night?

"No, but I like to read." Elle nibbled on some bacon, wondering where Kevin was fitting all of the food he was eating. It had to be triple what was on her plate. He washed it down with some orange juice and she found herself doing what she always said she wouldn't. She asked about his past. "Your mother said you went to college?"

"Yes, after I came back from Afghanistan. It was either sulk over not being able to reenlist or take action over my future." Kevin sat back in the stool and kept talking while she ate. His right hand rubbed his injury. "The rehab on my knee was quite extensive, so my studies gave me something else to concentrate on. Walking the campus also aided in rehabilitation."

"When did you get involved with the Heroes Benefit Society?" Elle figured she'd opened the door, so she might as well step right on in. It was liberating. "And what made you leave Wisconsin?"

Kevin's slow smile seemed to light up his face and somehow she sensed there was approval in that grin as well. A flash of irritation washed over her, feeling like he was laughing at her, but she forced herself to relax. Her initial reaction over a lot of things tended to be exaggerated and she didn't want to ruin a nice evening. One that she was really enjoying.

"I started out wanting to connect with those facing the same decisions I was facing. Turned out some of the men and women didn't want to accept their future." Kevin's smile disappeared, replaced by regret. "The adjustment from military to civilian life cannot be explained with words. I could see who they once were and what they'd become."

"Is that how you view me?" Elle pushed away her plate, suddenly not hungry. "You think of the girl that I used to be and wish I'd maintained that innocence? We're all given our path, Kevin. No one can walk it but us."

"There's that bad habit of yours. Putting words in my mouth." Kevin leaned forward to pick up a piece of bacon that she'd left on the plate. He lifted it to her mouth, waiting patiently until her lips parted to accept the food. "Is it so bad for me to see the good in people? When tragic moments take hold of a person's life that forces them to make choices they normally wouldn't make, that doesn't brand them a bad person. It's other people's judgments that do that and those people should be ashamed of themselves. You are right about walking in each other's shoes, but I don't need to do that to know that you did what you had to do to survive. Just as I had to do in order to endure my ordeal in combat, we sometimes have to do things that we wouldn't normally do given an alternative. We're creatures of our environment, but that setting can change if given the opportunity."

"Is that what you're offering me?" Elle asked, after having swallowed the bite he'd offered her. He brought the bacon up to his lips and ate the rest, his tongue licking his lower lip. What exactly *was* he proposing? "A change in my environment? I've already grabbed a hold of it, farm boy. There's no need to go further."

"Is there someone saying you can't have more? Or is it you're afraid to hope for more?" Elle was sure that Kevin wasn't really expecting a response, so she remained silent. He continued to stare at her as if he knew she was trying to figure it out, because in all honesty, she didn't know the answer. "I watch you when I'm at the club. When I take my turn as a Dungeon Monitor to ensure the scenes are in accordance with club policy, I see the yearning in your eyes when you happen to look over at the play areas. Do you know how long I've waited to satisfy that desire? To throw my vest down on the floor and become one of those Doms whose sub is restrained to a bench?"

Elle slipped off of the stool before he said another word, or worse, reached out for her. It was one thing to know how she felt in regards to observing the submissives being pleasured whereas it was another for Kevin to know. She'd also seen the other side of being a submissive—serving one's Dominant. Is that where he was going with this? She'd always wondered what it would be like, but did that make her like those women?

"Do you think I want to be a submissive?" Elle blurted out the question, for there was no other way to put it. She pulled the lapels of his robe tighter across her chest. "I spent years doing what men told me to do. I'm not about to do it again."

"Your mind certainly travels a hell of a lot faster than most people." Kevin stood up in between the stools, but leaned back against the counter and crossed his arms as if he had all the time in the world. "I was speaking in general terms of making love. You had sex with those men. There was no trust, passion, or caring involved. You're old enough and smart enough to know the difference. I was just pointing out the fact that you are a woman with desires and I want to be the one to tap into them because I don't think anyone has ever taken the time."

Another defensive barrier came down and her fingers loosened their grip on the material that was now bunched inside her palm. Elle shifted her feet on the hardwood floor, the sensation of her flesh suddenly making itself known. Kevin had the ability to take her mind off of everything but him. Hearing his words and knowing that he had no secret agenda caused a flush in places she'd not thought of in a long while. She wasn't used to simple and he had a way of making everything sound so easy.

"Does that mean I won't want to try things with you? Does that mean I won't tap into some submissive place inside of your heart and mind?" Kevin took a step away from the counter, slowly closing the distance between them. Elle's heart started racing and her palms started to tingle, sending streaks of electricity up her arms. Was this what the women felt at the club? Desire ripped through her at the opportunity he was presenting her with a chance to find out. She wasn't made of stone and the woman inside of her raged to claw its way to the surface, wanting to give him the chance to do all of the things he'd just said. "City girl, I want to explore every bit of you…physically, mentally, and emotionally. Yes, I'm a Dominant. I want to show you what I think is underneath all of those barriers that you've put into place. You're surrounded by the lifestyle almost every night. You might not have practiced and partook, but you certainly know all the rules and guidelines. All you have to do is say yes and select a safeword."

Elle's blood rushed through her ears, drowning out all sounds. The fabric of the robe became almost too much for her flesh and a vision of herself with it draped around her feet floated through her mind. What would his reaction be if she was to do that and stand in front of him bare? Kevin *did* make it seem so simple. He only wanted one answer and one word. One word. As if all of the events leading up to this hadn't altered her life in any way and he would accept one word to take things further. Her stomach felt like she was getting ready for the ride of her life and as if the tracks were set to go, her whispered reply flipped the switch.

"Yes. Firefly."

Chapter Nineteen

Kevin turned his head ever so slightly, straining to hear the one answer he'd been waiting on for more than a year. Elle's brown eyes were wide with apprehension and her knuckles had once again turned white. Her cheekbones were flushed while her lips parted as if she couldn't get enough oxygen. She was exactly how he wanted her and he had to clench his jaw not to just pick her up and carry her upstairs to have his way with her. This needed to be so much more.

"Let me see you and I want you to repeat your safeword just this once so that I understand you realize its significance."

Kevin had told her the truth. He wanted to know every nuance of her, in every way possible. If there was something Elle didn't like or that made her uncomfortable, he wanted to know about it. If he did something that caused her desire to ratchet higher, he'd do it again and again until she got her fill. When her pupils dilated and her breathing became shallower, he knew he'd have her strip again and again in the future. It almost killed him not to move from the spot he was in.

"Firefly."

That was all Elle spoke before her trembling hands fumbled with the thick navy blue belt. Once the material parted, Kevin was able to see her pale flesh, which looked like silk and practically begged to be touched. Her tiny belly button sat perfectly in the middle of her abdomen. He lowered his eyes, catching sight of her mound. What he considered a landing strip was situated perfectly over her clitoris and while he preferred his women bare, Elle was perfect the way she was.

"All of it."

Elle shrugged her shoulders ever so slightly, causing that material to fall around her elbows. It was as if she was taking her time in revealing herself to him in case he didn't like what he saw. Kevin wanted to assure her that would never happen, but his mouth dried upon the sight of her breasts. They would fit perfectly in the palms of his hands. Seeing the swell of her flesh made his cock harden. He hadn't even touched her, yet his fingertips felt as if he'd already traced the supple complexion. He tightened his grip on his biceps.

"Drop it."

The heavy material fell at Elle's feet, leaving her standing there in all her glory. The sight of her evaporated whatever oxygen had been left in Kevin's lungs. Though she was taller than most women he'd been with, there was a fragile air about her that he felt the need to shield. Pleasure and protect. He would show her the first and she would feel both by the time he was done.

"Widen your stance."

Kevin stayed where he was and watched closely as Elle did as he requested. A slight glistening appeared on her inner thigh, just enough so that he knew she was reacting the way he needed her to. He wished he could have questioned her about the men she'd been with, not in an insulting way, but to know if any had ever given her the pleasure that she deserved. In realization that she had probably never been treated the way she should have been and that they needed to keep her past separate from this moment in time, he slowly crossed the room and continued around her until her back was pressed to his front.

"Are you wet?"

"Kevin, I'm not good at—" Elle had immediately shaken her head at his question, her actions causing her hair to tickle his chest.

"It was a yes or no question, Elle," Kevin murmured against her head. She'd used his shampoo and smelling it on her emitted a distinctive scent that had his balls tightening. "I want a yes or no answer."

"Yes."

"Second yes of the evening." Kevin dipped his head and left a searing kiss on the back of her neck. "We're making progress. I'd like to see for myself though. Inspect what you expect. That's an old saying that I heard numerous times in the Corps. I'm thinking it translates just as well in this situation."

Gently, Kevin brought his hands down on Elle's shoulders. He kept them there for just a moment while he savored the heat from her body. She was truly standing in front of him, accepting his touch. It was beyond surreal and one he wanted to sear into his memory. Gradually he caressed her arms, her hands, and then transferred his fingers onto her hips. He stroked her abdomen and found it just as smooth as he'd thought her flesh would be. He heard her swift intake of air and then felt her go as still as the deer he'd see out in the field when they knew a presence surrounded them. Stopping for only an instant, he assertively moved his hand downward until his palm covered her silky mound. His middle finger sat securely over her clitoris.

"Mine." The word came out more guttural than Kevin had intended, but it was a primal instinct. Elle exhaled and amazingly, her body relaxed into his. Her tell let him know she responded to his commands and dominance, yet it was the wetness leaking from her core that assured him she relished what was taking place. "Do not move. I want to trace every inch of you and should the need arise to come, please do."

Kevin had been placing a kiss on her left shoulder when Elle's head whipped to the side, her darkened eyes connecting with his. The skepticism that shined through them tore at his heart. He'd been right and no one had ever taken the time to really get to know her body. Not wanting to release her pussy, but knowing that was what was best, Kevin ceased touching her and stepped around her until they were face to face.

With the back of his fingers, Kevin brought them to her forehead, trailing them across her questioning lines and then down her left cheek. Crossing over her chin, he completed his circle before tracing her nose. The minute he connected with her rosy lips, dragging his thumb over the plush flesh, her tongue reached out to touch the tip. As she had done to him, his eyes flew to hers, needing to see what emotion lay within.

Longing and something else so innocent that he couldn't name glittered through and caused his cock to throb. They had just scratched the surface of this connection that was between them and now, with just a tender caress, they'd unlocked an inferno.

"I love surprises," Kevin murmured, dropping his gaze once more to watch his exploration. "Don't you?"

Elle felt the world spinning around her while she remained locked in place. How could Kevin affect her this way with only his hands and his words? When he'd basically given her permission to come, similar to what she'd witnessed in the club, she didn't bother to hide her incredulity. She'd only ever come by her own hand; the men she'd been with were not worried about her pleasure. She couldn't come from just his exploration of her body. That was ludicrous. So why was she responding in such a fashion that she now doubted herself?

Elle thought about her safeword and where she'd heard that word before. It was from a particular scene she'd witnessed in the club. The electricity of that night's activities had energized the entire place. She recalled how the sub she watched screamed in ecstasy and how Elle had secretly wished to be in her place. Later that evening, when she'd been seeing to a guest's request in the lounge, she came across the same sub as she was cradled in her Dom's arms. She was obviously in aftercare as she softly wept and repeatedly whispered just one word over and over...Firefly.

"You are so beautiful, city girl." Kevin brought both hands to her shoulders, drawing her back into the present with the warmth of his palms. He kept tracing the edge of her arms and down to her hands. "More captivating than any skyline that a camera could ever capture."

By the time Kevin had worked his way up her sides, Elle's muscles were quivering. She couldn't withhold the cry that escaped her lips when he cupped her breasts, capturing her nipples in between his thumbs and hands. Her eyes involuntarily closed as pleasure wracked through her. There seemed to be a direct connection between her sensitive nubs and her clitoris, which now pulsated with her heartbeat.

"I absolutely love to hear you cry out when I give you pleasure." Kevin released his hold on her nipples, stroking the backs of his hands over her stomach and down her thighs. He leaned in front of her, covering every inch of her outer legs before starting to glide back up her inner thighs. Instead of continuing, he wrapped his arms around her until she could feel his breath on her mound. When his finger traced the crevice of her ass, Elle found herself standing as still as he'd originally wanted her to. It wasn't for the reason of his demand, but more so that she wasn't sure which side she wanted him to touch more. "I think I'd like to hear what you sound like when you come."

Each breath stroked her clit as if Kevin had actually used his tongue. She didn't even notice that his hands had moved until he stood up. His gray eyes seemed to be the color of granite, yet the heat that resided inside made them resemble a melting pot. It only fueled her body to give him what he desired. And just like that, standing in the kitchen without a stitch of clothing and reacting to just the warm tip of Kevin's finger on her swollen nub, her orgasm took hold and didn't let go until he did. The entire time her body enjoyed the contractions her pussy produced, Kevin watched her face and intimately took in every reaction. It was unlike anything she'd ever experienced before and had he not been there to catch her, Elle would have ended up on her knees.

"As much as I want you there, I don't think we're quite ready for that." Kevin's soft and tender voice washed over her as he spoke low in her ear. Her body still felt electrified and every word seemed to trigger another spasm. Swinging her up in his arms, he started through the house and up the stairs. "I did like the little mews you emitted. Very sexy."

Elle turned her face into his neck and pressed her lips against him for several reasons. One, she wanted to tell him that she was too heavy to carry but knew he'd only argue. Two, she was afraid she'd go into an uncontrollable laughing fit at having her strangled cries described as sexy. She was relatively sure the irrepressible urge stemmed more from the endorphins coursing through her body. Three, the time that had been spent in the kitchen seemed surreal and she didn't want to say anything that might alter the rest of the night.

"Back under the covers you go." Kevin carefully situated her on the bed and again, Elle refrained from saying she was a grown woman and not a child to be taken care of. She never stopped looking at him and was totally captivated when his large fingers, including the one that caused her body to explode, unbuttoned and unzipped the denim that kept her from viewing the rest of his glorious form. "You keep looking at me like that and I'm going to find it very hard to unearth the strength to do what I need to do."

Kevin's words didn't make sense but Elle chalked it up to her frenzied hormones. His jeans fell to his ankles and one by one, he kicked them free. The size of his thighs was corded with muscle, his abdomen was contoured to announce his physical well being, but it was his erect cock that captivated her. Long, thick, and with a pearl of pre-cum at the tip, Elle felt her body responding all over again.

"Scoot over." Kevin grabbed the comforter and lifted it higher, sliding his hard body next to hers. She reached for him, wanting and knowing what came next, but instead was stunned when he gathered her up and just held her. The sheets and comforter surrounded them, capturing their warmth. "Close your eyes. It's been a very long weekend."

Elle knew that sleep was in a far off place that she rarely visited. If Kevin thought now would be any different, he was sorely mistaken. Why weren't they going to have sex? It dawned on her that she hadn't really spoken since he began touching her and she didn't want to now, but the need for answers overcame her.

"Kevin?" Elle whispered, her head nestled into his shoulder although her body was far from relaxed. "Why aren't we doing more? You didn't…"

Elle was uncertain of how to describe what they weren't doing, knowing he would make it sound more intimate than she would. When Kevin didn't answer right away, she tentatively lowered her hand down his chest but he caught it before it moved any lower. The steel grip sent another wave of desire through her, yet she couldn't bring herself to tell him that the scene in the kitchen wasn't enough. She needed more.

"Close your eyes." It sounded as if his words were spoken through gritted teeth and she felt ire rise up, her hand closing into a tight fist. "Go to sleep."

"I don't want to go to sleep," Elle snapped, struggling to sit up. Although it was said in a normal tone, her words seemed to echo throughout the room. It was dim, but not so dark that she couldn't make out his features. He'd left the hallway light on, for which she was grateful. "We can't just…share something like that and then go to sleep. It doesn't work that way."

"It works that way if I say it works that way." Kevin refused to let her sit up. Elle emitted a deep frustrated sigh and settled back down, far from the relaxed state he wanted her in. She'd wait until he loosened his grip before slipping out. "You keep forgetting that I don't intend for us to be fleeting. When we're ready for something more intimate, we'll know."

Elle bit her lower lip to state that she damn well knew what she wanted, but discerned that would sound like a bitch. Instead, her mind raced with thoughts of what had happened, things she'd witnessed in the club, and scenes she wouldn't object participating in with him. Their relationship had gone from one big mind fuck to being physical. If she were honest with herself, it was both and that was why she was so on edge. She'd lost control of every aspect of her life. What was she to do now?

"Relax." Kevin spoke as if he'd heard her unspoken question, but Elle knew it was just because her muscles were taut and he could feel the tension radiating off of her. At least she was relatively sure he didn't have the power to read her mind. At this juncture, considering where she was, anything was possible. "I've got you. We'll wake up early, enjoy a nice breakfast while watching the snow fall, and talk about our week's plans. And maybe, just maybe, we can have a repeat performance of what happened in the kitchen. Those sexy little cries will get me through the day."

Elle inhaled and forced her body to relax. She pushed away the insidious fear that still crept around inside of her, baiting and taunting her that this would never last. She was truly afraid that the more he learned of her life on the streets, the more it would push him away. She would focus on the here and now, her different experiences having given her an unusual perspective. Would fear win out over hope? Or would hope instill faith in her as Kevin had once suggested?

The last few weeks had been leading up to this moment, albeit she would have thought they'd consummate their relationship together, and she'd answered him honestly in the kitchen when she'd said *yes*. She was ready to embark on this journey and see where it led them. She would also freely admit that she wanted the mental escape that the submissives at the club seem to have found, but knew that should they ever take their physical relationship that far, she would enjoy testing and setting new boundaries. She smiled against his chest and hoped that he didn't catch the motion. Tomorrow might just start out a little better than he'd described.

Chapter Twenty

Kevin stirred, not wanting to wake up from the dream that consumed his soul. Warmth coated him and he instinctively elevated his hips, wanting more. Silk, maybe satin, rubbed against his cock and he felt the building tension in his balls. Up and down, over and around, there was no getting away from the overwhelming heat that was tempting to pull his seed from deep within.

"Fuck," Kevin whispered, struggling to open his eyes. Sunlight didn't pour in like usual, giving him the indication that snow was falling. Either that or it was damn early in the morning. His room appeared the same and the warm spot beside him let him know that Elle was near. Everything was fine, except something wasn't quite right. He went to bring his hands up in order to rub his face only to realize his fingers were entangled in strands of mellifluous hair. Fuck. "Elle, stop."

With one long hard draw and a distinct flick of Elle's tongue, Kevin groaned when he felt the pressure of his balls erupt. Tightening his hold on her head, he kept her in place to receive his seed. He had no doubt this was exactly what she had planned, but nevertheless, it wasn't how he wanted the day to start. This was supposed to be about her, about acclimating her to his life and familiarizing her with the significance he wanted this relationship to have. His release was strong and by the time she'd drunk every last drop, Kevin seriously contemplated calling the office and telling Jessie that he wouldn't make it in today.

"Good morning," Elle murmured, slowly working her way up his body. He waited until she was directly over top of him before quickly flipping her over and pinning her to the mattress. "Oh!"

"Nymph," Kevin exclaimed before claiming her mouth. He kissed her until they couldn't breathe and then he relented, pulling away as they both gasped for air. "Ground rules. We need ground rules. This week will be spent getting to know one another, but on my terms. You had the run for almost a year, so now it's my time. Starting now. Take a shower and meet me in the kitchen. I never did manage to get your clothes washed, so borrow a pair of my sweats. We'll talk about the week over breakfast."

Kevin levered himself off of her and the bed, walking across the cold wood floor to grab some clothes out of his dresser. He made a mental note to buy some throw rugs, not wanting Elle to be uncomfortable. Flicking on the lights, he ensured the dimmer was activated so her eyes weren't bothered by the brightness. He nabbed the required garments and when he didn't hear the rustle of the sheets, turned back around. With her back against the headboard, she'd managed to tuck the sheet over her breasts and under her arms. Her black hair had come loose from its band sometime throughout the night and it draped over her shoulders. Rosy lips were visible and his dick hardened once more, knowing *it* was the reason for such a sensual look. She followed every movement he made, as if gauging his reaction of what had just taken place.

"Not all men are the same, city girl." Kevin couldn't tell what she was thinking, as her lashes came down just enough to cover the rich brown of her eyes. He didn't want to say or do the wrong thing here, but it was vital for both of them to be honest if they stood a chance of this lasting between them. He crossed back over the floor, needing to see her reaction in case he fucked this up, and sat on the edge of the bed. He reached out to firmly hold her chin, ensuring that their gazes were connected. "I love how you woke me up this morning, but I don't want that to be some sort of obligation from last night. Just because I didn't physically benefit doesn't mean I didn't obtain satisfaction. Being in your presence and being able to please you does that all on its own. Not all fulfillment is corporeal."

"And what if pleasing you gives me a sense of accomplishment?" Elle whispered the words, as if she too were afraid of muddling this moment. "I need to feel…"

"That your effort is substantial too?" Kevin could just imagine how hard it was for Elle to be truthful in this situation when her basic need was to withdraw any emotional strings left dangling in the wind. She was staying true to her word though and giving them a chance. That was all he could ask for. "The fact that you're in my bed, giving me access to your pleasure and willing to navigate this newfangled path we're on is all the effort I need."

Elle nodded slowly, as if she didn't really believe him. It was Kevin's job to make certain she did and he would spend every moment doing just that. The sheet had slipped a little, revealing a pert nipple practically begging for his attention. Releasing her chin, he guided the back of his fingers over the sensitive nub and was rewarded by her swift intake of air.

"You are hell on a man's resolve," Kevin murmured, knowing that if he were to touch her in any other way, he'd be buried deep inside of her within seconds. Forcing his limbs to do as directed, he stood. "Take a shower. If you keep testing me like this, your ass *will* be over that spanking bench."

Elle had taken care of the inventory and made sure the bar was restocked before heading back up to her apartment and grabbing her jacket. Monday was the day that she usually stopped in at Reformation and since Kevin had spelled out how their week was going to be spent, she knew that she'd have to keep that part of her schedule. As she walked into the bathroom to grab her hair clip, her reflection in the mirror caught her attention. Who was that woman staring back at her?

Elle still looked the same. Her hair was still black, her eyes were still brown, her features hadn't changed and yet there was a glow that she hadn't seen before. A smile. Happiness. Her heart fluttered.

She'd tried so hard to convey what she was feeling this morning, but the words hadn't come out exactly how she'd wanted them to. Reciprocating in the physical sense *was* how she was able to give back. How else was she to show her worth? Elle cringed at her thoughts and quickly grabbed the clip before making her way out of the apartment. It sounded like the same lame emotional and physical issues that every ex-hooker had. She refused to be in the same camp and having made it this far affirmed that she would continue and do her damnedest to give the effort that Kevin spoke of this morning. How hard could it be? Every normal woman seemed to be able to do it, why not her?

Frustration and exhilaration warred within Elle as she bundled up and walked the distance to the shelter. It always felt farther in the winter, with the wind whipping her about and the slick ice spots that she tried to avoid on the mostly empty sidewalks. The skyways were how the majority of people maneuvered throughout the city, but where she was going there was nothing of that nature. Finally arriving at her destination, Elle hurried up the stairs and through the front door.

Cinnamon and another delicious aroma shrouded the entryway, leading the way into the kitchen. Cam had a red apron tied around his neck and waist, along with a matching chef's hat sitting almost sideways on his head. Three girls, one of them Rachel, surrounded him at the table with cookie sheets filled with pink lady fingers lined up perfectly in rows of three.

"I can see I came at just the right time," Elle quipped, unraveling her scarf and taking off her gloves. "Any hot chocolate with that?"

"For you, dear friend, I'll even add on the marshmallows," Cam replied with a bow. As he busied making her drink, Elle removed her jacket and placed her stuff around the corner on a chair in the common area. Returning, she took a seat and knew immediately by the gleam in Rachel's eye that the girl was about to say something. What it could be was anyone's guess, but Elle instantly tensed. Cam beat Rachel to it. "A little birdie told me that someone's love life is spicing up just in time for Valentine's Day. Do share, beautiful lady."

Elle looked between Cam, Rachel, Molly, and Angela. All of them watched her expectantly, like she would share something like that with them. She had trouble just thinking about her relationship with Kevin when she was by herself. And how the hell had they known about her and Kevin? It wasn't like they were at any of the places Elle and Kevin had been.

"Who told you about Kevin?"

"I like the name," Cam said in approval, walking her way with a package of mini marshmallows. He set the bag down on the table with a wink. "Wait a second. I just connected the dots. Is this Kevin the one that came here months ago to question the tenants about the rapes and murders that have been taking place?"

Elle was too busy trying to figure out how they had come by the news to answer Cam's questions. He rarely left the center, so that left one of the women. Elle swung her gaze to Rachel, whose Cheshire smile said it all. It still didn't explain how she knew and it was starting to make Elle uncomfortable. She liked to fly under the radar. This was putting her in a damn red zone with flashing lights.

"Rachel? How would you know that I'm…that Kevin and I…that we're seeing each other?" Getting the words out almost strangled Elle. It was the first time she'd admitted it out loud. Swallowing in order to regain her voice, she continued her inquiry when Molly elbowed Rachel in the arm. Molly had known too? "Rachel?"

"A friend told me." Rachel shared a look with Molly and then with Cam, who suddenly seemed to be aware of the underlying tension. A friend? That didn't narrow it down and the simple statement made Elle all the more wary. She waited, knowing that was the best alternative to getting Rachel to talk. "Yeah, a friend. Said they saw you and Kevin together holding hands."

Cam set the hot chocolate on the table in front of Elle, but her stomach revolted immediately. A vision flashed in her mind of her and Kevin holding hands as he walked her into the club this morning. It was the only time they had done that publicly, besides at the hospital. The problem with anyone being witness to that is that Kevin had pulled his truck into the parking garage, which couldn't be seen from the street. That could only mean that someone had been inside the garage.

"Rachel, could I speak with you in private for a moment?"

"Oh, Elle, don't give her a hard time." Cam opened the bag of marshmallows and sprinkled some on the surface of her hot chocolate. "We're just teasing you."

"About what?"

Eric walked into the kitchen and straight for the coffee machine that was on the counter. He hadn't even bothered to look their way. His tone gave the indication that he was in a bad mood, but then so was Elle.

"Nothing."

"Elle's love life."

Elle and Cam spoke in unison, causing Eric to finally turn around, mug in hand. It struck her that Eric appeared exhausted, considering his eyes were bloodshot and there were discolored bags underneath. His features seemed to be set in stone although his surprise was evident. She wasn't sure she should be insulted or understanding that he would feel that way.

"Really? Who's the lucky guy?" If it had been any other person to say that, Elle would have taken it as is, but knowing Eric, he meant that in a derisive manner. He could be such an asshole. "Anyone I know?"

"No." Elle pinned her sights back on Rachel, who was now standing with Molly and Angela. All three appeared to want to leave, but that wasn't happening. At least not for Rachel. "Rachel, the living room please?"

With a defeated and dramatic sigh, Rachel moved around the table and walked into the common area. Cam was tsking, as if Elle was going overboard. She sent him a glare that had him holding his hands up in surrender. Eric watched the scene unfold in front of him as she scooted back her chair to follow Rachel.

"There's several people who know who Kevin is that we both know, but no one that should have seen Kevin and I this morning." Elle was very uncomfortable with the conclusions she was drawing, but she didn't want to jump to any assumptions before calling Kevin. "Unless they were in the parking garage. Is someone watching me, Rachel?"

"It's not what you think." Rachel crossed her arms and tapped her foot, obviously anxious to get this conversation over with. Regret was written across her features, but Elle was certain it wasn't regret for the right reason. "Don't be mad at Hash. He was in the area and saw you. That's all."

"In the area?" Elle wished that she had her phone in hand right now to let Kevin know what was going on, but it was in her coat pocket. Anyway, she needed more information. "Rachel, we were inside a parking garage. What was Hash doing there?"

"I don't know." It was a blatant lie and Elle was done with this conversation that was getting them nowhere. She'd had dealings like this the majority of her life, mostly arguing with the girls over whose turn it was to take the next john. Elle had learned early on not to take shit from anyone and when she'd stepped closer to let Rachel know that she'd had enough of this shit, the girl finally wavered. "He was just doing a favor for someone."

"This is your last time to come clean," Elle warned, standing her ground. "Why is Hash following me?"

"Bee wanted him to keep an eye on you," Rachel exclaimed, rushing her words together. "He wasn't convinced you were really leaving the streets and was willing to wait you out. Everyone knows that you were his go-to girl. The one who made him the most money. He took a big hit in business. He wanted Hash to keep tabs on you and to report back to him if Hash thought there was ever a chance that he might be able to convince you to come back and work for him."

Elle was instantly sick to her stomach. She turned away from Rachel, not wanting the girl to see her reaction. Vulnerability had no place on the streets and for a brief moment, that was what it felt like. It was as if she'd been drugged back into that helpless pit of vipers, wanting any piece they could get from her. Anger pushed out the disgust and she was even more grateful that Kevin had used his influence to keep Bee from harassing her during this past year. Bee was just smarter than the average pimp and found another way. What he didn't seem to understand was that it was her life. It was time she took matters into her own hands.

"Please don't be mad at Hash. He—"

"Stop." Elle walked to the corner and grabbed her coat, scarf, and gloves before finally facing the woman who reminded Elle so much of herself when she'd thought she knew all the answers. "It's time you grow up, Rachel. Hash is a low-level drug dealer that will never amount to anything. He'll obviously do anything for money, and in the end he'll pick the streets over you any day. As for Bee, he uses his street credo to keep his girls in line. God only knows if he's the one who's actually murdering those girls, but I'll be damned if he gets to keep his seedy little fingers in my life. Take a page out of this book, Rachel, and open your eyes to the risks of the profession. If you hide from it, you'll end up like Francie."

Elle walked to the door, hearing Cam calling her name. The last thing she needed was a lecture from him. He'd tell her that none of this was Rachel's fault and that Elle should be sensitive to her plight. Fuck that. Elle gave her time to Reformation to help, but Rachel's naiveté was going to get her killed. Someone had to be honest. She ignored Cam, slamming the door as she left. Slipping her arms into the sleeves of her coat, she'd made it to the sidewalk before looking back over her shoulder. Eric stood in the window watching her. She didn't need his shit now either and purposely turned her back toward him. Following the sidewalk, she pulled out her cell phone and shot off a text to Kevin. Their evening plans would have to wait. She had things to take care of.

Chapter Twenty-One

"So nothing on Bee?"

Kevin was sitting in the police station, looking over the latest reports that Taggart had put together. The tails that had been following specific targets had yielded nothing, and from what Taggart said were just calling unwanted attention from his superiors about the manpower he was using. He had to account for the money that was currently producing zero leads.

"I can't prove he was in the warehouse. Bee hasn't made a move against Rachel, but then again, I'm sure he's aware we're keeping our eye on her." Taggart brushed the crumbs of his stale donut off of his blue and white tie. "As for Rachel and Hash, they see each other regularly but their actions are habitual. As for the man who was murdered, we ain't got shit."

"What about surveillance cameras that are in that area? Any luck with those?"

"The gas station gave us the tapes. It covers the counter, but not the hallway where the phone is located." Taggart finished off his late day snack and then balled his napkin before trying for a three-pointer in the garbage can located six feet away. He missed. "There was a woman paying at the counter and she was verified leaving. Two men walked in after our victim did, only to grab some cigarettes and a couple of lottery tickets. They left. No one was seen and the clerk on duty didn't even realize there was an issue until a patrol car showed up."

"So that tells us something," Kevin surmised, leaning back in his chair.

"It tells us shit." Taggart reached over and grabbed the files that Kevin had put down. "We're still at square one."

"This is the problem with you detectives," Kevin said, ribbing the man good-naturedly. "Case after case starts to look alike, because they are alike. You can't separate the scenes and they all get lumped together. How many investigations do you have running?"

Taggart ran a hand over his face and then rubbed his chin. He didn't answer. He was overworked, underpaid, and still had a personal life to live. Add on murders, rapes, domestic violence, and every other damn crime his department was responsible for and it was lucky anything got solved. Kevin didn't envy him in any way. No wonder the parents of the first rape victim hired an outside agency.

"Look, I can have some of my contacts keep an eye on Bee if you need to pull back on the manpower. In exchange, can I have access to those tapes?" Kevin's gut instinct was telling him something was there and that they just needed to think outside the box. He and his team had the capability and time to see this through. "All of them?"

"Sure. You know Crest has gotten his hooks into the mayor. Your agency practically has carte blanche over our files." Taggart's words didn't contain hard feelings in any way, for which Kevin was glad. He always tried to maintain good relationships, but there were some officers on the force that played the power game. "I'll have them sent over."

Kevin would look at them first before handing them over to Taryn. Squid had a way with electronics and software that would pinpoint every coming and going along with who had the advantage to slip in the back entrance. This could be the lead they were hoping for.

"How's Emily? The guys went in for a collection of flowers. They should have been delivered today."

"Elle and I are heading over to the hospital in a couple of hours." Kevin's phone vibrated and he stretched out his body, reaching into the front pocket of his jeans. "I spoke with Jax this morning though and all seems to be returning to normal. They even moved the baby in so Emily could nurse."

Kevin's gut tightened as he saw a text from Elle had come through on his display. *Have something to take care of. Go to hospital without me. I'll have a taxi drop me at your place later tonight.* What the hell? Didn't they cover this already? She didn't get to back out now. He tamped down his anger as he thought of a reply.

"Everything okay?"

Kevin stood and grabbed his jacket. "It will be. Get me those tapes and I'll touch base in a few days."

With that, Kevin stalked out of the station. Ignoring the cold, he walked across the street to his truck ignoring the looks he received from bystanders in regards to his holstered weapon. Getting in, he threw his coat onto the passenger side seat and started the engine. Shooting a quick text off to Elle, he then tossed his phone in the direction of his jacket. He was done being patient.

✧ ✧ ✧ ✧

Elle's emotions were torn in two and she wasn't sure how to handle the upcoming confrontation. She paced her apartment, not even feeling the chill in the air anymore. She'd worked up a sweat on thinking of how she was going to confront Bee. She needed to be armed in case things went south, but he needed to know that it was unacceptable for him to be having her followed. God, it had been almost a year. She would have thought he'd given up any hopes that she'd fail in living a normal life. She'd had things mostly worked out in her head until Kevin had texted her back. That certainly hadn't gone as planned.

Spanking bench. Thirty minutes.

Was he fucking serious? Not a chance. It wasn't as if Elle had said she was cancelling their plans or that she was backing out of this newfound relationship. Honestly, Kevin was part of the reason she needed to confront Bee. She'd finally taken a chance on someone and she wasn't about to have that taken away by her past mistakes. Granted, going back over the text she'd sent, it could definitely be misconstrued. But she didn't have time to worry about that. Plus, she wasn't too sure about using the club equipment during closing time. It just seemed wrong, regardless of how her body responded to the words. She quickly left her apartment and took the stairs down to the club. She looked over at the play area as she crossed the floor to exit through the front entrance.

Once again, Elle's emotions were torn. She'd always wanted to know what that would feel like. As she exited the front door into the club's entryway, she turned around to make sure the door locked shut by watching the button on the access card device turn red. No doubt Kevin would use the garage and she wasn't about to run into him right now. This was something that she had to take care of on her own. She would deal with him and his hurt feelings later.

Upon leaving the building, Elle bundled up and dipped her head to keep the cold wind at bay. It took at least twenty minutes to reach her destination, but by that time she had everything mapped out in her head as to how she wanted this conversation to go. She needed to be the one to do this, not Kevin or anyone else. Bee wouldn't get the upper hand and once she'd stood her ground, he'd slink back into his sleazy hole and leave her the hell alone.

Taking a deep breath, Elle knocked on the door knowing full well it would be packed full of people. Men and women that she'd worked with and hadn't seen in a very long time. Bee always called a meeting to get a head start on the night's coup that might be raked in and she doubted that he would change his habits. It was hard to believe, but even in the dead cold of winter, people still paid to get fucked.

A couple of weeks ago she never would have done something like this. A warm feeling spread through her chest. She was standing up for herself and she was damn proud of how far she'd come. A little bit of guilt ate at her at the thought of Kevin back at her apartment, wondering where she was, but she pushed it aside when the door swung open.

"My pretty little Elle," Bee announced with a wide smile, although she did notice that he looked behind her. Was he still worried about Kevin? He should be more worried about her. "I knew you'd come back."

"I haven't come back to work for you, Bee." Elle kept her hands folded inside her coat pockets. "I found out through the grapevine that Hash has been keeping tabs on me. Let's be clear on something. I don't work for you anymore. I will never work for you. If I so much as see anyone that I conducted business with in my vicinity, I will call the cops and have you and whatever flunky you hired thrown in jail for harassment. Is that clear?"

Elle had spoken loud enough that the people within the run-down apartment no doubt heard every word. Voices became hushed, although it was evident from the murmurs inside that they were all questioning each other, trying to figure out what was going on. She knew it was a probability that he would make everyone leave, as Bee had a major anger management issue, so when his eyes grew dark and he stepped out into the outside hallway she wasn't surprised. Whatever he was about to say, he didn't want his minions to witness.

"You listen here, bitch," Bee muttered, not leaving more than an inch between them. She refused to be intimidated by him and stood her ground. Bee always took advantage if he thought he saw weakness. She'd learned that long ago. "If you wanted out, you should have left town. I've given you time to see that you don't fit in with those people. More then enough time."

"And what, Bee? You thought I'd come running back?" Elle tilted her head up, never once wavering her stare. When Bee's lip upper lip curled into that evil grin she knew so well, her grip tightened on the knife that she had hidden in her coat. "It's not going to happen."

"I'll tell you what's not going to happen," Bee exclaimed, spit practically coming out of his mouth. "You're not taking any more of my girls. I gave an order to them that there will be hell to pay if word gets to me that you're tryin' to change their mind, you hear me?"

"Is that why Hash is following me?" Now that made more sense than what Rachel had told Elle. Bee didn't like that she was assisting some of the girls out of the life. Either way, it was going to stop and she knew just what to say that would halt him in his tracks. It was her ace, the one that gave her the courage to do this, and it was time to play it. "I knew you weren't very smart. What do you think is going to happen if I turn the surveillance tapes of the club over to the police? You know that Kevin and his friends take security seriously and there are numerous surveillance feeds surrounding the building. One word from me and Hash is pulled in for questioning. We all know that Hash will roll on you to save his own skin."

Elle had no idea if there was such equipment installed around the building, but it was better to bluff and not blink than for Bee to think he had the upper hand. She also wasn't so sure that Hash would rat someone else out, but it got the reaction she wanted. The way Bee jerked back made her aware of his uncertainty. Bingo. Now she just had to follow it through.

"I saw Hash this morning and there is no doubt he was in an area of that building when he shouldn't have been. I'm thinking the police will find that very interesting. Don't you?"

"Hash was just doin' me a favor and keepin' an eye on you, that's all. There was no harassment." The door behind Bee tried to open, but he spun around and started spouting profanities before slamming it shut. He faced her once more, a deceptive smile now in place. "I jus' wanted to make sure you were safe, considering the murders and all. That's what old friends do, right?"

A chill ran up Elle's spin as she tried to decipher his meaning and his twist of the truth. She came up empty. Was he threatening her? Had she been right all along and he was the one that's been murdering those girls? Or did that fabricated tale just appear in the man's demented mind to throw the police off what he was really doing, which was threatening her away from his girls? Either way, she needed to drive her point home.

"This old friend can take care of herself." Elle took a step closer to him to stress her point. "I will not hesitate to turn those tapes over to the police if I so much as see one person who has a connection to you. You stay on your side of the line and I'll stay on mine. Are we clear?"

Bee didn't reply right away, just staring at her in a way that let her know he was calculating on how far he could push her. Elle tamped down her fear and anger that had taken hold the minute Rachel had disclosed what was happening. She made sure not to blink and give him any opening that would lead way to further threats.

"I'll stay on my edge of the street, pretty little Elle, and keep to myself. But we'll see how long it is before you're by my side and bringing me in the cash. The rest of the girls will follow your sweet little ass as well. It'll all come full circle."

"Is there something I should be aware of?" Kevin asked, the rich tenor of his voice that usually felt like molasses being poured over Elle's body having been overtaken by a rigid quality she'd never borne witness to. She would have spun to face him but his hands and body kept her where she was. "I'm relatively sure we had ground rules in place, Bee. From what I just heard, I'm thinking you didn't understand me correctly the first time."

Elle couldn't tell who was more shocked, her or Bee. Kevin, the mild-mannered, kind, generous, and thoughtful man, had turned into someone she didn't recognize. Of course, that was the man she knew. Bee probably recognized this one rather well. The only reason she was finally able to step to the side was because Kevin allowed it. When she saw his face, his features seemed to be made of stone and the gray of his eyes had darkened to the point that she would have called them black. How had Kevin known she would be here?

"Kevin, I can handle—"

"Go wait in my truck."

The lack of emotion within Kevin stunned Elle for a moment and it took her a few seconds before she could respond. This wasn't a fairy tale and he wasn't a prince riding in on his white horse. This was reality, her reality, and one that she was responsible for.

"No, I won't," Elle argued.

"Then I guess you'll stay to hear this," Kevin growled, not even bothering to look her way. He took a menacing step toward Bee, who'd backed into the closed apartment door. "I told you last year that Elle was off limits. You don't speak to her, you don't go near her, and you sure as hell don't get to keep tabs on her. You think you're the only one who has access to the information I need on the streets? You're one in a fucking million. Money is a beautiful thing, fucker."

"She came into my territory," Bee protested, raising his hands in mock surrender. "She—"

"Our business relationship is terminated." Kevin paused as if to ensure that Bee was clear on what was being said. "I suggest you tread lightly from here on out or this *will* become personal. If that happens, I will make it my mission that you spend some time in hell. You don't want that. It can fundamentally change a man forever."

Kevin spun on his heel, taking Elle by the hand. He didn't give her time to pull away or speak. She didn't resist, knowing that Bee had received his message regardless of who'd delivered it. She waited until Kevin opened the door and then situated herself between him and the opening. Crossing her arms in determination, she tilted her head slightly to look him in the eye.

"I had it covered."

"We'll talk about it back at your apartment." Kevin's jaw twitched. He was as perturbed as she was, but that was just too damn bad. "Get in."

"At my apartment? Let me get this straight. I do something you don't like and instead of going ahead with our plans at your house, you're taking me back to my place?" Elle couldn't believe Kevin had the audacity to call things off over a judgment she made while she was the one who'd conceded this entire time. "You—"

Kevin moved quickly and before Elle knew it, his hands were firmly cradling her face and his body was melded with hers. Her back was against the seat and she couldn't move, which was obviously his intention.

"You have a lot to learn, city girl," Kevin growled, his eyes dropping down to her lips. Elle wanted him to kiss her, to let her know that everything between them was okay. Having come this far, she wasn't ready for it to be over. "I'm beyond livid at this point that you would carelessly put your life at risk. We're going to the closest place we can have privacy, which is your place. Then we're going to have a long overdue talk. Now get your ass up in my truck before I do something else to it."

Chapter Twenty-Two

Kevin had been in a lot of situations where his emotions were at the height, but nothing had prepared for him to see Elle leaving the club through the main entrance as he'd been about to pull into the parking garage. She hadn't seen him as she'd been walking in the opposite direction. The stiff way she held herself as she'd marched toward her goal told him that she was resolute in whatever she'd had planned, but nothing had prepared him for what he'd just witnessed. He'd always thought seeing red was an expression, but now he knew better.

The ride to the club passed in silence, for which Kevin was grateful. He needed to get a handle on the rage and terror that was still pulsing through his veins before saying another word. One that he might regret and if he'd learned anything over the course of his family life it was that hurtful words said in anger couldn't be taken back. It was the same for a Dominant with his submissive, not that they had that type of relationship quite yet. If a submissive deserved to be chastised or punished, it should never be done in anger. He was wise enough to know and heed both.

"You wait for me to come around to your door," Kevin said quietly as he pulled the truck into the parking garage. He drove slow, taking the time to search the area. Other establishments shared the private garage and the slots were emptying out as the business day ended. "Make sure you have your card key in hand."

"It's not like someone is after us, Kevin." Elle twisted her body so that she was facing him, although he noticed that she slid her hand into her coat pocket and pulled out the access card anyway. "Hash is harmless and was only reporting back to Bee what he saw. You said yourself that you don't think Bee killed those women."

"Until I look into it further, we're not taking any chances." Kevin pulled in between two yellow lines close to the entrance door and shoved the vehicle in park. "As for me not believing that Bee is the suspect that I'm after, that doesn't mean he isn't dangerous. Fuck, the people he surrounds himself with are merciless, only out for themselves. Do you really think it's wise to go to his place of business and threaten him while the other girls watched? Are you trying to force his hand? The man is a coward, I know, but cornering him is the last thing you should have done. He could make the biggest mistake of his miserable life and try to hurt you. Then I'd go to jail for killing a damn pimp."

"Is that what you think about me? Or did you forget that I was part of that life?"

Kevin cursed as she shoved the door open and jumped out of the truck before he could turn off the engine. Doing so now, he quickly copied her actions and was at the door before she could she swipe the card through the slot, gaining them entrance.

"That isn't what I meant and you know it." This was why Kevin kept his mouth shut when his emotions ruled his head. "Swipe the damn card."

Elle shot him a glare and did just that, not because he told her to but because it was what she was going to do anyway. She practically stomped up the steps and he used the time she took to gain entrance into her apartment to dampen his rage. She didn't get the right to have the corner on that emotion when what she'd done was reckless, idiotic, and downright dangerous. It didn't help that he was too damn young to have a heart attack, but being around her sure as hell upped his chances.

"Feel free to leave." Elle entered the apartment, not bothering to look back.

"Like hell I'm leaving," Kevin exclaimed, not believing that she couldn't see this from his side. He shrugged out of his jacket and threw it toward one of the chairs, not caring that it landed on the floor. If she wanted to have this out now, then so be it. "What the hell were you thinking? Just answer me that, will you? What would possess you to confront a criminal on his turf when you know damn well what he's capable of?"

"That I'm an adult woman proficient at looking after myself." Elle reached into her pocket and pulled a switchblade out of her jacket. Kevin stared at it in disbelief. Really? A knife? When she presented a can of pepper spray from the other side, he purposefully put a hand over his mouth and brought it down over his lips to prevent himself from yelling in anger. It was damn hard when she continued to tell him what her intentions were. "He was having Hash and whoever the hell else watch me, Kevin. That's fucking wrong and you know it."

"Did you ever hear me say that what Bee was doing wasn't wrong? My point is that it never occurred to you to call me."

"I told you before that I appreciated the warning you gave him, but why is this your problem?" Elle yanked her zipper down and took off her coat after setting her items on the table. "I went to the center today and Rachel slipped up, letting me know she knew about you. Us. That means Hash had to have been *in* the garage."

"Us?" Kevin waited for the word to sink in and considering she said it first, he would think she would get its meaning. He had no such luck and he knew he'd have to push her harder. "That would imply togetherness. You know, a partnership."

"I know what it means, farm boy." Kevin would have laughed at her attempt to point out he was a redneck at heart had he not been so fucking pissed off. She risked her life over her inability to commit to something other than herself. Couldn't she see that? "That still doesn't give you the right to control every aspect of my life."

"I don't control *any* aspect of your life, Elle. At least not yet." Kevin couldn't resist that last sentence and didn't wait to see her reaction. He walked toward her small kitchen and set about making the coffee. She'd mentioned previously that she didn't have alcohol in her apartment and he didn't feel like running down to the club. Plus, they needed to talk this through before she reverted back to her old ways. He couldn't handle that so he tried a different tactic. "When we parted this morning, we were both in agreement that we wanted an exclusive relationship. We even had the week mapped out, considering our hours are somewhat different."

"Having a relationship doesn't mean you get to know everything I do," Elle argued, still standing in the same spot he'd left her. She didn't seem to know what to do now that he'd taken over her usual nervous activity. "A situation arose, I went to handle it. If you hadn't shown up, it wouldn't have ended any differently. Bee would still know that I'm not a pushover and leave me alone."

"For someone who keeps bringing up her background and experience with the human element, you're being damn naïve." Kevin shoved the white filter into the holder and then filled it with grounds. "The reason I warned Bee to stay away from you when you first got out of the business is that scumbags like him don't like to lose. You leaving caused him to take a hit. As for him biding his time like he has, that's on me. I should have been paying closer attention. Regardless of the reason, be it he wants you back working for him or he's angry that you're stealing more girls away from him, I should have known that Hash was keeping tabs on you."

"I'm not your resp—"

Kevin had just hit the brew button when Elle started talking, but by damned would he allow her to finish. It took two steps to have her in his arms and have her lips covered with his. By the time he was done claiming her mouth, he had a handle on his patience. At least as much as he would this evening.

"If I was working a case and got hurt, would you not come visit me in the hospital?" Kevin kept his hands on her shoulders, fearful that he would bend and have her over his shoulder and on the way downstairs where he could do wicked things to her until she saw things his way. He knew it couldn't happen that way, but damn, it would be so much easier. "If I needed help, would you not be there?"

"Of course I would, but I didn't need—"

"What if you're right and he is the killer?" Kevin asked, knowing he had to paint a brutal picture for her. "If you had given him reason to suspect you know, which talking to Rachel who puts him at one of the crime scenes regardless if we can prove it or not, then he would have snatched you up as if you were nothing but a scrap of paper. No knife or spray would have kept him from taking you and those people that you once considered friends wouldn't have said a goddamn word. He would have raped you and then strangled you with whatever he could find and if needed, his bare hands while you struggled for your last breath. I would have found you in some abandoned warehouse with half your clothes torn off and—"

Kevin stopped before revealing too much, not because he didn't trust her, but because it was his job. There were facts, like the lipstick that was smeared on the two murder victims that weren't shared with the public and as for Elle, she didn't need to know the rest. From the way the color faded from her face, he'd painted the picture he'd needed.

"You scared the shit out of me, Elle." Kevin laid his forehead on hers, needing her to understand the fear that encompassed him when he saw who she'd sought out. "We've just started our journey and for you to waltz right up to that douchebag was just too much for me. You aren't alone anymore. You aren't and you have to come to terms with that. I'm in your life and you're in mine. That means us. Together. Partners."

"I didn't mean to scare you," Elle whispered, finally reaching out to him physically. He felt her small hands on his waist and the heat seared into his skin, as if reassuring him that she was all right. "I'm not used to calling someone else when I can—"

"Handle it yourself, I know. But your actions don't affect just you anymore. Everything you do, every word you say, or action you complete affects me as well. Don't think I don't know this is a two-way street. I'll live up to my end of this bargain, but you can't shortchange me."

"This terrifies me." Elle's body shook with every word. Kevin couldn't name the emotion that expanded his chest at her admission. There were a million ways this conversation could have gone, but Elle's willingness to finally open up to him told him more than those three vulnerable words. "If I call you when I need you and you're not there..."

"I will always come to you when you call for me." Kevin wrapped his arms around her waist and pulled Elle tightly to him while lifting her up and claiming her lips once again. Her legs wrapped around his waist and when she tried to take control of the situation, he tangled his fingers in her hair and pulled. The slight gasp that escaped her throat caused him to harden and he wondered how he'd get through the night. Maybe it was time to change tactics once more. "Always."

Elle stood in front of her bathroom mirror and seriously contemplated going downstairs to raid the stash of vibrators that Lauren kept on hand to sell to their customers. She looked at herself with contempt and then yanked her hair back, using a tie to wrap a semi-bun on the top of her head. Kevin had resorted her to thinking about taking matters into her own hands when she'd never had any interest in that before. Sex had always been about work, and this last year she'd just been grateful that she didn't have to even think about it. Now he had her body on edge with just a kiss. If he wasn't going to do anything about it, than she just might have to.

"Suck it up," Elle muttered to herself, ignoring that her nipples were protruding underneath her tank top. She went about tying her pajama pants while giving herself a little more time to cool off. "If he can go without, so can you."

What was with that shit anyway? Was there a reason they couldn't consummate their relationship? She knew he wanted them to get to know each other better, but at this rate she'd catch fire and die. From what she saw five nights a week in the club, no one else seemed to have this issue with their men. Her thoughts went to Emily and Lauren. Maybe she would ask them their advice. Tomorrow was perfect, since Lauren had asked if she wanted a ride to the hospital to visit Emily and the baby. Feeling better and even a little emotionally lighter, Elle finally took a deep breath and exited the bathroom.

"Keep me posted on what you find." Kevin held his cell phone to one ear while walking toward the kitchen. He was shirtless once again, with the top of his jeans unbuttoned. She almost missed his motion, asking if she needed anything. Elle shook her head, wondering what he'd think if she tried to cover him up. If he was going to hold out on her sexually, it wasn't fair that he kept tempting her. "I'll be in the office in the morning, but I can stop by the station before noon. I have a call into Max regarding Hash as well. If the DEA has the little shit in their sights, they should have known he was trolling around Elle. All right. See you then."

"Taggart?" Elle had yet to meet the officer officially heading up the investigation. He wasn't a member of the club and though Kevin spoke highly of him, they didn't seem to hang out after business hours. "I take it you told him about Bee and Hash?"

"Yes." Kevin placed his mug in the sink and then walked her way. Reaching for her hand, Elle didn't think twice to place her hand in his. "But I don't want you to worry about Bee right now. We're taking a little walk."

"A walk? I just got ready for bed." Kevin's suggestion threw Elle by surprise, but she still followed him to the door. "Wait. Don't you need a shirt?"

"Not that kind of walk." Kevin led her to the door and pulled her through, turning to close it. She tried to warn him that she didn't have her access card when he patted his left back pocket of his jeans. "I want to get to know you better and I have just the way to do that. Trust me."

Trust him. Two words that sent her heart racing, but she'd jumped off the bridge by telling him what scared her most not a couple hours ago. As he kept leading her down the stairs and into the darkened club, it wasn't just her heart that was being affected. Desire spiked and she swore to herself that she'd have to kill him should he not do what she wanted to.

"Stay right here." The words practically purred from Kevin's throat and Elle was more than willing to do what he requested. He went about turning on the lights, although the main lamps throughout the club were a dim golden hue that centered mostly on the play areas. He left the bar encased in darkness and was by her side within moments. She didn't have long to wait for him to explain what he was doing and she squeezed her legs together in anticipation while her breath was stolen from her lungs in trepidation. "You and I are both aware of our affinity for the lifestyle, but seeing as we're both somewhat new to the ways things are done, we'll take it step by step. While you have your fears, don't think I don't question every word I say or action I take. I want to erase any reservations so that I can give you what you need. Can you trust me to do that?"

Elle looked up at him in surprise, never having known he felt like he was walking on eggshells around her. Kevin never showed doubt and she was coming to realize that it was his self-assurance that was carrying her further into this relationship by the day. If what he said was true, then any more confidence would have her on her knees in front of him. Which was technically where they both wanted her to be. Could she handle what came next?

"Yes."

Chapter Twenty-Three

"Tell me what you see."

Kevin stood directly behind her, his bare chest against her back. She felt his heat through her thin tank top and his skin that touched the flesh on the back of her arms was distracting. He asked her a question when all she wanted was to feel him touch her. The palms of his hands practically blistered her shoulders.

"Um, the St. Andrew's Cross?"

"That was a question."

"Kevin, I work here." Elle caught her breath when Kevin's fingers trailed down her arms and encircled her wrists. She waited for him to do something, anything, but nothing happened. "I know this place by heart."

"What I know is that you're going to experience that spanking bench and it won't be for pleasure," Kevin murmured, his voice vibrating in her ear. Elle tilted her head slightly, savoring the sensations. "You're a puzzle, city girl. One moment I'm pushing too hard and fast. Another, I'm going too slow. You know what I've decided?"

Again, the underlying dominant tenor of his rich voice felt like glaze being applied to her delicate flesh in slow brush strokes. Her mouth had gone dry and there seemed to be butterflies on the loose in her stomach or she'd have responded to the question. As it was, she closed her eyes and waited for him to answer.

"I've decided to take the reins, starting now. There will be no testing my will in the morning, there will be no pouting when I suggest that we spend the night getting to know one another better, and you will not seek release unless it's by my hand. Your pleasure equals my pleasure. That's what makes me happy."

Elle's eyes flew open and she would have spun on her bare heel had he not tightened his fingers on her wrists to hold her in place. How the hell had he known what she was thinking? He hadn't been in the bathroom with her and he wasn't a mind reader. She couldn't say that him taking charge in the bedroom was anything less than what she truly wanted. Before, being paid, she'd been the one who had to entertain. It wasn't just handing over control that seemed to consume her and Kevin seemed to know or else he wouldn't have said her pleasure was what made him happy. A sliver of fear ran up her spine that this was too good to be true, but was quickly erased when he released her wrists and placed one hand around her throat and one hand low on her abdomen. The secure way he held her made her feel protected.

"Now look at the St. Andrew's Cross, but don't say a word."

Elle did as he asked, not understanding why they were doing this. She looked at the black X covered in smooth black leather. It was sitting on a stage surrounded with black velvet rope slung between antiquated brass poles. The wrist and ankle cuffs hung from a link, waiting for a submissive to restrain. She could practically feel the soft fur on her skin.

"Do you see the bondage table? Imagine yourself spread eagle and blindfolded, awaiting my touch. What do you crave? Feathers...fire...wax?" Elle parted her lips to answer, but his low growl abruptly stopped her. Why did that affect her so? "Not a word until I give you permission."

"Look at the suspension beam and visualize yourself poised above with your movements limited to what I deem necessary." Kevin gracefully moved her slightly, so that the third play area was directly in her sights. Elle had witnessed countless submissives being suspended from that beam and she had often wondered what it would feel like. "I wouldn't allow you to hang from there without some type of decoration. I know of someone who will adorn nipple and clit clamps with the most stunning chocolate diamonds money can buy. Just think of how the color would complement your eyes."

With each play area Kevin pointed out, Elle's body responded and she knew that if he were to cup her mound, he would find that her panties were soaking wet. Her nipples throbbed as the blood rushed to the tips and her breasts felt fuller. Why he wasn't touching her in the places where she wanted it most frustrated her, but she wasn't sure she wanted to experience any of the BDSM furniture quite yet. She had no doubt that's where she would end up should she speak and the prospect alone excited her to an extreme level.

"The stocks in the next area will hold your top half secure while I have your bottom half to pleasure. Or flog. Or cane. I guess it would depend on what we would be using that piece of equipment for, but I can guarantee that your nipples would have small weights on them so your breasts aren't forgotten."

Had Elle had the slightest interest of being a Domme, she would have spun around and ordered him to have sex with her right then and there. But there wasn't a bone in her body that screamed dominant when it came to sex and his words only seemed to melt said bones. She was relatively sure he was now holding her up by his body. His rigid cock outlined by the heavy denim lying perfectly in the crevice of her ass told her that he wasn't unaffected. He went on to point out the other areas, those with beautiful gold cages to hold a submissive, a Sybian horse to be used in multiple ways, and a free stage to be used in any way a Dominant saw fit.

"Look," Kevin whispered in her ear, his warm breath causing havoc with her senses. He moved her body just so, giving her the perfect view of the spanking bench he'd mentioned multiple times. Elle immediately pictured herself over the soft black leather, her arms and legs strapped tightly to the sides while her ass and pussy were exposed to his view. "Do you know what this little experiment showed me?"

Experiment? Elle was still trying to control her body and biting the inside of her cheek to keep from begging him to have sex with her. She wasn't quite sure what he was referring to, but couldn't prevent a little swivel of her hips to let him know she was ready for more of whatever he had in mind.

"Every time you looked at something that would bind you, your heartbeat sped up." Kevin traced a finger down the side of her neck, showing her how he knew that. When his hand pressed further into her abdomen, Elle knew what he was going to say next and her face flushed in his precision. "If I mentioned restraints, your muscles contracted. Are you wet, Elle? Would I be able to take you right now?"

"Yes." Kevin would be able to take her now with no other foreplay required. Elle's body was strung to the breaking point and although she tried to turn around and face him, he wouldn't allow it. "Please, Kevin."

"Do you know what it was like for me to watch you manage this club and have men and women lust after you? I couldn't touch you, I couldn't socialize with you, and I couldn't claim you." Kevin's harsh tone was like biting glass hitting the memories he pulled up and she could only listen. "I lusted after you for a year and could only protect you from afar. Yet you casually waltz into a setting that would place you exactly in the same situation I tried to keep you from. At first, I thought it best to take things slow. Now I see what I have to do to cement the beginning of our relationship. And mark my words, city girl, this is a no holds barred kind of relationship. Total honesty and open to vulnerability…on both of our parts. I won't have it any other way."

The more Kevin described the way things were going to be and the longer he carried out this conversation, Elle finally understood that the entire time they'd known each other was just a preface to this time and place. She wasn't one to believe in fate, but if anyone were to ask her at this moment, she would have declared it existed. Understanding this led her to the realization that she needed to live one day at a time and not worry about the future. It was how she could protect herself should all of this disappear. She could give him what he asked for as long as it was day to day.

"We start now." Kevin released her, which sent a chill over her heated skin. She startled in surprise when his fingers slipped inside her pajama pants and slid them down her legs. "Step out, one leg at a time."

Elle bit her lip, lifting one foot and then the other. She glanced over her shoulder at the door and for a brief second, wondered if someone might stop by the club. Although she didn't have to worry about Jax or Emily, Connor or Lauren were prone to stopping in.

"Something you want to ask me?" Elle looked down to see Kevin's hungry gaze taking in every inch of her. If she told him she was worried about being caught playing in the club, would he put a stop to everything? That was the last thing she wanted, yet if she could just call a timeout to contact Lauren, then Elle would be assured they wouldn't be caught in the act. "You said you could trust me. Do you?"

Those words seemed to cause her racing heart to come to an abrupt stop. Trust was so fleeting and yet she knew that he would be the first person she would go to if needed. He probably didn't believe that after today, but it was the truth. Which brought her right back to his question.

"I trust you more than anyone I know." Elle hadn't lied. She also didn't add on an amount or percentage to that because she just didn't know how much. Trust wasn't something that existed in the lifestyle she'd previously led. "Is that good enough for now?"

"For now," Kevin replied, his warning just under the surface. He gracefully brought her panties down her thighs and over her knees, eventually letting them drop to her ankles. "You have only one thing to worry about. Me."

Kevin's plan to take things slow and ease them into this new relationship went up in smoke the moment she'd admitted her fear of him not being there for her. It was the most sincere thing Elle had said to him and he wasn't about to let her doubt what they'd started. Seeing her disappointment when he told her to take a shower while he made a few calls solidified his need to alter his strategy. He'd needed the time to contact Jax to let him know there was a slight change in plans, as well as Max and Taggart regarding the case. He also used those spare minutes to stage a scene that she would never forget and imprint on her mind and body that she belonged to him. He pushed aside all doubt, knowing there was no room for that now.

When Elle stepped out of her panties, he brought the satiny fabric to his nose and inhaled her sweet fragrance. When he looked up and saw her pupils dilate in response, he knew it wouldn't take her long to achieve her release. Wanting to prolong this for her as long as he could, knowing her orgasm would only be that much more intense, he slowly rose and stepped in front of her.

"I love the way you smell. Separate your legs."

The tiny stuttered gasps that escaped Elle's lips went straight to his cock and he clenched his jaw to prevent himself from throwing her down on this cold hard floor and sinking balls deep into her. He would make this first time between them everything she'd ever imagined. She fantasized about being bound to these pieces of furniture and he would do his best to live out every one of them. She eventually separated her legs and he noticed they were exactly shoulder width apart. Elle had definitely been paying attention to the submissives who frequented Masters.

Kevin held up one finger. Elle's brown eyes widened as he gradually lowered his hand and swiped the digit through her folds, truly experiencing how wet she was. Drenched would be the better adjective. Those little mews that he loved so much started deep in her chest and only stopped when she saw that he licked his finger clean.

"You taste heavenly." Kevin stepped away from her and he waved his hand to the spanking bench. "Situate yourself, and when you do make sure your pussy is as far on the end as possible. I want total access."

Kevin could tell by Elle's hesitation and then her unsteady walk to the large black device that she was still climbing higher with desire. It was his job to see to it that it went as elevated as possible. He'd witnessed countless Doms throughout this last year. Some were Sadists, some were into the ownership of a woman, and some simply liked the kink the lifestyle offered. He personally loved the idea of owning the pleasure of a woman. It was his way of owning her heart and since that was what he desired of Elle, he would damn well see to it that she was pleasured every day of her life.

"Like this?"

Elle's voice was breathless as she asked her question. Fuck. She wasn't even bound to the bench and the way her pussy gleamed from the golden lighting above was something to behold. Her smooth ass looked like cream, without one blemish. Her legs were folded up on the knee rests, her crevice opened to reveal her dark rosebud, which led to her open labia and engorged clit. Kevin gritted his teeth, trying to gain the control he needed to continue.

"Just like that, Elle." Kevin moved and secured her wrists and ankles, knowing if he were to lay one finger on her beforehand he'd never start. They needed to establish some boundaries when in a scene and doing so now would give him time to regain his control that he felt slipping. "Are they comfortable? Not too tight?"

"Fine."

Elle had whispered the word, her head turned just so in order to keep him in her line of sight. Kevin leaned down, wanting her to feel secure. Her hair was already tied back, so he was able to trace her high cheekbone. Her facial structure had always been a draw for him, highlighting her beauty.

"When we're in a scene, you are my submissive. I am your Dominant." Elle had spoken little of her time on the streets and Kevin didn't want to do anything that might trigger bad memories. This was one of the reasons he hadn't wanted to accelerate their relationship, yet there was no going back from here. He would have to make do with this small conversation and keep the scenes light until he learned more of her past. "Do you have a preference on what you'd like to refer to me as?"

"Sir."

"Sir it is." Kevin switched the knee he was leaning on, needing to adjust the denim that was restricting his blood flow as well as ease the ache from his old injury. Hearing that word fall from her lips had more of an affect on him than he'd ever dreamed. "I'm keeping this scene light until we discuss your soft and hard limits. I'm sure you know all about them, considering you have every submissive fill out a form if they are not already collared."

Elle nodded, her eyes locked on his. He saw a slight movement of her ass and knew that this conversation was just adding to her longing. It sure as hell was doing the same to his. They still needed to go over a lot more if they were to incorporate this type of kink into their relationship, but for what he had in mind it would suffice.

"Are you aroused?"

"Yes."

Kevin smiled and waited, knowing she would eventually figure out why he wasn't moving. Her fingers were digging into the palm of her hand and her toes were curled into her foot. She still wore her lightweight tank top, but that was fine for now. They had time ahead of them and he had no doubt he would give attention to each and every part of her body.

"I like to hear my title fall from your lips, city girl. Answer me properly."

"Yes, Sir," Elle said after having cleared her throat a couple of times. Her eyes were bright and the more she tried to move her bottom half against the unresisting leather, the further away her look became. Kevin knew when it came time for light impact play, with say, maybe a flogger she would reach subspace rather easily. "I'm very aroused, Sir."

Kevin stood and purposefully took his time running his hand over her back and arms as he circled the bench. He didn't think Elle was ready for anything more than bondage at this point, but that could change depending on her responses. By the time he was standing behind her, with a view that left his cock throbbing, he could see she was ready for him. Her cream shimmered on her rosy labia, which was blossomed to reveal her entrance. He couldn't resist taking his finger and slowly inserting it inside her snug sheath.

"Mmmmmm, Kevin." Elle tried to move on Kevin's finger, but she didn't get far. "Please."

Kevin pulled his hand away, not saying a word. He knew from observing the newer submissives at the club that it wasn't an easy transition to give up total control. The reward was more than worth it, but Elle didn't know that yet. It was his job to ensure she found out. That started now.

"You're forgetting something, Elle."

"Sir." Elle groaned the word, as if she was fed up already with the protocol. "Please."

Kevin couldn't resist smearing her juices and coating her clit. Elle's cry traveled through his blood and he found himself kneeling in order to get a better look at her. She was absolutely fucking beautiful.

"You should see yourself," Kevin murmured, although loud enough for her to hear. He slowly worked the pad of his index finger over her clit, never letting up. "Pink. Wet. Engorged. Needy. So ready to come for me. Are you ready to come for me, city girl?"

"Yes. Yes. Yes, Sir."

Keeping up the manipulation on her nub, Kevin used his other hand to gather more cream and gently touched her anus. He was rewarded with a gasp and her body tensed, awaiting his decision on whether to breach that specific hole. He didn't. Instead, he just gently kept massaging her dark penny until each of her muscles relaxed.

"I've never…I've never done that. In all my years, I only allowed vaginal."

Elle's words were muffled, as if she didn't want to bring up her past during this moment either. Kevin was glad she made that confession, although it didn't help the state of his dick. She certainly knew how to torture him.

"I'm glad to know that. It gives me something to claim as my own and it will be something that each of us treasure when the time comes. Today won't be that day though. It's something that needs to be worked on over time." Kevin saw her small entrance contract as he continued to rub her clit and knew it was time. He finally pulled away, although she emitted a small cry in protest. "I take it that anal sex is on your soft limit list?"

"Yes, Sir," Elle whispered, trying to twist in her restraints. He was as anxious as she was and he quickly shed his jeans and donned the condom that he'd had secured in his back pocket. "I think I'll have a lot to add to my soft limits."

"I'm glad to hear that." Kevin laughed softly, ready to take this scene into a totally different direction. "I'd like to introduce you to a lot of things I'd enjoy, city girl. One of them is making love. Is that what we are doing?"

Kevin witnessed her body going stock still. He stood there, with his cock in hand and ready to claim her, waiting for her answer. He needed it to be the right one or else he wasn't sure what he would do. This wasn't just sex. Hell, for that matter, this wasn't even making love. He'd never experienced anything like this and it sure as fuck superseded anything he could put into words.

"I need to hear you say it."

"Making love, Sir."

Elle said the words, although Kevin had to strain to hear them. That declaration was all he needed to step forward and place his tip at her entrance. He could already feel her heat and she had yet to even open for him. Pressing forward inch by agonizing fucking inch, he didn't stop until he was balls deep into her pussy.

Elle tried to move against the bench and it wasn't until Kevin opened his eyes that he realized he'd been as still as she'd been earlier. He'd wanted to savor this moment and imprint the vision of her being at his mercy, yet accepting who he was, into his mind. It was euphoric.

"You are everything I will ever need." With every word Kevin spoke, he stressed them by thrusting into her. Her pussy contracted around his cock, but he knew it was nothing compared to the intensity of what was to come. Over and over, he drove into her and he relished in the cries that escaped her lips. The cute little mews he was coming to love spurred him on even more and he kept up the pace until her sheath grabbed hold, practically baiting for him to switch the flip. "Come for me."

On that command, Kevin rubbed his thumb over her anus knowing it would trigger a different set of nerves. Elle cried out and Kevin wasn't far behind as they both catapulted over the precipice he'd set them on. His release was so strong that he had to lock his knees to keep from toppling over on her. Refusing to pull out of her quite yet, he leaned forward and placed soft kisses up her spine while the two of them caught their breath.

"You okay?"

"Mmmmm."

"That's not an answer," Kevin replied, smiling against the back of her neck. He reached under and pinched her nipple, causing her to yelp. "Are you okay?"

"Yessss," Elle hissed, moving a smidge to place her forehead against the black leather. "That was wonderful."

Kevin tightened his hold on her nipple, loving that she liked to have her breasts played with. The moan vibrated through her, stirring life to his cock. At this rate, he'd never get her unbound.

"Title?"

"Sir," Elle responded with a throaty laugh. Oh yes, this was going to be one hell of a ride and he'd make sure they both had front seats, side by side. "That was wonderful, Sir."

Kevin released her nipple and leaned up, slowing pulling out of her. Their groans mingled together and although he needed to shed his condom, he took care of Elle first. Once she was released and sitting up, he went about rubbing her wrists and ankles, stealing a couple of kisses every now and then.

"Go on upstairs and take another hot shower," Kevin instructed, after having already gotten her panties and pajama bottoms. "I'll tidy up down here and make sure the bench is cleaned properly. Connor gave us use of the club during the closed hours as long as we still followed the rules."

"So Connor knew we were here? As in, the club? Using the equipment?"

Elle's wide eyed astonishment made him smile and Kevin couldn't resist pulling her off of the bench to claim her lips once more. When she'd glanced at the door earlier, he knew exactly what she'd been thinking. It was the wondering that sometimes upped the naughty factor, and in this case worked like a charm. As much as she tried to play it safe now, there was still a little daredevil underneath her poised exterior.

"Yes, Connor knows and he promised to call before stopping by. Now go take that shower while I finish up down here. If you're still in there when I come up, I'll join you."

Kevin released her and watched as she clutched her clothes and streaked through the club. Elle glanced back at him right before climbing the stairs that led to her apartment. He caught the smile she gave and his chest tightened. He wanted that look on her at all times and he would do his damnedest to make that happen. If that took multiple visits to Bee, via either verbal or physical lectures, so be it. That scumbag would not fuck up this new path he and Elle were taking.

Chapter Twenty-Four

"Stay inside today," Kevin said, taking the last sip of coffee in his mug. He set the empty cup down on the table and picked up his holster and weapon, slipping the leather over his shoulders. Elle watched the way his muscles moved beneath his black long sleeved shirt and wondered how she never noticed the size of his biceps before. She bit her lip to keep from begging him to stay longer. It wasn't as if they hadn't spent most of the night having sex. She mentally shook her head. Making love. "Before you get your feathers all ruffled by my request, I just want to confirm that Bee understood our conversation with him last night as well as have a talk with Hash. Notice the word *our*. I wasn't happy that you went off on your own, but you handled yourself well. You're no pushover and that message came across."

Elle smiled and knew she'd never admit to him that her thoughts were on their night of lovemaking instead of focusing on his words. Kevin had racked up enough ammunition on her as it was. She was like putty in his hands now. She wrapped her fingers around her own mug, not needing the warmth like she used to since Kevin had turned up her heat. She'd confessed to leaving it a few degrees cooler so that she could save money. The surprise on Kevin's face that turned to anger had stopped her in her tracks and she realized that he thought Jax and Connor didn't pay her much, which was so far from the truth it was laughable. Elle had ended up sharing her obsessive thoughts of having this job yanked out from under her and that she felt an insane need to save every penny.

"Elle? Are you even listening to me?"

Elle had just taken a sip of her coffee when she caught sight of the bemused look on Kevin's face. Choking on the warm liquid, she held up a hand when he went to pat her back. He looked so baffled that it was endearing.

"I'm fine. I'm fine." Elle placed her mug beside his on the table and then wrapped her arms around his neck, leaning up on her tiptoes. "Let's see how I can do an official morning after. Thank you, Mr. Dreier, for a lovely evening. And yes, I will stay inside today. I have tons of paperwork to catch up on, new memberships to verify, and so on. Well, how'd I do?"

"Okay," Kevin said, nodding his head as if he suddenly had an epiphany. "I've figured it out. Where is the tough, independent, city girl that can't help but argue with logic? She seems to have disappeared."

Elle leaned down and bit his shoulder, causing him to bark in laughter. He pulled her tighter to him, even lifting her up higher, and kissed her hard only to then nibble on her lower lip. She knew that was his way of reinforcing that it was his job to bite and not hers. She didn't care as long as he kept it up.

"I'm still here, farm boy, but I don't argue with logic. I just disagree with the lack of common sense that you seem to sometimes view as logic." Elle laughed when he dropped her, only to then pull her close to him once more. "Go do your job,

Mr. CSA agent. Don't worry about me. You know that Jax and Connor have this placed armed to the max."

"Just stay inside," Kevin said with exasperation, finally releasing her to put on his jacket. "I'm swinging by the hospital to see Jax and Emily before heading into the office. I'll drop by my house later this evening to grab a change of clothes before coming back here."

"You don't have to," Elle replied softly, walking him to the door. She hoped he didn't take her up on the out she'd just given him. "You know the club is open until the wee hours of the morning."

"Which is why we'll be here instead of my house. I'm sure I'll head up here to sleep before your shift is over, but I want to be close to you. Is that a crime?"

"No, it's not a crime." Elle caught the door as he opened it and finally turned to face her. "And I'd like it if you were up here waiting for me when I close up the club."

"Ahhh, more admissions," Kevin exclaimed, stepping into the hallway before turning back once more. "Keep them coming, city girl."

Kevin winked before walking down the stairs but then turned to face her right before she was out of sight and raised an eyebrow. Elle rolled her eyes, knowing he expected her to shut the door to activate the automated locks. Waving her fingers, she stepped back inside to do just that.

Elle leaned against the door with a huge smile and feeling more lighthearted than she'd ever dreamed possible. She was happy. It was different than being content and she was determined to enjoy every second of it. This is what it is like to date someone and something she'd missed out on. It was more than dating and she knew that, but couldn't quite quantify exactly what they were. Boyfriend and girlfriend? Lovers?

Dominant and submissive? Was there even a title for what they were?

Hearing her cell phone ring, Elle's smile grew even larger thinking it was Kevin. She moved quickly across the floor and picked up the device. Disappointment settled in when she saw Lauren's number displayed across the screen, but then she silently admonished herself. Kevin hadn't even had time to reach his truck and she really did need a friend. A friend. Elle loved the way that sounded.

"Hello?"

"I hear we need to call before stopping by," Lauren said in humor, her light voice coming through the speaker.

Elle felt the need to talk and so far, Lauren had lived up to the true meaning of *friend*. Elle had never experienced that before and found that she liked it. A lot. She flopped on the bed and felt like the teenager she never had a chance to be.

"Then it's a good thing you called. Can you stop by the bakery for those blueberry scones? I've got lots to tell you."

✧ ✧ ✧ ✧

"Anything?"

Kevin spent the morning going over the statements from the murder at the gas station. The male victim had been a homeless man in the area. The slice across his throat had been clean and quick, indicating that the perp had caught the man by surprise. The target had been found lying in a pool of his blood on the dirty floor. No one had even known he was there until the cops appeared. No witnesses to the crime.

"Yes," Taryn replied, reaching for her tea. This one smelled like orange slices rubbed on the bottom of sweaty feet. Kevin swallowed, trying not to breathe in the rank aroma as he walked around her desk to look at one of her monitors. "I was able to access cameras that had been at the intersections closest to the gas station. I ran all plates that were in those two vicinities. If your perp was in a vehicle, he had to go one way or the other."

This was it. Kevin's heart sped up as the opportunity to nab this fucker just got a little closer. He gave the tapes to Taryn instead of looking them over himself. She was better at this shit anyway. He'd also placed a call into the parents of Becky Rattore earlier this morning, explaining why he and the police thought this killing was in relation to the rapes and murders of the other victims. Everyone involved needed this case solved, especially the future victims.

"Tell me you got a vehicle on tape pulling into the gas station that matches the time of the killing." Kevin leaned down and rested his hands on the desk, staring at the video feed. "License plate?"

"I wish I could tie it up in a bow for you, but I'm not quite that good." Taryn looked over the top of her black-rimmed glasses as she lifted her eyebrows. She then hit a few buttons on the keyboard causing the screen to change on the monitor. "What I did find was one particular vehicle crossing this intersection at least seven times in one hour. Taggart didn't think outside the box, although with his caseload that's to be expected. He was right when he said the surveillance feed at the back of the station is out. We got nothing there and there are none in the vicinity that would give us access to the perimeter."

"Seven times in one hour?" Kevin kept his eye on the screen, knowing Taryn would pull up the make and model of the vehicle. "Were you able to run the plates?"

"That I was." Tarn spun the wheels of her chair, holding her tea up in order not to spill a drop, and turned her focus on another monitor. Kevin swore she had more screens than NASA, but if it aided Taryn in her job, he didn't give a shit if she stole them from the control center. "The silver four-door SUV is registered to one Eric Bennett."

Kevin stared at the screen in absolute shock. He was well aware of who Eric Bennett was, along with his brother Cam. He'd even met them once when he'd interviewed some girls who were staying at the shelter after Becky's family hired him. To know that Elle was potentially putting herself in the line of a killer made his blood run cold.

"Unless Bennett lost a dog, I can't fathom any reason he'd drive back and forth across that intersection that many times. I pulled up his information. It's in the folder under your nose." Taryn leaned back in her chair, stretching out her boot-covered calves and crossing them at the ankles. She sipped her tea and when her gaze swung to her door, Kevin looked in that direction. Lach was standing in the doorframe. "Lach, I have that information you wanted."

"It can wait." Lach was wearing his black leather jacket and looking like he wanted to be anywhere but here. Kevin didn't know the man well, like he did Jax, Connor and Ethan, but from what he could tell, Lach was all right. He needed to be constantly working, no down time, and an office setting was not ideal to his personality. Kevin itched just looking at him. "I need to speak with Crest anyway."

"He sort of just stays under the radar, doesn't he?" Taryn asked as both she and Kevin watched Lach walk across the hall and enter Crest's office. "Solid guy, don't get me wrong. But he's hard to read."

"Took a bullet meant for Lauren. That about sums it up." Kevin looked down at the monitor, his mind already back on his case. He knew that driving through an intersection multiple times wasn't enough to obtain a search warrant, but would Taggart bring him in for questioning? Only one way to find out.

"I want to keep these tapes and still look for leads, but is there a way to just send the clips of Bennett's vehicle doing the drive bys to Taggart?"

"Is there a way?" Taryn smiled and rocked back in her chair. "Oh, Kevin, there's always a way. Go. Do your thing and let me do mine."

Kevin nodded, knowing she was right and wanting to speak with Taggart as soon as possible. He felt better knowing that Elle had agreed to stay inside today and that he would see her later this evening. He could concentrate on this new lead and hope to have answers by the time he showed up at the club. If Taggart couldn't get a search warrant or bring Bennett in for questioning, Kevin would have to follow up on his own and hope like hell he wasn't screwing up this case by tipping their hand.

"Taryn? Is there something that you're keeping from us?" Jessie asked, walking into the office with a dozen red roses in a matching vase. Baby's breath was strategically situated between the leaves while a white envelope sat in a long stemmed cardholder. Jessie's wide smile was brighter than the flowers. "These are absolutely gorgeous."

"Unless they're literally from the UPS man, I have no clue," Taryn said, her blonde brows furrowed, letting everyone know she didn't like surprises. She set her cup on the mug warmer that was attached to her monitor by a USB cable and then stood, holding out her hands. "Here. Let me take those."

Kevin didn't want to seem rude, but he didn't need to stay here to watch the women fawn over flowers. He picked up the folder and walked around Taryn's desk, inching his way toward the door when Taryn cursed louder and better than he'd heard anyone in this office perform.

"Get Crest," Taryn said with a catch in her voice. "We've just heard from Ryland."

Chapter Twenty-Five

"That's bullshit." Kevin threw a pencil down on his desk and sat back in his chair. The one wheel squeaked as usual, but he paid little attention. The day had gone from bad to worse and Taggart wasn't making it any better. To add on to an already fucked up day, Kevin's knee was killing him. "Bennett casing the crime scene should be enough to pull him in for questioning. What the hell do you need? The man to show up at your desk and confess?"

"You're well aware that it's not enough evidence." The background noise of the police station made it hard for Kevin to hear Taggart. "I'll contact evidence and pull the surveillance videos from the other crime scenes. There were no cameras surrounding the abandoned warehouse where Francie McQueen was killed, but we did get one surveillance feed where Daisy Scott was murdered. If Bennett's vehicle appears on that video, it'll be enough to bring him to the station. Until then, you'll have to be patient."

"You know me better than that. Now is not the time for patience." Kevin could hear Lach, Ethan, and Crest having a conversation about the package Taryn received today. Things were heating up on their search for Ryland and Kevin needed to be kept in the loop. It also reminded him that he needed to explain to Elle exactly who Ryland was and how dangerous he could be. "I've got to go. When I have something, I'll call you. How's that sound?"

Kevin was aware he came off sounding like an arrogant jackass, especially considering Taggart's hands were tied in the form of regulations, but Kevin was done playing by the rules. Taryn could get him what he wanted, but first, this Ryland thing needed to be taken care of. Kevin hung up his office phone and was about to join the team at the conference table when his phone rang once more.

"Dreier."

"Kevin, it's Max." Unlike Kevin's previous call with Taggart where the background noise was distracting, it sounded like Max was in a tomb. There was a slight echo to his voice. "I got your message concerning Hash, but we're more concerned about Gibson's run for the territory. We don't have Hash under full surveillance. What we do have is someone on the inside of Gibson's circle. Trust me, Bee's vendetta against Elle isn't even on the radar compared to the drug war about to take place between Gibson and Carlos."

"All right," Kevin sighed, adjusting his holster. "Do you mind keeping me apprised of the situation? I have some snitches that may be involved that I need to cut loose from the payroll if they're about to get rolled."

"Will do."

Max disconnected the call before Kevin could ask him anything else regarding this drug dispute between two common criminals. It was unusual for the man to end the call without some bullshit about how the Vikings hadn't made the Super Bowl, but Kevin chalked it up to the vast pressure that Max must be facing regarding Gibson. Kevin once again set the phone in the cradle and then proceeded into the large area where everyone seemed to have migrated. The only one absent was Jax.

"What have I missed?"

"You know that Ryland sent me flowers. His gesture is doing exactly what he wanted it to do," Taryn said from where she was standing next to the microwave. The odor of sweat filled the air and he knew she was making another cup of her god-awful tea. This time there was a hint of spices, yet it didn't smell like anything he'd ever consume. "Crest is sending Ethan out of the country to where the call originated."

"And that's a bad thing, why?"

Kevin swept his gaze over the other team members. Crest was standing at the table with his arms crossed, and from the look on his face didn't like that Taryn was questioning his judgment. Ethan sat in one of the conference table chairs with a bemused look on his face while Connor tossed a yellow stress ball in the air. Lach was leaning against the far wall, close enough to hear but far enough not to engage.

"Because he's trying to spread us thin," Taryn declared, finally taking her tea out of the microwave. She leaned back against the small counter, explaining her reasoning. "Jax is out of the office, staying with Emily and Derrick. Your case is heating up and Lach is heading out to save that woman again. That leaves Crest and Connor."

"What woman?"

Ethan, Connor, and Kevin all asked the same question at the same time. It wasn't that they weren't seeing the logic in what Taryn was saying or that the conversation still wouldn't proceed, but the way she worded her sentence made it seem that there was something more going on with Lach.

"It's nothing." Lach returned their stare, although it was deadpan. "Red Starr HRT is still unavailable. I'm covering for them."

"If Ryland wanted to take us out one by one, he would have tried something when Connor was in Switzerland." Crest uncrossed his arms and leaned down onto the table, placing his palms flat and punctuating his words carefully. "Ethan is going to Bali, not because the call to the flower shop originated from there, but because you linked Yvette Capre to the area. That was the woman's last trip before she was murdered and we know she's tied to Ryland on a personal level."

Kevin tilted his head in agreement, knowing that with every case all leads needed to be covered. Ethan had the ability to get in and out of an area undetected where most would set off alarms with the slightest movement. Kevin had a feeling Crest was keeping Connor close just in case Emily had a setback and Jax needed support.

"Sounds like good judgment to me, Taryn."

"Then let me go with Ethan." Taryn's fingers whitened on her cup. Kevin knew this was personal to her which was why if he were Crest, she wouldn't go anywhere near Bali. Kevin still didn't know the specifics and he wasn't sure he wanted to. "I can access mainframes of the places Yvette visited, should she have used their computers. I can do the same with the surveillance cameras to see if she met with anyone, especially Ryland."

"You can do all of that here when Ethan gives you the information," Crest countered, not backing down. "We have open cases that need your assistance…here. Jessie's making Ethan's travel arrangements. While we're waiting for him to reach his destination, you can help Kevin. Connor took over the counterfeiting case and I'm sure he'll need some data. Lach might need you to access satellite images and you certainly can't do that from Bali. You're stationed here. Understand?"

"Yes."

Taryn's word was clipped and her anger was evident, but to her credit she didn't argue further. Everyone disbanded and Kevin went back to his cubicle to write down the information he needed. Once he had it in hand, he made his way to Taryn's office knowing full well she'd be defensive after what took place. Tough shit. He had a case that was on the verge of being solved and he needed her expertise to shut the lid.

"Can you pull something for me before I leave for the day?"

"I don't have anything else to do." Taryn was typing furiously on her keyboard, not even bothering to look his way. Her black-rimmed glasses were sitting low on her nose and she looked every bit the librarian, pursed lips and all. Kevin knew better than to point that out though, knowing full well she wouldn't laugh at the comparison. "What is it?"

"I've written down the dates and times of the previous rapes and murders. Can you pull up the surveillance videos from all locations and send them to my laptop? I'll be working from a remote location tonight."

Taryn was so caught up in her resentment of not being sent out into the field that she didn't even question Kevin about where he'd be. It was just as well. When she acquiesced with a nod of her head, he figured that was good enough. He knew that once she got out of this funk, Taryn wouldn't be able to help herself. She'd start scrolling the feeds to find a link to confirm that Bennett had been near the previous crime scenes.

Kevin left Taryn's office to gather up his coat, phone, and laptop. He'd swing by his place for a change of clothes and then head to Elle's apartment. While she was working, he'd use the time to go over what Taryn sent him and by tomorrow morning, have enough to justify questioning Eric Bennett on his own. Kevin barely missed running into Lach as he came around the cubicle.

"Flight out to Africa?"

"No." Lach continued on his path to the front door with a wave goodbye to Jessie. He opened the glass door that led to the hallway. "The woman decided to help out on a mission in Iraq, giving food and medical supplies to the far reach areas."

"She in trouble again?" Kevin and Lach headed down the hallway and pressed the down arrow for the elevator. "And just who is this woman?"

"Her name is Phoebe Dunaway." Lach stood facing the elevator, his eyes on the numbers above. He didn't give much away, but Kevin didn't need to be a psychiatrist to know he was radiating tension. "She's not in trouble yet, but she will be when I get there."

"So this is personal?" Kevin was surprised that Crest would have signed off on something like that with everything going on. "Just tell me to fuck off if you want, but are you two together?"

"Stan Louis Dunaway."

The response didn't really provide an answer. The elevator doors opened and both men stepped inside. Lach pressed the ground floor button while Kevin connected the dots, and he was damn glad he didn't get drawn into that mess. Stan Louis Dunaway was a congressman on the verge of putting his hand in the ring for the presidential race. Talk about a clusterfuck.

"So Dunaway wants his daughter back in the States? The way you were acting, I thought it was more personal."

"I didn't say it wasn't." Lach sighed and tilted his head to each side, a pop sounding with each movement. It was evident this woman had gotten to him. "Dunaway doesn't control his daughter, but he wants it stressed to her that she needs to return home where she'll be safe."

"And you feel the same?" Kevin was starting to see the humor in this, but kept a straight face. Lach didn't have a handle on this Phoebe Dunaway and she wasn't being as cooperative as Kevin was certain most women were around Lach. He had that type of personality. "Not all women do what their father tells them to, especially if she has a mind of her own. If she's old enough to make her own decisions, you can't force her to come back. Do your job, tell her what her father wants, and let her decide. It's not like you can kidnap her."

Lach finally looked in Kevin's direction and he knew that was exactly what this man would do, although not for the reasons her father wanted her home. Lach wanted Phoebe Dunaway and she was being careless, placing herself in danger. Kevin had to wonder just how deep their relationship really was, but decided against asking. Lach looked like he was stretched thin and Kevin wouldn't be the one to snap that last string.

The elevator doors slid quietly open and Kevin stepped out first, looking around the main lobby. He and Lach headed for the parking garage in silence. Hoisting his laptop bag higher on his shoulder, he reached into his pocket for his keys. He needed to have one more serious conversation with Bee to make sure the fucker knew who he was dealing with. As for Hash, Kevin knew it wouldn't take much influence to make the little shit hide away in a gutter for the next year.

"You have time for an errand before you head out?" Kevin turned his head Lach's way, smiling. "It might help relieve some of your tension."

✧   ✧   ✧   ✧

Kevin opened one eye and read the green digital numbers on Elle's bedside clock. It was going on four in the morning. He heard the click of her door and knew she was done for the evening. Their schedules were certainly off this week, considering he usually kept later hours himself, but this case required a lot of daytime work. He still needed to speak with Elle regarding Ryland and the evidence he'd found on Bennett. Right now, Kevin would make do with the time they had and discuss things with her before heading out at seven in the morning. He'd gotten a solid five hours sleep and that was enough for now.

Remaining silent, Kevin cocked his head and listened to the sound of Elle as she went about her routine. After he and Lach located Bee and had another discussion with the pimp, along with finding Hash with Rachel on one of the street corners, the chats went as well as Kevin thought they would. Both men were well aware of where they stood and shouldn't cause Elle any more problems. Kevin had then swung by his house and grabbed an overnight bag. By the time he'd made it to the club, the doors had already opened and the play areas were being well used. He didn't stop to think that Elle would be uncomfortable in any way when he'd walked up to her and kissed her on the lips in front of everyone. Her face flushed in a graceful manner and he brushed his lips across her forehead, making sure that every Dom in the place knew that he was staking his claim.

After whispering an instruction that he wished for her to do upon closing, Kevin then spent the rest of the night in Elle's apartment reviewing the tapes. He didn't find exactly what he wanted, but another little piece of evidence presented itself. He would question Eric Bennett tomorrow, with or without Taggart's assistance. It was nice not to have to follow those types of regulations.

"Was it a good night?"

Elle had quietly tiptoed around one of the partitions, and although he couldn't make out her features due to the darkness, her gasp echoed in the apartment. Her figure was too close to the bed and before he could say anything he heard the bump of her foot and saw her shadow hop up and down.

"Damn it, that hurt." Elle sat on the edge of the bed, rubbing her toe. "I thought you were sleeping."

"I was." Kevin waited and pondered if she'd mention his earlier request. When she started to take off her heels, he leaned up on one elbow. "Now I'm wondering if you've followed through on your task."

"Lauren stopped by this afternoon, so I knew she wouldn't be in tonight to technically buy it from her." Elle reached over and turned on the side table lamp, casting the room in dim lighting. In her right hand she held a brown paper bag. "I called her though and asked if it would be all right to buy the ones that were in her display case in the back of the club."

Kevin grinned, just imagining that conversation. He liked that Elle was forging friendships and knew that once Emily was out of the hospital that Elle could add to the list. As for the display case that Lauren and Connor had set up at the back of the club, he'd seen the items that had been in there and wondered which toy she'd purchased. He reached for the bag.

"I, um, also brought up something else from the stockroom. I'll have to repay Jax and Connor, but I'll just add money to the till in the morning." Elle kept talking as he opened the bag and pulled out a bottle of lubricant. "There's no need to mention it to them. Technically. The Doms and subs buy stuff all of the time, so this is no different. Like I said, I'll just put the money in the drawer and since I've started to keep tabs on the accounting, it'll be recorded correctly."

"Elle, enough." The last thing Kevin wanted was for her to be nervous. Upon walking into her apartment this evening, a list of her hard and soft limits laid on the table. The first item noted on the soft list was anal sex. It was his job to fulfill all of her wants and desires. "Stand and undress for me."

"Maybe we should do this when you're not so tired," Elle said in slight argument, as if her rationalization would give her a pass. "There are other things on my soft limit list that—"

"Stand."

Kevin only said one word, knowing the inflection in his tone would be enough to relay his determination. She was in a pantsuit that hugged her frame just right, but it certainly didn't give him the advantage that a skirt would. She finally stood, and when her fingers started on the buttons of her suit jacket he threw back the covers. He couldn't contain his grin when her brown eyes went directly to his already hardened cock.

"You keep doing as I instructed while I take care of some things."

Kevin purposefully didn't elaborate, knowing her overactive imagination would do what he needed done. He had no doubt that even the thought of the butt plug in his hand being inserted in a place where she'd never been breached had heightened her body to a level that only desirable fantasies could achieve…that is, until reality took over. He wanted, needed, to be the one that gave her that.

It didn't take Kevin long to wash the implement and as he did so, admired the beauty of the chocolate diamonds at the base of the plug. The adorned jewels were a sight to behold, but he knew that once this was seated in her anus with his cock in her pussy, one look would send him over the edge. He'd make sure she was well and truly ready before he entered her.

Making his way back through her apartment, Kevin found her standing at the end of the bed. Her position mimicked those of the submissives in the club. Her fingers were laced behind her head, her shoulders were held back, and her legs were spread with her feet shoulder width apart. Her back was to him, so he had a perfect view of her shapely ass. He fought the urge to lean down and leave his teeth marks in the unblemished flesh. Sometime soon, she would have beautiful red handprints that showed she belonged to him. As it was, his balls drew up while his dick started to throb.

"I see you've been paying very close attention to the submissives. Does it heighten your desire to stand like them? Did you wish it was you restrained on some of the equipment this evening?"

"Yes, Sir." Elle's voice was laced with longing and he now wished that he'd stayed in the club for part of the evening. Watching her witnessing the members engage in scenes let him know what excited her. "I thought of you often, Sir."

"That makes me happy to hear." There was something in her voice that made Kevin suspect there was a scene in particular that struck a chord within her. "Did something specific take place that you would want to add to your soft limits?"

Elle didn't answer right away and Kevin wasn't sure if she was debating on telling him or that his touch was distracting. He'd held off as long as he could, but her fair skin called for his caress. He trailed a finger down the graceful curvature of her spine and over her crevice, making sure he kept his stroke soft. Soon enough, she would feel the intensity of what was about to occur.

"Elle, I asked you a question." Kevin lightly tapped her left cheek and relished when his pat caused a small ripple throughout her ample flesh. "You, of all people, should know that hesitation is not acceptable."

"I know that, Sir." Elle hissed in surprise when Kevin wrapped his arm around her body and placed a hand over her right breast, making sure her nipple was in between his fingers. "I was trying to put the scene into words, Sir."

"It must have been quite a scene, city girl."

"A sub was restrained to the bondage table, the one where the legs split so her Dom can position her legs wherever he wishes." Elle's knuckles turned white as Kevin continued to manipulate her nipple that was caught in between his fingers. "The Dom then used various vibrators and asked that she control her orgasms while he played."

"What fascinated you the most?"

"The vibrators were used in…both." Elle held her breath as if awaiting his reaction. He loved that she found the lifestyle so interesting, as well as arousing. "Sir."

"You mean her pussy and her ass?" Kevin figured that the tricks she'd been with had requested she say or do many different things that she'd rather forget. How she still maintained an innocent quality regarding sexual acts intrigued him and he wanted to tap into that unclaimed area. It pleased him that there were still things he could teach her and make pleasurable. "Bend over and place your elbows on the bed. This will give you the opportunity to grab a hold of the comforter should you need to. Spread your legs farther apart. If you so much as move them, I will pause this scene in order to obtain a spreader bar from downstairs. It won't be the only thing I bring up should you make me have to do that."

As Elle got into position, Kevin couldn't help but catch the small smile on her face as she laid her cheek on the white cotton comforter. He knew it would be wiped from her face soon enough and allowed her to enjoy the thought of tempting him with paddling her ass. He had no doubt she understood which implement he would obtain should he have to leave this room and from her reaction, she'd enjoy it very much.

"I do want to say how much I love the plug you've chosen. You remembered my remark regarding the chocolate diamonds." Kevin couldn't resist running his finger down her parted crevice and over her tight anus, puckered in anticipation of what was to come. "I don't think we should wait to see how you look, do you?"

"No, Sir," Elle whispered, her lips against the comforter.

Kevin reached forward and picked up the lube that she'd purchased earlier in the evening. Flipping the cap, he put a generous amount on his finger. He warmed it up by smearing the gel on the pads of his digits and then applied it directly where it needed to be. Elle's perfect stance seemed to brace, but to her credit, she didn't move.

"I think we'll improvise, considering this is so new for you." Kevin pulled away and walked back to the bathroom. He pulled the sash from her robe and when he couldn't find anything similar in her laundry hamper, he headed back to where she waited. Right before he went to sidle around the partition, he caught sight of her jacket. Her soft black scarf would do just fine for what he had in mind. "This is perfect."

Kevin returned to where she waited and went about securing her ankles to the two end legs of the bed. He'd laid the plug on the comforter where she could see and noticed that her cream now coated the inside of her inner thighs. He took a moment and licked it away, appreciating her taste. The way her small cries were being emitted, he continued to alter the scene, wanting her to get the maximum enjoyment with her first foray into anal play. Staying on his knees, he took the lubricant and applied more on his fingers, as well as the plug.

"I think I want to enjoy the taste of you as your ass acclimates to this toy you've chosen." Kevin used his tongue and glided it over her enlarged clitoris while at the same time using his thumb to work more lube around her puckered hole. He could feel her tense, but to her credit, she didn't move her upper body out of position. He would hate to have to halt the scene to carry out his promise of going downstairs for more restraints and a paddle. "I want you to relax, Elle."

Kevin didn't let up on her nub, twirling his tongue around and around her button. He mimicked his motions with his thumb, knowing she was waiting for him to finally breach her hole. Elle's juices started to flow and the moment he felt her push back slightly to get more of what he was offering, he slowly pushed through her sphincter.

"Kevin, Sir, please," Elle whispered, her torn emotions evident. "I – I need more."

"I'm glad to hear that." Kevin did nothing more than continue to lick her clit and slowly thrust his thumb in and out of her anus, wanting her to get used to the sensations. It seemed as if her juices were on a continuous flow, her body obviously liking this tiny invasion. "But for now, this is what you'll get."

Kevin sustained the slow onslaught for a good ten minutes, enjoying her mews as they got louder and louder. Her clit was now red with need and engorged with the need for release. Her sphincter had relaxed and was now contracting around his thumb in obvious craving. Without letting up on her nub, he used his free hand to obtain the plug. The stillness of her body alerted him to the fact that she'd been staring at the toy while she enjoyed his actions.

"Are you going to accept this beautifully decorated plug for me, Elle?" Kevin finally pulled back, wanting to witness this erotic act. He gradually drew his thumb out of her now loosened hole. "City girl?"

"Yes, Sir," Elle said, her voice muffled against the comforter.

Kevin squeezed the tube of lubricant, applying more of the gel inside her crevice. A muscle in the back of Elle's leg started to twitch the moment he placed the plug at the entrance of her anus. As gradually and as carefully as he could, he pushed the tip inside of her and watched in amazement as her hole opened to receive what he was giving her.

"God, Elle, that is the most beautiful sight I've ever seen. The only thing more lovely would be if it were my cock." Kevin continued to give her more, her cries getting louder with each inch. "I think I'll have you walk around the room for my enjoyment once this is seated within you."

"I – it burns, Sir." Elle said the words, yet her body reacted on its own by pushing slightly back against the plug. "I need—"

"What I give you," Kevin replied, finishing her sentence. He doubted that was what she wanted to convey, but that's what was going to happen. "Your body wants more, Elle, and I'm here to see that you get what you need. Push back, Elle."

"Oh!" Elle had done what Kevin had asked, and to his amazement he saw the entrance to her pussy contract. She was experiencing a small orgasm from the plug alone. "Oh!"

Kevin used her release to his advantage and pushed the toy the rest of the way in, her anus closing around the base and securing it inside of her. To Elle's credit, she never moved her upper body with the exception of her hands, which were now entangled in the sheets and comforter. He quickly untied her ankles and stood up, taking a step back to admire the view.

"Fucking gorgeous." Kevin took a hold of his cock, slowly wrapping his fingers around the base and squeezing, needing to delay his release. "I want that stroll around your apartment. Stand."

✧   ✧   ✧   ✧

Elle took her time but eventually, she was able to stand and face him. She wondered what Kevin saw when he looked at her. Her cheeks felt flush, as well as her body, and she couldn't seem to draw enough air. Even though she'd already had an orgasm, she knew walking around would get her to that place again. Who knew that forbidden area had so many nerve endings?

"Walk to the bathroom and use the mirror on the door to see what I'm seeing." Elle did as he instructed and once she was halfway to her destination, his words distracted her and she almost missed a step. The plug rubbed and elevated her desire to reach behind her and move it around. "You came without asking, city girl. From this point on, you will not have an orgasm without being given permission or there will be consequences."

Elle wanted to turn and see if there was disappointment on his face. She'd often wondered how the submissives at the club handled it when their Doms were displeased in their behavior. She kept walking and finally reached her destination, slowly twisting so that her ass was toward the mirror. Glancing over her shoulder, she couldn't hold back her gasp at the sight. In the middle of her crevice was the base of the plug, the chocolate diamonds practically sparkling. Her anus throbbed around the large silicone material, letting her know that she could easily come again.

"I want you to come stand before me with your legs spread wide." Kevin sat on the end of the bed, his cock in his hand for a front row seat as she walked back toward him. "Using your cream, I want you to rub your clit until you're on the verge of coming. You will not stop, but you will ask me permission for your release."

"Kevin, one stroke and I'm going to—"

"If you forget my title one more time, you won't be getting another orgasm until our next scene," Kevin stated, setting the ground rules. Elle enjoyed these scenes immensely and found she was more prone to this lifestyle than she'd originally thought. "Now stand before me and pleasure yourself."

"Yes, Sir," Elle whispered, slowly getting into position although she was sure there was uncertainly written across her face. "I will pleasure myself for you."

Elle had her gaze on his cock and noticed that his fingers were wrapped around the base. She'd love to get on her knees and lick the pre-cum that had pearled at the tip, but she knew that he wanted to watch her. Maybe he would allow her to please him afterward. Elle slowly dipped her hand and gathered the cream from her previous release. She was careful to not touch her clit just yet, in case one touch sent her over the edge.

"Use your other hand and fingers to pull up on your mound and display your clit. I want to see it swell as you rub it."

Elle felt her anus clench on the base of the plug and knew that this would be a challenge, but seeing his intense gray eyes locked on her pussy gave her an insane need to show him she could please him. Carefully, she used her left hand to pull up on the skin and felt the cool air hit her clit. She bit her lip to keep from moaning aloud.

"That's right," Kevin urged, all the while slowly pumping his cock.

Elle wanted to walk over to the bed and straddle him, taking him inside of her. The more this scene continued, the more her anus burned. She wouldn't have thought that possible, for the entire time he'd pushed the toy into her, she'd thought she'd split in two. The burning and slight pain had almost been too much, but she'd persevered. Now it was as if she couldn't get enough of the bite the plug provided. Knowing it was going to be overwhelming, she was already wincing when her moist fingers came in contact with her clit.

"Ohhhh, my God," Elle murmured, closing her eyes as she tried to control her response. Her inner thighs started quaking and she could feel the contractions of her entrance start. "Sir, may I please come?"

"No." Kevin said the word, but it came out a bit strangled. Elle opened her eyes to find that he once again had his finger wrapped tight around the base of his cock. Pride swelled inside of her as she was shown just how affected he was. "Control it, Elle. I want you to rise higher before allowing your body the release you're about to experience."

Elle tried to breathe through her nose but the more she stroked her clit, the more lightheaded she became. What felt like electricity was shooting up her inner thighs and straight to her clit. The plug seemed to swell in size, causing her ass to burn even more so than before. She was going to come and she wasn't so sure she would be standing when it was done.

"Sir," Elle practically hissed, not able to formulate her words in the way she wanted. "I need—"

"Relax into it, Elle," Kevin instructed. He was a blur now, blending into the tunnel that now consisted of her vision. "Do not come until I tell you to."

Stroke after stroke, Elle's fingers rubbed her overly sensitive clit until it was painful. Not having the plug being shifted by his hand or the walk he'd had her take was almost just as excruciating. Suddenly it felt as if she were floating.

"Come for me."

Lights exploded within her vision as blood rushed to and from her clit, causing her pussy to contract painfully around nothing. The plug shifted on its own as her anus produced spasm after spasm on the base. She needed his cock but didn't have any oxygen left as her body succumbed to the most intense orgasm she'd ever had.

"Fucking gorgeous." Kevin had come to her and when she would have leaned into him, felt him shift until he was standing behind her. "Bend over and wrap your elbows around your legs."

Elle was still trying to draw air into her lungs when Kevin's hand on her back didn't give her much choice but to do as he said. She bound her arms tight around her legs as his fingers bit into her hips, pulling her back toward him. With one thrust, he managed to get halfway into her pussy.

"Yes, Sir, yes," Elle chanted over and over as his invasion prolonged her orgasm.

Not relenting, Kevin continued to thrust in and out of her until he was seated fully inside of her. Even then he didn't relent and kept driving his cock into her until she screamed his name at the extended release. With each assault, he managed to shift the plug and it felt as if she was being fucked in both places. It was euphoric. Even with the blood pounding in her ears, Elle heard Kevin shout his release.

Elle wasn't quite certain how she ended up back on the bed, but she had heard Kevin mention that he needed to take care of the condom. She wasn't alone for long and when he went to take out the plug she resisted, wanting to keep the full feeling that seemed to satisfy her body. He wouldn't hear of it and removed the toy, cleaning her with a warm cloth and eventually snuggling in next to her. Something niggled at the back of her mind as she melted into his arms.

"Thank you, Sir," Elle whispered, wanting to see the look on his face when she said those words but not having the strength. She'd seen it done at the club and the satisfaction that the Dom seemed to obtain from those words was indescribable. She'd have to say them again to see if Kevin felt the same. "I'm so tired."

"I've got you," Kevin murmured against her hair, tightening his hold.

Elle knew that she wasn't prone to sleeping for hours after having arrived home from the club, but she couldn't stop her eyes from drifting shut. She felt warm and cared for…secure. She didn't want it to end and finally surrendered to the dreams that awaited her.

Chapter Twenty-Six

"I'm in that area a lot," Eric Bennett replied as he unzipped his jacket. "I couldn't say I was there on that day in particular. What is this about, anyway?"

"Video surveillance puts you in the area on the date in question." Kevin had been about to park in front of Reformation when he saw Bennett pulling out in his SUV. Following at a discreet distance, they'd ended up deep into the heart of St. Paul. Kevin waited to confront Bennett until they'd both reached a building that housed several corporations. Now, standing in the lobby, the question and answer session was just beginning. "I was hoping you could assist me in what you may have seen."

"Was the gas station robbed or something? I don't think I can help you. Or is this about the rape of the girl that Elle tried to help? I know you came by Reformation to talk with the women a long time ago. I think the only one that's left from back then is Teresa, but she's scheduled to move to her own apartment next week. You'd still have time to speak with her though."

"A man was murdered inside the gas station and we're look-ing for any leads to who may have killed him." Kevin detailed the convenience store and specifically mentioned the cross streets, all the while watching Bennett's features closely. His blonde hair was immaculate although there was something that seemed off that Kevin couldn't put his finger on. "The girls weren't the ones who passed by the station seven times within the hour on the evening in question. That was you."

Elle had been sleeping so soundly when Kevin had needed to head out for the day that he'd left her a note saying they needed to talk later that night before her shift began at the club. He'd also asked that she still continue to keep her distance from the center, but he knew she'd assume that it was in regards to Bee and Hash. He'd clear everything up this evening.

"As I said, I'm hoping you can remember the events of that night," Kevin replied, noticing that Bennett had clasped his hands in front of his groin. The nervous gesture didn't surprise Kevin in the least. His gut still told him that Bennett was guilty of the rapes and murders. Taggart wasn't keen on Kevin questioning Bennett, but it was the only way to move this forward. "With your line of work, I would assume you would want to keep the streets clean of murderers. The women come to you to seek refuge."

"I do everything I can to help the women that come through the doors of Reformation. If I was in that area, it was probably due to giving someone a ride." Bennett licked his lips a few times, letting Kevin know his anxiety was rising. The man was doing well in maintaining eye contact, but Kevin could palpably see Bennett's concern rising with each breath. "I don't keep a calendar as things pop up unexpectedly. I guess I'm not understanding what a man being murdered has to do with the case you were working on."

"I didn't say they were related," Kevin replied, wishing he could tell what Bennett was thinking. "Do you feel you could pinpoint who you may have been helping that evening?"

"Wait. You don't think I had anything to do with that man's murder, do you?" Bennett asked, the feigned surprise sure as hell not putting this man as a graduate of acting classes. He brought one hand up to run over his hair while giving a smile that didn't quite meet his eyes. "I put all my time and energy into locating funds for Reformation. Ask Elle. She'll tell you that."

"I don't need to ask Elle," Kevin said, not taking his eyes off of his subject. They were in the middle of a busy lobby, with men and women dressed in business suits having to go around them. Kevin didn't mind, as it seemed to cause Bennett to be a little distracted. "You must have gone back and forth on that road at least seven times. For it to be just giving someone a ride, that appears to be one too many times. I'm just wondering why."

Bennett looked around the large marbled entrance and Kevin tensed, feeling as if this might be headed for a chase. Instead, Bennett seemed to relax and let his hands fall to the side. The son of a bitch was about to play the cop card. Fuck.

"As I said, I'm in that area a lot for business. I'm sure if the cops need me to give a formal statement, they'll be in touch." Bennett's shoulders straightened, letting Kevin know that confidence was starting to settle in. He was like an inflated balloon, and unfortunately Kevin didn't have the ammunition to pop the fucker. "I don't remember what the name of the agency is that you work for, but if you'll give me your card, I'll be sure to call you if I remember anything. Or I could always just tell Elle."

"Elle's a little busy, so I doubt she'll be visiting Reformation any time soon." Kevin kept his voice even, hoping his point got across. Eric Bennett had done something on that night and Kevin wanted him scared enough that he panicked. Once Kevin left this building, he would have Bennett under twenty-four hour surveillance. He pulled out a business card and held it up between two fingers. "I look forward to hearing from you."

Kevin waited for Bennett to take the card before turning and walking out of the glass doors. It was time to call in some favors on the streets. Every second of Bennett's day and night was about to be monitored and reported to Kevin. In the meantime, he had to deal with two separate issues. One, he needed to find one more piece of evidence in order to convince Taggart to bring Bennett in for questioning so that alibies could be provided, and two, he had to convince Elle that going to Reformation wasn't safe at the moment.

✧   ✧   ✧   ✧

"Maybe I should have gone with the bear that had the white fur and blue paws," Elle said as she and Lauren walked down the hall of the maternity ward. Distant infant cries, breakfast trays being stacked on the carts, and the drowned voice over the loudspeaker all mingled together to give a chaotic feel. It wasn't pleasant. "What if someone already gave this one to Derrick?"

Elle had never bought a present for a friend, let alone a baby. Holidays had always been the prime time for working the streets and no one ever remembered birthdays. She held up the baby blue bear with white ears. What if Emily didn't like it?

"Elle, she'll love it," Lauren assured, putting her arm through Elle's. "And these donuts you bought at the corner bakery will be her favorite. She's probably going into sugar withdrawal."

"Jax wouldn't allow that to happen, would he?"

"Jax can be overbearing and protective. He's on this health kick because she's breastfeeding," Lauren replied, taking the last step to where Emily's door was located. She tossed her auburn curls over her shoulder and adjusted her purse strap before knocking on the door. "A little sugar will do her good."

A distant *come in* could be heard. Lauren placed her hands flat on the silver lever and pushed until they'd gained access. Emily was in bed, her brown hair a tangled mess held on top of her head with a tie, holding a bundle of blue. As Elle and Lauren took closer steps to the bed, Emily's eyes lit up with a smile.

"Hi! Oh my, are those blueberry scones?" Emily traded her blue bundle for the white paper bag that was in Lauren's hands, immediately opening the sack and breathing in deep. "I'm in heaven. Sit down while I stuff my face. We're safe for a while too. You guys have perfect timing. Aunt Beatrice just went downstairs for an early lunch and Jax went into the office to get an update on Ryland."

Elle clutched the bear and wondered what exactly she was doing here. Yes, she and Lauren had forged a friendship, but Emily was talking about things that Elle wasn't following. Lauren held Derrick in her arms, instinctively rocking back and forth. Derrick's eyes were closed and he seemed rather content. Elle hoped to hell she wasn't offered the chance to hold the baby. Kevin's nephew was one thing, but Derrick was so small. What if she dropped him?

"Connor told me all about that last night. Elle, can you swing the one chair my way?" Lauren maneuvered her purse off of her shoulder and sat down once the chair was close enough. She kept her jacket on, so Elle did the same. "How are you feeling today?"

"Tired, but Jax has been my rock." Emily took one of the scones out of the bag and immediately sunk her teeth into the pastry. She chewed slowly while savoring the taste before continuing. "It helps that Derrick is an absolute angel. He hardly ever cries and pretty much sleeps in between feedings. The nurses keep telling me how lucky I am."

"You are," Lauren answered, patting Derrick softly on his diaper. "My sister's children were colicky. Both of them."

Elle sat on the other chair, sitting closer to the edge. She still held on to the bear, but she didn't mind. These two women continued to talk and it was apparent their friendship ran deep. The fact that they would extend their circle to her was heart-warming and the more time that passed, the more comfortable Elle started to feel.

"Elle, is that for Derrick?" Emily asked, licking on one of her fingers.

"Yes." Elle held the bear toward Emily, setting the stuffed animal beside her on the bed. "I wasn't sure what you needed, but Lauren mentioned that Derrick's room is blue."

"It's perfect! Thank you so much." Emily used her non-sticky hand and caressed the fur. "I want to hear everything that I've missed. And by that, I mean you and Kevin."

"I'm not sure where to begin." Elle shifted her stance on the chair, delaying her need to answer by unzipping her jacket. "It's all so new and I don't want to jinx it. You look wonderful, by the way."

"I wouldn't say that." Emily took another bite and then licked the corner of her mouth to get a crumb. "There's a mirror in the bathroom, and if the bags under my eyes are any indication I'll be needing Lauren to take me to that spa she goes to for a facial. And Jax? I'll be lucky if we have sex within the next year. He's been treating me with kid gloves."

"Oh, he's just worried about you," Lauren replied, still patting Derrick who was now staring up at her. He had his father's coloring although with his mother's brown hair. He was absolutely beautiful. "Once you get your check up and the doctor tells Jax that you're healthy, things will go back to normal."

"Really? We're talking about the man who feels the need to carry me to the bathroom if I so much as have to pee?" Emily rolled her eyes and quickly took another bite of her scone. "Even the nurses are ready to kick him out."

"Jax is worried that he'll lose you." Elle said the words softly, knowing that if the roles had been reversed, Emily would have been just as protective. It was the way of it and something that Elle had witnessed over the last year. They loved each other. "It was a really close call, Emily. I don't think I've ever seen anyone so scared as watching Jax waiting to find out if you made it through the surgery."

Emily's blue eyes softened as she wiped her mouth with a tissue she'd gotten from her tray and then leaned back against her bed. The adoration that she displayed even talking about her husband was obvious. With the scenes that Elle and Kevin had been having, an idea formed that had her smiling.

"You know, if you're worried that he'll treat you with kid gloves the rest of your life, I might have an idea to change that." Elle even had Lauren's attention with that statement. "I know it will be a couple of months, but when the doctor gives you the all clear, I'll make sure that the club is clear while Lauren babysits Derrick. You can orchestrate any scene you want."

"You know that's called topping from the bottom," Emily responded, a twinkle in her eye. She loved the idea and Elle liked that she was contributing to this recent friendship. "I will take you up on that offer. I like your spunk, Elle. And from what I hear, so does Kevin. Okay, I want the scoop. Start talking."

"He's…." Elle was still having a hard time believing the turn her life had taken. She wasn't sure she could even put into words how Kevin made her feel or what he meant to her. What she did know was that every day was a gift and she was enjoying every second they spent together. Her clamp on the fear that sprung up every now and then was well in control. It only surfaced when she thought about the night that got her into prostituting herself to begin with. "I'm happy."

"I'm so glad to hear that, Elle. You deserve to be happy."

Elle's phone rang, the abrupt high tone causing Derrick to whimper and Lauren to pat a little faster. Elle quickly twisted so that she had access to her coat pocket and pulled out her cell. Reformation's number appeared on the screen. She hadn't been back to the center since Rachel had fessed up that Hash had been keeping an eye on her for Bee. Kevin's note this morning indicated he wanted her continue to keep her distance for a while.

"Hello?"

"Elle? Thank God," Cam said, his voice sounding as if he'd run a mile. "Eric just got back from an appointment. Your new man thinks he had something to do with the murders. You have to fix this!"

Elle was well aware of Cam's penchant for overdramatizing things, but no matter how this boiled down, it sounded as if things were as bad as he was saying. Eric? He wasn't her favorite person, but she couldn't see him as a killer. She had to give him credit for bringing in the money in order to keep Reformation running year to year. He worked hard and the girls who wanted to turn their lives around prospered from it. She wasn't sure why Kevin would think Eric was involved, but it wasn't him.

"I'll be there in fifteen minutes." Elle disconnected the call and then immediately searched for the taxi service listed in her phone that she used when she was too far away from her destination. Once her ride was scheduled, she stood and made a face of apology. "I'm so sorry, but something's come up that I have to take care of."

"Elle, you didn't need to call a taxi," Lauren said, standing and then leaning down to hand Derrick to his mother. "I can take you wherever you need to go. It's probably better we stick together anyway now that Ryland has made contact again."

"Ryland?" Elle looked between the two women. There was obviously something she didn't know, but it was going to have to wait. She'd listen to the full version of the story some other time. Maybe they would provide a short synopsis. She was needed at Reformation. "If you can explain in five minutes, then go for it. Otherwise, you'll have to catch me up some other time."

"You know that man that the agency took down right before Jax and I got married?" Emily asked, repositioning Derrick. She adjusted him so that he was against her shoulder, with one of her hands securely around his head. Waiting for Elle to nod, Emily continued. "Well, he escaped from a federal prison and no one can locate him. He sent Taryn flowers to the office, almost as if he was goading us. Ryland's made it his mission to know everything about me, the team, and their family and friends. Ethan was sent out to look for him. This man is really dangerous, Elle."

Elle knew she had a look on confusion on her face, but couldn't help it. Why would Kevin have kept this from her? Yes, it was his work, but she had a right to know if it affected her. She knew that Emily had some sort of past that wouldn't leave her alone, but Elle had never felt that she had the right to ask questions. But if what the girls were telling her was true and Kevin was in trouble and by extension her, he damn well should have told her.

"I'll call and cancel the taxi," Elle informed them, coming to a decision. One that she knew Kevin wouldn't like, but that was just too damn bad. "Lauren, you can tell me the entire story on the way to Reformation."

Chapter Twenty-Seven

"**Y**ou did what?" Kevin needed to have a conversation with Crest regarding his life insurance. Elle was driving him straight to his death. "If Cam Bennett told you what I suspected of his brother, why the hell would you go to Reformation?"

"Because Cam called me," Elle replied, placing her hands on her hips. She was getting ready to go downstairs to open the club when Connor had called him, letting Kevin know where Lauren and Elle had been all afternoon. "He was worried about Eric and I don't blame him. Eric is not a murderer, Kevin. And why wouldn't you have told me you suspected him to begin with?"

"I was going to tell you tonight. I didn't know you were going to drag your ass and Lauren's to the center on the day that I questioned Bennett." Kevin rubbed his chest to relieve the tightening that had been there since he found out what Elle had done. He should have contacted her the minute he left Bennett standing in that building. It had taken the rest of the day to get things communicated with his contacts on the street to set up around the clock watch on his target and he'd spent the last hour reviewing new evidence with Taryn at the office. "We talked about you being careful, Elle. What happened to that agreement?"

"Maybe the same thing that happened to it when you kept information from me regarding Ryland," Elle exclaimed, reaching for her suit jacket and shoving the sole button through the hole. "I mean, an assassin who murdered numerous people to try and kill Emily because of information she had? He sounds dangerous, and if he's targeting you then I have a right to know. Isn't that what you told me? That this is about *us*. Together. Remember those words?"

Kevin took a deep breath and counted to ten, knowing she had a point but not wanting to admit it at the moment. The information she obviously knew about Ryland wasn't public knowledge nor would it ever be. Kevin had known that he had to forewarn Elle regarding the cold-blooded killer, but if she kept putting herself in danger, it wouldn't matter because she'd already be dead.

"You're right, Elle. I should have told about Ryland sooner, but Ethan's out of the country working on a lead now and this case is heating up. We have more pressing issues with the fact that you continuously put yourself in danger. Eric Bennett may have killed those girls and I need you to stay away from him until I've wrapped up this case. That includes his brother and the center."

"Eric didn't do it," Elle protested, reaching for her access card and sliding it into her pocket. "Cam and I mapped out the dates of the rapes and murders. Eric was out of town for two of them, at meetings trying to gain more donations."

"I never said I suspected him of raping or murdering those girls, Elle." Kevin knew that Bennett wasn't stupid and would assume that's where he was leading with his questioning, but it made him livid that they would bring Elle into this. "Don't get me wrong. I do think he's our suspect. But I specifically questioned him regarding the murder of a homeless man."

"That's not what Cam said," Elle said hesitantly, finally slowing down enough to really look at him. Kevin needed for her to tell him everything that happened before she went downstairs to work. "He's under the assumption that Eric feels you suspect him of the rapes and murders."

"If Bennett feels like that, than there's a damn good reason. He did it." Kevin waited until he had her full attention. "Was Eric Bennett at the center when you and Lauren went there today?"

"No. It was Cam, who seemed heartbroken." Elle picked up the travel mug that she'd filled with coffee earlier. She stopped long enough that he could see the flash of pain cross her face. She needed to understand that there were certain things that she couldn't be privy to. "Kevin, I honestly don't think it's Eric. The cops don't either, or they would have already brought him in for questioning. And before you ask, I'm not going to stop volunteering at the center and giving the girls advice that I've had to learn the hard way. Girls that Eric have given a new start, by the way."

"You are so fucking stubborn," Kevin muttered, not knowing what else he could say to get through to her how dangerous this situation was. "Answer me this. What if I'm right and he's the killer? You're putting yourself at risk every time you go there. He's not going to politely ask to rape and murder you, Elle. He's going to just do it."

Elle opened her mouth as if to tell him something but then changed her mind. Unease travelled up Kevin's spine but before he could ask her what she was going to say, she brushed past him and picked up a pencil and clipboard that had been sitting on the table. She looked the utmost professional with her hair twisted at the nape of her neck, her business suit molded perfectly to her body, and her coffee and paperwork. She looked as if she was entering a courtroom.

"I need to get to work," Elle said quietly, looking as if she'd just lost a battle.

"Is this about me not telling you about Ryland?" Kevin asked, feeling a little lost here. She needed to throw him a bone. "I already told you I'm sorry about that. I should have warned you earlier, but he's out of the country with Ethan on his backside. I need you to worry about your everyday activities, Elle. You're putting yourself in the sights of a killer."

"Eric isn't a killer, Kevin." Elle looked toward the door as if she wished she were anywhere but standing in front of him. Unease returned and he found himself straightening his back for what she was about to throw at him. "He's the man I slept with when I was seventeen years old. I traded sex with him for a decent meal. And afterward? He introduced me to Bee. He's the one that got me into the lifestyle."

Kevin felt like he'd been blindsided by a landmine. His vision tunneled and ringing echoed through his ears. He struggled to accept what Elle was saying and found he couldn't. There was absolutely no way that the woman he loved sold her body to a man that he suspected of brutally raping and murdering women for his entertainment.

"What did you just say?" Kevin could barely hear his own words.

"Kevin, I was seventeen years old, living on the streets and hadn't eaten in days. I was standing on the street and wondering what I was going to do when Eric was driving by. He stopped and mistook me for one of the street girls."

"We're talking about the same man who runs Reformation for women who want to get off of the streets? Are you fucking kidding me?"

"Not back then," Elle argued, still standing by the door. She gripped the clipboard in her arm, holding her coffee with the same hand. Her right was gripping the doorknob. "A couple of years later, I heard Eric and his brother opened the doors of Reformation. I honestly didn't even connect Eric to the man I'd slept with until I met him. It wasn't like we'd exchanged last names. He was twisted in his thinking back then, rationalizing that him paying for sex was aiding the girls. I don't know much about his or Cam's childhood, but I do know that Eric turned his life around and has now dedicated his existence to Reformation. It doesn't matter how he got there, only that he works hard at raising money for the center."

"Doesn't matter? You're standing there, telling me you fucked Eric Bennett and that he introduced you to your pimp. How the hell did you think I would react?"

"Better than this." Elle opened the door and walked out into the hallway. His first warning should have been the coolness within her brown eyes. They didn't sparkle like they had these last couple of weeks and a stillness that he hadn't witnessed for almost a year appeared throughout her stature. He wanted these last five minutes back to start over. "If you'd have asked me that question last week, I would have said your response was spot on. This morning? Well, I guess it takes more than faith to turn a hooker into a lady, huh?"

"Don't you walk away from me, Elle," Kevin warned, taking a step forward. "We're not done talking."

"We're done. Just like I knew it would be the minute you learned the dirty details of what I had to do." Elle took a step toward him, but didn't cross the threshold back into her apartment. The regret and shame that was written across her features reached out and struck him that he'd totally fucked this up. He knew what was coming and he was helpless to stop it. "I slept with men for money, Kevin. That's a fact that I can't change. I sucked their cocks, I played their naughty daughter, I dressed up as their nurse, mother, and God only knows what else for whatever cash they would offer."

"Stop it."

"No." The word got stuck in Elle's throat but her eyes remained dry. Kevin felt a fear unlike anything he'd ever experienced. She had showed no emotion. It was as if they'd never existed. "You need to know. I did it in cars, hotel rooms, back alleys, and anywhere they could spread my legs."

"Do you think any of this matters?" Kevin shouted. "I know what the hell you did, Elle. It's what you chose to do about it that I love. I love that you had the strength and the courage to take my hand when I offered it. I love that you maintained your compassion, a naiveté those men couldn't strip from you, and your pride that can sometimes be your worst enemy. I love you."

Elle had begun shaking her head the minute Kevin started speaking, but that didn't deter him in the least. It was time she knew how he felt. That no matter what they disagreed on, what they learned of each other, or what came their way…he would love her with everything he had. She didn't get to ignore that or run away from it.

"You love the idea of what I am," Elle whispered, stepping back. "The real me is nothing like who you just described."

✦   ✦   ✦   ✦

Kevin sat in one of the sitting areas that gave him a full view of Elle while she worked. He nursed his rum and Coke, blocking out the music and cries that were coming from the play stations, trying to come to terms with what she'd told him earlier. She didn't just stop at saying that Bennett was the man she'd slept with, which didn't matter to Kevin. He knew she had a past and was well aware of how she'd made her living. It was how Bennett had served her up on a platter to Bee that had his stomach churning with acid until he was ready to hurl up the measly lunch he'd managed to have that afternoon.

"You look like someone ate your Cheerios, man." Connor sat down across from him, still in his jacket. It was obvious he wasn't here to play, which meant he was here in an official capacity as owner. "I take it you spoke to Elle regarding her trip to Reformation today?"

"You could say that." Kevin took another drink. Elle was speaking with Max, who was the Dungeon Monitor on duty this evening. "Bennett is the prime suspect and Elle just dropped the bomb that he's the one who got her into prostitution."

Connor sat back, a whistle hissing through his lips as he digested that bit of information. He turned his baseball cap backwards like he did at the office when he needed to think something through. Kevin hoped his friend could come up with something good, because Kevin was coming up with zilch.

"How did you handle that announcement?"

"How the fuck do you think?" Kevin barked, agitation shooting through him. His knee now had shooting pain from his race down the stairs to get to Elle before she entered the club. "My initial reaction wasn't good and I made myself sound like a total ass."

"Not to rub salt in the wound, buddy, but you knew about her past."

"Which is why I tried to fix it, but the damage was already done." Kevin downed the rest of his drink. "I fucked up royally."

"Oh, man." Connor placed his elbow on the arm of his chair, rubbing his forehead as if Kevin didn't already know his mistake. "Tell me you didn't say the L word after that kind of argument."

"If you're trying to make me feel better, you're doing a poor fucking job," Kevin growled, slamming his tumbler on the side table. "I know it was bad timing, but it still doesn't change the fact that I love her. I'll wait until she closes down the club and then I'll talk to her again. The longer this sits, the more she'll believe she's right."

"Then what are you waiting for?" Connor asked, shaking his head. "I'll cover the club while you sort things out with Elle. You don't want to have this hanging over both of your heads the rest of night."

Kevin knew he was right and he was just about to take Connor up on his offer when he felt his cell phone vibrate. Technically members weren't supposed to have their cell phones on in the club, but Kevin hadn't been thinking about that rule when he'd followed Elle down the stairs. She'd gotten to the back door and let the other employees inside before he had a chance to catch her. He reached into the front pocket of his jeans, ignoring the looks that were directed his way, and retrieved his phone. Displayed across the screen was Taggart's name.

"Please tell me you're going to bring Bennett in for questioning." Kevin didn't bother with the pleasantries. If he had solid concrete evidence that Bennett was the guilty party and wrap this case up, he'd be able to take the day off tomorrow and show Elle that he meant every word of what he'd said tonight. "He's the one."

"The DNA finally came back on the first murder. It doesn't match the DNA that we recovered from the rapes, but there *is* something you have to see. Meet me at the station. I'm filing an affidavit with the judge for an arrest warrant."

Taggart disconnected before Kevin could ask whom the warrant was issued for. Was Taggart suggesting that the rapes and murders weren't connected? Had they been working the wrong angle from the beginning? It didn't make sense, as the lipstick used on the murder victims had also been used on the rape victims. They'd just been beaten unconscious and had no recollection of the makeup being placed on their face. Taggart had to be wrong.

Kevin stood and adjusted the leather strap on his holster. Looking around for Elle as he shrugged into his jacket, he couldn't locate her. He did see Lauren by the display case, adding additional items.

"Listen, the DNA came back and Taggart's getting ready to issue an arrest warrant." Connor stood and walked with Kevin toward the back entrance where the parking garage was located. "Do me a favor though. Tell Elle that I had an emergency. Stress to her that every word I said was true and that we'll talk in the morning. I don't see her out on the floor, so she must be in the stockroom. If I go in there right now, I won't be leaving. This case needs to be over so that Elle and I can concentrate on us."

"I hear you." Connor slapped Kevin on the back as they approached the back door. "Go. Don't worry about Elle. Lauren and I will pass on the message."

Kevin turned once more to scan the crowd, hoping to catch a glimpse of Elle. Flint and Shelley were using the St. Andrew's cross. Mistress Beverly had one of her subs in the open area, displaying positions for the newer submissives to see. Dante was flogging Casey while Brie was getting a punishment from her new Master on the Sybian. Mistress Vivien was giving Kimmie a lesson in posture while Max was handing off his vest to Nick. Swinging his gaze to the bar, he saw the normal crew. Elle was nowhere to be found. She must be out front with the new hostess, showing her the ropes. He contemplated back-tracking and going through the front, just to plant a kiss on Elle so that she understood he meant every word, but decided against it. He'd finish this case with Taggart and then show her without words that her past didn't matter. It was the here and now that was most important to him…and that was Elle.

Chapter Twenty-Eight

Elle barely managed to make it two hours into her shift before she couldn't take it anymore. Having Kevin watch her from one of the sitting areas was just too much. She didn't know a person could physically hurt from emotional damage. That's what it felt like too. Damage. To her mind, to her heart, and to her soul. The moment he'd said those three words, she knew that was how she felt about him. If she thought for one second that he truly believed what he was saying, she'd have handled that situation entirely differently. But she knew better. Kevin didn't love her. He loved the idea of her.

Seeking Lauren out, Elle was grateful when her friend didn't hesitate to take over the club this evening and didn't even ask why. At least one positive thing had occurred upon Elle extending out of her comfort zone. Not looking back in case she faltered upon seeing Kevin, she walked through the front door and quickly explained to Hannah, the new hostess, that she should go to Lauren with any questions. Dialing for a taxi from the entryway because she didn't want to have to reenter the club to walk upstairs and retrieve her cell and jacket, Elle waited inside the door and mentally tried to make the driver appear sooner. She needed to be anywhere but here.

"Come on, come on," Elle muttered underneath her breath.

Did she really think that Kevin would have reacted any different upon hearing about Eric, her belief that he'd changed, or her path into life on the streets? Elle had known it could possibly change once he got a true visual of what she'd done and who she was. People didn't like to think of the choices they would make when being placed in a survival setting. The streets were just that.

Elle cracked the door, allowing cold air to breeze into the entryway. No taxi. She let it click shut, resting her forehead on the hard surface. She needed to be away from here to clear her mind. She needed to do something that made her feel worthwhile.

"Elle, are you okay?"

Elle turned to find that Max was being handed his jacket from Hannah. She remembered him saying that he had to leave early this evening and that Nick would be taking over as Dungeon Monitor for the rest of the night. He was a really nice man but she didn't want to make small talk.

"Yes, I'm just waiting for a taxi."

"I'm heading out," Max said with a gesture of his hand. "I can give you a lift."

"No, thanks." Elle tried to smile, but she knew it came across as forced. She didn't want Max to give her a ride to Reformation for he might mention something to Kevin. She knew the two of them spoke on a regular basis. Right now, she needed distance to figure out how to accept what had happened this evening. "I appreciate it though."

"Really, it's no trouble." Max opened the door, triggering Elle to cross her arms to ward off the cold. "Honestly, I'm surprised you're not getting a ride from Kevin. Everything all right between the two of you?"

"Oh, look," Elle exclaimed with relief, "there's my ride. Have a good night."

Elle swiftly made her way across the sidewalk without glancing back. She reached for the cold handle and swung the door to the back of the cab open. Climbing in, she rattled off the address before looking back and seeing Max standing there watching as the driver pulled away. She hoped that he went about his business and didn't say anything to Kevin. All she wanted was a few hours where she could be herself.

Reaching into her pocket, Elle pulled out the cash that she'd placed there in order to pay for the items that she'd purchased the other night. Thinking about that night caused a sob to well up in her chest and she let the green paper fall to her lap as she covered her face. She needed to regain her composure, but knowing that she'd lost everything she'd loved was harder to accept than the night she'd decided how to survive. It was a hell of a time to realize that she loved Kevin. Wiping her eyes, she then counted how much money she'd need for the ride and pocketed the rest. It didn't take long to reach Reformation. After paying the driver, Elle quickly exited and slammed the door.

The porch light was on, illuminating the steps up to the front door. Knowing this late that Cam and Eric would have locked up for the evening, Elle rang the doorbell and waited. After what felt like an eternity, the door finally opened to reveal Cam holding a cup of his famous hot chocolate. The familiar sight finally caused her tears to fall. Cam didn't say a word and folded her gently in his arms.

✧ ✧ ✧ ✧

"Where's Taggart?"

Kevin felt antsy and apprehensive upon walking into the police station, knowing full well it had nothing to do with the case and everything to do with Elle. Maybe he should have had it out with her before leaving the club. At least to point out how wrong she was. Once again, she was trying to put words into his mouth and trying to alter the way he felt. He didn't love an idea…he loved her. Absolutely. Totally. Infinitely. What was it going to take to make her believe that?

"Went to speak with the judge personally," Detective Schragg answered as he walked by Taggart's desk.

"Fucking great," Kevin muttered underneath his breath as he sank into Taggart's beaten-up old leather chair. Phones were ringing, the copier machine was whirling, and stale air permeated the ventilation. This place would suck to work in. He ignored the distractions and started shifting through the folders on Taggart's desk. Kevin knew that his friend would have left the information for him to review while he ran his errand. Nothing. "Beetle, did Taggart leave me anything?"

The robust detective that was sitting at the desk in front of Taggart's turned around in his chair and shook his head. A phone was tucked in between his shoulder and ear, letting Kevin know why he wasn't replying. Kevin nodded his appreciation and then sat back to wait. He pushed his fingers against his tired eyes, Elle appearing in the darkness. Maybe he should call the club, make sure that Connor gave her his message. At least he'd be able to hear her voice. Kevin took out his cell phone and continued contemplating, wondering if a call would make it better or worse.

✧ ✧ ✧ ✧

"What made me think that this would work?"

"Because it can?" Cam asked, sitting on the couch with Elle. The girls that were present had retired to their rooms upon her arrival. She knew it was because Cam shooed them out and she didn't argue. Rachel wasn't around, which turned out to be a good thing. The last thing Elle wanted to do was argue about Hash and Bee. "Elle, it sounds to me as if he accepted all of you. Besides Kevin thinking that Eric is guilty of murder, he seems like a good guy. So you two had a fight. I'm sure it won't be your last."

"It was a little more than that," Elle admitted, tightening her hand on the warm mug that Cam had supplied her with. The marshmallows were melting into the hot chocolate, but she didn't care. It wasn't like she was going to drink it and she doubted that Cam would have the stomach for his after she told him the truth. "I told him that I slept with Eric."

"You told him…" The look of confusion on Cam's face turned to hurt and squeezed Elle's heart. "You and Eric had a relationship? Why didn't I know about this?"

"It was a long time ago, Cam." Elle leaned forward and placed her cup on the coffee table. The common area was cast in soft lighting from the side table lamps and where it usually generated a comfortable atmosphere, she was feeling anything but. "I was seventeen. It was one night. I didn't see the need to say anything once I started to volunteer here. Eric's changed over the years. I'm sure you know that. You're his brother."

"Oh my God. Eric's the one that introduced you to Bee, isn't he?" Cam placed his mug next to hers, leaning forward to grab a hold of her hands. "You should have told me, Elle. We don't talk about our past very often, but our mother was a prostitute. She, well, she did what she had to do to support us. It was hard on her, and eventually she just gave up. A man brutally raped her and the internal damage was just too much. I knew what my mission was in this life and that's what Eric and I have created here."

"I understand all too well," Elle said, squeezing his fingers. She felt bad that they were raised in that life. "Which is why you should understand that women like me don't get happily ever afters."

"That's where you're wrong, Elle. I've seen and even had a hand in helping these girls obtain a life. Obtain happiness. You've come such a long way. Don't give up just because you two fought about Eric. I'm sure the evidence will eventually exonerate him and Kevin will have another suspect. As for you and Eric, that certainly explains the tension that surrounds the two of you. Have you ever talked about it with him?"

"There's nothing to say." Elle released Cam's hands, needing to stand. She walked around the room, looking at various pictures positioned on the furniture and hanging on the wall. In one of the pictures was a red-haired woman, a child on each side of her and one in her arms. Her lipstick appeared brighter in color than anything else in the photo, but the woman's smile didn't quite reach her eyes. "I can see how hard Eric works for Reformation. I know he's changed."

"So if you believe Eric has changed, why not you? Why do you think you're the only one who still has to suffer for the decisions you made when you were young?"

"Your mother?" Elle asked, pointing to the frame while looking over her shoulder for Cam's reaction. She purposefully didn't answer his questions. "She's beautiful."

"That photo was taken right before she went to work the streets that night," Cam said, his voice low as if he were taken back to that time. His eyes were glued to the photo and Elle felt a twinge of guilt for using it to make her point. "She used to put on this red lipstick when she went to work. That's how we knew she'd be gone for the night and that we would have to fend for ourselves." Cam tilted his head and then focused his gaze on her. "I know where you're going with this, but it isn't the same. Your circumstances are different. Do you want to know what I think?"

"Not really, but that has never stopped you before." Elle turned, crossing her arms and knowing what he was going to say before he said it. "Go on."

"I think when Kevin told you he loved you...you panicked. You did what came natural and instantly went on the defense. Now it's time for you to face the truth. You are worthy of love, Elle, but it's up to you to accept it. You said Kevin keeps bringing up this courage that you have." Cam reached for both mugs and once they were in hand, stood up and walked her way. He handed her one and then continued to clink the cups together. "Show Kevin he's right."

"What if he doesn't take me back?" Elle whispered, looking down at the creamy liquid that was now cool. "What if I've really messed up this time?"

"Love doesn't take a hike just because of a disagreement," Cam scolded. "Take Rachel. She's up in her room packing, getting her things ready to move in with Hash. Granted, they'll have a rough haul of it if Hash doesn't get his crap together, but Rachel refuses to give up on him."

She shook her head in disappointment, hoping that Rachel would come to her senses. Elle heard a vehicle pull up in front of house. Looking out the sheer curtains, she could see that it was Eric's SUV. Thinking back to how adamant Kevin was about Eric being the killer, she decided it was best that she leave. She had a lot of making up to do as it was, but first, she needed to call a taxi.

"Cam, thank you." Elle reached out and hugged him tight. Here she thought she hadn't had friends before Lauren and Emily. How wrong she'd been. Just as wrong as she was regarding Kevin's feelings. He *did* love her. "I'm going to have a small chat with Rachel while I wait for my taxi. Then I'm going to dig real deep for this bravery that everyone says I have. It's got to be in here somewhere."

"It was always there, Elle. You just needed to be shown."

Chapter Twenty-Nine

"**W**here the hell have you been?"

Kevin stood upon seeing Taggart walking toward his desk. He was holding up papers in his hand as if in victory, but Kevin had yet to see the prize. He'd been waiting for more than an hour and he'd been about to abandon whatever the hell it was he was doing here to go back to the club. He couldn't take that Elle really believed he didn't love her. If it was one thing their lifestyle in BDSM would achieve, it was that she didn't get to say how he felt.

"I've been wheeling and dealing, my friend. Thanks to you, I was able to get two arrest warrants signed." Taggart folded the papers and shoved them into the inside pocket of his suit jacket. "Did you look at the file?"

"What fucking file?" Kevin growled, sick of being kept in the dark. He swept his hand over the mess of papers. "You didn't leave me anything."

"The hell I didn't." Taggart shuffled some papers around on his desk until he came up with a manila folder. He held it out for Kevin. "It's right here."

Kevin yanked the folder out of the detective's hand, looking down at the tab. It was blank. Instead of roaring in anger that he couldn't possibly know what the folder had contained, he gritted his teeth and opened the front to reveal the papers inside. A bunch of nonsense glared off of the page.

"Taggart, I'm in a fucking bad mood. Translate."

"We leave in three minutes," Taggart said after twisting his wrist to see his watch. "I picked a few men to go with us to serve the warrants and they're getting ready now. You know how we got the DNA results from the first two rapes? We didn't get a hit in the system. Well, the results from the first murder came across my desk this afternoon. They don't match the assaults but this fucker was in the system. You're not going to believe it."

"What do you mean, they don't match?" Kevin dropped the folder on Taggart's desk. "When both Becky and Melanie were beaten unconscious, lipstick was applied to their lips that matched that of both murder victims. We're looking for the same guy."

"The DNA didn't match, but the lab made note of the markers." Taggart reopened the folder and shifted through the papers until finding the one he needed. He held it up for Kevin to see. "Look at the comparison. You, my man, should be given a gold medal. If it weren't for you, I would never have made the connection. The hit in the system didn't hurt either."

Kevin still wasn't quite sure what he was looking at, but the longer he stared at the analysis, the more he saw the similarities. He couldn't believe it. This was going to crush Elle. Fucking A.

"Siblings? Are you telling me that Cam Bennett is in on this with his brother?"

✧   ✧   ✧   ✧

Elle came down the stairs after a hopeless conversation with Rachel. The girl was hell bent on being with Hash and nothing anyone said was going to change her mind. Elle didn't know if it was love or a last grab of keeping a hold of something that was comfortable, but Rachel had made her decision.

"I can't believe you would have done that to her, Eric." Cam's voice rebounded from the kitchen and Elle knew that he and Eric were talking about her. She didn't want to be caught in the middle, but had no choice but to walk past them. "She was innocent and you all but handed her on a silver platter to the one thing that ruined our lives."

"You knew what I'd been doing. I know it was wrong, which is why I'm trying so hard to make up for it now. Did you tell her that I had alibis for the nights of the rapes?" Elle stood at the base of the steps, knowing she should cough or make some sound to alert them that she was there but his next words stopped her in her tracks. "Did she believe you?"

Elle took a slow step back up the wooden staircase, her heart racing at what Eric had just implied. She hadn't wanted to believe Eric could be guilty, but the way he'd asked his question made it seem as if Cam had known all about it. Her heel missed and she winced as the noise caught their attention.

"Elle, how is Rachel?" Cam asked, as if she hadn't just overheard something so monumental. Had she misinterpreted it? "She still packing?"

"Yes." Elle cleared her throat and decided to just go with the conversation. She tried to appear calm and pasted a smile on her face. "I think my taxi's out front. Cam, thanks for the talk."

"Anytime, sugar."

"Wait." Eric stepped in front of Elle, blocking her way. "I'm sure you overheard us. Did—"

"Eric, she's had a long day and an even longer night," Cam rebuked, putting his arm around her. Elle swallowed, not liking the feeling of being smothered. Something wasn't right with this scenario and she needed to leave. She needed Kevin. "Elle relayed your message to Kevin. I'm sure he'll look into it and he'll realize that you're not guilty of those horrible crimes."

"Speaking of Kevin, I just talked with him," Elle said, lying through her teeth. She'd left her cell phone in her apartment, but they didn't need to know that. She'd called for a taxi using the club's phone. "He's waiting for me at the club. Cam, thank you so much for your advice."

The moment Elle stepped away from Cam, his hand slipped off of her shoulder. Eric moved to the side, but he didn't look happy about it. She didn't care as long as she got out of there. It wasn't like there weren't people in the house should either of them try to hurt her. All she would have to do was scream.

"I'll walk you out," Cam offered, following her through the main area. That was the last thing she wanted. She wasn't sure what just happened, but she knew she was safer away from here. "Do you want one of my jackets to wear back home?"

"No, thanks." Elle felt better as she reached the front door. She'd feel safer if she were within Kevin's presence. She refused to think that he wouldn't accept her apology…on multiple counts. "And no need to walk me out. Like you said, it's cold. I'll touch base in a few days."

"Okay." Cam held the doorknob as he wrapped one arm around him to ward off the chill. It amazed her that he didn't seem at all shaken that she'd walked in on him and Eric. "Let me know how it goes with Kevin."

Elle waved a hand behind her, walking quickly down the steps and sidewalk to where the taxi waited. She was confused by what had happened, not knowing the meaning behind Eric's words. Was she just so distressed over what had happened with Kevin that her perception was skewed? She couldn't help but glance behind her and was relieved to see that Cam had closed the door.

"Oh!" Elle exclaimed, having bumped into someone. Hands wrapped around her arms to steady her as her head whipped around to see who it was. "Max."

✧   ✧   ✧   ✧

Kevin scrambled to get a hold of his team as he followed behind Taggart. Crest was immediately available and stated he would pull Taryn in to monitor surveillance feeds should a chase occur. Jax agreed to go to Max Higgens' apartment, keeping watch in case the man went home. Kevin knew that Max had been leaving the club early and he saved calling Connor last. He dialed the club all the while the fact that Cam Bennett wasn't the murderer reverberated through his head. It was Max Higgens.

Max Higgens. Biological brother to Cam and Eric Bennett. A respected DEA agent and Kevin's friend. According to what Taggart had unearthed in a couple short hours, Max Bennett had been given up for adoption in his young teens and he'd taken the surname of his new family. There wasn't anything in the man's file that would indicate he had mental issues and had it not been for the evidence of one lone hair at the murder scene matching Max's DNA that was on file, the man never would have been caught.

"Hannah," Kevin said into his phone once the hostess answered, "this is Kevin. I need speak with Elle or Connor."

"Well, Elle left an hour ago, but I can get Connor," Hannah replied, her voice soft and hard to hear over the revving engine of his truck. Kevin had to be mistaken when she said that Elle had left. "Hold on while I find him."

"Wait. Hannah, what did you say about Elle?"

"She left. But like I said, Connor is here. I'll find him and bring him the phone."

"Hannah, do you mean Elle went upstairs to her apartment?"

Kevin tightened his grip on the steering wheel and slowed when Taggart stopped at a red light. He'd gotten word that Max was meeting a couple DEA agents at their office, which was located on Washing Avenue South. They would serve the warrant there and then proceed to Reformation to issue one on Eric Bennett.

"No, Elle called for a taxi. I'm not sure where she went." Kevin sat at the intersection even though Taggart had already pulled forward when the light had turned green. Everything around the truck seemed to come to a standstill. Lights flashed by, vehicles honked, cars sped around him but nothing registered. Elle wasn't at the club. She wasn't safe. He couldn't protect her. "Connor, Kevin is on the phone."

Kevin slowly pulled the truck forward, his first instinct to drive in the direction of the club but knowing he needed the facts first. Hannah must be mistaken. Connor would have called to inform him that Elle had left. Hell, Connor wouldn't have allowed her to leave after the fight they'd had. His friend would get on the phone and tell Kevin that Hannah was mistaken.

"Kevin, what's up?"

"Tell me that Elle is there with you." Kevin practically spit every word out due to the fact he couldn't get his jaw to loosen. "Tell me."

At first, there was silence. Gradually, the background noise came to the forefront and Kevin could hear the faded music, along with the murmurs of the crowd. Eventually, Kevin heard Connor's breathing getting heavier all the while signaling the worst scenario that Kevin could encounter.

"Fuck. I don't see her. Almost the minute you left, we had issues with a Dom not stopping when his sub called out her safeword. I've been dealing with the situation and haven't had a chance to speak with Elle." Kevin could almost visualize Connor walking through the club, looking for Elle. The terror that constricted his chest told Kevin all that he needed to know. "I see Lauren talking with Mistress Donna. Hold on a second."

Muffled sounds were all that came through the phone's speaker. Kevin pulled behind Taggart at the DEA offices and put the truck in park. Taggart exited and he didn't look back as he walked into the building with a handful of officers surrounding him. Kevin didn't budge. Nothing was more important to him than finding Elle and being assured that she was safe.

"Lauren said Elle came to her a while back, claiming that she needed some time to herself. I'll run upstairs and check her apartment."

"She's not there," Kevin replied, his words sounding distant even to himself. Movement out of his peripheral vision didn't cause him to look at who it was. It wasn't until a knock sounded on his window that he sprung into action. "Find Hannah and figure out what taxi service Elle used. Find out where she went and call me back."

Kevin tossed his phone onto the passenger seat and then rolled down his window. Taggart was standing there, his facial expression saying it all. The officers stood behind him, ready for their orders.

"Higgens isn't here and they don't know his location. Has Jax contacted you? Is Max at his apartment?"

"We're picking up Bennett first," Kevin ordered, putting his truck in reverse. "Elle isn't at the club. My gut is telling me she's at Reformation. Someone from the courthouse could have alerted Max and that's why he's not here. He's running and he's got the contacts to do it. I want Bennett arrested now."

"Let's roll."

Stepping on the gas, Kevin swung the large vehicle around letting the wheel slide through his fingers. Taggart shouted to his men their new course of action. Elle would only go to one place and Kevin didn't need Connor to verify that. She just placed herself into the hands of a rapist. Putting the truck into drive, Kevin left marks on the road as he sped towards his destination. He refused to believe anything other than the fact that he would reach Elle in time.

Chapter Thirty

"Wait!"

Elle watched in disbelief and fear as the taxi pulled away from the curb. When she attempted to step around Max he blocked her path. Stumbling back, her heel snagged on some ice but she caught herself before she fell. In her mind she knew that Max had just sent her cab away but her brain couldn't connect the dots.

"Max, why would you do that? And why are you here?" Elle could barely see his expression in the dark, as the streetlight did not illuminate the area well enough. Had Kevin sent him? She looked back up at the empty porch. "I need to use your phone and call Kevin. I think he was right about the case he was working on."

"Kevin's wrong." Max reached forward and grabbed Elle's arm a little more forcefully than needed, bringing her attention to the forefront. "My brother didn't murder those girls. I did."

Shock reverberated through Elle's system at Max's confession. This wasn't really happening. Brother? What was he talking about? Confusion scattered her thoughts as she instinctively tried to get away. His grip was too strong and he continued to drag her to his vehicle.

"Max, what are you talking about?"

"We're taking a little drive. I overheard Kevin and Connor at the club tonight. Eric kept saying that you'd learned your lesson, but that obviously isn't true." They were no more than eight feet from the car. If Max were to get her inside, Elle had no doubt that he'd kill her. Her life would be over, there would be no future, and more importantly, she wouldn't have the chance to spend her life with Kevin. "You should have taken the new beginning you were offered. Instead, you're just like her."

Elle calculated her odds and knew they weren't good. Max always carried a weapon, just like Kevin. She saw that he had one holstered under his jacket, but it was better to take a gamble now then solidify her fate by being put into his vehicle. The second he reached for the handle, Elle used all of her weight and yanked her arm from his hold. She stumbled but instead of falling into the snow, she was able to maintain her balance and run into the yard.

"Really?" Max's laughter seemed to echo throughout the darkness, but never once did Elle look back. She continued to run through the yard and in between the houses. "This is your own doing, Elle. You're mine now."

There had to be someone around, maybe someone walking their pet or taking out the trash. Reformation was in a relatively iffy neighborhood, but it still contained residences that were close together. Elle kicked off her heels, adrenaline rushing through her to the point she didn't even feel the bitter cold snow on her feet. She was almost to the back of the house when she saw the kitchen light shining through the window. If Max admitted his guilt, then that meant Cam and Eric were innocent. She could hear his pounding feet getting closer, so she veered off but miscalculated the turn. Her foot slipped and there was nothing to grab hold of as she fell into an abyss.

Hitting her shoulder, back, and hip on the cement stairs, Elle landed directly on her back. Air whooshed out of her lungs as she stared up and into the cloudy sky. The darkness was lighter above, allowing her to see the shadow that formed at the top of the steps.

"This couldn't be more perfect," Max stated with complacency, standing there with his hands on his waist. "See, all I have to do is snap your neck and they'll think you got yourself killed. This is priceless."

Elle's eyes watered as she tried to drag oxygen into her lungs. When she saw Max's shadow move closer, she knew that he was descending the stairs and he would not hesitate to do what he said. Panic seemed to spur her on like a jackrabbit running from a predator. Air hissed through the small hole that appeared in her trachea and she lunged for the door handle, astounded when it actually turned and she stumbled inside the darkened basement.

"Why make this harder, Elle?"

Max's question appeared closer and Elle quickly turned and shut the door, fumbling with the handle and praying there was a lock. Not finding one, she whimpered and quickly felt with her fingers up the seal until locating a metal latch. She'd just started to slide it through the bolt when she felt the door shake and spring toward her. The pin had been far enough in that the door held, but her finger got caught and she yanked it back in pain. She instantly felt wetness and knew she was bleeding, but she didn't care. She reached back up and secured it in place, all the while hearing Max's expletives through the wood.

"Cam! Eric!" Elle continued to yell their names as she tried to maneuver around in the darkness. She bumped into countless items as she tried to make her way across the room. It was pitch black, but she knew there had to be stairs somewhere that lead up to the kitchen. "Cam!"

Elle forced herself to stop and listen to see where Max had gone. Was he still at the door? Would he be able to use his strength to break it down? All she could hear was her own breathing. As she stood there a little longer, pain started to radiate through her body from the impact she took falling down the stairs. There would be time later to see what her injuries were, but getting to a phone and calling for help came first. She spread her arms in front of her to prevent herself from running into anything else when blinding light had her holding her hands up to her eyes.

"Elle?" Cam's voice came from her right and Elle turned quickly, trying to get her eyes adjusted to the brightness. "Is that you?"

"Cam!" Elle still had no idea where Max had gone and she was afraid he'd make his way into the house. "Call the police. Right now. The man who murdered those girls is outside."

"What? Oh my God, Elle," Cam exclaimed, finally appearing in front of her. Concern was written across his features. "You're bleeding. Come upstairs and tell me what happened."

"I'm telling you, Cam," Elle insisted, shoving his hands away as he reached for her. She smeared the blood that was running down her forehead. "Max Higgens is outside and he just confessed to the murders. I know you don't know him but—"

"Max? Of course I know Max." Cam once again extended his hand but Elle stepped back, not believing what she was hearing. "He's our brother, Elle. He didn't kill anyone."

"Yes, he did," Elle stressed, lowering her voice as she tried to look around Cam to see if anyone was coming down the stairs. "Cam, I don't care if that man is your brother or not, but he just confessed to me that he's the killer. We have to call the police. Now."

"Cam, why don't you go upstairs and make sure that the women didn't hear anything."

Elle jumped upon hearing Max's voice and once Cam stepped to the side, she could clearly see him standing a few feet away holding a gun pointed in her direction. Eric was standing next to him, shifting his stance from side to side as if he was uncomfortable with the way this situation was shaping up. Elle didn't like it either, but for obviously different reasons.

"Max, what are you doing?" The incredulity in Cam's voice was evident, but at the moment, Elle wasn't sure what was going on. Her instinctive need to survive was all that she was certain of and she glanced back to look at the exit, wondering if she could make it before being shot. Would Max shoot her, taking the chance the girls would hear the sound upstairs? "Put that thing away."

"Cam, you always were too soft." Max took a step forward, but Eric placed a hand on his arm.

"Don't. He's innocent and this is all my fault."

"Somebody needs to tell me what is going on," Cam exclaimed with a tremor in his voice and reached out for Elle's hand. She didn't want to take it but she was afraid of the consequences if she didn't. She still didn't know if any of them were innocent. "Eric, say something."

"I – I couldn't help myself," Eric stuttered, a pleading tone in his voice that made Elle's stomach revolt. "I'm the one that raped them. I was just trying to show them what would happen if they started down that road, Cam. The one Mother took.

Every time I would see that date on the calendar, I would fight the urge to do something…but eventually my rage finally took over."

"You sexually assaulted those girls?" Cam sounded appalled, but Elle didn't know if this was some other trick they were playing on her. Her best bet was to let them continue to talk while she figured a way out of here. "Why would you do that?"

"To *show* them," Eric stressed with a sick intensity that made Elle's stomach hitch and her skin crawl. "Mother was raped repeatedly until she died, Cam. The same will happen to these women if they don't learn. I was teaching them a lesson."

"You murdered them!" Cam directed his accusation toward Max while he tightened his grip on Elle's fingers. She had been watching Max the entire time and his weapon didn't waver. The barrel was steady as she looked down the opening. "Eric, you have to turn yourself in."

"He's not going to do that, Cam." Max tilted his head as if he were talking to a child. He was the youngest, yet it seemed as if he were in charge of the sibling relationship. Elle shifted her feet to give her a better view of the stairs but realized that she and Cam would never be able to get around Max and Eric. She looked around for some type of weapon. "He didn't murder the women. I did. It didn't take a genius to figure out the dates. After all, Mom would go out to make extra cash every three weeks. I knew it was Eric, but he was getting careless by putting lipstick on the women. He didn't beat the third victim uncon- scious. She saw his face and she was going to go to the police. So I took matters into my own hands, just as I took care of that homeless man who'd called the station to give them a descrip- tion of me."

Cam dropped Elle's hand and placed his palms over his face, as if he couldn't accept what Max was saying. She didn't blame him. The more this ludicrous conversation continued, the more certainty settled over her that this wasn't going to end well. Her teeth were starting to chatter, but she wasn't sure if it was due to the cold, her bare feet, or the fear of dying.

"This isn't happening. We can fix this," Cam said desperately, his hands dropping to his sides. The devastation of what he was finding out was evident in his voice but Elle couldn't worry about that now. She took a step back as Max extended his arm. "Don't! Not like that. I meant if the two of you turn yourselves in and confess, the authorities might be lenient. You're one of them, Max. They'll give you a light sentence."

Max laughed and shook his head while Eric seemed to be loosing his grip on sanity. The man's eyes were shifting back and forth and the more worked up he became, the more Elle felt panic rise up within her. Regardless of how Cam thought he could talk rationally with his brothers, it was a losing battle.

"First, I was careful and left no trace of evidence." Max stepped forward. "Eric isn't in the system, so they'll never tie the assaults to him. The only thing I couldn't let go was leaving them without Mom's calling sign. Eric was a genius. They looked just like her, lying there all pale with nothing on but red lipstick."

"Oh, Max." Cam's words were almost a plea for Max and Eric to say this was all a nightmare. "Mom wouldn't have wanted this."

"Mother only thought of herself," Max spat out in disgust. "This is how tonight's going to happen. I'll let you handle this *need* Eric has to teach the hookers a lesson while I deal with Elle. She's the only one who's between us and freedom."

Cam shifted between her and Max, concealing her from his view. Elle quickly looked around and saw a crowbar sitting in a wooden crate. Grabbing it, she held it behind her back and gauged the distance to the back door. It was too far. Regardless of how of cold the air was in the basement, she felt her palms perspire and she prayed that she wouldn't lose her hold on the steel weapon.

"Listen to what you're saying, Max." Cam backed up a step causing her to do the same. "You took an oath to uphold the law. This is wrong. You are not a murderer."

"I'm a brother. I'm Eric's brother. I'm your brother. I will do what I have to in order to protect my family." Max's voice seemed to be getting closer and Elle brought the crowbar in front of her, ready to swing should Cam move out of the way. "You might be the older one, Cam, but I'm the one who's in the position to make this go away. All you have to do is walk up those stairs as if nothing has happened here and let me take care of the rest."

"Eric, can't you see how wrong this is?" Cam's desperation was evident and Elle knew they only had seconds before the decision was taken out of his hands.

"Don't be this way, Cam," Eric pleaded. "Max understands how family works. Come upstairs with me."

"I'm not letting you kill Elle." Cam altered his stance and Elle twisted so that she would be able to run when he did. That was their only choice. "Put the gun down."

"That's not going to happen, brother."

"Run!"

With that one scream, Cam threw himself at Max. Elle immediately turned to run for the back door but Eric grabbed her by the arm. Instinct took over and she swung the crowbar. The metal made contact with his shoulder hard enough that he released her but she knew that it wasn't enough. She couldn't get the momentum behind the tool for another swing and did the only thing she could. Eric lunged and when he came at her once more, Elle used every ounce of strength she had to jab the straight end directly into his stomach.

It seemed as if time stood still as Elle connected her gaze with Eric, whose eyes were wide with surprise and disbelief. Releasing the crowbar, she stepped back and watched in horror as he fell to his knees. His hands grabbed the metal protruding from his stomach and a strangled cry came from his parted lips.

"What have you done?" Eric whispered.

Chapter Thirty-One

K evin entered the residence with Crest by his side. They covered each other as they maneuvered into the house through the front door. Side table lamps were lit and there were cups on the table, but no one was in sight. Silence hung in the air but was interrupted by a shuffling sound in the kitchen. Taggart had entered behind them and had taken position on the far side of the room. Crest and Kevin both waited for his cue before proceeding toward the kitchen.

Upon arriving at Reformation, Kevin felt stark terror shoot through him upon seeing Max's undercover vehicle parked at the curb. Had he been tipped off? Did he know that they were after him and his brother? Elle was inside with both of them and Kevin didn't know if she was fine, hurt, or worse…dead. His first instinct was to rush inside, but Crest had pulled up the moment Kevin opened the door of his truck. Connor had phoned on the five minute trip and relayed that the taxi service had definitely dropped Elle off at the center. He was already in his vehicle and headed to their destination, saying he'd join Taggart's men at the back of the house. Kevin thought they'd only have to deal with Bennett, but now that he knew Max was on the premises, all bets were off.

Crest made a hand signal to signify that one person was in the kitchen. Kevin swiftly turned the corner. Within seconds, he had the woman against the counter with his hand over her mouth.

"Where are they?" Kevin whispered, catching Crest closing the refrigerator door in his peripheral vision. "Where are the Bennett brothers?"

The scared brunette shook her head, terror shining in her eyes. Kevin distinguished she was telling him the truth and he couldn't stop his heart speeding up at the thought that the men had already gotten their hands on Elle. Crest tapped him on the shoulder and nodded behind him. Kevin turned to see an open door on the opposite side of the room. Taggart slowly joined them, indicating that he would take care of the woman. Kevin gradually pulled his fingers away from her mouth, demonstrating that she should remain quiet with his other hand. Her eyes widened when she caught sight of his gun.

Not having their earpieces that the team usually wore in situations like this made Kevin feel as if he was at a loss. If that door led to the basement, then Connor would be able to access it from the outside. Unfortunately, Kevin had no way to relay that piece of information. Cautiously crossing the kitchen floor, he took his time looking around the doorframe.

"Eric!"

Kevin immediately recognized Max's voice and from the pitch of the man's tone, there was no time to waste. Furtively taking the stairs, Kevin prayed that his knee wouldn't give out or that his weight and that of Crest's didn't alert the men below that they were descending. The moment Kevin hit the hard floor, he took in the scene before him and swore his heart stopped beating.

Cam Bennett was lying on the floor, trying to sit up while holding the side of his head. Relief surged through him at seeing Elle. She stood toward the back of the basement with blood running from her forehead down the side of her face, her hair half undone from her clip, and standing on the cement in bare feet. There was no color in her face and her lips were tinged blue. In between Cam and Elle stood Max. It was only when he moved to the side that Kevin was able to see that Eric was kneeling on the floor.

"Max, it's over," Kevin announced, his words echoing through the basement. He hoped that Max still had some reason left within him. Finding out that a man he considered a friend was capable of murdering women shook Kevin to the core. He refused to believe that Max didn't have some sense of benevolence left inside of him. If not, Kevin wouldn't hesitate to shoot if it meant keeping Elle safe. "Hands in the air where I can see them."

"Kevin," Elle whispered, her need to come to him evident.

Kevin shook his head slightly, needing her to stay where she was. Angst rose inside of him that she wouldn't heed his command. Crest finessed his way around a workbench and a couple of boxes to give him a better angle while Kevin continued to walk in a straight path to where his targets were located. Elle's brown eyes didn't waver from him, for which he was grateful.

"You know I can't do that," Max responded in a much too casual way. He had yet to turn around and face Kevin, putting him at a disadvantage. This wasn't going to go down in an amicable way. He kept his weapon trained on his target. "Elle, tell your lover what I have pointed at you."

"H-he's got a gun." Elle continued to watch Kevin as if she was waiting for him to give her a signal. The bravery she was exhibiting made him so proud, but it was diminished by the fear running through his system that this could end with her life. "His finger is on the trigger."

"Your brother needs help," Crest stated from his location on the left hand side of the room. "He's bleeding and unless we get someone in here to help him, he's going to die."

"While we wait to see who blinks first," Max said, "I'm curious as to how you figured it out. Or did one of the girls upstairs overhear what was taking place and call the police?"

"I know how much you like perfection, Max, but just because you're a DEA agent doesn't make you infallible. There's enough DNA evidence to put both you and Eric away for life. That is if he doesn't die first."

Kevin was finally close enough to see what Crest was talking about. Eric Bennett had a crowbar lodged in his stomach. His hands were wrapped around the middle of the tool, but as if Crest's words on his mortality finally hit home, Eric moved.

"You bitch," Eric screamed, diving forward.

Crest shot his weapon first, applying the required four pounds of pressure required to discharge his Match Grade Model 1911A1 loaded with 230 grain Hydra-Shock rounds travelling at nine hundred and thirty feet per second. It sounded as if a cannon had been fired, but before anyone had perceived the thunderclap of the shot, the damage had already been done. The high performance round impacted its intended target and dramatically demonstrated exactly what a .45 ACP round was designed to do. The round hit with nearly a thousand foot pounds of energy. Lacking any sort of body armor, the point of entry yielded to the irresistible force and upon contact with its first reasonably hard object, the bullet destroyed Max's shoulder joint and mushroomed into the size of a half dollar coin. Kevin had no doubt that the hardened tungsten penetrator stuck to the mass of shattered bone and ruined muscle tissue. Max would never have use of his right arm again. He dropped his weapon and thereby removed his ability to threaten Elle.

Kevin fired his 9mm Beretta 92FS, ensuring that Eric didn't reach his target. Elle's scream mingled with the reverberations as the back door of the basement burst open, shards of wood splintering into the air.

"You're safe. You're safe. You're safe." Kevin didn't remember closing the distance between them. All he knew was that Elle was in his arms...safe. Alive. "You're safe."

"I love you," Elle murmured against his neck, her hold on him as tight as his was on her. "I'm so sorry I didn't listen to you. I thought I wasn't going to be able to tell you that I really do believe you. You do love me. I know that, Kevin. I know that."

"God, you scared the hell out of me." Kevin knew he had to let her go and assess the damage she sustained, but he couldn't bring himself to let her go quite yet. "When are you going to get it through your head that I mean every word I say? When I say you're beautiful, you're stunning. When I say you're intelligent, you're damn smart. When I say I love you, I fucking adore everything that makes you who you are."

"I know. I know."

"Kevin, Taggart called for ambulances when he headed back upstairs," Connor said in a soothing voice. He was handling the situation as Kevin would, not knowing exactly what Elle had gone through before they got there. He tightened his hold on her, not wanting to ever let her go. "Paramedics need to check Elle over."

✧ ✧ ✧ ✧

"I'm fine," Elle answered, pulling back slightly but not loosening her grip on Kevin's neck. She couldn't seem to get enough heat from his body. It sounded insane, but she would have crawled inside of him had physics allowed. "I just fell down the stairs outside."

"You're bleeding." Kevin tenderly took one of Elle's arms and released her hold on him to holster his weapon. He brushed the flyaway strands away from her forehead for a better look and he winced at what he saw. She assumed from the blood that it was a gash, but the aches and pains that were starting to settle in were more of an all over thing. A trembling had also commenced in her limbs, surprising her. "You might need stitches. Anything else hurt?"

"I just want to go home."

For the first time since Kevin had appeared, his face softened and he gathered her up once more. Elle didn't complain when a sharp pain resounded through her side, as she wanted his warmth surrounding her. Unfortunately, he must have heard the hiss that escaped her lips.

"You need to be looked over, city girl."

When Kevin stepped back, Elle had a clear view of the scene behind him. Officers encased the area while paramedics hovered over Max and Eric. Crest was helping Cam sit up on a crate. She'd only seen him a couple of times before, but something told her he was in charge and not the police. He exuded confidence and power, with his black suit and a long matching dress coat that appeared to cost more than her entire wardrobe. He kneeled in front of Cam, comforting her friend. Cam.

"I have to go to him, Kevin." Elle placed her unsteady hand on Kevin's arm. "Cam tried to save me. He had no idea what his brothers were doing. He's got to be devastated. What I did to Eric—"

"You did what you had to, Elle," Connor replied. The three of them looked on as one paramedic that knelt over Eric shook his head. Elle tried to feel remorse that the man was dead, but the only thing she felt was guilt for the part that she took in taking his life. If what she heard during the confrontation was true, he'd assaulted those women in the worst way while Max took their lives to cover up his brother's crimes. Her culpability stemmed from taking away Cam's brother. "Do not feel guilty for defending yourself."

"Cam will be all alone." Elle leaned into Kevin and it wasn't until he stiffened that she saw what caused his reaction. Max was sitting up, a scowl on his face with his eyes locked onto them. Taggart stood guard while the paramedics cut off his jacket and shirt to reach his wound. This man who took the lives of two women and who knew how many countless more would spend the rest of his life behind bars. It almost wasn't enough. "Although maybe that's a good thing."

"Cam's got you and he's got the girls that rely on him upstairs."

Kevin led her around the left side of the basement, obviously not wanting her near Max. Elle wasn't about to argue. She'd had all the excitement she could handle today. As they approached Cam, her friend looked up at her with devastation in his eyes. Although she didn't know what he was going through, she did understand what it was like to feel as if she were alone in the world. One day she would share with Cam the joys of allowing someone inside. She squeezed Kevin's hand as they stopped in front of a very devastated man.

"Cam, I'm so sorry." Elle thought she had her emotions under control and was surprised by the catch in her voice.

Regardless that Cam had a full beard and mustache, it was apparent that his lips quivered. Releasing Kevin's fingers, she lowered herself to her knees in front of Cam. "I can't imagine what—"

"It's me who should apologize, Elle." Cam shook his head but never once looked at Elle. His tortured gaze was on Max, his younger brother. "I should have known. I should have put two and two together. I knew there was something wrong with Eric, but I just didn't want to face that he wasn't *there*, you know? As for Max, he was always closer to Eric. If only I'd—"

"The only person to blame for those assaults and murders are the culprits themselves," Crest stated.

"It's time that the paramedics look the two of you over." Kevin reached for another crate, pulling it over so that Elle didn't have to leave Cam's side. "Be a good girl."

Elle didn't want Kevin to leave her, but she knew that he had business to take care and that he wouldn't be far away. The betrayal he must be feeling in regards to Max Higgens must have hit him hard though he didn't show it. It would hit the members of the club just as much, considering they'd taken Max in as one of their own. She knew that she would have nightmares about tonight for a very long time to come, but as long as Kevin was by her side, she'd be able to get through anything. Another sob rose up, catching her unexpectedly.

"I will always come when you need me," Kevin whispered fiercely in Elle's ear. He said it in such a matter of fact tone that she didn't doubt him in the least. "I love you, city girl."

✧   ✧   ✧   ✧

"Have you read him his rights?"

Kevin was disgusted as he looked at who he thought had been a friend, a protector of people who'd taken an oath to serve. Max Higgens had betrayed his family and friends. Worse, he'd taken the lives of two innocent women and would have continued to do so had he not made the mistake of leaving behind trace forensic evidence.

"Yes," Taggart answered, abhorrence lacing his tone. "And now we've got the media surrounding this place. I'll have to make a statement, but this is going to hit the airwaves like a fucking bomb. The DEA will need to be on board. The families will have to be notified."

"I'll contact Becky's family as soon as I know that Elle is all right."

"It's because of Eric that she has a life." Max struggled against the men that were trying to place him on a gurney, but when Taggart stepped forward, he complied. It didn't matter as Taggart cuffed him to the metal side rail and that his other arm was useless. The detective would remain by his side on the way to the hospital. "If those other women had made a different choice, I wouldn't have had to do what I did."

"Your brother was a sick and twisted man." Kevin looked for an ounce of the man that he thought he knew, but the Max he'd shared meals and laughs with no longer remained. "You're no better, Max. Those women were doing what they had to in order to survive. They did nothing worth the sentence you gave them."

"They're whores, Dreier. They needed to be taught a lesson or wiped from this earth. We do it to scum every day of our lives. They are no different."

"Take him out, Taggart," Crest ordered, coming to stand next to Kevin. The paramedics folded the gurney and carried Max away, who seemed content to have the last word although agony was now written across his features. It was a good thing he was taken out the outer door instead of having to pass by

Cam and Elle. Kevin didn't want the fucker anywhere near his girl. He glanced over his shoulder to see Elle sitting with Cam, comforting her friend. "The medic gave her the all clear. She'll be sore and should probably go for some x-rays, but she refuses."

"She had an intimate relationship with Eric Bennett early on," Kevin confessed, needing to get it off of his chest. He rubbed a hand over his heart. How was Elle going to handle that when the dust settled? He would do whatever he needed to in order to ensure she didn't feel guilt over something she couldn't control. "He got her into prostitution, yet we now know that in his twisted mind, women should be punished for that."

"No one can say what flips the insanity switch inside a person's mind." Crest turned as well, both of them now facing where Elle and Cam sat reassuring each other. "What you can control is your own actions. Which is why once you've spoken with Becky Rattore and her parents, you'll take the rest of the week off to spend with your future wife."

Kevin shot a glance of surprise Crest's way to see that he was already looking down at his phone as if this had just been another day at the office. Wife? Kevin smiled slowly, knowing not to argue with his boss. He had a tendency to be right, and the moment he was spot on. At some point Elle would be Kevin's wife. He'd known it the second he'd seen her and he'd invested the last year getting to this point. The year to come was going to be the best of their lives.

"Thank you." Kevin didn't have to say anything more, for he knew Crest would understand what those two words encompassed. Just as Elle knew that he would always be there when needed, Kevin knew the same of his team and mentor.

"I'll keep myself available though, just in case something comes up with Ryland."

"Do that." Crest placed his cell back into his pocket and turned to go. "Gut instinct is saying he'll turn up soon. Keep an eye peeled."

Kevin continued to watch Elle as the place around them started to fill up with more officers and forensic personnel. Coming from the main level of the house were voices carrying down the stairs, letting Cam and Elle know that the women wanted to know what had happened and if everyone was all right. The left side of Cam's face was already sporting a bruise from where Max had probably pistol whipped him. The entire story would come out once Cam and Elle gave their statements, which for Cam would occur soon. For Elle, he was taking her ass to the hospital regardless of her hardheadedness. If the medic advised she needed x-rays, then she'd have them. Taggart could personally take her statement at the hospital. After that, he was taking her home—their home in the country, where no one would bother them.

"Elle, it's time to go," Kevin said softly, not wanting to startle either one of them. He held out his hand and Elle immediately reached for him. He prayed that it would always be so. "Cam, is there anyone we can call for you? I know how hard it is for me to accept a friend could possibly do the things that Max did, let alone for you as his brother. Elle has always spoken highly of you. If there's anything we can do for you, all you need to do is ask. What I'd really like right now is to take her to the hospital. I'd feel better if a doctor looked her over."

"Yes. Yes, I think that would be best." Cam wiped the corners of his eyes and stood up, holding out his hand. "Thank you, Kevin. I'll be fine. The girls are upstairs and I'm sure they are wondering what happened. It's going to break their hearts that Eric is responsible for the tragedies of their friends. I'm not sure if they will even trust me after all of this."

"Cam, you are not your brothers. You are innocent and you will hold your head up high. Those women upstairs love you and they'll rally around you." Elle winced when she stood as well causing Kevin to place his other hand on her waist. He couldn't stand that she was in pain and he wanted her at the hospital ASAP. "I'll stop by in the morning."

"Afternoon, provided she's cleared by the doctor," Kevin revised, shooting Elle a look that dared her to argue as he shrugged out of his jacket. He put it around her shoulders, patiently waiting for her to put her arms through the sleeves and ignoring the cute scrunch of her nose. Once she'd done what he needed her to, he zipped the coat up to her chin. "Elle will be sleeping in and then we'll *both* be by to see if you need anything."

"Thank you. Both of you." Cam's eyes caught someone behind Kevin, so he turned to see who it was. One of the detectives stood there, notebook in hand. "Go. Get Elle checked out. Once I give my statement, I'll have to tell Liv, Molly, and the rest of them what happened. They deserve to know the truth."

Elle gave Cam one last hug and then she and Kevin stepped aside to let the detective do his job. Needing to have her in his arms once more, he pulled her close. They stood there, soaking in the fact that they'd pulled through this. He knew that their time on earth wouldn't be enough for him, but he would strive to make every second count. Needing to see her face and assure himself that she was truly all right, he drew slightly away.

"How's my city girl?"

"Thinking I'd rather be country," Elle replied, a tremulous smile on her lips. There were still some unshed tears lining her lashes. "Kevin, I thought I'd never get to tell you how much I love you. I was so afraid you would walk away in the end that I refused to believe the truth. What we have isn't something that I have to fear, but something I should embrace. It's truly love."

"We'll build on that until we have what my parents have, Elle. You can have it all and I want to be the man that gives it to you. Anything your heart desires, I'll make sure you have." Kevin reached down and swung her up into his arms. There was no way in hell she was walking out there in her bare feet. Not wanting her to catch sight of what was left of the scene, he walked around it so that her back was to Bennett's body. She instinctively snuggled deeper into him as he walked up the cold cement stairs and into the dark night, which was now glowing red and blue from the cruisers' lights. "Let's get you to the hospital and then home. Our home."

Chapter Thirty-Two

Six months later, Elle entered Reformation to see five women sitting in the living room drinking coffee and tea that Cam had supplied them with. Assorted pastries were sitting on two trays while fruit was situated on another. The women were new to the center, while Liv, Molly, Teresa, and Angela were well into living their fresh starts. Rachel had returned to the streets, living with Hash but working for Bee. Not everyone wanted to be saved.

"Just the person we were waiting for." Cam came out of the kitchen holding two mugs with what was hopefully coffee. He'd trimmed his red beard so that it was closer to his face, giving him a more professional look. Handing one steaming cup to her, he winked. "I saw you drive up in that fancy new car of yours. I've got to admit, the color suits you."

"Why? Because the black matches my hair?" Elle shook her head in amusement. Fancy didn't come close to describing her compact, dependable Saab that Kevin had talked her into. He claimed that she'd needed to get her license and a vehicle if they were to continue to live in Eden Prairie. It had taken him close to four months to pry her hands off of her savings, but it was only one more step in believing that her life as she knew it would last. As for the color, Cam had been on a rampage trying to add different shades to her wardrobe. "I'll have you know that the color black is classic. Kevin loves the suits that I wear to work."

Elle neglected to say that was because she wore nothing underneath them anymore, unless it was the chocolate diamond body accessories that he'd purchased. Kevin liked to sit in the club during play hours and watch her work, visualizing what her body looked like underneath. At first it was awkward but as the night wore on, Elle's desire had been so heightened that the moment she'd locked up, they'd enjoyed the club until the sun broke over the horizon.

"From that smile you're wearing, I take it Kevin's home from his business trip?"

"Not yet. He's due home tomorrow." Elle sipped her coffee and let out a hum of appreciation. The brew was good but not as good as Kevin made. Her heart felt a ping of sadness. He'd been gone almost two weeks, along with Crest and Ethan. She missed him. "Let me talk with the girls about the job fair that's happening at the Metrodome this weekend. It'll give them most of the week to prepare."

Elle spent the rest of the morning passing out brochures and explaining the process of the job fair to the women. Cam listened in although he'd lost his interest after a while and busied himself in the kitchen. He'd been putting up a good front, but she knew the upcoming trial was weighing on his mind. Max had pleaded not guilty, claiming any evidence at the crime scene must have come from Eric. It was both her and Cam's testimony that were key and neither one of them were looking forward to it. As for Eric, his funeral had taken place a few days after the coroner's office had released his body. The only ones in attendance had been Cam, Kevin, Elle, and Liv. She'd gone to show support for Cam. No one expected anything less, but it was still heartbreaking to watch Cam bury the brother he'd remembered from his childhood. Not the man he'd become. Elle breathed a sigh of relief the moment Teresa entered the house.

"This is Teresa and she's going to share her knowledge regarding paperwork for grants in order to attend the community college." Elle made the introductions and then grabbed her cup, which had been empty for quite some time. She needed a refill and wanted to have a talk with Cam. "I'll be in the kitchen should anyone have any more questions."

Elle left the group in Teresa's capable hands and walked out of the room to find Cam sitting at the kitchen table, staring off into space. He wore a short-sleeved buttoned dress shirt with a pair of dark jeans, but his apron was clutched in his hands. Lately he hadn't had the urge to bake and she felt helpless in his struggle to accept the things that had happened.

"You know, all you have to do is ask and I can take time off at the club to run Reformation while you take a well deserved vacation." Elle offered up her suggestion, having already talked to Kevin about it. They'd spoken every day that he was away, giving her updates and letting her know what they'd found on Ryland. Apparently he'd been in contact with a plastic surgeon in Greenland. The fact that he might have changed his appearance had upped the stakes. As for the team members still at home, their day-to-day lives still had to go on. She looked at Cam, awaiting his answer. When he just smiled in a regretful manner, she knew he wouldn't take her up on her offer. Which was why she'd called in some reinforcements. "Lauren and Emily? Would you two come in here please?"

Both of her friends had arrived when Teresa had, just in time for Elle's talk with Cam. She knew that he'd hem and haw over leaving the center, but he needed some time away. Lauren walked in first, her red curls surrounding her face. The sun had caused her freckles to darken, giving her that fresh outdoor look. Emily gracefully entered behind her friend, little Derrick sitting on her hip and looking around. When his gaze landed on Elle, he clapped his hands. She reached up from where she was sitting and the little boy practically launched himself at her, giggling when she widened her eyes in surprise.

"Now that's not something I would have thought I'd ever see," Cam said, his smile enough to brighten his eyes.

"I resent that," Elle replied with a chuckle. "I'll have you know I'm very good with children."

Kevin had taken Elle back to his family home a couple of months ago, and while it had taken time to get used to the chaos, she found that she didn't want to be anywhere else. She'd spent extra time with Kevin's mother and sister, along with his sisters-in law. In doing so, Elle was surrounded by the children. She'd been able to relive her childhood through them in that short week, from playing tag to catching lightning bugs in the fields. She'd felt free and sharing that with Kevin made it all the more special.

"So when are you going to get married and have one of your own?" Emily quipped, pulling out a chair and taking a seat. "You know there's bets around the office as to who bites the bullet first. Connor or Kevin."

"How much is the pot?" Lauren asked, joining them at the table. "I think we should raise the stakes, because I have insider information."

"Shit! You set a date, didn't you?" Emily put a hand over her mouth and sent a look Derrick's way. "Remind me to put a dollar in the cuss jar. Jax and I are trying but it's so damn hard."

"Two bucks." Elle shared a look with Cam, who seemed more relaxed than she'd seen him in a while. "But you can earn that back if Lauren is saying what I think she's saying."

"Connor's dad is insisting we have a full blown church wedding and Connor doesn't want to let him down. It'll take at least a year to plan, with my sister living in Florida and Connor's father's side of the family in Jersey. We're shooting for next summer."

"What about a honeymoon?" Elle shared a look with Lauren, leading her exactly where they needed the conversation to go. Cam had no idea where this was headed but she hoped that he took them up on their offer. When they had originally come up with the plan, it had been regarding vacations. "Any special place in mind?"

"I know it's silly, especially when we could go anywhere in the world, but I really want to go to a Sandals Resort. I just can't choose between the one in Barbados or the one in the Bahamas."

"I love the beach." Emily placed her elbows on the table, playing along. "Don't you, Cam?"

Ever since that fateful night, Lauren and Emily had rallied around and joined Elle in making sure that Reformation kept their doors open. Cam had to take over Eric's job in raising money for the center, and at times worked round the clock. It was time to convince him that he needed a break.

"I can see where you three are going with this and—"

"Before you say no, let us have our say." Elle waved a hand toward Lauren, who had her part all planned out.

"I seriously can't decide between the two. I'd love it if you could test out both locations for me, say a three day stay at both resorts, and then tell me the pros and cons to each."

"The three of us can cover the center while you're gone, and you said yourself that you were going to find someone else to volunteer their time here who was better at marketing to bring in the higher donations needed to keep things running." Elle bounced Derrick on her knee as she continued to convince Cam that he needed this. "Cam, the trial is starting in the next couple of months. You haven't been able to sleep, you work all of the time, and—no offense—but you look like shit."

"One dollar for you," Emily murmured, sitting back in her chair with a smug smile.

"I would have just stuck with the fact that I need him to scout the two locations," Lauren said in a stage whisper. "And maybe throw in the fact that he might meet someone while sunning it up on the sand. That's always a hook, line, and sinker kind of thing."

Cam started laughing at their antics, which was what Elle wanted to see. He'd always been the carefree one, and recently the light in his eyes had been extinguished. She wanted it back, along with his famous hot chocolate that he hadn't made in what seemed like forever.

"What do you say, Cam?" Elle took Derrick and held him up, letting him use his legs while he bounced up and down. The baby smell that had yet to leave him wafted from his hair and she couldn't help but take a deep breath. She caught Cam's eyes and saw a little glow that made her heart warm. "Will you take us up on our offer? Go on vacation. It doesn't need to be Sandals, but Lauren is serious about those two places being her choices. Will you let us take over for a week while you take a break?"

Cam looked down at his hands, which made Elle realize that he was trying to hide his emotions. She shared a smile with her friends, knowing that he was going to agree. Things were shaping up and now she just had to wait until Connor was back in town so that she could discuss her future with him and Jax. Cam had found his fundraising person; he just didn't know it yet. Once he returned from vacation, she planned to discuss with him her thoughts of turning Reformation from a nonprofit organization into a not-for-profit organization. This was something she wanted to do, and with Kevin's support she'd finally found her niche.

"Thank you." Cam held his hands out to Lauren and Emily, each of them taking one. It was Elle that he made eye contact with. "You're dear friends that I treasure very much. Before those women descend into this kitchen and you change your mind, I'm going to go pack."

Elle held up Derrick's hand and waved, letting Cam know he was off the hook. Sure enough, he must have heard Teresa wrapping up her speech, for all of the women came into the kitchen. Cam was long gone, leaving the three of them to finish up answering questions regarding wardrobe, possible interview questions, and inquiries about schooling. She noticed that the blonde named Whitney didn't seem inclined to join in the discussion. Elle was afraid she might be one of the ones that didn't make it, but at least she was being given the chance. Looking around the group of women, Elle felt pride that she could give a piece of herself to each of them. She finally found a place where she was needed and could contribute to better others.

"Hey, I think you're wanted in the living room," Emily said, holding out her hands for Derrick. The baby squealed, bending his knees erratically. Elle lifted him up, allowing Emily to take him and wondering if Cam had changed his mind. "Come on, big guy. Let's finish our business here and get you home for a nap."

"Excuse me." Elle left the kitchen, although the conversations seemed to be wrapping up anyway. She walked through the doorway, thinking of the various reasons she could come up with to convince Cam that he needed this vacation more than anything. "Cam, what if I—"

Elle stopped midstride when she saw Kevin standing in the middle of the room. Even though it was the dead of summer, he still wore denim that encased his thick thighs that she knew were corded with muscle. His chest was covered in a white T-shirt that had three buttons at the top for style, although she knew he could care less about the accessory. She enjoyed it, for it showed a little of his tanned chest. His hair needed a cut but she wouldn't complain since she loved running her fingers through the thick strands. He looked so damn good that she stared at him for a moment before launching herself into his arms.

"God, I missed you," Kevin whispered against her ear. "These two weeks felt like two months."

"You're not telling me anything I don't know." Elle had her legs wrapped around his waist while her arms were wrapped around his neck. Pulling back, she searched his gray eyes. "You're home, right? You don't need to turn around and leave again, do you?"

"No." Kevin snuck in a kiss and then returned her stare. "I promise I'm home for at least a month. Jax and Lach will take the next rotation, unless something urgent comes up that needs all of us."

"So we can go home right now and have the next two days to ourselves?"

Kevin must have heard the excitement in her voice, for he raised an eyebrow. The stern look he gave, which was meant to get her to fess up, caused her to laugh hard enough that she almost fell out of his arms. She'd spent most of the two weeks he was away arranging things to be perfect for his return. There was nothing he could do to get her to spill.

"Farm boy, take me home."

Chapter Thirty-Three

Kevin waited for Elle to pull her car into the garage before doing the same with his vehicle. Maneuvering slowly inside, he put his truck in park and turned off the engine. There was a glow to her that made his entire body warm at the knowledge that she was happy. He'd spend every waking hour making sure she stayed that way.

Stepping off of the running board and closing the door, Kevin met her in front of the vehicles and didn't hesitate to dip her into a kiss. Elle gave as good as she got and by the time she was standing upright, they were both out of breath. Two weeks was a damn long time to be away from her, but the results of their investigation produced solid leads that put them one step closer to capturing Ryland. Kevin wasn't so sure that Crest wanted him apprehended so much as eradicated, but that problem was for another time.

"Show me this surprise you have up your sleeve," Kevin ordered, patting her on the bottom. It was Monday and Elle's day off, so she was wearing white shorts with a black T-shirt. She'd lifted her sunglasses up so that they sat on her head, pulling her hair behind her ears and revealing her chocolate eyes that sparkled with mischief. "I saw you smiling in your rearview mirror the entire ride home."

"Follow me." Elle entered their home and only stopped briefly to turn off the alarm as she continued until she came to a stop at their bedroom. He raised an eyebrow wondering what she could have done that excited her this much. She'd been talking of a new bedspread, but he didn't see how that would get this reaction. Then again, he was known to be wrong on a few occasions. After she threw the door open and he followed her inside, he immediately noticed the wooden wall partitions on the far side of the room. "Go and look at what's on the other side."

Kevin smiled at her enthusiasm as he passed her, walking across the large area rug that they'd purchased a few months ago. The rich tones complemented the wood of the furniture and added a homey feel that made him contemplate building a fireplace with a brick mantel. It was easy to picture Elle lying on the floor in front of the flames and the various things he could do to her body.

"You're taking too long," Elle complained, coming up behind him and giving a light push.

"That's what you said right before I left for my trip and look how well that turned out for you." Kevin looked over his shoulder to see the light flush on her cheeks and he knew that she was thinking of their last night before he had to leave for Greenland. "Speaking of which, have you been preparing yourself like I asked?"

Elle's face went from flushed to an all out red coloring her high cheekbones. Her response was exactly what Kevin wanted, for it told him that she had listened to his instructions. His cock twitched in anticipation of the afternoon to come. He'd see what she wanted him to and then he'd have her in bed within five minutes, making her detail her two weeks verbally while he readied the items needed for their scene. Two weeks had been a damn long time.

Kevin finally walked around the partitions and stopped in his tracks. Elle never ceased to amaze him but this one surprise took the cake. A brand new black leather spanking bench, similar to the one at the club sat right in the middle of where the small sitting room had been. He didn't know what happened to the furniture and honestly, he didn't care. Walking further into the hidden area, he saw the items that were hanging on the wall. Various implements, such as paddles, floggers, and crops, were lined up with special hooks. Shelves had been hung underneath and were holding numerous dildos, vibrators, plugs and diverse lubricants. It was their own mini play area.

"Very well done, city girl," Kevin said, making certain that his approval came through. His dick was now hard as nails. "I couldn't have done it better myself. Undress and place yourself over our new piece of furniture. Today is the day that I will truly claim you."

From Elle's gasp and her quick response to shed her clothes, she knew exactly what Kevin was referring to. She'd unconsciously saved a part of herself that would only ever belong to the two of them. Much to her dismay, he'd purposefully waited and made sure she was properly prepared by gradually progressing through the different size plugs. She was now on the largest and therefore ready to take him.

"Yes, Sir."

Kevin left Elle behind the dividers while he walked to the side table where he kept his weapon. Removing his holster, he pulled his gun out of the leather and placed them side-by-side on the hard surface. He then kicked his boots off along with the rest of his clothing. His balls felt heavy and his cock throbbed, but he knew it would be quite a while before he got any relief. There were times they made love in bed and numerous areas throughout the house, but with each passing week, their scenes lengthened and tested both of their soft limits.

"Elle, are you ready for me?"

"I'm ready, Sir."

No matter that Kevin knew what he would see when he walked back behind the partitions, the sight took his breath away. Elle had removed every stitch of clothing and she had situated herself on the bench just as she had in their very first scene. The summer had given her flesh a sun-kissed look, and while she certainly distracted him, he had to ensure her safety for their upcoming play. It was to his advantage though, seeing as the more he spoke the wetter she became. He did so as he secured her wrists and ankles.

"I see the distance between your lovely ass and the dividers are perfect for the floggers you purchased." Kevin placed a finger inside the cuff, ensuring the restraints weren't too tight against her skin. "I think we should test it though, don't you?"

"Yes, Sir." Elle was slightly breathless and he saw that even though her head was turned to face him, her eyes were glued to his cock. He bit back a moan when the throbbing intensified. At this rate, he'd need a cock ring. "I do think you should test them out."

Kevin bit back a laugh when she used the plural use. Elle always made their playtime exciting by trying to top from the bottom. He adored her fiery nature but loved when she succumbed to him even more. The journey made it that much sweeter. Standing, he noticed her eyes following his dick. It wouldn't be long until they were closed in pleasure. Letting the anticipation build, he walked back and forth in front of the floggers and crops, touching each and every one of them.

"I wonder which one would leave the more beautiful streaks across your bottom." Kevin wrapped his hand around some of the handles, wanting a comfortable hold. "I do think you need to have a plug inside of you while I make your ass blush."

"The glass plug is—"

"I'm relatively sure I didn't ask you a question," Kevin chastised, purposefully releasing the flogger and reaching down for the plug that contained a flatter base that wouldn't get in the way of the flogger that he'd chosen. "This plug will do nicely, although I do realize that it is of a larger size. If you've been stretching yourself like you've been instructed, you shouldn't have any problem taking this inside of you, correct?"

"Hmmm." Elle rubbed her cheek against the soft leather as if she was keeping herself from responding the way she wanted. Kevin smiled, knowing this plug was the one that gave her a burn that lasted for hours afterward. It was nothing compared to what she would feel with his cock. "I have been preparing myself, Sir."

"That's good." Kevin chose a water-based lubricant, and while he was applying it to the plug saw something that caught his eye. "My, you have a wonderful assortment of implements."

Elle was moving herself against the bench, obviously trying to gain some friction on her clit. What she didn't know was that her little nub would go untouched until he was about to enter her. He wanted her pearl so engorged and sensitive that one touch would set her off.

"Let's see how well prepared you've made yourself, shall we?"

Kevin didn't wait for her answer, but instead stepped behind her and ran a hand down her smooth cheek. He could see her pussy glistening but he resisted the urge to taste her. That was for another time. Taking the lubricant, he held it in the air and squeezed the bottle, watching as it dribbled down her crevice. It kept traveling until it met up with her cream.

"Are you ready, Elle?"

"Yes, Sir." Elle was restrained to the point where she didn't have much leeway to move, but Kevin could easily make out the upward movement of her hips. He placed the tip of the plug against her anus, pushing ever so slightly to cause her sphincter to part. "Oh, Kevin. Sir. Please more."

"I love when you ask for more, Elle," Kevin said, watching in fascination as her dark penny continued to open and accept what he was giving. He continued to push the plug deep and knew the moment she felt the burn start to grow. Her moans became deeper and her muscles tensed. "Relax. Breathe through the burn. You can take much more for me."

Kevin continued to work the plug, noticing that her juices were now running onto the leather. Elle loved the slight bite of pain and used it to heighten her arousal. The large plug was almost in when he encountered a slight resistance.

"Push against it," Kevin ordered, not relenting. This plug *would* be inside of her while he flogged her pretty ass. He needed her fully prepared for when his cock took its rightful place. "Do as you're told, Elle."

"Yes, Sir." Elle carried out those words until they sounded like a hiss, but she did as instructed and instantly the plug was in and her anus was wrapped tightly around the ridge. "I need to come, Sir."

"Thank you for telling me." Kevin walked back over to where he eyed the beautifully adorned clamps. The chocolate diamonds matched the gems that hung from the clit clamp he'd purchased right before leaving for Greenland. They too sparkled as they lay there. He changed his mind about touching her clit. "Maybe these will help you ward off what you are not allowed to have until I give you permission."

Kevin picked them up and turned toward her, holding them up in his hand for her to see. Her eyes widened but it was easy to see that her arousal ratcheted up a notch. A light perspiration coated her skin and he saw that her nipple was hard as her breast dangled on the left side. Leaning down, he withheld a grimace as the ache in his knee let itself be known. There was no place for that right now.

"Lick my fingers." Kevin held up his hand and when her lips parted, he settled his digit inside. Her tongue moistened his finger and thumb without hesitation. Using the dampness to his advantage, he pulled and rolled her nipple until she was crying out. "The additional stones that were added will tug on your nipples nicely. Every time you shift, you'll feel the weight and know that you are not allowed to have your release without my permission."

"Sir, I need to come."

"That's nice," Kevin acknowledged, knowing exactly how far he could push her. He watched her face closely as he fastened the clip to her nipple. Her lips made a perfect O, although no noise escaped her lips. It wasn't until he'd affixed the other clamp to her right breast that she cried out. "Nice and snug."

Kevin could see a slight tremor tear through Elle's body. Her fingers were curled into her palms and her toes bent as he walked behind her, knowing full well what was coming. It was then that he noticed the stool off to the side. Leave it to Elle to think of his knee and the trouble it gave him when he knelt down. He'd have to remember to thank her later. Pulling it close, he sat down and took a moment to savor the view of her pussy. He must have waited too long for her liking, for she tried to shift her body. He chuckled when she gave a throaty groan, knowing the clamps were now swinging. That was nothing compared to what she would feel on her clit.

"I had heavier stones added to your clit clamp, Elle." Kevin used his left hand to try and wipe some of her cream away, but damn if she didn't continue to dribble. Doing the best he could, he gently took hold of the swollen nub and carefully extended it, not wanting her to obtain her release just yet. When she started chanting his name, Kevin knew she was too close. He shifted her plug and allowed the burn to take the edge off. "This clamp is going onto your clit and you will not come. Do you understand me?"

"Yes, Sir. It's just so hard."

"It will be worth every tortured second." Kevin quickly attached the clamp, ensuring it was tight enough to stay in place. Elle made a noise that he'd never heard and damn if it didn't vibrate his cock. Pushing the stool away with his foot, he wrapped his fingers around his base and squeezed tightly. "Very good. Give yourself a minute to adjust and then we'll see about creating a lovely red shade to your backside. It will give me a beautiful picture as I claim your ass."

Elle was practically whimpering but Kevin knew the slight stings she would receive from the flogger would offset the pleasure she was feeling. Choosing the one that best fit his hand, he situated himself in a better position. The first time he'd flogged her, he found that she preferred a particular rhythm. It had carried her to subspace for the first time and she'd been euphoric. He wanted her there again, where she felt her body float and it was his to do with as he wished without her feeling an overwhelming need to come. At least not yet.

"We'll start off slow," Kevin explained, taking his time and slowly showering her with the strands of the flogger. He started with her back, not wanting her to feel the plug shift quite yet. "Feel the kisses of the soft leather."

Gradually, Kevin worked Elle over, raining down the threads. Over and over, from her back to her buttocks to her legs. He kept her guessing as to where they would land, but kept up the same pressure until he saw her relax against the bench. Adjusting his swing so that the pressure was harder, he could see her clit clamp swinging. The motion was carrying her into that special place and gone was her pleading for an orgasm—in its place was silence while she floated to euphoria.

Kevin didn't stop until her flesh was a nice pink. Working her back down, he slowed his swing until eventually he was using the strands to caress her skin. Her breathing was even and her eyes were closed. Allowing her the enjoyment of subspace a little longer, he quietly laid down the implement and went about sheathing a condom on his cock and lubricating it well.

Taking his place behind her, Kevin used his hands to knead her sensitive buttocks. He did this until her breathing altered, alerting him that she was finally coming back to him. This was where her desire would be the highest and he knew it was time to finally give them what they both needed. He gently took the base of the plug and slowly pulled until her sphincter gave way.

"Hmmm."

"That's right, Elle. It's time to take what's ours." Kevin removed the large toy and placed it on the shelf to be cleaned later. Returning, he could see that her dark hole was slightly open and ready to receive him. "I want you to stay relaxed and when I tell you to push back against me, you're to do it."

Elle murmured something against the bench and Kevin smiled when she tried to lift her hips toward him, causing the heavy gems to sway. She moaned a little louder but remained still, obviously wanting the movement to stop in order to prevent herself from coming too soon and without his permission.

Kevin appreciated that the bench was at the perfect level for his cock to enter her without him having to bend his knees. He held himself steady as he placed his tip at her anus. Holding her hips with his hands, he pushed forward and felt her sphincter give way to allow his crown to pass through her tight ring. The rush of pleasure that hit his balls was almost pure agony.

"All mine, Elle. You're mine and will forever be mine."

Elle's entire being felt like she was floating yet she was experiencing everything that was being done to her body. The warmth of the leather beneath her, the tug on her nipples, the throbbing in her clit, and Kevin's cock within her ass combined together to amplify her already sensitized form. It was a mixture that was being stirred together to ignite into something she'd never experienced.

"Yours, Sir." Elle had waited such a long time for Kevin to claim her in a way that no man ever had. This was something special that would only belong to the two of them. "All yours."

Kevin continued to work himself inside of her, the burn intensifying to the point where she didn't know if she wanted him to stop or to keep going. She could hear his words of encouragement over the rushing through her ears, telling her to push out and accept more of him. He was wider and longer than any plug she'd used but never once did she consider using her safeword. The fire intermingled with her pleasure and was taking her to that precipice where they would fall together.

"Come for me, Elle."

At the same moment that Kevin said those words, he quickly pulled off her clit clamp. Blood rushed to her sensitive nub and the first wave of her release crashed down. She had to close her eyes to keep the room from spinning. The sudden spasm grabbed hold and was so strong that when Kevin drove the rest of his cock into her, it only caused her orgasm to become stronger. Crying out, she rode the waves as she felt his fingers tighten on her hips for leverage, plunging himself over and over into her ass and not letting up until both of them were satiated.

"I love you, Elle Reyes."

Elle opened her eyes to find Kevin kneeling in front of her, releasing her wrists and ankles from their restraints. She had no idea how long she'd been there but suddenly she felt the coolness of the air conditioning. Goosebumps trailed over her skin and uncontrollably she started to shiver. This reaction had only happened once and that was when she'd reached subspace. She knew that it had occurred again, but before she could say anything he had her in his arms and was walking towards the bed. It wasn't like she had to tell him anyway. He always knew what she needed.

Finally managing to open her eyes, Elle saw that instead of going to bed, he'd brought her into the bathroom. Candles were lit, the shades were drawn, and the large jet tub had bubbles higher than the edge. Kevin stepped into the water and when he sank both of them inside, the hot water coated her skin and eased the heightened sensitivity she couldn't seem to shake.

"Here," Kevin said, shifting her so that her back was to his chest, "rest against me."

"Hmmm."

Elle couldn't form a coherent word yet, so she did as he said and relaxed her body against his. Gently, she felt him using the sponge to wash along her arms and over the front of her breasts. She peeked through her lashes and saw that the clamps were no longer on her nipples, but she couldn't recall him taking them off. The hot water warded off the shivers and sleepiness overwhelmed her.

"Sip," Kevin ordered, causing her eyes to open. A bottle of water was being presented to her and she parted her lips. Her head was resting back against his shoulder, but she didn't need to lean forward for he brought the bottle to her lips. She greedily drank up what she needed until he pulled the container away. "I'll let you rest for a while, but then we need to eat. You need to get something into your stomach."

"Did I mention that I'm glad you're home?" Elle closed her eyes and snuggled deeper into him, not wanting to move.

"I got the gist." Kevin chuckled and she felt the vibrations in his chest. She felt so safe within his arms and when they tightened around her, she turned her head and planted a kiss on his cheek. "Hopefully I'll be home for a while."

"That would be really, really nice," Elle said, her voice surprising her as it came out in almost a purr. She was coming down from subspace nice and slow and would have to tell him that the bath idea had really worked well. Last time she'd cried afterward for a time but couldn't give him a reason. At the moment, her body felt well used and satiated, although her ass could still feel his presence. "Thank you for making this such a special moment."

"No, Elle. I should be thanking you." Kevin's arms tightened around Elle, pulling her slightly higher against him so that he was nuzzled against her neck. "You willingly gave me a piece of you that will forever be mine. I will treasure that and you for the rest of my life."

"I love you, Kevin." Elle lifted her lashes and waited for him pull far enough away so that she could see the gray of his eyes. They were soft, appearing like cotton in which her heart was wrapped within. "It was your conviction that brought us here and renewed my faith in love. You have my heart, my body, and my soul in your hands. I believe that you will never let me fall."

"There are no words to express how honored I am with the trust you've placed in me." Kevin kissed her tenderly on the forehead, letting his lips linger. "Know this…I will show you every day how much you are loved, city girl."

Epilogue

Crest glanced at the clock on his wall, noticing that it was well past midnight. He picked up his mug, saw that it was empty, and set it back down on his desk with a thud. The lights in the office had been shut off hours ago and he was going over paperwork using his desk lamp. It was easier on the eyes, but it was time to call it a night. All he'd wanted to do was get through the SITREPs that Kevin and Ethan had submitted earlier that day, but the extra hour had turned into much more. Both men were positive that Ryland obtained plastic surgery from a Dr. Robert Malik, located in Nuuk, Greenland. Unfortunately, the surgeon was dead and his clinic had been burned to the ground, taking with it any trail of paperwork.

The additional information that Taryn had come across hadn't been shared with the team. Crest was giving her time to come to terms with the intelligence that she'd come across, seeing as how it affected her personally. Her mental and emotional state needed to be one hundred percent healthy if she was to continue to work on this case or else he'd have to pull her. Taryn was well aware of this and she'd chosen to take the next few weeks off. Fortunately the only open assignment was the counterfeit case and Jax pretty much had that wrapped up. Ryland had taken much of the office's time, but their efforts were paying off. They were getting closer and Ryland was feeling the heat.

"Gavin?" Jessie's voice drifted through the office and when he glanced up, she materialized in his doorway. She'd left around six o'clock this evening, claiming she had plans. As she stepped across the threshold, he saw that her long brown hair lay in waves over her right shoulder. She'd changed clothes from earlier and was wearing a simple black dress, although her accessories were red. He kept his gaze on her face while he held the pencil steady in his hand, waiting to see what she needed. "Ethan texted me. I'm surprised that he's not here yet. I'm arranging a flight for him to Canada. Dr. Malik's nurse, the one that you and Kevin couldn't locate, just contacted her family to tell them that she was safe and sound in Ontario. According to his intel, once she heard that Dr. Malik had been murdered, she was terrified that she was next."

"I'll join him, so go ahead and reserve a private jet." Crest shoved the pencil in its holder and went about straightening the papers in the folder. Jessie could file them at a later date. "Alert the rest of the team and keep them on standby."

Crest stood up and walked to where his coat rack stood in the corner, assuming that Jessie would leave his office and head back to her desk. He hoped like hell that he and Ethan made it to Malik's nurse before Ryland did. If he and Ethan could obtain a sketch of Ryland's new appearance they'd be ahead of the game. Picking up his jacket, he turned to find Jessie waiting for him. He stayed where he was, searching her green eyes for answers. She was now standing in front of his desk.

"Elle's twenty-five," Jessie announced as if this was new information to him. Crest didn't know where she was going with this and his look must have conveyed that. "Kevin doesn't have an issue with her age."

Crest knew exactly where this was going now, and so far he'd been able to ignore this...thing...whatever it was that was between them. He wasn't about to get into the matter now, for Christ's sake. Jessie shouldn't want to either because all it would do was end her employment here. She should know that this wasn't something that he was going to discuss. He'd made it abundantly clear through his actions that their relationship was purely business.

"I'm glad to know that." Crest leaned over his desk and picked up the manila folder. He held it out for her to take. "Would you please file these SITREPs?"

"Is it my age?" For the first time since Crest had known Jessie, there was a vulnerability within her eyes that slashed through his barriers. Didn't she understand that this wasn't the time or place? She didn't know when to stop. "I went out to dinner with Taggart this evening. Did that not bother you in the least? If it's not my age, then tell me what it is that is holding you back."

Crest's palms itched to take Jessie by the shoulders and shake some sense into her goddamned head. He threw the folder back on his desk, mentally counted to ten, calling on his patience to see this through without damaging her heart. She was a good girl who deserved a hell of a lot better than a shadow of a man in his mid-forties whose inclinations ran darker than she'd ever seen at the club.

"Jessie, I'm going to say this once and then we're going to forget we ever had this conversation." Crest stepped closer, but the foolish girl didn't back away. If anything, she stood taller in her heels and tilted her head back to meet him eye to eye. The sparkling dare that shined in her emerald eyes called to something deep within him that he had thought had been locked up to never be seen again. "You deserve a man who can give you what you need. I've seen things, done things that have darkened my soul to pitch. Nothing and no one can take those scars and make them pretty again. I see the way you look at me, Jessie. I'm nowhere near the man you think I am. You don't want to know me or see into the pit that is who I am."

The hurt in Jessie's eyes tore at his chest, but Crest knew she needed to hear these words. If he left the country and came to find her gone he would understand. What he would never reveal to her was that seeing her in this office every day was a light that he looked forward to seeing. It was a warmth that should she leave would never return. Knowing it was a mistake but not able to help himself, he slowly reached out and cradled her face. It was the first time, and the last, that he would voluntarily touch her. Leaning down, he kissed her forehead tenderly, savoring the fragrance of her hair and the softness of her skin.

"Take the time I'm away to decide if you want to continue to work here." Crest stepped away, allowing his hands drop to his sides. "This agency that I've created is also a family, one that you're a part of, although I will understand if you can't stay. You will always be welcome here as long as you accept where I stand on this. There will never be an *us*, Jessie."

"Thank you, Gavin, for your honesty." Jessie squared her shoulders, and just like that the hurt in her eyes was gone. Crest couldn't say what replaced the emotion. His guard rose a few more inches, not sure of what she would say next. "I'll think things over while you're gone. Right now I'll make those arrangements for you and Ethan."

Jessie reached past him, picking up the manila folder he'd tossed onto his desk. Her perfume was light but just enough that it filled his senses. Crest warily watched as she walked out of his office, mystified by her change of attitude. He'd thought his words would end this cat and mouse game they'd engaged in for the last couple of years, but for the first time, he couldn't get a read on her emotions. The ringing of his cell phone tore his attention away from the empty doorway.

"Crest."

"I'm requesting a few weeks leave," Lach stated, his voice sounding far away. There was no greeting, no reason for his request. Crest didn't expect any, as this was Lach's disposition. "Do you approve?"

"Approved, but stay on call." Crest walked out of his office and into the large common area, seeing Ethan strolling in with a duffle bag slung over his shoulder. "Ethan and I are following up on a lead and may need you at a moment's notice. Are you somewhere close?"

"I will be within a day or two." There was slight static interfering with Lach's words, but Crest could still make them out. "Keep in touch."

Just like that, the call ended. Crest knew that Lach had taken a personal interest in Phoebe Dunaway, but he wasn't so sure that was in his best interest. Getting involved with a presidential candidate's daughter wasn't the wisest choice, but his team had their own lives. He certainly wasn't one to give advice on women. Crest pocketed his cell and joined Ethan at the conference table.

"Ready? We'll swing by my place so I can pick up some things before heading for the airstrip."

"The two of you have been added to the manifest," Jessie said as Crest and Ethan walked into the entryway. She was standing at the door, her red purse dangling from her shoulder. A smile that didn't quite meet her eyes graced her matching lips. "Have a safe flight."

With that, Jessie was through the door and letting it swing closed before either man had a chance to say goodnight. Crest continued across the entryway until he was standing in front of the glass, witnessing her walk down the hallway. His hands curled into fists as he saw Detective Taggart waiting for her. The man wasn't good enough for Jessie. Regardless, this was how things were meant to be, but that didn't mean life wasn't a bitch at times.

"I've changed my mind. We'll take separate cars," Crest said, watching the couple enter the elevator. Jessie's gaze connected with his before the doors slid closed. No, Taggart wasn't the man for her. She could do a hell of a lot better. "I'll meet you at the airstrip. I have a phone call to make."

~ THE END ~

About the Author

First and foremost, I love life. I love that I'm a wife, mother, daughter, sister…and a writer.

I am one of the lucky women in this world who gets to do what makes them happy. As long as I have a cup of coffee (maybe two or three) and my laptop, the stories evolve themselves and I try to do them justice. I draw my inspiration from a retired Marine Master Sergeant that swept me off of my feet and has drawn me into a world that fulfills all of my deepest and darkest desires. Erotic romance, military men, intrigue, with a little bit of kinky chili pepper (his recipe), fill my head and there is nothing more satisfying than making the hero and heroine fulfill their destinies.

Thank you for having joined me on their journeys…

Email:
kennedylayneauthor@gmail.com

Facebook:
https://www.facebook.com/kennedy.layne.94

Twitter:
https://twitter.com/KennedyL_Author

Website:
www.kennedylayne.com

Newsletter:
http://www.kennedylayne.com/newsletter.html

Books by
Kennedy Layne

KENNEDY LAYNE

CAPTURED
INNOCENCE

CSA CASE FILES 1

Captured Innocence
(CSA Case Files 1)

When former Marine, Connor Ortega, was ordered into the offices of Crest Security Agency on a Saturday morning, he didn't expect the latest case to hit so close to home. A submissive has been murdered in a particularly vicious manner and to bring her killer to justice, he must go undercover. Not hard to do considering he's already part of the BDSM lifestyle.

Lauren Bailey, a local vendor of bejeweled erotic implements, lives vicariously through her clients due to her fear of bondage. When Connor's dominant side can't resist trying to ease her anxieties, she accepts his proposal and agrees to his one stipulation…keep things casual.

When the killer sets his sights on Lauren, Connor is forced to rethink their relationship. He has the training it takes to catch a murderer, but does he have the courage to escape his inner demons and capture Lauren's heart?

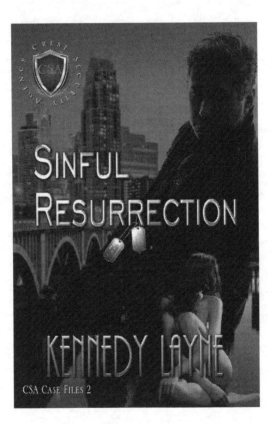

SINFUL
RESURRECTION

KENNEDY LAYNE

CSA CASE FILES 2

Sinful Resurrection
(CSA Case Files 2)

Sins of the past have been resurrected, predetermining their path to love. Can they overcome the treacherous obstacles set before them?

Jax Christensen likes his life just the way it is. He has his work, his club, and the occasional naked submissive to take his mind off everything else. He doesn't talk about the past, as there is no point in reminiscing about things that cannot be altered. His chest has an empty hole where his heart used to be, but he's grown accustomed to the constant pain. It's become the only thing that reminds Jax that he's alive.

Emily Weiss has never forgotten the one and only man she's ever loved. She's hidden for two long years in an attempt to protect Jax and herself, desperate to try and stay one step ahead of those who want her dead. She has information that could destroy the United Nations. Unfortunately, they want to eliminate her first. Emily's exhausted and wants more than anything to feel safe once more. That was how she felt in Jax's strong arms and she longs to be there again.

When Jax sees that Emily has risen from the grave, his heart and soul are full of anger and regret. He'll never forgive her lies and deception. He will, however, keep her safe. He hates her for what she's done, but he doesn't want her death on his conscience. He'll protect her and then walk away.

Secrets are revealed and the danger is more sinister and deadly than anyone could have guessed. Jax and Emily are forced on the run and the passion they once felt for one another burns even hotter and brighter the second time around. Jax doesn't know how he'll walk away this time or if he even wants to. Emily is determined to expose a high-level official within the United Nations and walk away unscathed. She wants a second chance with her first love—even if it kills her.

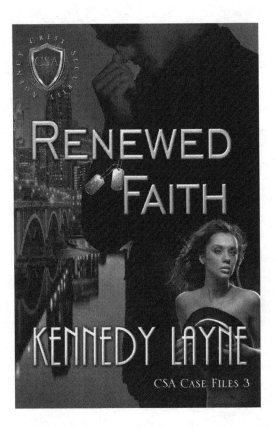

RENEWED FAITH

KENNEDY LAYNE

CSA CASE FILES 3

Renewed Faith
(CSA Case Files 3)

Is it possible to renew one's faith in love?

Injury ended former Marine Kevin Dreier's enlistment much too soon, leaving him with unwanted pins and screws in his right leg to serve as a constant reminder of what he'd lost. Being a team member of Crest Security Agency, however, gives him a sense of purpose and accomplishment. The determination that makes him good at his job is the same drive he'll need to win over the woman he wants in his life.

Taking charge of her destiny, Elle Reyes has spent the last year working hard to make something of herself. She's found a reputable place to live, saved a little money, and even secured a managing position at a club. She's finally safe, content, and in need of nothing more, but she knows she wouldn't have been able to turn her life around without Kevin's assistance.

When Kevin loses a family member, Elle is convinced this is her chance of returning a favor and repaying a debt. Accompanying him to visit his family and offer support, she is faced with the reality that warm and loving homes are real. She's torn between what she knows to be the truth and the tempting hope that something more exists.

Upon their return, Kevin's current case crosses paths with Elle's past. Secrets and lies encircle them as a killer ups the stakes in a cat and mouse game meant for only one winner. When time runs out, Kevin intends to be the last man standing—in life and love.

Made in the USA
Charleston, SC
07 April 2015